P9-CAO-478

Praise for
Caprice Crane's first novel,

# *Stupid and Contagious*

"With this winning romantic comedy, former MTV head writer Crane delivers a first novel reminiscent of Laura Zigman's bestselling *Animal Husbandry.* Crane makes light comedy, usually so difficult to create and sustain, look effortless."

> —*Booklist*

"Crane's . . . style of writing is both endearing and hysterically funny."

> —*Star Magazine*

"A truly exceptional book—funny, twisted, clever, mean, and always brilliant."

> —Anna Maxted, author of *Getting Over It*

"So much fun . . . snappy dialogue . . . Crane's giddy, playful prose feels fresh."

> —*Publishers Weekly*

"Heaven Albright, the irrepressible and sexy heroine of *Stupid and Contagious,* is bursting with humor that is smart and infectious."

> —Brian Doyle Murray, co-writer of *Caddyshack* and
> contributing writer for *Saturday Night Live* and *SCTV*

# forget about it

## caprice crane

NEW YORK   BOSTON

5 Spot
Hachette Book Group USA
237 Park Avenue
New York, NY 10017

Visit our Web site at www.5-spot.com.

5 Spot is an imprint of Warner Books. The 5 Spot name and logo are trademarks of Warner Books.

Printed in the United States of America

First Edition: August 2007
10 9 8 7 6 5 4 3 2 1

Library of Congress Cataloging-in-Publication Data
   Crane, Caprice.
      Forget about it / Caprice Crane.—1st ed.
      p.   cm.
      Summary: "From the acclaimed author of Stupid and Contagious comes a hilarious new tale of a woman who fakes amnesia in order to leave her mediocre life behind and live a life that is truly unforgettable"—Provided by publisher.
      ISBN-13: 978-0-446-69755-2
      ISBN-10: 0-446-69755-9
      1. Chick lit. I. Title.
      PS3603.R379F67   2007
      813'.6—dc22
                                                                    2007000475

*For my father, Les Crane,*
*to whom I can attribute my twisted sense of humor.*
*Blame him.*

# acknowledgments

To Caryn Karmatz Rudy, you are awesome. Thanks for being all I'd hoped for in an editor. Thanks to my agent, Jenny Bent, for believing in me. Thanks to Amy Einhorn for taking the first chance. Thanks to my agent Adam Levine, my manager Dave Brown, Endeavor Agency and Trident Media.

Thanks to my family: my mom, my dad, my stepmom, and my grandmother, none of whom are depicted in this book despite the "Frownies" reference. Thanks again to my dogs, Chelsea and Max, for the unconditional love. I know, I know, I'm fooling myself—they're in it for the food.

Thanks to my friends, who make life better: Rick Biolsi, Adam Carl, Dahlia Cohen, Jim Cotter, Tajma Davis, Denise Diforio, Ralph Fogel, Ellen and Irwin Frankel, Glen E. Friedman, Jonathan Fuhrman, D. B. Gilles, Jeff and Claudia Goodman, Devon Kellgren, Scarlett Lacey, David List, Jacqueline Lord, Nez Mandel, Cristina and Cade Mcnown, Makyla Oakley, Terrell Owens, Missy Peregrym, Simone Reyes, April and Erik Rofe, Paul Romaldini, Jeff Schneider, Lisa Singer, Lou Stalsworth, Sky and Victoria Stone, David Vanker (for so many reasons), Joe Vernon, Amanda Voelker, Fran Warner, Kim Whalen, and Harley Zinker.

Thanks to everyone at 5 Spot/Warner/Hachette: Rebecca Isenberg, Tareth Mitch, Rebecca Oliver, Brigid Pearson, Penina Sacks, Martha Schwartz, and Elly Weisenberg. Thanks to all the wonderful 5 Spot writers I've met and adore.

And a big thanks to all the readers who read my first book and wrote me to tell me they loved it. I love you *more*.

# forget
# about
# it

# 1.
# my first marriage

I got married when I was seven years old. I remember it like it was yesterday. I married my next-door neighbor Todd Beckett. Typically male (though atypically unaware of the delights of conjugal benefits, as that wasn't in our second grade curriculum), Todd was against the whole affair—totally commitmentphobic—but he went along with it since we had nothing better to do that day. My best friend, Catherine Parker, presided over the ceremony.

It was the middle of July, but it was perfect wedding weather: breezy, seventy-five degrees, and a clear blue sky. I felt lucky that I could wear my best outfit—cutoff Jordache jeans shorts and a rainbow-striped bathing-suit top. Cat wore her favorite color-patched Dolphin shorts and a hand-me-down Van Halen T-shirt that wasn't handed down as much as appropriated from her older brother, and Todd wore a Hang Ten shirt and cords. The ideal weather was lost on him; Todd always wore corduroy pants and Vans no matter what the outside temperature was.

The ceremony was set up in my parents' backyard right under the swing set, where we stood before Cat, who eyed us gravely and began: "And do you, Jordan 'Jordy Belly' Landau, take Todd Beckett to be your awfully wedded husband, to have and to hold, in sickness and in health, till death do you part?" I forgave Cat for invoking the jelly bean–inspired nickname my stepfather had given me—I knew she was mad that she had to play justice of the peace rather than bride.

"I do," we each said.

"I now pronounce you man and wife. You may now kiss the bride. And you have to hold it for three Mississippi seconds."

And then we kissed. Well, our lips touched, and we didn't move a muscle as Catherine counted out one Mississippi, two Mississippi, three Mississippi. And that was that. Me, barefoot with flowers in my hair. A simple ceremony. No family arguments. No stressing over having invited too many people. No registry nightmares. No problems. But there *was* cake. We'd always seen couples in movies smearing cake all over each other's face, and we thought that was an integral part of getting married.

"Time for the cake!" Cat shouted, and we geared up to get messy. I had taken two chocolate Sara Lee cakes from the freezer and set them out to thaw about an hour before our ceremony. I'd placed one right on top of the other in an attempt to create the tiered effect of wedding cakes I'd seen in movies. I surreptitiously swiped at my confection's double-decker side and popped a sugar-coated finger in my mouth. They were thawed and ready. So I took a handful of cake and smeared it all over Todd. Then he took a fistful and smeared it back on me, careful not to get any in my hair. At first. Until he noticed how much I appreciated his keeping my carefully feathered bangs icing free. Good-bye, feathers, hello, frosting. Cat dared to laugh, so we both smeared a few handfuls over her. Partly for revenge, but mostly so she wouldn't feel left out.

I remember that we'd recently seen *The Karate Kid Part II*, and there was some kind of ceremonial bonding ritual in the movie where a Japanese couple drank tea from each other's cups, so we thought that maybe we should have a bonding ritual too. It was too hot for tea, so Todd and I each chewed a piece of grape Hubba Bubba bubble gum, blew a bubble, and then moved in close to each other so that our bubbles would touch and stick together—thus bonding the two of us for life. And as a wedding present Todd gave me a whole unopened pack of Watermelon Wave Bubblicious.

It was a hell of a day. What I remember most is how simple it all was. It probably took two minutes from my hatching the day's activity to "I do." That was before I had the chance to be scared I may have gotten pregnant from our three-second kiss. The more I thought about it, the more nervous I got, so I grabbed Todd and tugged at his arm.

"Do you think I could have just gotten pregnant from that kiss?" I whispered.

"I don't know. Do *you*?" he asked.

"If I *knew*, I wouldn't be asking." And we stood there and looked at each other for a moment, Todd's eyes blinking, eyebrows raised.

Then he shrugged. "Well, we *did* just get married, so if you are pregnant, I guess it's okay. I think it would be worse if we weren't already married."

"I think so too," I said.

Problem solved. The celebration resumed, and we consummated our marriage with a game of tag.

My marriage to Todd was perhaps my way of trying to create a union more perfect, or at least less disastrous, than my own parents' marriage. I remember the day my first dad sat me down and put a hand on each of my shoulders. He looked me square in the eye and said, "Jordan, I want you to know that I love you very much, and I want you to always remember that." I remember feeling a sense of dread, although I didn't know what the feeling was exactly—I just knew it didn't feel good, so I distracted myself by studying the hairs that were growing just a teensy bit too far out of his nose. "Do you know that, Jordan? Do you know that I love you as much as I'm capable of?" he asked. I blinked and watched the one gray hair that was peeking out of his left nostril like a little mouse amid the other black ones, checking to see if the coast was clear. "Jordan?"

"Yes, Daddy."

"You understand that?"

"Uh-huh . . . ?" I said, with less certainty then he'd probably have liked.

"I may not see you for a while," he continued, "but that doesn't mean I won't be out there somewhere . . ." His words then drifted off with a theatrical pause. His nose hairs whistled slightly in the silence. I was mesmerized. Then he snapped back, ready to make his final point. "I just want to make sure you know that you are loved by your father, so that you don't grow up to be a man-hating lesbian."

I was barely *five*. A million thoughts raced through my head—a million questions that I wanted to ask him—but I felt paralyzed. Why are you telling me this? Where are you going? When will you be back? What is a lesbian? And most important, are you ever going to cut your nose hairs?

Nothing came out of my mouth. Well, none of the elevendy-million questions that whirled through my brain like a meteor shower, blasting through my mind until they'd exhausted their energy and faded away. The only thing I uttered was "Okay."

And he nodded, said, "Good girl," and then he was gone.

When my mom came in from the backyard a few minutes later, she didn't believe me when I told her that I didn't think Daddy was coming home. She got angry at me for saying such a terrible thing and asked me if I "thought I was a psychic." I told her no. I told her that I wasn't a psychic and I wasn't a lesbian—because even though I didn't know what either thing was, it just seemed like the right thing to say and I could tell my mom needed some reassurance.

"WHAT?" she yelled. And then I explained—told her everything he'd said, as nearly as I could recall it—and I must have captured the sense of it pretty well because afterward she went into the bathroom and cried for three and a half hours.

When she finally came downstairs, her face was dry and her head held high. She'd obviously spent some time in her fancy clothing closet; she wore a black dress I'd never seen with a double strand of pearls around her neck. The effect was classy with just a hint of sexy—and frankly this moment destroyed the little black dress for me forever. She took me into my room, put my fancy velvet party dress on me, and combed and fastened my hair with two ribbon barrettes. She then sat me down and told me that we were starting over. And that was exactly what we did.

Three years later I had a brand-new life, complete with a new house, a new dad, and a new baby sister. You'd think I'd be scarred from all this, and maybe I am, but at the time I really didn't suffer. Walter Landau quickly came into our lives, married my mom, and told me to call him Dad. My mom called him my "new and improved dad," but I didn't really see what had been so bad about the old one. He gave me Mrs. Butterworth, a brown mixed-breed mutt of a dog who had a white stripe on her head that looked like nougat. Mrs. B. was my best friend in the world. She sat under my feet at the dinner table, followed me everywhere—even if I was just going to the bathroom, where she'd wait outside the door—and slept with me every night. I had a happy family, my best friend, Cat, and my new husband, Todd.

Cat, Todd, and I were the three musketeers. We did everything together. Cat and I were polar opposites, lookswise. I had long brown hair, and she was blond. I was fair with freckles all across my nose, and she was perpetually tan. We were both about the same height, but she was always thinner than I was. We became blood sisters by pricking our fingers and holding them together. We were too young to know about AIDS and how that sort of contact might not be the best idea, but that was a simpler time when the first grade was considered early to be having unprotected sex and shooting heroin, so everything turned out okay.

My wedding had taken place a month before my birthday, and I remember that for that particular birthday I desperately wanted a metallic-blue Schwinn bicycle with a banana seat and a white wicker basket with neon flowers on it. I wanted that bike more than anything in the world, and when my dad told me to go outside to get the newspaper that fateful morning, I caught my first glimpse of my dream bike—the coveted Schwinn. I shrieked a joyous victory scream so loud it set off a river of tears from my baby half sister, kicking off a bitter rivalry that would last for two decades.

My memories of childhood are mostly pleasant up to that time, and I half suspect it's because they're not memories at all but stories built up around photographs and home movies I've seen. Because the truth is that after my father walked out on my mom and me, she cultivated a deep-seated fear of abandonment and destitution. She responded by becoming an abject materialist in every aspect of her life, and my new family would essentially become an uneasy alliance between a man who made a lot of money and two women who liked to spend it—those women being Mom and my sister, Samantha, who would grow into a carbon copy of my mother. And then there was me. I was in the mix with them, but more like a leftover ingredient from the failed family than a perfectly blended addition to the new one. Maybe that was all just in my head. Like the time Samantha told me that my father must have had some seriously powerful *ugly* going on for me not to have gotten *any* of Mom's good genes. Maybe that was just sisterly ribbing. If the issuing of *cracked* ribs is normal between sisters.

If our memories were true records of everything we've seen and felt, a lot of us would probably be overwhelmed or even horrified by what was going on. But I arrived at my eighth birthday in good spirits. Though I already had my first set of wheels, my first day of school, and first marriage . . . my first car, first job, and first sexual indiscretion were still years away.

Life was good. I *loved* being me.

# 2.
# gutter chic

By the time I'd turned twenty-five years old I *hated* being me. I loathed every single thing about my life. I'd long ago traded in my Schwinn for a ten-speed Cannondale and I hated that bike, probably as much as I'd loved my Schwinn. It wasn't the bike I hated so much as the experience of riding that bike in city traffic. Making it to twenty-five was no small feat considering the fact that I lived in New York City and narrowly escaped death by yellow taxi and MTA bus daily.

Navigating New York City streets on two wheels is a tricky affair, made even trickier by the fact that I was usually riding to work, so I had to keep the overall effort level at minimum to avoid sweating in my work clothes. With a salary that put me in the economic company of migrant farmworkers, I was bicycling not because of some noble impulse to save the world from global warming or love of the outdoors but because a cab ride to work was about as affordable as a European vacation, and both the bus and subway would have meant a long walk and a transfer. When I was little, bike riding was all chasing around after nothing, going to someone's house or the little store four blocks away for candy. Now that it had the purpose of getting me to my job at Splash Direct Media—the midsized advertising firm I'd hung my hopes on, which was nearly as rewarding as cleaning toilets at Grand Central—it was turning into a royal pain in the ass. Even so, weather permitting, I was pedaling. And dodging.

My latest pet peeve was the on-your-left riders—the people who passed me as I was trying to remain sweat free and yelled "on your left" as they zoomed by and glared at me. I heard the words "on your left" so often that sometimes I felt as though I was becoming a conservative by default.

Technically, I was not supposed to say anything back when they passed. They'd told me they were passing, and I was just supposed to be aware. But I got bored, so occasionally after they'd said "on your left," I'd reply "on your right." And if I was feeling really ornery, I'd shout back a non sequitur, mostly to entertain myself. "Follow your dream!" I once told a sleek spandex-clad bicyclist who I could have *sworn* was Lance Armstrong. Two blocks later, he wiped out into a garbage truck, still looking back at me with newly discovered angst.

Sometimes I'd find myself at a stoplight next to a bike messenger, and we'd do the nod. I was always tempted to race when the light turned green; and more often than not, that scene from *Better Off Dead* would come to mind, and I'd have the soundtrack of a teenaged Asian Howard Cosell egging me on in my head. Most of the time I ignored it.

But the worst part about riding my bike was getting doused with a mud milkshake, which seemed to happen about once a month. Some yuppie princess would be in her Range Rover, applying her lipstick, barking into her cell phone, and would barely miss running me over but succeed in soaking me in muddy water, usually when I was a block or less from work. Typically, I would pedal away from this scenario, sporting a dark ring from the calves down, whether I wore pants or a skirt with bike shorts underneath, and higher up, dark smudges would dot my thighs and occasionally my blouse and sleeves. I say "muddy water" because to anyone outside of New York, that's what it would be; but the truth is, the water that pools on the streets of New York is often a toxic fluorescent-green muck, so gross that you *wish* it was good old-fashioned mud.

Those days were less rare than I'd have liked. So much so that it was like God was playing a cruel joke on me, and all the random extras in my life were in on it. I wondered if one of God's assistants had communicated my schedule to him on a day that he had a cold, so he interpreted every third Monday as Mud Day.

When this happened, it usually left me no time to go home and change my clothes. And as I trudged through the halls at my office, I got curious looks from coworkers and upper management, who were wondering what was wrong with me and why I kept coming to work looking like a Jackson Pollock.

Of course, on a day when I got splashed I'd also inevitably run into Mr. Billingsly, the president of the agency. And that day, I did.

I saw him coming from all the way down the hall and tried to keep my head down so he wouldn't recognize me, but, as fate would have it, we were walking straight into each other so he was bound to see me. It's ironic, because most of the time I felt like I was invisible at work, and the one time I *wanted* to be, it was like I was dressed in neon. Billingsly was completely intimidating, but you'd never think so at first glance because he resembled an overfed grade school principal, someone who might dress up like Santa Claus at Christmastime—white hair, red face, plump, dimples. But the minute he opened his mouth, the facade was ruined: his withering comments would have made Rudolph's nose shrivel up and fall off rather than light his way. Luckily, Billingsly was always in a hurry so any interaction was usually over as soon as it began. *But not that day.*

"Is everything okay, Jordan?" Mr. Billingsly asked me.

"Me? Yeah! Great!" I said until I realized that he was referring to my current state of dishevelment. "Oh, you mean *this*? It's the new thing. Gutter chic," I said, trying to make the best of things.

"Leave it in the gutter next time."

Since that didn't work, I decided I'd try another tactic. "I got splashed. I'm making a statement. Maybe I could be the company mascot. Kind of like 'Splash,' " I said as I bent forward and did jazz hands.

Mr. Billingsly stared for a second, not amused, then decided the interaction wasn't worth his time and walked briskly away. And I was reduced to a mud-soaked loser.

The quick and dirty rundown of Splash Media was this: We were totally dysfunctional. The account people's job was to make sure all client issues were handled, and in a good agency, they generally do a good job of keeping just about everyone happy. But *our* account people were mostly sniveling sycophants who went around pissing off their colleagues and might just as well have worked for the clients instead of Splash. They'd go to creative and "gently" give them client direction, like this: "I'm totally with you guys on this, and I think they're nuts, but let's just go along with it for now." Then they'd take the reworked creative to the client and present it like this: "I'm totally with you guys on this, and I think it needs work, but the ideas are all there." Deviously working both angles, they essentially acted like weather vanes going in whatever direction the hot air was blowing.

Our creative people were mostly prima donnas who thought that everything they shit out was gold. You'd change a word or shrink a graphic, and they'd scream like you had just taken their bottle away from them. Of course, my resentment was intensified by the fact that I desperately wanted to *be* one of them.

Our production staff consisted largely of well-meaning, friendly people who were under the despotic rule of Marilyn Mason. She was a master of the form of psychological manipulation known as active aggression. This differs from passive aggression in that she was always trying to get her way—and didn't give a *damn* who knew it. As a result, our production department was always in a sort of angry panic. Because her name was so close to Marilyn Manson—and because from there it was just a hop, skip, and a jump to "Charles"—we called the production team the Family. They had a similar messianic sense of purpose, believing that without them nothing could be done—and if they were so inclined on any given day, we'd all be dead. Figuratively. We hoped.

I worked in traffic and had done so for two and a half years. Traffic was the eyes and ears of every department in the company. We saw the underbelly, we saw everybody's skeletons, and *most* of us used it for good. There was a pretty high turnover in traffic, but the people who stayed and wanted a career in advertising usually made the leap to production. Some went to account management or jumped ship and went to work for the clients. None of those routes interested me in the least, and my career misdirection had given me a very bad case of bad attitude, despite my normally sweet and pliant disposition. Splash tried to gloss over our shit jobs by adopting a new P.C. title for us—project managers—but no matter the title, I knew we were simply corporate gophers. We put all the meetings together, shuttled jobs from department to department, and, in my humble opinion, basically ran the joint.

Most of my days involved juggling a dozen streams of contradictory input, placing a hundred calls, trying to retain consciousness through meeting after excruciating meeting, checking the proofreaders for comments, battling with creative on deadlines, dealing with some condescending hack at a studio, taking a set of mechanicals on what is called a "round," and then getting it all back to each department to make sure their changes or issues were addressed. As much as it aggravated me, this allowed me to keep my finger on the pulse of the entire agency, and it was my best source of cardiovascular activity because it was no secret that I loathed the gym.

I took the job because I wanted to get my foot in the door of an oversaturated market. Ask a waiter in New York what they really want to be and odds are about 90 percent that you'll get, "An actor." Ask the dishwashers, and odds are about the same that you'll get, "A copywriter." I also believed that working in traffic would give me access to all the ad campaigns. The creative director I worked for more than anyone else was Lydia Bedford—the most respected creative director in the entire shop, but she was also known for putting the "pain" in *campaign*.

Nowhere in my job description did it ask me to write, proofread, or edit headlines, taglines, or ad copy—but occasionally I'd be handed something, get a better idea, suggest it quietly and as though I were joking, and almost every time, my little tweak would ferret its way into the comps—and sometimes into a campaign. Lydia loved to take advantage of my creative zeal and my willingness to be exploited. And I didn't mind. Especially the time Lydia was having personal problems and pretty much abandoned work for two weeks. She was there but she wasn't *there*. So I developed a print and direct mail campaign for an online IKEA competitor and from the ground up did *everything* myself. The client loved it. The agency loved it. And the consumers loved it. Small detail: I got zero credit, but that was okay because I figured it was only a matter of time before Lydia acknowledged my contributions and I moved up.

I wasn't the only one looking to move up. Kurt Wyatt, another guy in traffic—a guy who started seven months *after* me—seemed to be angling for my promotion. I could just tell the guy was looking for a payout, but he wasn't doing anything to earn it.

That's actually not true. He was doing the *schmooze*, which was the part that I hated. But creatively speaking—he did zip. I didn't like to go out every night with my coworkers. Most of them weren't people I'd spend time with if I wasn't *paid* to do so.

The agency had developed an after-work drink schedule that had certain days as occasions. The only problem was, with Monster Mondays, Terrible Tuesdays, Wicked Wednesdays, Thirsty Thursdays, and Fucked-up Fridays *every single day* was an occasion. In order to partake in the after-work schmoozing, not only did you have to have a completely empty social calendar, you had to be an alcoholic. Kurt went every single night, played the game, and kissed ass. Sometimes I went to just keep up with Kurt, and it was always awkward. I'm just not good at small talk. I hate it.

I hate after-work small talk almost as much as I hate being asked "How was your weekend?" by someone who couldn't care less every single Monday morning. On an elevator. Or in the kitchen area when I just want my much-needed coffee. Or as I'm running past trying to get proofread copy back to creative only so they can decide to change something at the last minute and get it rushed to the studio, but certainly not before I tell How-Was-Your-Weekend Harry how my weekend was, only to have him glaze over when I answer him or, worse, just walk away mid-sentence.

I was gainfully employed, and I suppose I should have been thankful. But my job felt like a trap. Every time I tried to get out, I got slapped by some blockheaded business school washout or some self-important, A/X black-mock-turtleneck–wearing frustrated artist or a ponytailed, crimson-lipped harpy raging about a hairline placed too far left of the column to meet PowerPlace Gym's new graphics standards and now the client is going to throw a fucking *fit* and can't we get even a simple god-damn graphic fix right in this fucking place?! (end quote).

Of course, you may look at my life and say, Count your blessings and quit grousing. In which case, you'd have been welcome to it. With so much talk about identity theft, I sure wasn't losing any sleep. Mine was there for the taking.

So after my humiliating Billingsly moment, I settled in to my cubicle in the pit, a shared area of all the traffic people. My desk wasn't as littered with personal items as most people's because it was such an open space that I felt like anything I *did* display would be scrutinized and judged. Therefore, the only items that I'd decorated with were a self-consciously ironic poster of David Hasselhoff, meant to amuse, and a picture of Johnny Cash flipping the bird, meant to ward off post-weekend discussions or technically *any* discussions.

I opened my in-box to a barrage of e-mails from my mom and dad. This was a constant, major annoyance that I'd brought on myself. One day, a few years earlier, I had an uncharacteristic fit of pique at my mother's blatant disregard for my feelings/opinions/etc., and my sweet-natured stepfather came up with this solution (which was simply awful, but I felt too embarrassed by my childish display to call it off): They would copy me on every single e-mail they wrote to each other. Most of the time the e-mails had nothing to do with me and ranged from the mundane to the ridiculous to the "Oh my God, that's none of my business, why oh *why* would you want me to read this?"

I decided for the fiftieth time that I was going to put a stop to it. I picked up the phone and called my mom, only to have her put me on hold while she spoke in bastardized Spanish for about six minutes to the housekeeper, who has stayed in that house over ten years with only one possible explanation: a devout Catholic, she must be angling for canonization.

When my mom finally directed her attention back to the phone, she asked me if Dirk, my boyfriend, was going to be coming for Thanksgiving. For the record, I never thought I'd date a guy named Dirk (or Kip or Chet for that matter), but Dirk wasn't his actual first name. His name was Michael Dirkston, and there were a few Michaels at the school he went to, so they shortened his last name to Dirks, then Dirk, and it stuck. Dirk wasn't too pleased with this forced nickname at first, but when he found out Dirk was actually a Scottish word for a long dagger, he decided it was fitting.

"No, Mom," I said. "I told you already. Dirk can't make it that night. He's busy."

"Too busy for you?" she asked, and I could hear her eyebrows rising over the phone.

"Yes, too busy for me." It wasn't worth arguing.

"Well, I don't understand that."

"He has his *own* family, Mom."

"The men in my life *always* made me their top priority." Which was why she had to hear that her first husband had left her from her five-year-old. I somehow managed to keep this nugget to myself, so she bull-dozed on. "And Dirk is a wonderful boy, Jordan. Have you done something wrong?"

"No, I haven't done anything *wrong*. Unless not being related to him is wrong. He's going to be with his *family*." It was always suggested that something was my fault if it wasn't going according to the ideal plan. Plus, Dirk majorly kissed my mom's ass, always stroked her ego by refer-ring to her as my other sister, *and* was a lawyer—fitting in perfectly with every mother's doctor/lawyer dream for her daughter—so she thought he could do *no* wrong.

My mother is five foot two and weighs about a hundred pounds. She is sheer physical perfection. She has the Sally Hershberger shag and is always dressed a decade too young, but manages to pull it off. I am five foot seven and what you would call normal. My mother likes to bring to my attention that she is very small boned and so is her carbon copy, my sister, Samantha. The two of them share clothing I couldn't even hold up to me without crippling anxiety that the seams might rip in fear, and neither of them understands how I became so big boned. Their gleeful repetition of this conversational gem does wonders for my ego.

I wasn't really unhappy Dirk would be skipping the family meal. *Last* Thanksgiving, Aunt Sally and her third husband, Stewart, were play fencing with the carving knife, and in one deft turn, Stewart acciden-tally stabbed Walter in his right forearm. Walter, being the easygoing guy that he is, joked that it wasn't Thanksgiving until someone got stabbed. The Thanksgiving before, my mom was on a fanatical (read: psychotic) nut craze, due to the wealth of news items on their health benefits, and insisted that every dish include nuts. Green beans with almonds? Fine. Sweet potatoes with toasted walnut topping? Fantastic. Pecan pie? Of course. But cashews in the gravy? Just. Plain. Wrong. And then there was the Thanksgiving before that, when my cousin Jeff had a few too many Sam Adamses while watching football, waiting for dinner to be served. Just as the spread was finally laid out, Jeff threw up *right* next to the stuffing and the visual similarity put me off stuffing for life. No, I can't say I minded Dirk's taking a pass.

I was in the middle of trying to change the subject when Lydia walked by. The best way to describe Lydia would be to say she looked like a macaw. She had a really angular face that was always bright red from using too much Retin-A. She looked like she went to the dermatologist for a chemical peel every morning before work. She had a pointy nose and tiny beady eyes. Her dyed red hair was naturally curly, but she blew it out to make it straight nearly every day. This was *supposed* to achieve a put-together look, but the damage to her hair from the constant coloring and blow-drying unfortunately created the look of a before model in a Frizz-Ease commercial. If I were her, I'd have left the natural curls. It certainly would have softened her up a bit, but she insisted on making it look like she'd been electrocuted.

"Uh, Jordan, could you put a hold on the personal phone calls until you've solved my KidCo dilemma?" Lydia said in that too-tightly-wound, falsely sympathetic way she had, as if I'd spent the better part of the morning on the phone. I mean, I *had*, but it was only five minutes into that morning and my coffee hadn't even kicked in yet.

"Mom, I have to go," I said, and hung up the phone. Art, the mail guy, high-fived me as he walked past without making any eye contact and without any change in facial expression. That was our thing, the unacknowledged high five. Art and I had the ideal acquaintance relationship. We had more than a nod but less than the bullshit pleasantries that come along with most acquaintances. I'd notice if he was gone, but I wouldn't feel the need, or even have the number, to call him up and find out why. It was the perfect office relationship.

I opened up the KidCo document in my in-box and understood why Lydia was in a frenzy. Her ideas sucked. Maybe *sucked* is too strong a word, but they weren't inspired. They certainly weren't the kinds of ideas that got her where she was today.

Before I could wrap my head around any concrete thoughts to help her, I heard the ding of my in-box and opened it to find an e-mail from my father to my mother, which I had been cc:'d on.

From: wallygator317@hotmail.com

To: judypatootie521@hotmail.com

Subject: Chicken tonight . . . or fowl overload?

Patoots—Chicken tonight? Or is it too soon, since we just did chicken Wednesday? Also need to know if you're into fava beans, because I'll get those too. Nice side dish.

I wondered how two people could be married for twenty years and not know if their spouse liked fava beans. And marveled once again at why my stepdad felt compelled to copy me on this.

Bicycling home after work, I got cut off several more times and yelled at by a mustachioed cabdriver talking on his cell phone.

"Watch out, motherfuck!" he called out after he ran me off the road.

"*Er!* Motherfuck*er*!" I corrected.

"Motherfuck you too!" he replied. God Bless New York.

*   *   *   *   *

I got off my bike downstairs in front of my building and was preparing to haul it up the front steps when I saw my friendly neighborhood homeless lady.

She stepped up close to me, then gave me a serious sidelong glance. Her voice carried a sense of desperation. "'Oh, Mama, I'm in fear for my life from the long arm of the law . . .'"

I took the cue, looking side to side first, then directly at her. "'Hangman is coming down from the gallows and I don't have very long,'" I answered, and she nodded her trademark long-necked nod and went on her way. She and I had been trading song lyrics for almost as long as I'd lived in this apartment. Most of the stuff she throws out would scare the bejesus out of you if you didn't know she was quoting songs. I saw her approach a man in a long overcoat once and practically reduce him to tears with, "'Borderline . . . feels like I'm go-ing to lose my mind.'"

When I walked into my apartment building, I got on the elevator at the same time as the creepy flattop guy who lived three doors down from me. He was one of those extreme muscle-bound guys who always wore spandex shorts and some variation of workout gym shirts, usually of the Tiger Schulmann variety. He smiled a toothy grin, and I pressed our floor button a few extra times. This is not a man that I would ever be attracted to. I need to clarify that before explaining that he also had the most massive penis I had ever seen, amplified every day, no matter the weather, in his black spandex shorts. It was proudly on display for all the world to see, garish and out of place as the Washington Monument, and it was always an effort not to look at it. I'd lived in the same building for four years (that includes four freezing New York winters) and had never seen him in anything but those shorts.

"Hi, Jordan," he said, all teeth. I'd never told him my name, but he'd been using it for the past three years.

"Hi," I replied, content in not knowing his.

"When are you going to take me up on that street ka-ra-*tay* lesson?"

"Oh . . . I don't know," I said politely. Meaning, *never*.

"New York is a dangerous place," he said as the elevator doors opened, facing me, his gargantuan penis taunting me. "Anytime you want, you should come over to 5B and let me show you some moves."

"Ha, ha," I said back, which was again, me saying that I was not interested in him, or his penis, showing me any moves at any time, in any apartment, in this lifetime, ever.

I ducked into my apartment and started rifling through my mail. Nothing good. A Citibank bill. Overdue. My rent bill. Also overdue. A Williams-Sonoma catalog. An offer from Capital One, devilishly tempting me to transfer funds from my *other* overdue credit cards. An envelope of ValPak coupons. A solicitation from one cable TV company to transfer from my current one, whose bill, had it been among the day's catch, also would have been overdue. And a handwritten note from my landlord: *Still haven't seen your rent check for last month. This pattern of lateness is going to leave me with no choice. Please remit forewith with all due haste.*

Worse than the simple scolding for my tardiness was the trumped-up legal overtone of the note. "Forewith?" Obviously he'd miscopied the missive out of a bad landlords' handbook, but the implication was clear: improve my cash flow or I'd be out on my ass. The first homeless Landau. Soon I'd be out quoting song lyrics with my friend full-time.

I was thinking of making an indie film about myself. I was going to call it *It's a Miserable Life.* It was going to be about a woman who thinks things would be better off if she'd never been born, and, after spending a day with her, her guardian angel actually *agrees*.

# 3.

# consider it kissed

I'd been going out with Dirk for the better part of two years. We were sort of in one of those holding patterns: We weren't happy, but we didn't completely hate each other. We started dating two years after college, and as bad as things were in recent months, it never outweighed all the good that we'd had when we first got together.

We first met at Slate, a sports bar in midtown, when there was a big Notre Dame game on.

Dirk worked at Stanton, Seal, Shafer & Long LLP doing corporate transactional law—buying and selling, taking companies public, mostly doing mergers and acquisitions. Typically it took eight years to become partner, but Dirk seemed to be on the fast track and was trying to make partner By Any Means Necessary. He had to bill at least twenty-five hundred hours a year, which pretty much meant working ten to twelve hours a day and sometimes weekends.

It was a source of immense pride for Dirk that he worked a ton of hours yet still managed to go out for drinks even more than *we* did in advertising. I'd sworn I'd never date a guy who ever said "I like to work hard and play hard," but I gave him the benefit of the doubt.

I was out with a girlfriend and we were in our looking-for-men-where-men-are phase. She had decided that men were not in produce aisles and bookstores as everybody thought, and that we needed to hit sports bars on game nights, steak houses on weeknights, and strip clubs on any night that we could muster up enough nerve. Steak houses didn't sound like a great idea to me. Sure, there may have been packs of men there having dinner. But they were having *dinner*. I mean, wouldn't it be a little creepy to just hover around the table, like dogs looking for a bone?

And strip clubs . . . I wasn't quite comfortable with the idea of that. Plus, it would send the wrong message. It wasn't like I was a regular at Flash Dancers, and I wouldn't want a potential mate to think I was. Or that it was okay for *him* to be, once we started dating. It would be false advertisement. Bad enough that I was wearing a Wonderbra. So strip clubs were out, and that left sports bars.

I first spotted Dirk when I was playing a game of pool; I happened to be having an uncharacteristically great game. He was tall and well built, brown hair, great eyes that crinkled at the sides when he smiled. He looked like a young George Clooney. Devilishly handsome. Full of confidence. The kind of guy any girl would look twice at.

I noticed Dirk watching me, so I tried to look extra cool taking my next shot. Of course I *scratched,* but that was when he came over and introduced himself. I should have known then—he preyed on the weak. He had those boyish good looks and more charm than Bill Clinton on intern orientation day. So naturally I fell for him.

Dirk and I had both just been through the postgraduate shock syndrome—him from Columbia Law School and me from NYU undergrad—and we helped each other out of it. For some people I knew, college was like a free-for-all, a four-year run (seven in his case) of irresponsible sex and intoxication—like getting paid to hunt for bedmates and not worry about anything real. Then there was the after-college dry spell, the where-did-all-the-free-sex-go? period. Topped off with the fact that you can't schedule your job like you did your classes so that you have no work before 11 A.M. or on Fridays. Real life was a hell of a letdown.

We both had been dating around. For me, a big reason for dating Dirk exclusively was that it had been hard to stay focused on several men at a time. For Dirk, I think it was the realization that if you date many women, you're paying for a lot of dinners and not necessarily going to be getting any sex, but if you date *one* woman, you'll definitely get sex and probably cut your dinner bills in half. Dirk was nothing if not practical. Not exactly what you'd call a romantic approach, but there we were.

At first he was unsure of the whole boyfriend-girlfriend thing, but one day about three weeks in, something changed. It was Christmastime, and they were doing the big lighting of the tree in Rockefeller Center. We'd both been living in New York and of course seen the giant lit-up tree in years past, but neither of us had ever been to the actual *lighting* and we thought it would be fun to attend. It's always a big event, with thousands of people cramming into nearby blocks to see pop stars lip-synching Christmas songs and witness the first lighting of the tree. They'd been talking it up on TV and the radio for the whole week beforehand, and we knew it would be a madhouse, so we decided to get there early.

It was by far the coldest day of the year, and for some crazy reason we decided to walk there. It wasn't that far from my office, but as cold as it was, we still froze. About halfway to Rockefeller Center, we stopped in a Starbucks to thaw. I got a peppermint latte and he got a Chantico chocolate drink, which he'd dubbed "crackito" because it was so addictive, to warm us up for the rest of our journey.

We talked and laughed, and the freezing walk felt warm and fun. As we neared Rock Center we worried that we wouldn't get a good spot, what with all the news coverage and anxious locals and tourists, so we picked up our pace to an almost run for the last few blocks.

When we got there, it was surprisingly desolate. There were a few signs up, telling people where to go, but *no* people. We crossed the street at Saks Fifth Avenue and walked right into Rockefeller Center. Empty but for a few ice-skaters on the rink. The tree was there but it wasn't lit up.

Then we saw the sign that advertised Tuesday's tree lighting. It was *Monday*. We were early. By twenty-four hours and twelve minutes. We looked at each other and cracked up so hard that our eyes started tearing. Maybe it was from the cold, but we were in bona fide hysterics. He kissed me next to the unlit tree, and I swear I saw the lights go on for one split second. We'd enjoyed ourselves so much, holding hands on our walk and showing up in time to find out we'd totally blown it, that it was decidedly more fun than if we'd actually been fighting our way through wall-to-wall people. In fact, we had so much fun doing it wrong that we decided we didn't even want to do it right.

I thought we'd live at that peak, but we started our descent almost immediately, like an Everest expedition hurrying to get back down before the oxygen ran out and the storm hit. Still, I looked back fondly on the high points, believing beyond hope that we'd see them again.

To this day I still haven't seen the lighting of the tree. But from that moment, everything changed with Dirk and me. For the better *at first.* Where before he wasn't into having a girlfriend, suddenly he started inviting me to office functions. I was introduced to all the partners, and they quickly took me into their tight-knit family—and were also not too shy in suggesting Dirk and I start our *own.* I don't know if it was that they thought we were a terrific couple as much as they liked their lawyers to have mortgages, spouses, and kids . . . so they couldn't quit.

As heavy as his workload was, he would call me every few hours just to hear my voice. (*Later* he would call "just to hear my voice," but it was actually to make sure I was home so he wouldn't get caught doing whatever he was doing elsewhere.)

But in those first few months he made me feel like the luckiest girl in the world. We'd walk down the street and he'd hold my hand, and he had that cocky swagger and I somehow just felt cool, which was something I rarely felt. We'd cook together. Well, technically I'd cook for him, but he'd hang out with me and do an Olympic gymnastics judge play by play.

"Now, Jordan's cracking an egg," he'd say. "Let's see if she can manage to avoid the shell-in-yolk blunder that's so common in this move. The level of difficulty is about a seven, but Jordan happens to be very skilled in this event." Sometimes he'd even hold up a sign with a score. I'd pout if I got a lower score than I deserved, but he was usually pretty fair.

When we first started dating, our sex life was pretty hot. He had a couple years on me and was a lot more experienced than I was—he sort of helped me come into my own. I don't think I'd ever been on top before I dated him. In fact, I think I may have been the most boring lay on the planet. But nobody'd ever complained, so I didn't know any better. Most guys were just happy to be getting laid, period. But Dirk showed me a whole new world, and for that I'll be eternally grateful.

The point is, we bonded. We had such a romantic first six months that for every time he was an hour late, there was a time he *tried* to make me breakfast in bed, Eggs Benedict burned mercilessly, but still there on a tray with a rose and a homemade coupon for "one delicious nonburned breakfast at our favorite diner." And for every time he didn't show up at all, there was a time when he showed up uninvited because he just couldn't wait to see me. And that bond was so strong that it carried me through the tough times, hoping that we'd find our way back. I *tried* to bring the romance into the relationship again every now and then. Usually I failed miserably.

So there we were . . . two years later, and things had certainly changed. At least between us. Dirk's apartment still looked and smelled like a frat house. He shared a one-bedroom apartment with Jim Murphy, a fraternity buddy (and law school dropout) whom he somehow couldn't let go of—as if living alone would somehow mean he was officially a grown-up—so we rarely had his place to ourselves. Not that I necessarily *wanted* to spend that much time there, beer paraphernalia everywhere—still emanating the faint stench of stale booze—moose antlers that he'd won in a poker game, and of course his prized possession: the Farrah Fawcett poster from the seventies where you could see her nipple.

Every now and then, after he'd had a few beers, he'd point her nipple out to me, as if it was the first time he'd noticed it. I never knew if he was expecting me to high-five over it or tear open my shirt in jealous competition or something, but I'd usually just nod: Yes, it is indeed Farrah Fawcett's nipple.

We'd planned to have a night alone, and I brought candles that I'd picked up at the Pottery Barn over to Dirk's to add a little ambience. It was one of my latest attempts at trying to breathe a little life back into our evaporating relationship. I was cooking a romantic dinner for us and, God knows why, had even brought flowers to complete the mood. I moved the flowers into several different spots on the table to get things just right. Then I took out one of the candles and placed it between our two settings on the table. "Love Me Tender" came on the radio. Dirk started singing along, doing a very bad Elvis.

"I love this song," I said. "At least I *did* prior to this rendition."

"I'll 'love you tender,'" he said. "I'll love you so tender you won't even be able to ride your bike home." And then he smacked my ass and walked out of the room. Quite the charmer, he was.

When I went to light a candle, I burned my finger on the match.

"Ouch!" I screamed, but Dirk didn't even look up from the television. I grimaced and tried again, louder this time for effect. "Ouch!" Still nothing. "I just burned my finger," I said. "Wanna kiss it and make it better?"

"Consider it kissed," he said without looking. What was *that*? I could have gotten mad at this. I *should* have. I could have said, "Consider yourself fed" and taken my gourmet meal elsewhere, or "Consider yourself fucked" and taken my gourmet vagina elsewhere. But I didn't. Instead I said, "Gee thanks," and I stayed and continued to cook until I heard a knock at the door.

"Are you expecting someone?"

"Yeah," he said. "Tony and Greg are coming over to watch the game . . . I forgot to tell you. Think you're making enough for all of us?"

"Um . . . Dirk?" I paused to gather my thoughts, my left leg jiggling anxiously. "I love all the guys you work with . . . especially Tony and Greg . . . but I thought this was going to be *our* night. Isn't that why Jimmy isn't here right now?" I asked as I continued stirring the pasta.

"It *is* our night. *Every* night is our night, baby."

"But I thought we were going to have dinner just the two of us. Like you said. I hate to sound like the naggy, whiny girlfriend, but lately it just doesn't seem like you really want to spend any time with me." As soon as I said it, I wished I hadn't. If I hated to sound like the naggy, whiny girlfriend, then why did I finish the sentence? Why did I *start* the sentence? I stirred the pasta furiously, frustrated at the both of us, and came dangerously close to whisking the water right out of the pot.

"Jordan, do you realize that before I was with you, I dated three, four, five girls at a time? I dated more people at once than you've been with in your whole life," he said, his eyes leaving the TV screen for the first time that night. "And I *know* you know how many girls *come on* to us when we do Boys' Night at Keen's . . ." He waited for some kind of acknowledgment, but I just kept stirring, annoyed by his line of reasoning, so he went on. "The fact that I now choose to be with *only* you is a *really* big deal. You need to *appreciate* that."

"I do appreciate it," I said, one salty tear falling into the pot.

"Good. So you'll make enough for everybody?"

"Yeah, no problem."

"Cool," he said. "I know I said it would be just us tonight, but . . . forgive and forget." "Forgive and forget" was Dirk's favorite saying and my guiding principle for the majority of our relationship. I did a lot of forgiving but, truthfully, not as much forgetting. Dirk's lame attempts at impersonating a boyfriend—or even a human—were pretty much impossible to erase from my mind.

Yes. I was a total loser. I know it. I shouldn't have let him treat me that way, but I'm admitting this up front because the evening only got worse. I spent the night watching them watch TV and high-five over whatever ridiculous thing they were bonding over at that given moment. High fives were really big with Dirk. I made a promise to myself that the next guy I dated would never high-five. Ever. Except maybe the occasional ironic post–high-five-aware high five. After all, everything in life has a parody phase.

After about two hours of this fun, the beer ran out. I was already bored so I halfheartedly offered to go to the store and pick some up.

"Thanks, sweetie," he said, and kind of ruffled my hair. I know you shouldn't offer to do anything you don't really want to do, so I sort of got myself into that, but right then I heard a thunderclap and looked expectantly at Dirk, waiting for him to change the plan. "Uh-oh . . . don't forget an umbrella," he said with an almost innocent smile. I was constantly shocked by how low he'd go, and this night was no exception.

"Don't make her go in the rain, man. Jordan, *I'll* go," said the always-chivalrous Tony.

"No, no. I *offered*," I said, sort of baiting him, hoping Dirk would realize the offer was *pre*-weather situation and grow a conscience.

"You sure you don't mind?" Tony asked, looking back and forth between Dirk and me.

"Not at all. I *love* going out in the pouring rain," I said, oozing with sarcasm. The only problem was, sarcasm is generally lost on those who partake in the non-ironic high five.

"Cool, thanks," one of them said. The deafening sound of thunder that erupted simultaneously made it difficult to identify who was talking.

And there I was, off on a beer run at 10 P.M. in the pouring rain. I actually heard Dirk joking to his friends about how well trained I was as I was walking out the door. I was tempted to lay into him for basically calling me a poodle, but I hated confrontation and I didn't want to prove him right by being a bitch; so I just went out to get the beer.

I got completely soaked on my way to the deli. It was one of those Manhattan rainstorms that pounds down diagonally so no matter how you hold your umbrella, you're *gonna* get soaked. I was so cold, sopping wet, and frustrated that I was near tears by the time I got to the store. I surveyed the different beer brands, and when I finally decided on Pete's Wicked Ale, I realized that Dirk had conveniently forgotten to give me money. Even more conveniently I didn't have enough cash on me, and the nearest ATM was three blocks away, so out I went again into the storm. This time I *was* in tears. Just for a minute. It was one of those non-cry cries. Like when you get choked up at an AT&T commercial but the next second you're on to a Tide commercial, and just like *that*, you couldn't care less about the girl calling her dad on a Sunday, because it is *all* about that grass stain and whether or not it's gonna come out.

When I got back to Dirk's, I tried to join the conversation or at least start one, but they kept shushing me, so I fell asleep on what Dirk referred to as his "Man Chair." When I woke up a half hour later, the guys were gone and Dirk was passed out on the couch. I got up and smelled the flowers that I'd brought over, thinking of that saying about stopping to smell the roses once in a while. They didn't smell very sweet; in fact, they turned my stomach, so I hurled them in the garbage can. I tried to say good night to Dirk, but he wouldn't wake up. Considering that evening a train wreck, I saw myself out.

# 4.

# he peed in my closet

As soon as I got home I called Todd. Trusty Todd. My best male friend and former husband from age seven. I threw down my bag and took off my still-damp sweatshirt, waving my arms over my head in self-directed disgust, while I recapped the unfortunate evening I'd just suffered through. My frantic motion and bra-clad figure was no doubt creating a spectacle for anyone who should happen to be peering in through my tiny window. A horrible thought crossed my mind: What if Spandex Man could see in my window from *his* and saw my distress as an invitation to come save me with his ka-ra-*tay*? Suddenly, desperate to leave the building, I asked Todd to meet me for late night coffee.

My relationship to coffee was like no other. Much like my relationship to Todd. Both perked me up when I was down, helped keep me going when I was low on energy, and made me have to urinate constantly. There *is* a downside to having a friend who's a laugh a minute. Todd had grown up well. He was skinny but not in a nerdy way. He was more of that *hipster* skinny. He lived in T-shirts of bands a normal person would never have heard of, jeans, and Pumas. He worked as a graphic designer at another ad agency, and although his was a *real* agency peopled by something other than misfits, he got it when I complained about the bullshit I dealt with and, in our own private game of My Job Sucks Worse poker, he would see my ad woes and raise them with his own.

As we were picking where to meet, I noticed a large cockroach unapologetically crawling up my wall. I recognized him. I'd seen him before and named him Major Deegan after an expressway here in New York. Major Deegan briefly stopped when he saw me, and we had a bit of a stare-down. A Mexican standoff with *la cucaracha*. Me and the roach. Each claiming our rightful territory. This was New York, after all, and anyone knows that a New York apartment for under $1,200 a month comes with roaches. In any other part of the country $1,200 would rent you a pretty decent place. In New York, it will get you a shoebox-sized apartment with dozens of six-legged roommates who won't contribute to the rent yet still feel free to leave their shit all over the place.

I was so focused on the roach that I couldn't even hear Todd speaking into my ear anymore. Finally the roach got bored and continued up the wall and I returned to the conversation, during which we'd apparently agreed to meet at Cozy's Soup 'n Burger.

"See you in fifteen," he said. I put a dry sweatshirt on and headed out the door, knowing full well that I'd feel infinitely better once I'd bitched and moaned to Todd, and Major Deegan would be happy to have the place to himself.

On my way to meet Todd, I walked past my lyrical drifter, and she stopped to look me up and down. Then she said, " 'Now there's trouble bussin' in from outta state . . .' " and she whipped her head up, one eye on me, waiting.

" 'And the D.A. can't get no relief,' " I replied, both eyes on hers, head bowed a little. She accepted my reply with what looked like it was going to be a sly wink, but was actually the beginnings of a sneeze. Springsteen. I wasn't going to miss *that* one. As we both continued in our different directions, I wondered if she ever thought about me when I wasn't around and tried to come up with a lyric that would stump me. Or maybe if that would make me like every other person she accosted, so my actually knowing the proper response was a welcome relief.

When I got to Cozy's, which was our favorite twenty-four-hour diner, Todd was already seated at our booth and had us each a coffee and slice of cake. One cheesecake and one chocolate blackout cake. Todd was the perfect gay male best friend except he wasn't gay. He actually got more chicks than any guy I knew—including all of Dirk's lothario law buddies. There was something slightly Woody Allen–ish about Todd but only in his neurosis and brilliance, not in the looks department. The hipster-cool thing that women in New York seem to flock to was working for him big-time. Yet as much play as he got, *none* of the girls stuck—and not for a lack of their trying. There was always something he'd find wrong with them—some ridiculous thing, like finding a copy of Jewel's poetry book on her bookshelf or a Phish bootleg in her CD collection or a pair of Uggs—and that would kill it.

Todd *hated* Dirk.

"You must, *must* stop seeing him," he urged.

"He's not that bad."

"No, you're right." He shifted in the booth and looked alarmed. "In fact, Jesus, I think he's right here—I'm sitting on him! Oh, no, wait—it's just a *festering boil on my ass*. You can understand the mix-up."

We sat there quiet for a moment. I knew he wasn't finished. He was planning his strategy. He'd remind me of some of the unspeakable things that Dirk had done and I would defend him until I couldn't anymore and we'd both know that he was right and I should break up with Dirk but that I didn't have the balls to do it.

"He forgot your *birthday*," he began.

"I hate birthdays anyway."

"Nobody hates birthdays," he said dismissively. "People hate getting older, but everybody loves a birthday."

"No, I actually hate birthdays," I countered, standing.

It was true. It had started on my sixth birthday, when I thought for sure my dad would be there, because even though he said he might not see me for a long time, I really didn't think he meant *that* long and he'd surely be back for my *birthday*. He, of course, was a no-show. And then there was my ninth birthday, the year we had boys *and* girls. Walter had planned a hip-hop dance party because hip-hop was taking off and he thought the kids would love to dance. Boys stayed on one side of our house, girls on the other, and the only mingling was a softball that got hurled by Billy Engbert, which was meant to just show off his throwing arm, but landed square in my face. And who could forget my fourteenth birthday, which got *completely* overlooked, in what I thought was an homage to *Sixteen Candles* and surely a practical joke to be revealed at my surprise party—a party that never took place. For these and several other unfortunate birthday debacles, I genuinely didn't like birthdays. Todd was going to lose this one. So he tried another route.

"He hit on your sister."

"He was just trying to get to know my family."

"In your family do you greet new people by sticking your tongue down somebody's throat?" he goaded in a decibel way too high for a place called Cozy's.

"There was no tongue," I defended. "And Sam is a slut."

"Fine, so they're *both* assholes. That doesn't make *him* any less of an asshole!"

"I know . . . I know."

"Do you need me to go on?"

"I think so." I shrugged.

"Fine. He peed in your closet. I mean . . . *there are no words*."

"I already told you! He was sleepwalking after having many, many beers that night. He thought it was the bathroom." Todd's look said, Come *on*—who are you trying to kid? "He did!" I squealed.

"He didn't go to your grandmother's funeral."

"Funerals weird him out. He doesn't like *dead* people . . ."

"And the rest of us just *love*'em. C'mon, Jordy! He's a total asshole. As your husband, I demand that you break up with your boyfriend. Don't you have to listen to me or *obey* me or something?"

"Fine. I've heard enough for tonight," I said. "I'll think about it." Dirk *was* a jerk and I knew it. If I could only hold on to the feeling I had right that minute, then I'd have the courage to break up with him. But I'd head home, go to bed, wake up, and it would be a new day. I would be filled with the same naive hope that maybe this day would be different. I'd think that maybe he'd do a turnaround and be nicer, treat me better, remember how things used to be, and try to recapture what we had, making it all worth it. Maybe. Yeah, sure, and maybe they'd also invent that pill where you could eat whatever you wanted and never get fat.

The rehabilitated Dirk was an illusion, but a necessary one. I held onto the fantasy that things would be like they were in the beginning because, besides my issues with confrontation, I just didn't like to give up. You may think that's a weakness, but you can also look at it as a strength. A strength of hope and a resolve to continue to work at something because I didn't want to accept failure. Even though sometimes the strength it takes to admit failure is probably worth as much as the determination not to quit. So there you have it. I was stuck fighting for a relationship with a boyfriend who, truth be told, I'd much rather forget ever existed.

# 5.

# will copywrite for food

I came home and checked my answering machine. Another message from Citibank. Delete. I rifled through my drawer to find the actual bill and marveled at how much I owed, considering I had so little to show for it. That seems to be the universal thing with credit card debt. Yeah, here's $11,000 spent, but where's the car? Where's the stereo system and sixty-inch plasma TV? What did I spend that money on? Did I eat it? All I ever really paid for was food—but could I possibly have eaten $11,000 worth of food? I may have a hearty appetite but, Christ—not that hearty.

I rushed to my full-length mirror in sudden certainty that I must weigh a minimum of six hundred pounds. And . . . nope. Yet I found myself torn between relief and feeling somewhat let down that I wasn't worth my weight in credit card debt.

My financial squeeze was just that—too little room between income and expenses, like an impatient cabbie trying to create a third lane on a two-lane side street. Scrape. Fast fact: $30,000 in school loans, plus eleven grand in credit card debt, plus monthly rent, utilities, health insurance co-pay, and all the niceties (such as food) don't exactly fit into a $34,000 annual salary after taxes. Shocker, right? The school loans might have been avoided, but I'd made a valiant, half-serious offer to cover a portion of my costs, and my mother had never been so proud—or so careful with money.

Needless to say, a portion is more than you might suspect. I wasn't ever extravagant. I believe the appropriate term is *stupid*.

I tucked the bill back into my desk, ironically in between two pages of my Zagat guide, and started to write in my journal. I decided to make a list of Dirk pros and cons. Sometimes when you lay it all out in black and white it can help you see things more clearly. It started out as a list and morphed into a pie chart. That was scary. Knowing how much I got charged for food, I realized I'd best keep pie out of this. I quickly shut the journal and moved to the computer—resulting in an entire PowerPoint presentation. This was a little *too* clear, so I just closed the document and didn't bother hitting *Save*.

Feeling crummy sometimes has its advantages. Creative genius often stems from complete misery. I was feeling sufficiently bad about myself and had nothing *better* to do, so I tidied up my apartment and started thinking about work stuff. Specifically, I was thinking about this KidCo campaign that Lydia was working on. KidCo was a regional kid's activity center, much like Gymboree, with play classes for all ages and a wide variety of art, music, and fitness events. If I were a kid, I would honestly have a hard time choosing among them. And suddenly the ideas started flowing. I rushed to the computer and stayed up half the night writing them out, ready to be presented in the morning.

\* \* \* \* \*

When I raced into Lydia's office she looked less than pleased to see me. If I hadn't been there for a couple years, I'd have worried that I'd done something wrong. But, knowing Lydia as I did, I could tell that this was just her usual look of disapproval. She often looked as if she were smelling something rancid. I made the mistake once of asking her about it, because she genuinely looked like she was in discomfort.

"Do you smell something bad?" I had asked.

"No," she'd said, looking side to side, suggesting I was out of my mind. "Do you?"

"No."

And then we stood there looking at each other for an awkward moment. She stared at me, seeming mildly horrified yet interested, like I was Tara Reid on the red carpet, nipple exposed to the world, smiling for the camera—and then raised her eyebrows as if to ask me, Is there anything *else*?

"Okay, then. Great. I was just taking a poll," I said. "That will be three 'No, I do *not* smell anything bad' and one 'Yes, I *do*, but it's probably just my flatulent cubical mate.'" This was my attempt at humor. One of several daily failed attempts that I'd learned to accept as more nuggets for the old humility treasure trove. She looked at me blankly and then gave me about seventy-five hours of busywork to ensure I didn't go around the office taking any more polls.

So that morning when I ran in there all gung ho to tell her my ideas, her look was much the same. She was on the phone. She pulled the phone away from her angry, angular jaw.

"What is it?"

"So I think I've got some great ideas for the KidCo TV campaign." I beamed.

She acted perturbed by the interruption, but I could see that she was excited underneath her winter-like exterior. This was validated by the fact that she told whoever she was on the phone with that she'd have to call them back. She never got off the phone for me. She acted distressed and exasperated, but I *knew* she was eager as a virgin on prom night to hear the concepts.

"What do you have?"

This was my chance. I was going to wow her with my ideas and finally get to start writing copy around here. My only involvement with traffic would be avoiding it on my daily commute. I'd be a brilliant copywriter. I took a deep breath.

"Okay. I have a couple of ideas . . . a few on the same variation. Picture a boardroom with a bunch of kids in grown-up suits talking marketing strategies—IPOs, etc. It's a cute visual even by itself. Then the V-O comes. 'At KidCo, *our* boss is your five-year-old.'"

Lydia just sat there looking at me. She cocked her head. I wondered what was going on in her brain. She wasn't giving me much to go on, so I told her my next idea.

"Okay, visual effect: First kid draws another kid tumbling that morphs into a live kid tumbling into a sea of balls that splash up into the hands of a juggler, whose feet become the feet of a new kid dancing with a teacher, whose hand points to a background that becomes a chalkboard with lessons that a kid studies while clapping in a circle with other kids singing and then falling down laughing. And this V-O: 'KidCo. Come to learn. Come to play. Come today.'"

She still didn't react, but she did write something down on her notepad.

"Go on," she said.

"Okay, this is a tryout for a Broadway show. From the dark of the theater seats we look up at the hopefuls on the stage—KidCo instructors and teachers and helpers. We hear a child's voice: 'Okay. I love what I'm seeing from Art; and Dance Class, outstanding; Gymnastics, beautiful work; Field Trips, Music, Languages, Reading, Snack Time—you're all definitely in.' Then at the end of the chorus line, we see a nebbishy guy in a suit with slumped shoulders. The voice pipes up again: 'Uh, Boredom? Thanks for coming. We'll call you.'" Then the voice-over tag— 'KidCo. Matinees daily. Enjoy the show.'"

Lydia wrote something else down. I couldn't quite get a read on her, but I had to think if she was taking notes, then she liked my ideas at least a little. I kept going.

"Now, new visual: Picture an assembly line with big boxes and a child sitting in every box as they move down the conveyor belt. The V-O comes in: 'At KidCo, we don't make *kids* . . .' And then we cut to a shot of a kid going down a slide, falling into a basin of colored balls. 'We just make kids *happy*.'"

Lydia smiled for the first time. Probably in weeks. I thought it was because she liked them. She liked me! I felt like Sally Field at the Academy Awards when she said "You like me! You really like me!" I was ready to burst. But then her smile turned derisive. Almost pitying. "Well," she said, "it's good that you're keeping yourself active. It's probably too late

for any of this to have an impact, though . . . we'll see. But keep dab-
bling, because you never know . . ."

"Okay," I said, completely deflated, still standing there, somewhat
shell-shocked.

"You can go now."

I was dismissed. But that was all right, because I knew that deep down
she was impressed. This had to be the beginning of my new career.

* * * * *

After work I met Cat at the gym for our biweekly torture session on the
treadmill. Cat was in much better shape than me, so it was always good
to have her running next to me for motivation's sake. Cat was my oldest
friend, next to Todd. She was more like my sister than my sister was, but
that wasn't difficult with a sister who still attempted to put my finger in
warm water when I came home for the holidays, trying to get me to pee
my bed. I told Cat what had happened at work that day.

"That's awesome! I see a promotion in someone's very near future."

"You think so?"

"Definitely! Those are really solid ideas. There are some big changes
about to happen in your life. I can feel it."

Cat could always "feel" things. She also "saw" things. Not things in
the future, but things that weren't there. People, to be more specific. Cat
saw movie stars, TV personalities, and celebutants about five times a day.
We'd be walking down the street and she'd insist that we just passed Jon
Bon Jovi.

"That was a woman," I'd say.

"Oh."

As excited as she'd get for each of these sightings, she always took it in
stride when I informed her that it was not, in fact, Elvis (I mean, c'mon,
he'd been dead for like half a century). I don't know why she tried so
hard to spot famous people. It may have been partly an antidote for her
work as a therapist—constantly hearing the mundane ins and outs of her

patients—and also because she was so happily married it was ridiculous, so seeing some hot star was her attempt to spice things up a little. Generally speaking, Cat was the most levelheaded person I knew.

Cat got married a year and a half after moving to the city, and she and her husband, Billy, had an amazing apartment in SoHo. Professionally, she was a prodigy, with a specialty psychology practice in an office on the ground floor of their building. She did a small amount of one-on-one and group therapy, but her largest client base came to her for drama-therapy and psychodrama, spontaneous role-playing during which her clients acted out fears, traumas, memories, et cetera.

"Keep going!" Cat said as she increased her speed to 7.5 on the treadmill, a speed I'd only read about in fitness magazines.

"When I get promoted, can I stop coming to the gym?"

"No." She cheered, "You'll be invigorated!"

I started slowing down my treadmill.

"Don't do it," Cat warned, sensing correctly where things were headed. "Let's role-play right here. It'll be fun."

"Oh no . . ." I said. "No, no, no."

In an effort to jolt myself out of my comfort zone and get a different part of my brain working, help myself both creatively and personally, nurture my spontaneity, and maybe just maybe develop skills that might one day vault me to sitcom superstardom, I'd foolishly let Cat talk me into doing a role-playing exercise a while back.

She was a great teacher, but I was a terrible student. Partly because it was Cat and—professional as she tried to be—with our knowing each other inside and out, I wasn't able be someone *else* without feeling totally embarrassed, and partly because I just couldn't let my guard down. It seemed I was destined to stumble through life unable to make Jordan Landau anything more than . . . Jordan Landau.

"You *got* the promotion. You are confident and successful . . ." she went on.

"Five point two . . ." I said as I slowed it further. "Four one. Three seven . . ."

"No role-playing exercise, no more actual exercise even—*however* . . . I'm going to exercise my right to go have some Ben & Jerry's. Right now."

Cat looked disappointed, but somehow I'd manage. I deserved it. This wasn't pity ice cream . . . this was celebration ice cream! I'd seen that glimmer of a smile on Lydia's mean face, even if she belittled me seventeen seconds after it. I knew she saw something in those ideas. I'd finally had a small victory at work! This was victory ice cream!

When I got outside, I could still see Cat through the window, and she me. She was watching me as I tried unsuccessfully to hail a taxi. And just when I had one, flashing his lights, signaling that he was mine, a girl ran out in front of me and stole it. Cat and I had a long history of cab debacles and I could sense her *willing* me to snatch it back, to be more assertive. I never had it in me to fight back when someone stole a cab from me. Part of it was my admitted distaste for confrontation, but the other reason was that life's too short to sweat things like that. People are *going* to steal your cab, and if that's their worst offense, consider yourself blessed.

I decided I had no business taking a cab anyway, so I took the M15 bus back down to St. Marks, and I stopped at the deli at Astor Place to peruse the ice cream section, which was seriously lacking. I debated between Brownie Batter, which is chocolate with the fudge brownie bits in it, and plain old vanilla. What I really wanted was *vanilla* with the brownie bits in it. The chocolate with the chocolate was just too much. Vanilla with brownies would be perfect.

I actually wrote a letter to Ben & Jerry's once and suggested that they create this flavor. Free of charge. I wasn't asking for royalties or a credit or anything. It would be reward enough for me just to have my flavor in *existence*. I mean, sure it would be nice if they named it after me, but with the names they chose—Chunky Monkey, Cherry Garcia—God knows what my flavor would be called. Jordan's Junkfood? Jolly Jordan? Worse, Chunky Jordan? No, they could just leave my name out of it.

Ben & Jerry's wrote back to me eventually, with a form letter (apparently I wasn't the first person to suggest a new flavor to them), and thanked me for my suggestion and included a coupon toward my next purchase of Ben & Jerry's ice cream. I'd had wild fantasies about a truck pulling up one day and these really incredible-looking guys coming out one after the next with crates of Gorgeous Jordan ice cream. A parade of ice cream hunks bearing brownie chunks on a vanilla ice cream red carpet. They'd be coming to surprise me because Ben & Jerry's had perfected my flavor and they wanted me to be the first to have it. And my ice cream hunks would be shirtless, of course, and sweating as they carried the boxes from the truck to my apartment. At which point it would only be right for me to invite them in for some ice cream, and well, you can guess the rest. (*Before* you guess the rest, I need to clarify that there wouldn't be an orgy taking place or anything—I'm not that kind of girl. I'd just pick the best one out of the bunch. *Now* you can guess the rest.) Anyway, they never showed up, so the coupon toward my next purchase would have to suffice.

I took the coupon to Ernie One-Brow, the guy with the Frida Kahlo unibrow who usually manned the counter at Delion. Consolation: He was sweating profusely when he grumbled about the coupon and angrily made change.

Anyway, I decided on Chocolate Chip Cookie Dough, and since I was already there, I got a pint of Peanut Butter Cup too. Just for emergencies.

Crossing the street at Broadway and West 4th, I saw Lyric Lady coming toward me.

She sidled up to me and leaned in, " 'Know it sounds funny but I just can't stand the pain . . .' " And she stopped. Waited.

I looked off and thought for a minute, I sang it in my head a couple time, and then *BAM!* " 'Girl, I'm leaving you tomorrow,' " I answered back. She looked at me and pursed her lips a little, eyes squinty, then she went on her way contentedly.

As I got out of the elevator on my floor, I had the great displeasure of seeing Tiger Schulmann Spandex Cock Guy, bending over into our trash room, dropping a stack of newspapers into our recycling bin. That thing was monstrous. Truly frightening. I practically ran past him so I wouldn't have to ward off another offer for private self-defense class.

Once safely inside my apartment, I immediately started to storyboard my ideas for KidCo. If anyone wanted me to take it any further or if it got brought up in a meeting, I wanted to be ready.

I hadn't even noticed that my answering machine was blinking. It said that I had one message. The automated voice that I'd come to know so well. The one that pronounced my name in a stilted rendering, with the accent on the wrong sylla*ble*.

"Hello, Jor*dan* Lan*dau*, this is Cindy from Citibank. This is a very important call. Your account is sixty days past due. Please return this call Monday through Saturday between 8 A.M. and 8 P.M. Eastern time." And then she gave the number, which I could never make out on the machine.

Did you ever notice that it's rarely good news when your bank calls? It's never "We just wanted to express our amazement at your rapidly ascending balance!" Or "We just want to say thanks for being you."

My financial situation was pretty much in the shitter. You'd think a college degree would get you somewhere, but the job market was so bleak when I graduated that I took what I could get with promise of a salary increase. I was still waiting for that increase. I just didn't know how to bring it up. Every time I almost did, I got squeamish, started sweating, and chickened out.

Yet I'd be damned if I was going to go crawling to my mother and stepfather for relief. I didn't believe in that sort of thing. That sort of thing being humiliation and guilt and lectures from one of the world's all-time spendthrifts about being more frugal. Self-reliance and personal responsibility are a good foundation. Back them up with a reluctant, condescending creditor and you're on your way to true financial independence.

# 6.
# fresh air will do you good

It was Saturday, and I had planned weeks earlier to have lunch with my mom. I took the train out to Long Island and was seated next to a guy who had quit smoking that day and felt the need to talk about it incessantly.

"It's not the first time I've quit," he said after he'd finally stopped talking, and I thought that we were finally done.

"Hmm." I nodded.

"Yeah, I quit once before . . . I mean, I've quit a thousand times before but one time for *real*."

"Yeah, quitting is hard." I thought a definitive statement and a look out the window would give him the cue that we we'd covered the topic.

"But obviously I picked it back up again. And you know when? Like four months later. I'd quit cold turkey. And I was fine. Completely fine. Then I was walking down the street and it hit me like a bolt of lightning. I needed a cigarette and I needed one that instant. I couldn't even wait until I got to a store or passed someone I could bum a smoke off. I just stopped *right* where I was and looked around at the ground. Sure enough, there was a butt. A beautiful butt." I could tell he wasn't going to stop. Smoking *or* talking. Ever. "I reached down and picked that butt up and oh man . . . it was *heaven*."

I got off the train an entire stop early and walked to my mom's house, which took an extra half hour. We lived in an affluent suburb—not nearly so much then as now. Home values are so high that they're inducing a kind of paralysis in some of the neighbors, like with a stock that keeps rising. You don't want to jump out now, because you'll kick yourself if it goes up more the day after you've sold.

Walking through the neighborhood, I had memories of my childhood. I passed the Andersons' house and remembered how awed I was by their Christmas decorations and how they always outdid every other house on the street. When I passed the Dickersons' house, I thought about the rumor that Mr. Dickerson was having an affair, which was so widespread that if he wasn't, he might as well have been. And I still scowled when I walked by crazy Mrs. Cooper's house—the woman who used to say that she'd have our dogs shot if we didn't stop them from barking.

When I got there my sister, Samantha, shot me a look that rivaled the best Mean Girl Junior High dirty looks. Both she and my mother looked completely surprised and none too pleased to see me. My mom regularly vacillated between wanting me around and wanting no part of me. But only since I'd graduated college and moved out. *Prior* to that, she always wanted to have me under her roof—not because she liked my company but more as a method of control. I was a part of her, certainly not her favorite part but a part nonetheless. An appendage. So my leaving somehow felt like an amputation—because it was always about her. Sam was still living at home, taking *one* class at the community college to justify it.

"Hey, *Jordan,*" said Samantha as she looked at our mom, seemingly wondering what the hell I was doing there.

"Hey," I said back. My mom just kept looking shocked to see me.

"Jordan, honey, what are you *doing* here?"

"We're going out to lunch today, remember?" I said, more annoyed than hurt. She almost always forgot when we had plans. And I swear she wasn't forgetful about anything else, but when it came to me . . . I don't know.

"Are you sure, J.?" she said, looking skeptically at me. "I told Samantha I'd take her shopping today." Sam was twenty years old, and she *still* couldn't buy as much as underwear without my mother's presence. And wallet.

"Yeah, and we're late!" chimed Princess Bitch.

"Well, I just took an hour-and-a-half train ride and walked forty minutes to come see you, as was the plan. Well, not the *walking* part. That was because of a psychotic nonsmoker, but the train was the plan. We had a *plan*, Mom," I found myself whining and hated it. Why did she drive me to this? Why did I let her?

I took out my day planner and even showed her where I'd written it down weeks earlier as proof.

"Oh, I'm sorry, sweetie. I penciled you in for tomorrow. I'd tell you to come shopping with us but . . . you really don't like to shop. Do you like to shop? I don't think . . ." She trailed off. No, she didn't think. At least not where I was concerned.

"I'll shop." I sighed. The truth was, I didn't mind shopping. I just didn't like shopping with *them*. Whenever the three of us shopped, they always got *two* of everything, same size, different color. Two Juicy Couture sweatsuits, size *zero;* two pairs of size twenty-four dark wash jeans; two pairs of size twenty-four light wash jeans; two *this*, two *that*, two, two, two, two, TWO.

It wasn't that I couldn't fit into their shared wardrobe that bothered me as much as the feeling of not fitting into my own family and having it so glaringly amplified.

My mom and Samantha shot each other a look. Mom's was telepathically asking Sam if it was okay if I tagged along. Sam's was telepathetically begging Mom *not* to let me. I knew she didn't want me to come shopping with them, and believe me, I didn't want to either. But seeing how annoyed Samantha was at my inclusion made it that much more enticing.

We were riding in the car, Mom driving, Sam riding shotgun, and me in the back. Mom and Samantha were gabbing away about inane crap while I sat getting whipped by my hair—all of the windows were open and my hair was blowing all over the place and all over my face. Samantha was planning her to do list.

"I'm obs*essed* with the new Jimmy Choo's! Everyone was wearing them in this week's *US Weekly*."

"But doesn't that mean that by next week they're going to be *out?*"

"No," she said. "Well, yeah," she added. "But, *Mo-om!* They're so cute!"

I couldn't take the hair in my face any longer. "Do you think you guys can maybe roll up your windows please?"

"It's a beautiful day, honey, enjoy it. You're always holed up in that city apartment. The fresh air will do you good."

If it wasn't already unbearable enough, as my mother was uttering the last word of her sentence and I was opening my mouth to object—a bug flew in the back window straight into my mouth. I started freaking out, making faces, flailing around, spitting . . . all of which my mom caught in her rearview mirror.

"Jordan! What's the *matter* with you?" Sam started laughing at me and shook her head.

I'd managed to get the bug out of my mouth, but I was fingering my gums just to make sure. The bug was gone. My hair was a rat's nest. I looked into my mom's eyes, still locked on me in the rearview. "*Nothing's* the matter."

"Honestly, Jordan, the way you act so crazy sometimes, I find it hard to believe that you're *my* daughter."

"Maybe she was adopted," Sam offered. "Was Jordan's *dad* so big boned?"

"She wasn't adopted, Sam, and yes, her real father was tall."

I sank farther into the backseat as the Sister Sledge song "We Are Family" taunted me in my head.

We were in the shoe section at Bergdorf Goodman when Samantha dropped the bird bomb.

"So you know I'm going to Cancun with Amy and Alex next week, right?" she said to what I assumed to be our mom but she was looking right at me.

"No, I didn't know that," I said. "Sounds like fun."

"Well, I thought you could watch Sneevil Knievel for me . . ." Sneevil Knievel was her *canary*. If she thought I was going to watch him, she had another think coming.

"I think that would be a very nice big-sisterly thing to do, J.," my mom said. "Oh, these shoes are to *die*! Are they to die or *what*?" she asked Sam.

"They're hot," Sam said, and then looked pleadingly at me. "It's only for a week."

"I'll drive you back into the city with the birdcage," Mom offered.

"Fine," I said.

"Awesome," Sam yelped. "I totally won't forget this."

*  *  *  *  *

Finally we got back to the city. The bad thing about shopping with my mom and Samantha . . . was shopping with my mom and Samantha. But the good thing was that I got the ride back into the city, which I hadn't planned on.

When I got back to my apartment building, birdcage in hand, my next-door neighbor had a giant box outside his apartment that I had to step over. This was a weekly occurrence. The guy worked in shipping at his company, and over-ordered toner and ink-jet cartridges, which he then sold on eBay for a hefty profit as a side business. I stood there, thinking about all the little secrets that you come to know about your neighbors and wondered why he was so cavalier about his stealing. What if I was a police officer? Or the daughter of his boss? The building super was guilty of it, too. He was a pot dealer for everyone in the building and probably beyond. I'd never seen inside his apartment, but from all the business he did I imagined it to be a full-on greenhouse. That coupled with the fact that when I moved in, he told me under no circumstances should I let any representative of the city including firemen, police, or any inspector of any kind into the building made him slightly suspect as a law-abiding citizen in my book.

Sneevil Knievel started to chirp, so I had to quit musing on my fate as keeper of every neighbor's dark secrets and quickly get us both inside. For once I had no debtor messages on my answering machine, so I turned on the TV and surfed around until I landed on an old favorite. *Regarding Henry* was on television. I changed into my pajamas and settled in to watch it. I wrote in my journal a little bit, further pondering the film, wondering what it would be like to forget *everything* and *everyone*, and soon after fell asleep.

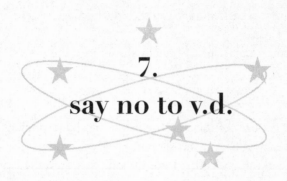

# 7.
# say no to v.d.

The bonds that people form with their college friends strike me as similar to those they have with their camp friends—profound, enduring, and strengthened by inside jokes, shared histories, and secret handshakes. I never went to sleep-away camp and always felt I missed out on the kinship that goes along with it. This set off a sort of social-misfit chain reaction for me—when I went off to college, I opted out of the whole sorority scene, pretty much also consigning my college friends fate to the fairgrounds of few and far between. Maybe all those happy campers understood that, by throwing themselves into some type of forced social activity, they'd be able to garner those everlasting bonds that set you up with lifelong friends with whom you can get together annually and rehash the glory days. I just didn't get it.

It wasn't that I swore by the Groucho Marx maxim of not wanting to belong to any club that would have me as a member. I simply never found a specific club that I could bring myself to be that passionate about. I was having enough trouble finding one *person* to be passionate about, let alone a whole club.

The night before Valentine's Day, sophomore year, I got dragged by my roommate to a frat party on the third floor of a building that housed five fraternities—one on each floor. The party was overcrowded and uncomfortably moist, so fifteen minutes in, I made my move—for the stairs, in hopes of beating a hasty retreat to the exit. One flight down, a door flew open and there stood a really cute guy I'd noticed a week earlier in line at the salad bar in the cafeteria. I recognized his aqua-blue eyes and remembered that they perfectly matched the stripes on his Adidas sneakers. I also remembered that he had stayed away from the carrots but gone crazy for the garbanzo beans.

This is going back a few years, so some of it's a little foggy, but I remember enough to know his conversation was so charming that I took a detour onto the second floor and into one of the bedrooms—it seemed like a college thing to do.

*Mr. Charm* and I made out on a borrowed bed for about an hour. There was no extreme touching, just your garden-variety smooch-fest. When we broke for some air, I remember him looking at me quizzically as he lit an American Spirit cigarette and inhaled the smoke through his nose.

"I've decided that I'm *not* going to pledge this fraternity," he said, looking somewhat wistfully out the window. "And I think I might be gay."

The clock said 12:01 A.M. It was officially Valentine's Day. Happy . . . Fucking . . . Valentine's Day. I'm sure I wondered why he'd bothered making out with me, and hoped *I* wasn't the final test to decide if he was going to switch teams, but I couldn't bring myself to ask him much less even *speak*. I just put my coat back on and returned to the stairwell, this time making it all the way out of the building, never to return.

And so, the next morning, still Valentine's Day, when I met Cat at a coffee shop between each of our campuses—my chin totally stubble-burned from the pathetic events of the night before—and saw her wearing an anti–Valentine's Day T-shirt that said, SAY NO TO V.D., I knew I already had the only friend I needed. Cat was attending Columbia, majoring in psychology with a double minor in irresistible smirks and disjointed hilarity.

I remembered that morning's gossip fest vividly as I walked toward Cat's apartment—now seven years later. We were having lunch with Todd at Jerry's on Prince Street, but I was picking her up at her place so I could see the renovations she and Billy had done. I got there about twenty minutes early and decided to wait outside, but then saw Cat through her office window, motioning me in.

When I opened the door and saw a woman in tears glaring at me, I was sure I'd misunderstood Cat and she had actually been waving me *away*. I started to back off, but Cat took my arm.

"Come in," she said. "This is Ruth."

"Hi, Ruth," I said to the glowering woman, and I gave Cat a quick hug.

"Hello," Ruth said in a stilted manner.

Cat shifted her feet back and forth for a second, and then gave me a big smile. "How would you feel about helping me for just a second?" she asked in the cheery voice that I recognized as her cover for complete exasperation.

"Me?" I said. "How do you mean?"

"Ruth and I are doing a psychodrama, and for some reason, her familiarity with me isn't allowing her to *believe* me as her mother. Could *you* just be Ruth's mother? It will only take a few minutes."

"Sure." I shrugged. "I guess . . . ?"

"Great," Cat said. When Ruth went for water, she leaned close to whisper, "Whatever happens, just listen and say you're sorry. I'll do the rest." Then with Ruth returning she spoke up. "You just stand *here*, and Ruth, now you tell your mother what you're feeling."

"Okay," she said, "You're . . . here. As my mother . . ." And I stood there and waited. Ruth looked at me and her chin started quivering. She looked like she was about to say something, and then she stopped herself. Then the tears started pouring out.

"Where were you?" she said.

We stood there, me looking at her, she at me, and I didn't know if I was supposed to answer her or not. I looked at Cat, and then Ruth stamped her foot.

"Look at me! I asked you a question. Where *were* you?" she screamed.

"I—I don't know," I said hesitantly. "But I'm sorry I wasn't . . . wherever I was supposed to be?"

"Soccer practice. You forgot to pick me up. Coach Bidwall had to take me home with *him* until he could locate you. More than once. Do you know what it's like to be waiting to get picked up and watch everybody else's parents come to get their kids and have nobody come for *you*?" She stuck her chin out at me. I wasn't sure if I was supposed to answer again. "Do you!?" she wailed and tugged at her hair, snot running from her nose to her upper lip.

I just wanted to have lunch with my friend. Suddenly I'm getting blamed for forgetting to pick someone up at soccer practice twenty years ago. I'd like to say I knew just how to handle the situation, but that would pretty much be a lie. My typical stance is on the sidelines, passive, letting it happen, rather than making it happen. I was tempted to play this one true to typical Jordan. But right then, I wasn't me. I was Ruth's derelict mom. Not heeding Cat's instruction, I spoke.

"Ruth," I said, not knowing exactly where the moment would lead; then Dirk's favorite standby occurred to me. "Could we start to forgive and forget?" I asked with a half smile, hoping to help defuse the little scene.

"I don't forgive you," she hissed. "Every insecurity I have to this *day* is because of you. And for the record, I *always* hated tofu and cod liver oil on a bagel. Why couldn't I have just cream cheese like *every other kid*?" She stared wild-eyed at me. I was the *avatar* of Ruth's derelict mother, which filled me with a certain odd pride and a sense of responsibility. Forgetting a soccer practice was one thing—but plain tofu and cod liver oil on a bagel? That's culinary torture. So I took my turn again, and I took her hand.

"Ruth, I can only say I'm sorry for everything that hurt you," I told her. "I always did the best I could with what God gave me. Now it's up to you."

Cat stared at me, her own eyes wild, more surprised than Ruth, who was now quiet. "Thank you," Ruth said, now less feral, with shoulders in a gentle arc. "Maybe we could get together sometime for bagels and cream cheese."

Not knowing to whom this was directed—me or Mother Ruth—I looked at Cat, whose jaw moved side to side signaling something nebulous.

"I prefer peanut butter on mine," I said uncertainly, which set Cat's jaw into higher gear, "but, yes, absolutely, yes." That broke the spell, so to speak. Ruth smiled and nodded.

Cat cleared her throat and announced, "Wow, we've made great progress today, Ruth. Our session is up."

"I think this was a real breakthrough," Ruth breathed, touching my shoulder. "Yes."

Outside afterward, Cat wouldn't look at me for a while. "I think what you did would really bother me, if I weren't so . . . stunned by how different you seemed." She looked up and met my gaze with a forgiving smile. "Maybe you both learned something."

"Definitely," I said. "No kid of mine is ever going to soccer practice without a cell phone." She rolled her eyes, and it was off to Jerry's, hold the tofu and cod liver oil.

*   *   *   *   *

When we settled into our booth, Cat reached into her coat and pulled out a small piece of paper. "I have something to show you," she said, and then turned the paper faceup and pushed it in front of me. It was a sonogram printout. I thought. I'd only really seen them in the movies.

"You're pregnant?" I beamed, and she nodded an enthusiastic yes. I looked at the picture and didn't want to insult her, but I wasn't sure exactly where the baby *was* in it.

"It's right there," she said, sensing my confusion. "That little thing."

"Aww," I said and gave her a hug across the table, careful not to squish her stomach. "That is so amazing, Cat. Congratulations! Were you guys trying?"

"Well, we weren't *not* trying," she said.

Most of my friends are single, but I do have a handful of married friends and it seems that the "not *not* trying" is the second phase of married life—at least from what I gather. If you ask a newly married couple if they're going to have kids, usually you'll get, "Not yet. We want to *enjoy each other* first . . . travel . . . etc." Then comes phase two: They've done enough of the enjoying just each other—or maybe even stopped enjoying each other entirely—and they may be ready to have kids. Yet they won't say that. They won't say they're "trying." And maybe it's because they don't want the pressure of people asking them how it's going, and that's understandable, but isn't "not *not* trying" the same as "trying"? Why the coded double negative? When Todd asked me that morning what I was doing later in the afternoon, I didn't say, "I'm not *not* having lunch with Cat in SoHo . . . so perhaps you'd like to join us?"

Anyway, Cat was pregnant and that was fantastic news. I adored Cat and was genuinely thrilled for her happiness. We talked about her amazing apartment and the amazing new neighbors she and Billy had befriended and how they had an amazing two-month-old baby boy, who was destined to be best friends with *her* baby.

When Todd showed up, Cat apologized for gushing about her "amazing" life and turned the tables on me, asking about Dirk. "And . . . ?" she said with a hopeful grin. "How's life in Dirk land?"

"Oh . . . you know . . ." I said, meaning "sucky," but I didn't want to complain. I always felt guilty telling Cat about my personal problems because she listened to people's issues for a *living*. Why should I make her suffer through it on her lunch break? She was intuitive enough to know that things weren't good and hadn't been good for a long while. By contrast, my life was looking like a shit sandwich compared to hers. Overworked and underpaid? Check. Slimy landlord in a barely heated crummy apartment? Check. Up to my diamond-studless earlobes in debt? Check (certainly no cash). Oblivious boyfriend I outgrew six months ago but don't have the balls to do anything about? Check, check, check.

Cat started asking pointed questions about Dirk. Specifically, about the romantic dinner that she knew I was cooking for him and how it went. I played it down, but even so it didn't sound good. Todd said nothing. But he shook his head in disgust.

"Why do you put up with it?" she asked.

"I didn't want to make a scene in front of his friends."

"Who *cares* if his friends were there? Who are *they*? You're allowed to stand up for yourself, Jordan." I always knew she meant business when she used my name. If ever she was taking me to task on something, she always used my name. And not "J" or "Jordy," like she'd call me any other day. *Jordan*. The equivalent of your parents calling you by your first and middle name when you're in trouble. Or all three names if you're *really* in trouble.

"I *know* I'm allowed to stand up for myself," I said.

"Then why *don't* you?" she said. "You can't let people walk all over you."

"You're right," I said, tongue firmly planted in cheek. "Next thing you know I'll be letting people drag me into their psych sessions." I paused for effect. "Oh, wait! That's already happening. You're *right*. I *am* in trouble."

I looked to Todd, hoping he'd back me up, but he took her side. "Not to mention that you deserve *so* much better than that meathead. There. Once. I'm allowed to say it once in every conversation, right?" He didn't wait for my answer. He just raised his eyebrows and pointed at Cat. "But Cat's right. And she does this for a *living*. What is it with you not standing up for yourself?"

"Yeah. Relationship advice from the guy who hasn't had a girlfriend for more than a *week* since . . . ever?"

"Not lately," Cat said, curious. "What's up with that? Dry spell?"

"At the moment, I'm over the promiscuity thing," Todd announced. "I'm too old for that shit."

"So you're cruising the Lower East Side for Miss Right?" I asked.

"She's not there," he said, and stood up to go to the bathroom.

"No," I said to Cat. "And he knows this because he's worked his way through the *entire* female population of Lower Manhattan, and he needs to find new pastures to plow."

"Someplace new to drill for the next gusher," Cat added.

"I was going for subtlety," I said, pushing away my tomato soup.

\* \* \* \* \*

When I got out of the elevator on my floor, I could already hear Sneevil Knievel singing, so it was not a big surprise to find another note taped to my door from my landlord. It said, "Please advice [sic]: It has come to my attention that there is a loud bird in your apartment. Pets require approval and we have no record of a preapproved bird in your apart-ment. We have already receive [sic] several complaints. Please silence the bird or we will require [sic] to take further action."

If it wasn't bad enough to get the scolding note on my door, the state of my apartment when I walked in was enough to send me over the edge. Sneevil had somehow managed to throw every morsel of food out of his cage and onto the floor, my desk, wedging seeds in between keys on my computer keyboard and somehow across the room and onto my unmade bed. My landlord was right—it was enough to make me sic.

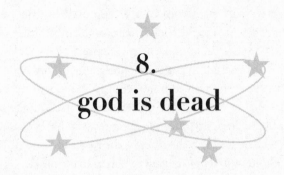

# 8.
# god is dead

Monday morning, I rode into work. Surprisingly, nobody cut me off on my entire trip. I decided that, if for no other reason, it was going to be a good day.

About three blocks from the office I heard someone scream my name.

I turned to look but couldn't see where it was coming from. I pedaled on, thinking maybe I was hearing things, but then a taxi coasted past me and a head poked out.

"Where's your helmet?!" It was Stu Elliot, one of my illustrious colleagues at Splash, who was almost at Lydia's level but who lacked the killer instinct (and trail of dead bodies) that would help him actually get there. I liked him. Working on his gigs was always less stressful than working with Lydia. I'd like to say it was because he valued my work that he cared enough to yell about my helmet, but this wasn't the first time someone had yelled something of this ilk from a passing car. People just love to be drive-by surrogate mothers.

I'm not one of those people who refuses to wear a helmet. I almost *always* wear it. Just sometimes if I'm rushing (or have a really important meeting and don't want helmet head) I forget (or forget on purpose). And really, I never shout at colleagues who are taking one of their infernal cigarette breaks that they forgot their nicotine patch, so why can't we just agree to all leave each other's self-destructive habits alone?

Finally in the office I stopped by the kitchen to pour myself my usual two cups of shockingly bad coffee. I was immune to the bad taste at that point and knew that one cup wouldn't do it, so I poured two cups at once, two cups that I'd pound in record time to save myself a trip. When I got to my desk, I was once again confronted by an e-mail from my father to my mother. Not only was it none of my business but also it nearly made my eyes bleed.

From: wallygator317@hotmail.com

To: judypatootie521@hotmail.com

Subject: Wally through the wall?

Patootie with the great booty—At work. Sam is asking for a new laptop. Should we indulge even though she still has no job? Eh, Dell can probably give us a good deal, right?

It had to stop. The copying of me on every single e-mail, the shameless spoiling of Samantha, and must he talk about my mother's ass? Blegh!

After about ten minutes of doing not a whole hell of a lot, it dawned on me: Lydia hadn't barked any orders at me or run around in apoplexy as she normally did on the day of a big presentation. We had the KidCo bigwigs coming in, and Lydia's pitch was being boarded up for the presentation. It was so eerily quiet, I wondered if she wasn't even *in*, so I got up from my desk and found her door was just slightly ajar. I peered through the teeny gap so as not to disturb her if she were indeed crashing to get something done. She was in there all right—and so was someone else, his back to me, sort of half sitting on the edge of her desk. From the perfectly moussed, bleached-blond-tip do and the little tweak at the front, like a tiny rhino horn of hair, I could see it was Kurt. Then I saw something that I didn't believe I was seeing at first, thought I was imagining, even hallucinating, so out of place and utterly discordant did it seem.

She was softly stroking his jaw.

Now, if I hadn't known better, *much* better, I'd have thought something was up. But I figured there must have been a reason. Maybe somebody had punched him and she was administering first aid. He'd certainly driven *me* nearly to violence more than a few times, so it was somewhat understandable.

Until I saw the kiss.

At least I thought it was a kiss. I backed out before they saw me and tried to wrap my head around what I'd just observed. Lydia and *Kurt?* In what alternate universe would Lydia give it up to a guy in *traffic*, probably ten or fifteen years her junior? I'd actually been under the impression that she had some sordid thing going with *Billingsly,* but it looked like I was wrong. *Way* wrong.

I felt sick and shaken, but there wasn't time for a reaction yet. I'd throw up into a corner waste can on my way home if I had a chance. Right now, we were into full-speed presentation prep mode. When Kurt slithered out of Lydia's office (I'd assumed a posture of intense interest in a sheet of foam core down the hallway in order to observe his exit), everything got back to normal. Lydia was running around between the studio and the conference room even more than I was. Which was kind of weird. Usually she had *me* doing all that, but she was totally hands-on this time. The only thing she had me do was get the comps from production and bring them to her. She pretty much did *everything* else.

I sat at my desk, contemplating if she could possibly be considering me more of an equal finally, and if *that* was why she wasn't ordering me around like a rented mule. Then I heard the ding of an incoming e-mail.

From: judypatootie521@hotmail.com

To: wallygator317@hotmail.com

Subject: re: Wally through the wall?

Re: Sam . . . already ordered one online. Great minds (and behinds) think alike. LOL!

Nauseating. Truly. I may have even thrown up a little in my mouth. Poppy seed bagel with cream cheese, honoring Ruth. I was getting a jump on my later release.

"Everyone . . . can I have your attention, please?" I heard Lydia say, so I deleted the e-mail and looked in Lydia's direction as a group of about ten or so people from traffic and creative congregated in our common area. "We have in our midst someone who's extremely bright and unappreciated very often, *I think.* This person's worked very hard and *wanted* this for a long time . . . so I'd like you to join me in welcoming them to the creative team."

I felt a rush of excitement and panic. I was right. Lydia *was* going to promote me. And publicly. So sudden! So unexpected! Yet so deserved! The girl who kept her nose out of trouble, but always did her best for the agency and was always there with a bright idea for a promotion or the perfect block of scintillating copy . . . it was my time at last. I'd suspected that it was going to be a good day, but I'd never allowed myself to think it would be *that* good.

"Effective today, there'll be one less traffic person." I held my breath and waited for it. "Our newest copywriter is *Kurt Wyatt*! Congratulate him," she said with as close to a smile as I'd ever seen struggle to dominate her thin lips.

I exhaled. No, I more than exhaled. I completely *deflated.* If I'd been a cartoon, I would have flown around the room like a balloon with a bad leak, zipping around in a whirlwind until there was nothing left in me . . . and then I'd drop to the ground. And probably get stepped on.

Kurt? Was getting *my* promotion? I was stunned. I didn't know what to say. Everyone was congratulating him, and I just stood there silent until he looked at me.

"I didn't know you wanted to be a copywriter," I said.

"Sure," he said casually. "It's always been my dream." No, it wasn't. It was *my* dream. I half suspected he'd found it while rummaging through the drawers in my cubicle and stolen it. He didn't give a damn about it, but since it meant *everything* to me, he thought he'd keep it, just to watch me disintegrate.

I was so frustrated, I bit my tongue—not as in stopping myself from saying something I'd regret but literally; it was bleeding. I stopped into the bathroom to rinse my mouth out on my way into the conference room where the KidCo presentation was taking place. Lydia was smoothing out her frizz in the mirror, but she darted out of the bathroom the second I walked in.

When I walked into St. Bart's conference room (our conference rooms were named after vacation hot spots), the presentation was just about to begin. I looked up at the board and stopped dead in my tracks.

Wow, I thought for a split second, there are my ideas, mocked up in glorious color.

Then I thought, *son of a bitch*, there are *my* ideas, mocked up in glorious color! My Broadway sets, my kids on the assembly line—all the ideas I'd brought to Lydia, shined, supersized, and on display. And she was pitching them as her *own*. No mention of me. She'd *stolen* my entire campaign! The frustration I felt boiling up inside was like nothing I'd ever experienced. A fury starting in the pit of my stomach, filling my lungs to a point that I'm sure I could have spat fire if I'd tried.

I'd have said something, or at the very least singed her hair with my breath, but the clients had already taken their seats at the table. At least that was the fine fiction I sold myself a few minutes after I stood just *outside* the room, my eyes closed to trap the tears that wanted to fight their way through. If I was being honest with myself, I'd admit that I would never have said anything, even if Lydia and I had been the only two people on the planet. And I hated myself for my lack of resolve. For my gutlessness. For being Jordan Landau once again.

\* \* \* \* \*

I walked away from the meeting and straight out the front door. I'd decided that at the very least I needed to take a long lunch. I unlocked my bike and started pedaling fast, even though I didn't know where I was going. When I got to 59th Street, I rode along Central Park and suddenly knew exactly where I was headed.

Alice's Tea Cup on 73rd and Columbus. It was the most enchanting little restaurant. Dirk brought me there when we first started dating, and it was so unlike him, I remember being totally floored and wondering how he'd found it. They served about a thousand different kinds of teas, and then you had your choice of scones or finger sandwiches of the traditional English variety. Everything was served on charming plates with matching tea sets, and I completely fell in love with the place. And even more in love with *him*.

We hadn't been there since, but it was such a sweet memory that it was exactly where I wanted to be, even if I was by myself. I locked my bike against a street sign that said NO STANDING. I remembered one time when I was a little girl and saw a No Standing sign for the first time. I contemplated the rationale. Why weren't people allowed to stand there? And if they were supposed to sit instead, why weren't there any chairs? Just as I was pondering this, I noticed a policeman approaching—looking right at me—so I screamed at the top of my lungs and dropped to my behind, skinning my left knee in the process. When my mother asked *what on earth I was doing,* I confessed I believed the policeman was coming to arrest me.

I called Todd on my cell phone as I walked toward Alice's and started to rant about Lydia and what an evil bitch she was.

But then I lost my voice.

At least I lost the power to use it for a minute. I blinked to make sure I was seeing correctly. Then I blinked again, thinking that maybe if I blinked hard enough it would go away. But it *didn't*. There, sitting at a quaint little table in the whimsical Alice's Tea Cup, was Dirk, or rather, *were* Dirk and some skinny blond girl, holding hands in the center of the table!

As if things weren't already bad *enough*. I was spiraling down the rabbit hole, not knowing *what* kind of mad tea party could possibly be waiting at the bottom.

"Jordy?" I heard Todd say. "You still there?"

I cleared my throat and peered into the window. They were oblivious to me. They were the only two people in the world. "I'm looking at Dirk," I said.

"Huh?"

"Dirk is about fifteen feet in front of me, at a place that I thought was *our* place . . . hand in hand with some other girl!"

"What a dick. Is she pretty?"

"Yes, Todd. She's pretty. She's pretty and skinny and she has *good hair*. I hate my life."

"Maybe it's his sister," he offered

"He doesn't have a sister."

"Fuck her and her hair. Go tell him to fuck off!" Todd yelled, but I couldn't move. I just *watched* them, phone stuck to my ear, Todd barking orders for me to go stand up for myself. I watched her laughing at the things he said, and I wondered if I'd heard them before. "Jordan! What's happening now?"

"He's moving her hair out of her face," I whispered, although I wasn't sure why I did.

"Maybe she's got some food on her face," he said. I didn't answer. I just kept watching. "What's going on *now*?" he asked.

"I can't see."

"Why not?"

"Because he moved his face in really close to hers."

"Oh *God*," he said.

"Well, that could be nothing," I offered weakly.

"Right. Maybe he's *eating* the food off her face," he said.

"Well, who knows, maybe he has some excuse . . . or something."

"What's with you?" he screamed. "Are you cultivating the art of being a doormat?"

No, I wasn't. I just didn't want this to be my reality. But it got worse. The next time I looked up they were no-doubt-about-it kissing. Full-on making out.

"He's kissing her!" I said, very much not in a whisper.

"God! That fucking asshole! Go *confront* him!"

"I don't want to confront him. I don't want to do anything! I just want it all to go away!"

"Jordan!" he said, "you have to *make* it go away!"

"I gotta go."

I hung up on Todd and stood there, taking one last look. I didn't *want* to watch, but at the same time I couldn't pull my eyes away. I was completely nauseated. And the added bonus: It began to rain.

I started back toward my bike and thought that maybe Dirk saw me. At least he looked in my direction. I didn't wait around to find out if he'd caught me catching him.

*     *     *     *     *

Riding away from the wreckage that was my relationship, I could barely see because tears were streaming down my face. I wasn't even crying actively. I was just riding my bike and the tears kept coming, flooding my eyes, and blurring everything in front of me.

I was thinking about all of the crap I'd put up with, all the times I should have broken up with him and hadn't. Now here I was, left with no choice.

I wondered how long he'd been seeing her . . . if there were others . . . if he was nicer to them than he was to me. I blinked back some more tears and noticed that someone had spray-painted on a wall:

GOD IS DEAD
—Nietzsche, 1883

Great. So, my asshole boyfriend was cheating on me, I didn't get the promotion, my boss had stolen and used my treasured brainchild, my credit card debt was higher than my pothead super, my family treated me like a dog treats a hydrant . . . and God had apparently been dead for 124 years. Turned out, this was *not* a good day. At all.

Then I was flying.

Flying, floating, free—but only for as long as it takes a human body to sail twelve feet in the air over a car hood and crumple, head and shoulder first, onto the street. I can't say exactly what happened, but I do remember a loud buzzing and a sensation like thunder trying to push its way up my spine out through my ears.

Someone said, "Oh my God!" about six times very fast. I kept my eyes closed, to keep the thunder from pouring out, but I could still sense a shadow blocking the light. I felt like half my face was sweating, so I stuck my tongue out to lick it, and discovered it was blood. I couldn't wrap my mind around anything that was happening. I grasped at thoughts, different people popped into my head—Kurt, Lydia, Dirk, Samantha, Spandex Cock Guy, all slipped through my mental grasp like so many greased pigs. Then I reached for those who were much closer—my mom, Todd, Cat—but even they eluded me, and it started to feel like I was drowning.

The voices said different things. "Is she okay? Who is she? Did you see it? Did anyone see it?" They hovered over me, and I heard again, "Who is she?" I heard them speaking and I could have said my name, but what was the point? Jordan Landau. Who was that, anyway? No one *I* wanted to be.

It grew darker, but I wasn't nearing death—it was just shadows, shapes. Through the slits of my eyelids I could make out very little.

One thing seemed certain. Somewhere above me was an angel. "Are you okay?" the angel said with panic on his sweet face. I turned my head toward him and felt my hair stuck to my face.

"No, no, n— I . . . *not* okay," I said, and everything began to swirl faster and faster, and I felt myself drifting inexorably. "I'm in such . . ."

"Pain?" he asked.

"No thanks," I said. "I've had enough."

# 9.
# do-over

I heard the ambulance wailing in the background and remember thinking briefly that it was something of a mating call—the siren reaching out to me. Or maybe just telling everyone else to get out of the way. When the medics got there, I heard one of them say something about immobilizing me. They rolled me around and started to cut my clothes off, checking for bleeding. I was rotating in and out of consciousness, and objects would zoom into my foreground, startling me beyond what seemed possible, and then get hazy and dissolve before my eyes. A neck brace was suddenly around my neck. I remember my forehead being taped to a board, which frightened me. Someone kept saying, "Stay awake, stay with me."

I overheard the other guy on the phone, talking to the triage nurse. He said I was early twenties and weighed 135 pounds. I wanted to tell him my weight was none of his damn business, but the "early twenties" comment gave me enough of a feel-good, so I just lay there while the other guy asked me questions, I guess to keep me awake.

"What was your first pet's name? How long have you been riding a bike?"

I knew that my first pet was a bunny named Thumper. I opened my mouth to tell him, but I felt dizzy again so I just shut my eyes. I heard the guy on the phone say "motor vehicle versus bicycle," and I distinctly remember thinking that it wasn't a fair fight.

Once we got to the ER, a whole *new* team of people started asking me questions, dizzying questions—not the inquiries themselves, which were fairly basic, but the speed at which they were getting thrown at me. What's my name? How old am I? Who is my nearest relative? But all of it, coupled with the pounding in my head and the fluorescent lights directly above me, was confusing and way more than I could manage to focus on. So I just closed my eyes—although I remember a single, heavy tear managing to sneak out and roll down my cheek.

* * * * *

The next thing I remember is a glaring light penetrating my eyelids. I lay still, eyes closed against the light, and concentrated on the sound of a man's voice turning into actual words. I hadn't opened my eyes yet, but I could hear someone talking.

"Everything looks okay so far, pupils normal, CT images show a hairline fracture to the skull. I want to do an MRI and possibly an EEG to check for damage to the brain. She'll be here at least overnight while we run some more tests."

"Thank you, Doctor," said a voice, unmistakably my mother, uncharacteristically weak. And then I started hearing the rest of them. Samantha was first.

"I can't believe she fell off her bike. It seems so *fifth grade*."

Then Walter chimed in, coming to my defense, "Sam, honey, she got in an accident with a car."

"I wonder if she can get her nose fixed while she's in here," Sam said hopefully. "Her nostrils sort of *flare*."

"Her nose is fine," assured my stepdad.

But then came Samantha again. "Or a boob job. Maybe some lipo?"

I opened my eyes and blinked a few times, still not believing what I'd just overheard.

"Well," said my mother, "if I was stuck lying in a hospital bed *anyway*, I know I wouldn't mind a few nips and tucks. But Jordan is comfortable the way she is."

And *still*, nobody noticed that I'd opened my eyes! They weren't even paying attention to me. They were too busy planning my plastic surgery. I didn't have a lot of experience waking up in hospitals after significant traumas, but I knew enough to know this was *not* how it was supposed to be. Finally my mom glanced my way and noticed that I was awake.

"Jordan, my God! Thank goodness! We were so worried about you!"

I just looked at her blankly. They weren't *worried* about me. They were dissecting me like a lab rat.

"Jordan! Hello?! Did she lose some *brain* cells while she was at it?" This came from my ever-sympathetic sister.

I wanted to tune them all out, but I'd already made the mistake of opening my eyes. I remembered the last conversation I'd had with Todd . . . him telling me to confront Dirk . . . me saying that I didn't want to, I just wanted it to all go away . . . him telling me that things just didn't go away—I had to *make* them go away.

"Jordan . . . are you okay?" That was my mother. It *sounded* like she was concerned but then as she was leaning in to look closer at me, I could swear she was staring at a zit on my forehead with disapproval. Even at a time like this! I desperately longed for a mother to comfort me . . . but not *my* mother. I wouldn't mind losing *this* mother for a while, find someone else for the job while this one went back to school and learned how to love.

All I knew was that I didn't want to listen to the petty ravings and psychotic self-centeredness of these people anymore. I didn't want to be related to them. I didn't want to know them. All these people around me and not a single good memory among them. As I scanned the room, it seemed that an odd, blue-tinged haze made everyone look somehow cold and small, and I wished I'd awakened somewhere else.

Or as some*one* else.

"Jordan?" my mother said again. And then it hit me. I *could* make this all go away. I could do in real life what I'd failed to do in my role-playing exercise with Cat.

I was about to embark on the performance of a lifetime. I needed a new start. I needed it more than anything I'd ever needed before.

I blinked a couple times and looked up at my mother. "Hello," I said in a confused and innocent tone. "Do I know you?"

My mother hesitated, as if not comprehending what I was asking. "Jordan? Honey, you're awake."

I looked at her. "Agreed," I said. "But who are *you*?"

In the background, Sam stopped twirling her hair and turned slowly to face me. "What'd she just say?"

I looked back and forth now from my mom to Sam to my stepdad. I settled on Walter. "I . . ." I kept my mouth open, then looked worried. "What am I doing here?"

"Maybe if we slap her, she'll snap out of it," Sam said, stepping forward to get a better angle of attack.

Walter raised his arms. "Hold on now," he said crossly. "Nobody does anything till I get back here. I'm getting the doctor."

They all stared. And I stared right back, as emptily as I could.

*     *     *     *     *

After I'd feigned utter ignorance of everyone in the room, everything that had happened, my workplace, my home, and all but the most mundane details, the doctor leaned in.

"Jordan?" he said.

I let my eyes drift as though he may have been talking to my mother or my sister or the nurse, who then looked at me quizzically. The doctor took his deep inhale and sized me up. With no reason to believe I was pretending, and a major head wound to support the possibility, he explained to my family that my amnesia could be a temporary reaction caused by the trauma of the accident.

I couldn't believe it. They were *buying* it.

The last time I'd attempted acting I was seven years old and playing a tree in a school play. I didn't have any lines, but everyone said I was very convincing. Now, all these years later, it turned out I had this hidden talent for playing the wide-eyed innocent without a clue. Who knew? All I had to do was act like I didn't know who I was or who anyone around me was and I was home free. Piece of cake. Why hadn't anyone else thought of this before? Or maybe they had. What if everyone who had amnesia was just faking, I wondered, taking much-needed breaks from their lives?

My family looked concerned, but for all I knew, they could have been just acting too. Maybe the whole family had this talent and none of us knew it. The doctor explained that they were going to consult a specialist. My stepdad frowned as he listened, and my mom came over and rubbed between his eyes to make him stop. She was the wrinkle-police; if anybody frowned in her presence she would put an end to it immediately. She even had these little sticky triangle paper things called Frownies that you put in between your eyes to keep you from frowning. I'm surprised she didn't carry them around and slap them on random strangers and passersby.

Samantha came over to the side of my bed and stared at me. I stared back. "You really don't remember anything?" she asked.

"I remember I have a bed, but I'm not sure where," I said apologetically.

"I'm your sister," Sam said, a little singsongy, as though I were an idiot.

I looked at her and then at my mom. "I like her," I said to my mother, smiling. "She seems so nice!"

"Oh my God," my stepdad said quickly with genuine alarm, "she really *has* lost her memory."

Just then Todd came running in, out of breath. He looked completely panicked, his eyes darting back and forth from the doctor to my family to me—then locking on me. I saw the fear in his eyes as he looked at me, and although my head hurt like hell and the room was spinning, I felt relief for the first time since I'd woken up. So far he was the only one who'd set foot in that door that I *knew* really cared about me.

"Jordy! Are you okay?" he said.

I wanted to answer, but I was also trying to be true to my untruth. So I glanced around with a blank expression and sought guidance from the doctor.

"She may not remember you," he said to Todd while looking at me carefully. Then he looked to my mom and Walter. "This might be a little distressing, with people who seem like strangers. I'm thinking—"

"No," my mom said, "this one's all right. We can limit visitors, but he's known her *forever*. She might even remember Todd. Sweetheart?"

"Are you part of my family too?" I said hopefully.

"She has *amnesia*," my mom said to Todd.

Todd tentatively stepped closer and moved a piece of hair out of my eyes. "Well," he said with his trademark goofy smile. "We were married when we were seven. I think *technically* that does make us family."

"Can I mention once again that I'm hungry?" Sam interjected. Walter looked perturbed and whispered something to her.

"So glad you're here, Todd," my mom said, and Walter whispered to her. "Jordan . . ."

She saw the questioning in my eyes.

"Jordan," she said with a hand on my arm. "Remember? Jordan, will you be okay for just a minute if we go to the cafeteria? Just a minute?"

"I'll stay right here," I said.

"This is Todd, and he'll watch over you. You can trust Todd. Honey, you grew up with Todd." The doctor took his leave, giving some private warnings to Mom and Walter. Then the four of them—the doctor, Mom, Walter, and Sam—filed out of my hospital room, looking back at the curiosity I represented.

Todd was there so they felt like they were now excused. They'd done their time, the new shift was in, and they needed snacks. I looked toward the door to make sure that they were gone.

Todd was stiff, standing straight up by the door, looking afraid.

"Can they see us?" I whispered.

"No," Todd said curiously.

"And there's no surveillance cameras?" I said. We looked from ceiling corner to ceiling corner.

I pounded the mattress with as much gusto as I could manage, tubes waving everywhere to get him to step closer. "Listen. I'm fine, Todd. It's me. I don't really have amnesia."

"What?"

"Shhhh! Look, I just need a do-over. My life sucks."

"What?" he said again louder, not necessarily asking me to *repeat* what I said, more insisting I *defend* it.

"Will you keep it down?!" I looked at the door but spoke to him. "I can't take it anymore. Everything about my life is a disaster, and I've had enough. So, starting today, I'm reinventing myself. But you can't say *anything* to *anyone*. Not your parents, not mine—*definitely* not Cat. Not your pet, not a stranger, don't write it, don't think it. Just forget I told you entirely. Pretend *you* have amnesia! At least as far as this conversation goes." He looked doubtful. "Please do this for me. You know you're the only one I can trust."

"You're insane!"

"No, you don't catch insanity from a head injury. I'm gonna stick with amnesia."

"Funny," he said, rolling his eyes in disapproval.

"Will you help me?" I asked.

"Absolutely not."

"Please?" I begged.

"No! Jordan, this isn't a joke," he snapped.

"No kidding. This is my *life*," I defended.

"There are doctors and your family . . . and other people involved here."

"Where are these people that you're talking about? My loving family just put you on Jordy duty less than five minutes after being told their daughter suffered a head trauma so severe that she can't remember who they are. 'Jeepers, Judy Patootie, let's go get some snacks and talk more about Jordy's plastic surgery now that she's regained consciousness and can hear us.' Oh, and I'm sure my loving boyfriend might swing by at some point later. Maybe he can bring his skinny yet busty date from Alice's Tea Cup."

Todd had started to turn a pale shade that made me want to ask the nurse if we could get him a bed in an adjoining room.

"Look, I know what's involved, Todd. And I'm sorry for wasting the

doctor's time—I am. But I'm not completely faking here. I'm hurt. I
have a fractured skull. That's *huge*. I do have a headache and you're making it *worse* by not saying you'll help me," I said, sensing that he was
starting to relent. I turned down the defiance and softened my approach.
"I *need* this. I can't take my life anymore. With as much physical pain as
I am in right now, I'll take my head trauma over my entire-life trauma
any day. I need to buy some time, Todd, so I can figure things out. Just
indulge me. *Please?* I need a break!"

"So take a vacation!"

"I can't afford a vacation! Please, Todd?" I looked at him pleadingly
and gave him the puppy dog eyes through my puffy eye slits. I even bat-
ted my eyelashes with effort, which made him laugh.

"Only because I love you so much."

"Yes!" I said, punching the mattress. "Thank you, thank you! Okay,
I need you to do me a favor. Find out everything you can about amnesia. Look on the Internet or ask around here. I need to make this seem
legitimate."

"And what do *I* get out of this?"

"I'm your wife, remember? 'For better or for worse'? Well, sophomore
year when I got drunk and we made out? That was for *better*. This? Is for
*worse*."

He rolled his eyes and slumped into the chair at my bedside, snatch-
ing the remote from my hands. Todd was the one person I knew I could
count on no matter what.

"I guess we'll be watching a lot of daytime television in here," he said.

"It'll be just like college!"

"Can I have your Jell-O?" he asked, already digging in.

"All yours."

"Excellent."

"See, this situation is already starting to pay off for you."

"Sure." He paused for a minute, fighting with the plastic on the Jell-O
container before finally pulling it off and staring intently at the Jell-O as
though he were looking through it.

"What is it?"

"The Jell-O is a start, but I was just wondering if the nurses would mind if we got drunk and made out."

As he dug into the Jell-O, I remembered clearly why he was my best friend in the world. I suddenly had the feeling that everything was going to be all right.

# 10.
# mercury and amnesia
# in retrograde

Samantha showed up at my bedside again early the next morning, peering into my eyes and cocking her head from side to side as though she'd chosen to impersonate Sneevil Knievel. I was surprised to see her, especially as it seemed she'd come on her own, but my mom walked in a few moments after her with a big flower arrangement covering her face.

"It's me," my mom said, from behind the spider mums and stargazer lilies. "Aren't these beautiful?"

"Yes," I said as she placed them on the table next to my bed. I reached for the card that was tucked into the arrangement between some baby's breath and a branch. I read the card aloud. " 'To Judith, Hang in there. The Rosens.' "

I looked up at my mom and wondered aloud, "Judith? Wow, I must be in real trouble. I could have sworn you guys told me my name was *Jordan* yesterday."

"I'm sorry, dear," she said, bustling awkwardly. "That shouldn't have been in there," she said and snatched the card back, tucking it into her purse. "Those were sent to the house. *I'm* Judith. I just brought them to brighten up the room. They were for the whole family. Including you. And, yes, your name *is* Jordan."

"Would it help if I showed you pictures?" asked Sam. "Maybe to jog your memory?"

"I don't know . . . What kind of pictures?" I said, sounding just the slightest bit panicky.

"Nothing incriminating," Sam said as she reached into her Prada backpack and pulled out a brand-new iPod, clearly purchased the day before as a way for my mother to console her daughter . . . the one *without* the skull fracture and amnesia. She started scrolling through the pictures one by one and showing them to me.

"Remember this? We were at summer school? I was the most popular girl and you didn't have very many friends. And I let you hang out with my friends?"

"No, I don't remember that," I said. "Is that me? Wow . . . and who is that pudgy little thing next to me?"

"Pudgy?" She balked. "I wasn't pudgy. That shirt was an extra large. It hung funny on me." And with that she snatched the iPod away and scrolled to another photo. "How about this? It was your prom and you got poison oak? Oh my God, you looked *awful*! And you didn't want to go but you didn't want to cancel. And then your date didn't even show up, so it didn't matter. Remember? This was you in your dress, waiting for him to come. You *must* remember that!"

I shook my head and smiled meekly. It was so thoughtful of her to try to jog my memory with the most traumatic events of my awkward past.

Then she scrolled to the next picture, glanced at it, and immediately tried to skip to the next one.

"What's *that* one?" I piped up.

"That one isn't going to jog any memories," she said. But I suspected I knew exactly which photo she didn't want me to see.

Then I saw Dirk. He was standing in the doorway, looking in at me, possibly waiting to see my reaction to him. I gave him a half smile and kind of raised my eyebrows. He walked in.

"Hi," he said and then kissed my mother on her cheek and crossed over to my bedside. "Remember me?" he asked. I tried to look as if I was straining to remember. I even furrowed my brow, something my mom would have loathed to see.

"No," I said. Sweet . . . innocent . . . vacant. "Sorry. I *don't*."

"I was your boyfriend. We'd been going out for like two years."

"Huh," I said and then realized he had used the past tense. Maybe he *had* seen me at Alice's Tea Cup. "You said you *were* my boyfriend." A sweet smile. "Did we break up?"

"No," he fired back at lightning speed. "I mean . . . you were totally into me."

"Totally? And you were totally into *me*?" I said, my voice rising with childlike hope.

"Well, yeah," he said. "Yeah. Sure." *Buzzz*. The correct answer would have been "No, I treated you like shit and cheated on you," but thank you for playing.

"Wow, I'm so sorry I don't remember you. I'm sure it'll all come back to me."

He looked confused and a little bummed out. I guess he thought that even after the trauma of a head injury and severe memory loss, I would *have* to remember *him*. I mean—he was Long-Daggered Dirk, after all.

"Well, I'll take you back to my place when you get out of here and I'm sure that will jog your memory. We've had a lot of good times there."

And in this awkward moment, with Sam pondering the meaning of "good times," I saw my opportunity and darted a hand out to seize the iPod and check out the photo Sam had tried to hide. Bingo. I'd gotten a good long look at it and stifled a laugh before she was aware of what I'd done.

There she was, arms encircling, lips attached to Bo Caldwell, *my then boyfriend,* whom my charming sister tried to steal from me and succeeded. Their relationship lasted the two weeks she worked him to betray me and an entire four days after I found out. The novelty wore off. She discarded Bo—recognizing, perhaps, that if he'd settled for *me*, he couldn't be much of a catch—and she moved on to someone else's boyfriend who was at least more age appropriate. She held on to that photo like a trophy. It was the first tangent proof of her evil victory. If I were her, I'd have just savored the memory and destroyed the unflattering photo—her hair tied up in a scrunchie that could not hide the unfortunate home-highlighting job she'd botched the week before. This one had earned a place in neighborhood legend. Suffice it to say that they weren't highlights as much as zebra stripes, which were aiming for blond but landed on orange. She'd cried for two days and demanded my mom's stylist fix the mess, but he'd thrown up his hands in defeat. Her look was completed by the braces she'd claimed had ruined two years of her life. All in all—heinous.

"You look so *in love*. Is this your boyfriend?" I asked sweetly.

"Unh . . ." she stammered.

Dirk caught a glimpse of the photo before she grabbed it back, and he started laughing *hard* at the hair. I looked at the pair of them, two incorrigible cheaters, thinking, This is my life? These are the people I surround myself with? This is sisterhood? And by the way, Dirk, I saw you with that toothpick with tits yesterday and I know that you're cheating on me and if I wasn't faking amnesia you would *really* get a piece of my mind right now! But I refrained from saying any of it. I had to. It was fun just watching him get all distressed because the mere presence of his handsome manly-man self wasn't jogging my memory.

Samantha and my mom left me to get reacquainted with Dirk. What I didn't understand was why he even showed up. Could it be that he actually felt a little guilty? "So you don't remember *anything* that happened right before your accident?" he asked, eyeing me closely. Aha—he *had* seen me at Alice's, then.

"I don't remember anything—period."

"Wow . . . that's . . . I'm really sorry to hear that," he said, setting off bullshit detectors everywhere. And then he sat with me for a total of four more minutes before saying he had to "bail," but that he'd be back to check on me.

*   *   *   *   *

Todd was at home researching amnesia for me so that I'd know the dos and don'ts of not remembering who you are and how you got wherever you happened to be. He called my room just in the nick of time. I'd practically memorized the hospital menu and was dangerously close to getting completely wrapped up in *All My Children*.

They have more useless meals in hospitals than you could imagine, and they trick you into thinking you have options by providing an actual menu. It's actually more like an SAT test, with the similar portent of a perilous future if you blow it. One page, double sided, with circles to fill in with a number two pencil. I'm not kidding. So you look and you shade. And sometimes you get surprised by what they bring you, either because you forgot what you picked or perhaps it's that what they bring just doesn't quite resemble what you thought you'd ordered—if it even resembles food at all.

"Two weevils started life together," Todd said, and instantly I knew it was going to be a joke. Todd was famous for his silly G-rated jokes.

"Uh-huh . . ." I answered.

"One was an immediate success; the other was a complete failure. Naturally, it became known as the lesser of two weevils."

"Very cute."

"Okay," he said. "So the good news is there really are no hard and fast rules. These people don't just forget their memories; they have no recollection of how they used to behave. Sometimes a different part of their personality emerges while their memories have submerged." He was sounding all doctorly—it was sort of cute. Amazing what you can find on the Internet.

"So a timid, pushover type might all of a sudden be aggressive and assertive?"

"If she were so *inclined*," he said, and I could hear the conspiratorial smile on his face. Some people in this world you can always count on. They will be there for you no matter what, through thick and thin. If memory serves—and contrary to present outward appearances, mine generally did—it was the comedian Dave Attell who said, "A friend will help you move. A *best* friend will help you move . . . a body." How right he was.

That was Todd. And, ironically, he was helping me move a body right then. Mine. The old me. Here lies the body of Jordan-the-Pushover, may she rest in peace. She lived a mediocre life, was loved by few, and is survived by her materialistic mother, her well-meaning but clueless stepfather, and her spoiled brat of a sister. In lieu of flowers please send donations to the New-and-Improved-Jordan fund. She will require tons of extra cash to buy a new wardrobe, eat at fancy restaurants, and perhaps take a class in something she'd always been interested in but never knew it.

"There is a ton of stuff on the Web," he went on. "By the way, did you know there's something called Korsakoff amnesia? People can develop that from drinking too much."

"And?"

"I'm just *saying*. I think I may have suffered from that in college and not even known it. I was graded unfairly . . ."

"Anyway . . ." I prompted.

"Okay. So there's this whole online site dedicated to amnesia treatment. But I couldn't get in. You need a user name and a password, and that costs ninety-nine dollars."

"Genius," I said. "They probably hope that the poor amnesiacs will keep *forgetting* that they signed up so they have to keep forking over the ninety-nine bucks."

"But what I did find out is that there are two main ways we access memory," he explained. "Recognition and recall. Recognition involves a process of comparison of info with memory. With recognition, an experience stimulates the memory. Because it's somehow *like* the memory, so it awakens the memory."

"I feel like I'm the one suffering in college, Todd."

"Could I make this up? Quit interrupting and listen. Recall involves a search of memory and then the comparison process once something is found. You recall by focusing your attention in the direction of a memory."

"Okay . . . so recognition is like a feeling of familiarity?"

"Exactly. Like recognizing someone you know."

"So it's possible to have recall without recognition?" I said.

"Right. But if you had recognition without recall, you'd be like me taking a test in school. I was fine so long as I was looking at the answer sheet."

"And I might not *recognize* my mother . . ."

"Yeah, but you might *recall* Angelina Jolie as someone famous," he said.

"And then *recognize* Ms. Jolie when she comes to visit me?"

"Yes. And when you guys start making out—"

"Are we doing my fake amnesia or your twisted fantasy?"

"Why can't we do both?" he implored. "Let's see what else. Okay, this is huge . . . There's also a big difference between what this one specialist called subconscious memory and process memory. Like the difference between emotion and pure facts . . . pictures . . . numbers . . . steps."

"So I still know how to ride a bike, but I don't remember a bad emotional investment like Dirk."

"Precisely," Todd said. "What else . . . what else. Oh! I can't remember any more data, but I did find some good stuff in this search. Like herbal treatments—"

"You're not supposed to be finding out how to *cure* me," I whispered, "you're finding out stuff to help me fudge this."

"I know. But there's a lot of interesting stuff. Brahmi booti is apparently big in herbal remedies."

"Brahmi booti?" I asked.

"Brahmi booty?" echoed the unmistakable voice of Cat. "Is that like Veggie Booty? Or Pirate's Booty? I *love* that stuff."

I looked up at her as she slowly approached my bedside with a sad smile soaked in worry. I felt terrible. Like I was deceiving my best friend. Because . . . I was.

"No, I didn't ring my call button, but thank you for checking on me," I said to Todd and hung up on him. Now, I was going to have to fake it in front of Cat. Here was someone who truly understood the mindscape. Who made a *living* off it. And who knew me well. It wouldn't be easy, but I had no *choice:* I pretended not to recognize her when she walked in. That was my least favorite part of the whole thing and it was already getting old. But I knew I had to get through this initial discomfort in order to re-create my life and reinvent myself.

"Hi," she said, with that feeling-sorry-for-me look that I totally didn't deserve. "How are you?" I couldn't know her. I had to think to myself, *You don't recognize this person.*

"Hi," I said and looked blankly at her.

"Do you recognize me?"

"Sorry," I said with an apologetic shrug.

"I'm Cat," she said with a reassuring smile. "We're best friends. Have been since we were kids. Me, you, and Todd. We're the Three Musketeers."

"I've met Todd," I said. "He was here. He's nice."

"How are you feeling? Does it hurt?"

"I'm doing okay, I guess. My head hurts," I said leaning over and indicating the general area of my head. "I'm sorry I don't remember you," I added pitifully.

"It's okay," she said. "You will. I'll help you get your memory back." And then she just sat on the chair at the side of my bed. We didn't really have a lot to say since we were essentially strangers, but she seemed unwilling to walk out—so we sat in uncomfortable silence for a few minutes.

Then something terrible happened. *All My Children* appeared on the TV, and sensing it was an escape hatch from the oddity of being with a best friend who doesn't know you, Cat began to catch me up. On everything.

"You're watching this?"

"Not really," I said and looked away indifferently. "Kind of hard for me to follow."

"Well, if you're going to *get* anything out of it . . ." And she commenced an epic verbal journey through a dozen seasons of *All My Children*, each new meaningless plot twist requiring a backfill of ten others to explain it fully, each new character's startling revelation leaving me closer to full anesthesia. Worst of all, I already knew every bit of it. I remembered every marriage, birth, brawl, affair, divorce, double cross, death, wait—she's not really *dead*! And I bore not only the shame of having devoted myself to so pointless a cause but also the boredom of having to relive every last moment of it. At one point, I began to think she was going to interweave the gripping history of the commercial breaks that had framed our story. But I smiled and remembered, This is why I love this girl. Now, if only I could reach the leg of her chair. And tear it off. And clock her with it.

"Hello!" I practically screamed when my mom showed up at last. "This is . . . this is . . ."

"I know who it is, Jordan," Mom said. "Cat, so sweet of you to come keep her company."

"Cat," I said, staring intently at my loquacious friend as she said her good-byes and choked back tears. "Cat. Cat." I pointed at her and let them know I was making a mental note of the fact. This was *Cat*.

"Thanks for coming to visit me," I said. I fought back an intense urge to ask her about the baby she was carrying, her husband, the apartment . . . but I remembered something: I wasn't supposed to remember *any* of it.

And I thought about the legend of a medieval French torture device, the oubliette. Prisoners were shoved into narrow holes in the ground and forgotten and left to die. Real amnesia must be like that, I thought. But in *reverse*. The agony of the struggle to recall . . . where the hell did I dig that hole?

* * * * *

"Jordan does, in fact, have a slight concussion," the neurologist said as he flipped back and forth between pages of test results. Eureka! A concussion would be a perfect accessory to my amnesia. "Loss of memory of events taking place before the accident is called retrograde amnesia."

I pretended not to have much interest, eyes wandering about the room, fingers twirling my hair. "Is that what she has?" my mom asked.

"We believe so. Jordan's concussion is the most likely cause of this type of memory loss. She'll probably experience some degree of post-concussion syndrome—fatigue, dizziness, headache, and difficulty concentrating. Even following the mildest concussions, there is generally some degree of temporary memory impairment."

"This *would* happen to Jordan," Samantha said. "Her life was so lame, who *wouldn't* want to forget it." And as she said that last bit, her eyes narrowed at me to see if she was actually onto something. My heart started racing, but instead of freaking out I licked my lips and pretended to have cotton mouth, to deflect from her vile existence. And the fact that she was right.

"So how long will this go on?" my mom asked, and I could swear the tone was impatience, the implication being this little bout with amnesia was a major inconvenience for her.

"The symptoms of post-concussion syndrome usually resolve within two to five days."

Two to five *days*! No, no, no, dear doctor! That was not going to work for me at all. I needed time. I wanted to milk this baby for all it was worth. I hadn't even *begun* to forget. Surely there was a mistake.

"However, the more severe the concussion, the longer these symptoms may remain. In cases of severe head trauma and concussion, it can take up to six months."

When I heard that, it was all I could do to keep myself from jumping up and down on my hospital bed. I'd just received a six-month green light! I was beaming. Grinning from ear to ear, and my mom looked over at me.

"Odd," the doctor observed. "Notice how she seems elated by the news. Clearly some elements of euphoric delusion." Right, I checked myself quickly. Who in her right mind would be so tickled by word of a concussion? I quickly changed my expression from one of glee to that of worry. Ecstatic to concerned.

Then back. Just like that. I was a natural.

Lights . . . camera . . . amnesia.

"So I won't know . . . I'll be like this for six months?" I asked.

"Hopefully you'll regain your memory much sooner. We have some encouraging new treatments that I'd like to get you involved in right away. We'll keep you here for another night and then move you into the rehab ward."

I feigned a hopeful look, though I knew that none of those treatments was going to work on me. And then a nurse walked in with a giant—and I mean *giant*—bouquet of flowers.

"Delivery," she sang out cheerfully as she placed the flowers by my bed. My mom looked all kinds of intrigued.

"Who are they from?" she asked.

"I don't know," I said. "Let's look at the card."

As I was opening the card, Mom was hedging her bets. "Must be Dirk. What a sweet thing."

"Travis," I said, and suddenly I wondered if I really *did* have amnesia. I looked at the card to make sure I was reading it correctly, and I even turned it over to make sure it was my name on the outside. "Do I know a Travis?"

"I don't know."

The nurse came back in with another gift. This time it was a humongous box of chocolates.

"These came too."

"*Those* must be from Dirk," my mom said with certainty.

I opened the card. They were from Travis *too*. I read it out loud. " 'Don't know what you like . . . just want to know how you are. Feel *terrible* about what happened. Hope you're all right. Travis.' "

"Who is Travis?" my mom asked.

"Do you think he was the guy in the car?" I wondered.

My mom swiped the card from me. "Let me see that." She looked at it and read it over about five times. "The nerve of him trying to weasel his way out of a lawsuit." She glared at the card. "Well, fat chance. We're going to get him for everything he's got!"

\* \* \* \* \*

It was nearly impossible to fall asleep in the hospital bed, and every time I did fall asleep, a nurse came in and woke me up to do a neurological assessment. They'd check my pupil size and start asking me random questions.

"Who is the president?" they'd ask me. "Do you know what time of day it is?" They weren't looking for an exact time, they just wanted to know if I could tell the difference between day and night. And my *least* favorite question, only because it posed such a major dilemma, was "Do you know where you are?" And every time I'd have to fight back the overwhelming need to screech, "You're in the jungle, baby!" in my best Axl Rose.

They'd have me squeeze their hands and then they'd press my feet and tell me to "push down like it's a gas pedal."

I was on a mannitol IV drip to reduce any swelling in my brain, so sometimes when they came in to wake me, they'd stay even longer to hook up a new drip. I'd have to do this three or four times during the night. It was exhausting. And even *more* exhausting when I got different nurses, who felt like they had to explain what they were doing every step of the way.

"This is dehydration therapy to reduce intracranial pressure by osmotic diuresis," the nurse would say. "Sounds complicated but it's basically a diuretic for your brain." They'd already told me this several times—the first time when my mom was in the room, and she looked oddly pleased by the explanation. *Diuretic* was a term my mother knew and loved, and she must have thought it meant I might lose weight. Only my mother would view a hospital stay as a lucky dieting opportunity.

# 11.
# i'm a c cup—dammit!

The next morning I got transferred to the rehab ward. I was assigned a new doctor, and subjected to about four thousand neuropsychology tests that I didn't want to pass but didn't want to fail. It was strangely taxing to guess which set of answers would indicate temporary, six-monthish amnesia resulting from a mild concussion, leaving the patient functional and not a danger to herself or others, and which would land me in a locked room under close supervision until I came out of it.

They eased into things with a Rorschach test, which was *tons* of fun. I'd always wanted to take one of those but never really had the occasion. There were ten inkblots, five of which were in black and white, three in black and red, and two multicolored. I was supposed to say what I saw in each of them and, distracted as I was by the whole how-deep-is-her-forgetfulness exercise, took it as an opportunity to have fun. Bizarre responses *could* indicate brain damage and neurological pathology, or they could merely demonstrate creativity and capriciousness.

When the doctor held up the first one, I said I saw a butterfly. It looked like a butterfly and I'd bet that 80 percent of the people who see that one say "butterfly." The second one looked like a blob, so I said it looked like an early Picasso. I said the next one looked like Florida.

When he held up the first black-and-red one, I said it looked like a gnome and then quickly changed my mind. "Arnold Schwarzenegger!" I shouted.

We moved on to a drawing test, which was meant to measure my visual retention. They'd hold up a drawing for ten seconds, and then I was supposed to draw what I'd seen. They were mostly simple geometric shapes, but I drew a tree and a rainbow when I got bored of the shapes.

When the doctor mentioned the new "treatments" that they were trying out, I had no idea what I was getting myself into. I found out all too quickly when I walked into the eighth floor room where they'd sent me and found myself face-to-face with an odd assortment of robed individuals—clearly patients—and a prematurely gray, long-haired Grateful Dead devotee who went by the name of Dr. Debra. She had a pair of glasses on a long chain around her neck. She wore a tie-dyed blouse and a peasant skirt that went to the floor. She stood up in front of us and pointed to her name, which was written on the chalkboard.

"I am Dr. Debra. Welcome to Dance Therapy."

I just looked around the room. I signed up for this? But then that thought I'd had earlier about people faking amnesia came back. What if I was right? What if nobody had amnesia, and there was a secret society of people who had done exactly what I had? Did they all know? How do I let them know I'm in on it? Do they know I'm in on it because they know that there is actually no such thing as amnesia? Are we a club?

It was freaking me out as I searched the eyes of every person in the room. I just wanted a sign. Something. But nobody was giving me *anything*. Was Dr. Debra in on it too? No, I decided she couldn't be. She had to have genuinely believed her throwback outfit would comfort her patients—after all, chances were good that she wasn't the only one in the room stuck in the seventies. "Let's everyone pick a partner or let me know if you can't find anyone."

People started pairing off. A man timidly smiled at me. He was bald on top and wearing a cardigan sweater that looked like it had belonged to his grandfather and then to his father, and now the heirloom and its cross-generational stench were finally his. He started making his way over toward me, and a quick review told me my escape routes were blocked.

"Hi. I'm Paul," he said.

"Hello."

"Begin to move your bodies and talk to your partner," said Debra. "Say whatever comes to your mind. Sway and convey, sashay and parley, glide and confide. Everybody move!"

I did *not* sign up for this. Paul embraced this thing wholeheartedly, and there I was, all of a sudden his dance partner. I had to do it. I self-consciously moved ever so slightly in what could I guess be called dancing if you're using the term very, very loosely. I don't like dancing. Never have. I guess because I'm not very good at it, but I really think dancing for the most part is embarrassing for all parties involved. Even those watching. Then Paul said something to me that I didn't quite know how to respond to.

"I'm eighteen," he said wistfully. This man was clearly in his *forties* and he looked it. "Why do I look so old?"

"Oh, you don't look *that* old," I said, trying to make him feel better.

"I don't look eighteen. They're trying to tell me I'm forty-seven. But I'm not. I'm eighteen!"

"Okay," I said. "I believe you. You're eighteen."

"Hold me," he said suddenly. "The prom committee isn't looking." Christ. What could I do? I put my arms around the poor guy and counted the minutes until it would be over.

I will say this: he was definitely *not* faking. And I started to feel tremendously guilty about my ruse. And in that moment I remembered something else I hadn't considered: Sneevil Knievel was in my apartment and nobody was taking care of him.

Samantha was obviously back from her trip, but she hadn't bothered to ask about the bird or get the keys to my apartment so she could take him back. What kind of parent *was* she? Clearly modeling herself after our own mom.

Todd would have to come get my keys so he could deal with Sneevil, but my phone access was limited, and as soon as I finally got back to my room and had a moment to myself, *Walter* showed up.

It was funny—the first day I was there everybody was interested, available, concerned. But now, only a couple days in, I was old news. And I could tell that he felt uncomfortable, but, bless his heart, he wanted *someone* to represent my family.

"So we've put together a file on you. The doctor told us it might help you remember," he said. He handed it over to me cautiously, like the contents of it would seal the fate of some undercover agent. Agent Jordan, posing as anyone but herself.

"Thank you," I said, knowing that it couldn't move the needle.

"We'll get through this, honey." The whole thing felt really strange, and it was. Then he kissed me on my forehead, and when he did, I felt incredibly small. Like a little girl, wanting, needing, craving attention from her father—from anyone—but not getting it. Or not getting enough of it or the right kind of it. I knew that the kiss was because he was leaving even though he'd just shown up. It was a consolation prize— an ice cream cone instead of pushing me on a swing for an hour.

"I know," I said. And I *did* know. But it didn't change my sudden wave of sorrow. He looked at me one more time before he left, and it felt like he was looking at what *could* have been. It was really odd. Like maybe he thought I was *never* coming back. I felt bad for him. He'd tried to love me the best way he knew how. I knew that. And for someone who wasn't actually related to me, he certainly put in more effort than anyone who *was*.

I opened up the file they'd made on me. There were *some* pictures, but it was mostly information. Information that was . . . *wrong*.

"This is all wrong!" I shouted. "This . . . this is bullshit! I don't weigh that much! How the hell do *they* know when I lost my virginity?!" Sam's handiwork was evident throughout. "And I'm a C cup, dammit! *Not* a B cup, thank you very much."

"Are you talking to me?" a nurse said hesitantly.

"No, I was talking to myself."

"Oh. Well . . . you have another visitor."

I looked up to see Lydia, the frizzy-haired, red-faced, evil idea-stealer from hell. What the hell was *she* doing showing up here? I wondered. And then she started talking . . . verrrry slooooowly, while the nurse made sure I didn't freak out at the strange woman.

"Hi. I'm Lydiiiiiaaaa. I'm your superior at Splaaash—an aaaaadvertising agency. We wooooork together."

Now, *this* was going to be fun.

"We do?" I asked.

"Yes, for twoooo years now."

"You're my boss? Do I make a lot of money?" She shifted her feet, and I could tell she was starting to get uncomfortable. It was great. The slow talking stopped and her needles sprang out.

"Well, *I* think you make a decent amount of money. Sure."

"Thanks," I said, piling it on.

"How do you feel?" she asked, leaning in slightly.

"Better, I think." I decided to milk the moment for all it was worth. "You seem so nice. It's all hazy to me now, hard to describe—like not having a reflection in a mirror. But I'll bet you and I work very well together."

"I . . . uh . . . Well, of course we do. We're like a team. I've been in-strumental in your career." She sat down in the one chair they'd desig-nated for visitors.

The nurse, sensing there wouldn't be a psychotic episode, said, "Buzz if you need anything."

Lydia cleared her throat. "Do you remember anything at all about work? Anything that happened before your accident?" she asked point-edly, leaning in, waiting for my answer. It took all my self-control not to read her the riot act.

"I remember odd bits and pieces. A building. A giant color printer spitting out posters. Phones that are too loud when someone wants you."

"The intercom," she confirmed, staring at me.

"But . . . people, things that happened. No, I can't really say that I do."

"Nothing that happened?" She perked up.

"Nothing with you. I . . . You're not familiar." I sighed and forced my eyes to well up a little. "I'm sorry. I can tell we weren't just coworkers. We were good friends too, weren't we?"

She breathed in deeply and smiled. "It's all right. We'll make *new* memories."

"Gosh, I sure *hope* so!" I beamed. "So we *were* good friends?"

"We were . . . *Sure* we were." Liar. Then again, who was *I* to judge?

"Like we had lunch together and stuff?" She tugged at a loose thread on the chair cushion, her eyes searching for somewhere to look other than at mine.

"On occasion," she said. What occasion would that be? I wondered. "Well, how do I ask this: Do you think that you can still . . . remember how to be creative?"

"I . . . I don't know. You mean . . . with ad stuff? I can try."

I could see her actually starting to sweat. There were little beads forming on her upper lip and her forehead was getting shiny. I think I watched her go through about seventeen emotions in a matter of three seconds. She was relieved that I didn't remember, nervous that I might not be able to do her job for her anymore, hopeful that I'd regain my memory for that aspect but fearful for the other . . . It was a hell of a thing to watch. Worst of all, she was trying to simulate kindness, which was just not in her biological makeup.

"Well, you just rest and get better now. And we all hope you come back to work very soon."

"Okay, I hope so, too. Thanks for visiting . . . friend!" I said, like a mildly retarded person.

Lydia got up and walked out. She looked back at me and smiled probably the fakest smile I'd ever seen. It was punctuated with her muttering "shit" under her breath, not quite as inaudibly as she'd intended. It was *delightful.*

* * * * *

After a week or so of different therapies and diagnosis, the days were starting to get predictable. I'd suffer through dance therapy, I'd go through a series of tests, I'd draw pictures, I'd meet with specialists, and occasionally they'd throw something new into the mix.

The doctors would sometimes speak in medical jargon that I didn't understand and refer to affected parts of my brain, like the hippocampus—a part of the brain that's "key in storing and processing declarative memory as well as episodic memory information." I was informed that damage to the hippocampus usually affected access to memories prior to the damage, which was what I was experiencing. I'd hear him speak the words but get stuck on the phonetic implications. I'd hear him say "hippocampus," and immediately I'd picture a college for hippopotami, and then take it a step further—and remember the Hungry Hungry Hippos, the childhood game of frantic marble-munching hippos, trying to see which one could eat the most. I'd remember a T-shirt I'd had, an homage to the game, which featured a shrugging hippopotamus and the caption: HONESTLY, I WAS NEVER THAT HUNGRY.

Then there were the odd visitors here and there whose line of questioning and intention were inscrutable. They weren't doctors or nurses, but they seemed to be there on official business. They'd ask me questions about my capacity to perform certain tasks, my function level, what I felt comfortable with . . . and they seemed very careful in trying not to offend me. They asked me about the medications I was being given, if I was feeling depressed since I'd been admitted, if I thought about harming myself, harming others, and about my general mental state.

I heard the words "capacity" and "consent" and my mind would invariably wander—drinking contests at college parties, the abortion debate, the Senate's "advise and consent" responsibilities on judicial nomination, the little signs on restaurant walls (I know the capacity of this room is not to exceed 241 persons, but what if it *does*?). All in all, my memory was exceptional. But what undoubtedly had grown worse since the accident was my attention span.

And there was something else I realized about my hospital stay—there were no cute doctors. I was spending most of my days watching soap operas, each of which has its own hospital filled with hot young doctors and nurses, and mine had zip. I made a mental note to send a letter to the network, putting them on notice that these programs are false advertising and that, were someone to make a trip to the hospital for the sole purpose of meeting a hot young doctor with washboard abs and a killer smile, they would be sadly disappointed.

Todd walked in and looked around, noticing the increasing number of floral arrangements that were taking over my hospital room. "Who are all of these flowers from?"

"The guy who hit me. He's sent me something almost every day. My mom wants to sue him, but he seems really nice."

"Now, that's the old Jordan talking. The new Jordan would say . . ."

" 'Baby needs some new shoes!' " I shouted, a little louder than I should have.

"Word up, sister," he said. "I stopped by your place like you asked. Your bird is psychotic, by the way."

"It's not my bird— Why? What's wrong?"

"He's just loud and he throws his seed everywhere. And I ain't cleaning it up. So you've got *that* to look forward to."

Then, my phone rang.

"Hi, Jordan, this is Lydia? Remember me? I was visiting you the other day? We work together?" Of course I remember you, you rapacious swamp sow.

"Oh yeah!" I said excitedly. "The nice older lady from the office."

"Well, I wouldn't call myself an *older* lady, Jordan. I'm only a few years older than you."

"That's what I meant. Older than me."

"I'm calling to see how you're feeling? If you remember anything about work yet?" Was she asking me? Or telling me? She was punctuating every sentence? With a raised pitch and a question mark?

"Nope. Not coming back just yet."

"Okay then. I'll let you go rest up some more."

"Okay, Lydia," I said as the cheeriest me I could muster, "thanks for calling!" And I hung up the phone and concluded just as cheerily, "You cradle-robbing, scum-sucking hag." Todd cracked up; he was clearly enjoying my fun almost as much as me.

* * * * *

My release date was still a few days away, but my mom had been talking to her loony friends, who each had come up with a surefire way to help me regain my memory. So she asked my doctor if I could be released to her care, so that I could partake in some of her cockamamy treatments. Agreeing that I wasn't dangerous to others or myself and not much of a flight risk ("We can be thankful that she seems totally devoid of the hostility and dementia that often accompany even mild amnesia," he'd declared after a few days of my amiable fakery), he consented.

*Finally* they were letting me out. I was at the nurses' station, looking over the release papers and feeling this overwhelming rush. I couldn't wait to start living my life as the new me, outside this hospital. Was it the new me? I wondered. The new fake me? If I faked it long enough, would I become that person? I could be as assertive as I made up my mind to be. Hell, I could be as "whatever" as I made up my mind to be. The world was my oyster. Starting now. And with a little rinsing of my memory, I could dispense with the bad like unwanted sand and oceanic grit. I turned to my mother, who had all my release papers in her hands.

"Okay . . . where do I sign?" I said, ready to embark on my new life.

"Your mother can do all that for you," said the nurse. Fine by me. Todd told me there is a school of thought in medical circles that holds that a good deal of so-called amnesia is garden-variety malingering, an effort to let life slide for a little while. Since I was a poster child for that school, I figured it was time for me to start receiving some dividends.

"Great," I said cheerily. "So on the next really nice day can you write me a note to get me out of work, then?"

"For what?" my mom said with a confused look on her face.

"No, I was kidding. You know how mothers write notes when their kids are sick and staying home from school."

"Are you feeling sick?"

"Never mind," I said. I didn't know whether she was slow on the uptake and never got out of her own head long enough to focus on me, but it was like so many moments with her—better just left alone.

Our first stop: the chiropractor's office.

I'd never been to a chiropractor before. There were scented candles burning and New Age music playing. *This* was more like it—screw all that hospital stuff. I didn't know if a massage came as part of the treatment, but already it was better than my sterile room at the hospital.

Dr. Mangere walked in and, before he even asked me my name, he carefully placed his palms on either side of my neck and wrenched it to one side.

"Ow!" I screamed.

No reaction from Dr. Mangle Me. He grabbed my head again and wrenched it to the other side.

"Jeez!"

"Do you remember anything now?" he asked, as if his practically breaking my neck had been the miracle cure.

"No!" I practically screeched.

"Come back in a week," he ordered.

"Yeah, I'll be sure to remember *that*."

Then he raised his hand and began to reach for me again. I put my arms out to block him and forcibly knocked his arms back with a move that was partly a quick double karate chop and partly a manic cheer— "DE-FENSE!" I mean, my neck goes only two ways and he'd already yanked it *both* ways, so I had to draw the line. Needless to say, he was a little startled by my block.

"I'm just reaching for the thermostat," he said as if he were talking to a crazy person. "It's a little chilly." Here at last, I'm sure my mother thought, was the hostility and dementia my doctor had missed.

"I thought you were going to yank me again," I offered meekly.

"No."

"Oh."

We stared at each other for a minute, not quite knowing where to go from there.

"Okay then. I'll see you next week," he said. "I'm reaching for the door now and I'm just going to turn the knob and walk out of this room."

Great. Now in addition to being an amnesiac, I was being treated like a dangerous nutcase. But you know what? I felt kinda good. Nobody had ever been scared of me before. I was always okay-by-me Jordan, walk-all-over-me Jordan, go-ahead-and-cheat-on-me Jordan, I'd-love-to-do-your-work-assignment-while-you-actually-have-a-life Jordan. This was cool. I mean, I wasn't going to go karate chopping every person I came into contact with, but I was enjoying mentally fighting back on behalf of the timid little wimp I'd been before.

# 12.
# my mother my sister

I was going to stay with my parents on Long Island for a few days—to ease my way back into life. The general consensus was that sticking me back into my apartment might result in me wandering aimlessly through Lower Manhattan and becoming a lead story on the local news (after the ever-popular "Fire in the Bronx" that I'd come to associate with the start of every news broadcast). Or I'd disappear in my nightshirt and turn up years later as a clerk in a fabric store in Oklahoma, married to a city surveyor, answering to the name Lulu (an extreme execution of the fake-amnesia gambit, one that seemed beyond necessary to me at the time). So the alternative was as much time as I needed at the 'rents' place.

Life in Long Island was just as I'd remembered it. Boring. My mom was annoying; my bedroom had been turned into a "study"; and Sam, not even knowing that she was *right*, was hell-bent on proving I was faking my amnesia in her latest attempt to get attention.

I was sitting in the breakfast nook, smearing low-fat cream cheese onto my bagel when she casually strolled in, with a loaf of nut bread in hand.

"Hey, Jordan," she said absentmindedly, not even looking at me, as she picked up the wall phone. "Mom wanted me to take this nut bread over to the Kornbluts' as a Thanksgiving gesture, but it's freezing, so I want to call before I walk over in case they're not home. What's their phone number again?"

I looked at the nut bread in her hand and shook my head sweetly. "Well, a nut bread. Our mother is a *dear*, isn't she?"

"Yeah," she said impatiently, still thinking she could trick me into re-
citing the number back to her instantly in a show of mnemonic strength.
"Huge dear. So what's the number again? I forgot."

"Um . . . try . . . wait, it's . . ." I said, and then paused for a second,
toying with her. She leaned in, her eyes slightly narrowing, an evil glimmer over the excitement at nabbing me. "Oh, what's that number for
getting people's numbers?" I said.

"Four-one-one," she said flatly.

I looked left and right. "Oh, I should write that down. I get so embarrassed asking these dumb questions all the time. But I could walk it
over there for you—if you can point out the house to me. You've been so
good to me, I'd love to do this for you."

"Never mind," she said, angry that her trickery hadn't worked. She'd
have to try harder than *that*. And she did.

One night while I was drifting off to sleep, I felt her form sitting at
the side of my bed. Figuring my guard was down, she softly said, "Hey,
Jordan . . . you know that silk blouse of mine that you've always wanted
to wear? I'll let you have it. But I can't remember if it was the Valentino
or the Chloé. Which one was it?"

I replied dreamily, "It was . . . the latte . . . You've got to be the dim-
mest barrista I've . . ." and then I pretended to drift off to sleep. She got
up and stormed out, careful to shut the door loud enough to wake me if
I *had* actually been asleep.

\*   \*   \*   \*   \*

Another idea my mom had was to take me to an herbalist, thinking perhaps that homeopathy would be the cure for my amnesia. Navigating
our way through Chinatown was no easy feat for my mom and me. First,
the guy's "office" was hidden in the upstairs of some out-of-the-way
building that was so narrow, I half expected that we'd enter not through
a door but a mail slot. But the more important obstacle was the knockoff factor. Trying to walk past a knockoff Hermès bag for my mother was
like a gay man trying to ignore an advance copy of the new Madonna
album a week before its release date. Not only did they have the Birkin

that she'd been wait-listed for, they had it in every color for one-fiftieth of the price.

"Who's going to know?" she repeated over and over, more in an effort to convince herself than anyone else. When all was said and done, she'd bought three bags in three colors, Chinese slippers ("because they're all the rage on *the Island*"), and a pen with a fifties pinup girl whose skirt lifted when you turned her upside down to write. This was for Walter. I made the mistake of asking why she was getting it for him.

"Because I'm going through 'the change' and he's not getting into my skirt anytime soon," she said. "It'll be a cute way of telling him to hang in there, and we'll be back at it soon."

Hearing about her going through "the change" and my stepfather under her skirt was far from cute—in fact, it was enough to make me nauseous.

Then she added, "I just don't feel very sensual lately."

If I never heard my mother say "sensual" again, it would be too soon. This was one of those moments when my mother tries to act like my sister and crosses that information threshold. I spoke to Cat about it once, and she said that when it happened, I should tell my mother in no uncertain terms that she is "crossing generational boundaries." But since I wasn't allowed to have any recollection of Cat or the relationship that my mom and I used to have, I had to just keep my mouth shut.

I must have looked sick, the nausea working in my favor, because she thought it was from the accident and focused once again on getting me to the Chinese herbalist.

When we knocked on the door at the top of four flights of rickety stairs, it took the guy about five minutes to answer. This was especially shocking because once we got inside, the space was so small that I wasn't entirely convinced that it was not just a closet with some spice racks.

This little guru dude looked exactly like you'd expect a 127-year-old man to look. Long white beard. Shogun mustache. Robe. Slippers. A caricature of himself. And tiny. He had obviously been expecting me—without asking a single question he immediately started putting together some weird concoction, which he then thrust into my hands.

"You take-a these herb. They get memory back. You remember first time you suckle mother's breast even!"

"Hmm," I said. "I'm not looking to go back *quite* that far." The last thing I wanted to think about was suckling on my mother's breast. There was that *nausea* again. And when I knocked the elixir back, it tasted like the street below smelled. Rotting vegetable with a bile chaser.

They looked at me, and I looked back. He sensed what my mom was waiting for and laughed lightly. "Not now. Not like a . . ." He sought the word, then interlaced his fingers and flung them apart with a boom sound effect. But I, who had drunk the thing, wanted to correct him. Inside me, it *was* like interlaced fingers being flung apart and going boom. *Now.*

"Yes, it takes time. We understand. Thank you, sir," my mom said and then bowed. She *bowed*. Maybe some people could have pulled that off without appearing condescending. Not my mom. It was bad. Awkward doesn't even begin to describe it. And worst of all, I could tell that she felt really "hip" doing so.

When we walked out, it took all my self-control to keep from giving up the ruse. I didn't want to appear too unwilling. But her aimless meandering through the memory-recovery playbook was oddly self-indulgent. Like it just wouldn't do to let a recovery run its course.

"You know, all of these 'treatments' are pretty random." I said. "Do you think if I went back to work, maybe that would help jog my memory? You know, being in familiar surroundings." She sort of ignored me. I continued, "My boss did come visit me. She *said* they wanted me back."

"Would you mind terribly if we stopped at Century 21 while we're down here?" It's like we were from different gene pools. And hers was tainted with insatiable need for stuff to jam into her overflowing closets.

*     *     *     *     *

We got home, and I'd barely had time to fake an attempted memory when the doorbell rang. I walked over to the front door and through the peephole, saw a man I legitimately didn't recognize. He looked waxy. Like a character straight out of Madame Tussaud's. He was smiling before I even opened the door—like it was permanently plastered on his face. And it wasn't an attractive smile either—giant yellowed teeth, which he'd neglected to brush after lunch. A lunch that clearly included spinach. I opened the door a crack.

"Hello?" I said.

"Jordan?" the man asked.

"Yes . . . ?"

"I'm Ben Waronker, the hypnotist. I spoke to your mother on the phone. We have an appointment," he said, looking at his watch and then showing it to me, "right now."

"Oh," I said, without opening the door. Then my mother interceded, flinging the door open and grabbing his hand.

"Mr. Wonker—"

"Waronker," he corrected.

"This is a such a pleasure," she continued. "I've heard your radio ads for years. I never thought I'd need to call on you."

"I do a lot of smoking cessation," he said sympathetically.

"Mom!" I said sternly, then caught myself. "I'm awfully tired."

"Perfect," she said. "Jordan, sweetheart, I know you've been through a lot, but I want you back. Just like before. And so I'm willing to try anything. Say you are too, honey."

We were gradually making our way down the list to electroshock therapy, so I'd have to come up with something before then.

"I guess," I said, although I wasn't sure. I knew I could fake amnesia, but I wasn't positive I could fool a hypnotist. Still, I'd always figured it was a hoax, based at least partly if not wholly on will, so if I didn't open myself up to it, hopefully he wouldn't get me to fess up.

"Where is comfortable for you?" he asked. "Is there a room in the house where you might be inclined to experience deep peace?" If there *was*, I'd certainly never found it in the eighteen years that I'd grown up there.

"The living room is fine, I guess," I said. "Right in here." I directed him into the living room and my mother followed us, pretending to fluff the overstuffed pillows on the couch.

"First of all, I want you to throw out any preconceived notions you may have about hypnotherapy. I don't dangle a watch in front of your face and try to get you to run around acting like a chicken in front of people. And I'm nothing like those guys you see on TV," he said and then cocked one eyebrow. "Unless you've seen *me* on TV."

"I haven't."

"Then you're in for a treat. I'm not just here to help you regain your memory. I'm here to help you discover strengths that you never knew you had. I firmly believe that ninety percent of our untapped potential is stored in the subconscious mind, so all we need to do is learn how to access it and then start using it. Sound good?"

"Anything to get back a little more of me," I said earnestly.

"Close your eyes," he said. "Relax . . ." It was quiet. Until I heard the shuffle of my mother's feet. I opened my eyes and saw my mom still hovering.

"Should we be alone?" I asked. "I feel a little self-conscious."

"I'm gone," my mother said, and Mr. Waronker nodded for me to close my eyes again.

"Let go of all of the day's worries . . ." he said.

"Tell her that when she wakes up," I heard Samantha shout from the next room, "She'll remember she owes me seventy-five bucks." Then there was some general shushing, followed by Sam saying, "It's *true*!"

The hypnotist got up and closed the door. Then he settled in where he'd left off.

"Detach from your body . . . release from your own identity and merge with the universe . . . you have no limitations . . . you are everything . . . you are pure . . . you are aware . . . you are relaxing . . ."

As I drifted off, I started to feel dangerously at ease. He lowered the tone of his voice, and it *did* feel like I was on the verge of that profound rest I experienced after working an all-nighter on a rushed campaign.

"You're relaxing . . . everything is floating away, nothing to worry about. All the cares, all the cares of the day, all the cares that . . . hung about you through the week."

I spoke up dreamily. " 'Seem to vanish like a gambler's . . .' "

"'Lucky streak!'" he continued anxiously, thrilled by the apparent breakthrough. "Tell me, what do you see?"

"A door."

He paused. Maybe he hadn't expected anything to come of it either. "Reach for the door," he said. "Open the door."

"It's locked."

"Do you have the key?"

"No."

"Okay . . ." he said.

"Wait," I exclaimed. "It wasn't locked. It was only stuck."

"So open the door," he urged a little edgily.

"It's open."

"What do you see?"

"I see a face," I said.

"Describe it."

"It's like wax."

"What else?" he probed.

"The nose is grotesquely large and the teeth—horrifying, misshapen, yellow." I lifted my arms and made little pointing motions. "With bits of . . . spinach plugged into them."

"Okay . . ." he said somewhat hesitantly. "What else?"

"Glasses."

"Wait a minute," he said. "Are the glasses on the face wire rimmed?"

"Yes."

"And the body it's attached to . . . is it wearing a V-necked sweater . . . ?"

"With a crest from the New Hyde Park Country Club."

He sighed. "Well, we've succeeded in recovering your memory of opening the door twenty minutes ago when I got here," he said. "And I *floss*."

\* \* \* \* \*

None of their tricks were working, but that didn't mean they were giving up. My mom was determined to bring my memory back and Sam was determined to prove me a fraud. Her pièce de résistance came later that night. Fighting off Dr. Wax Museum's voodoo wasn't any harder than defeating a four-year-old at Trivial Pursuit, but the ordeal took a lot out of me all the same, and I needed some rest. I was lying on my back, eyes closed, listening to the rain hit the windowsill like I used to when I was a little girl. Then the door flew open and Sam stomped in, wearing a pair of ridiculous Chanel motorcycle boots. Dissonance at its finest.

"I went to check on Sneevil today . . . your bird?" she said, and then waited for my response.

"I have a bird?" I asked, using every ounce of my strength to *not* attack her.

"Yup."

I had to admire her skills. I couldn't own up to knowing Sneevil was *her* bird, but the thought of having an avian Liza Minnelli for a permanent roommate made my head hurt. She was good, I had to admit.

"Well, I should thank you for checking on him."

"It was really my pleasure," she said. "You got more flowers too. Like three different shipments. I took one for the table tomorrow night." Tomorrow night? Then I remembered. It was Thanksgiving.

"Knock knock," said Dirk, peeking his head into the room. "Your mom let me in."

"Dirk," Samantha said. "Nice. Making the trip to Long Island!"

"I wanted to check on J," he said. He *never* called me J.

"Thanks, *D*," I said, with a big smile. He twisted his face subtly—a reaction to being called D, I surmised. Hey, if *he* was making up new nicknames, so would I.

"I figured I'd be with the fam for Turkey Day, so I wanted to make sure I stopped by before all the mayhem," he said. "Remembering anything yet?"

I looked up and saw that he'd already directed his attention to the TV before I had a chance to answer. More accurately—his attention was focused on a set of Xbox controls.

Sam noticed, too. "Wanna *go*?" she said to Dirk, and he was already sitting on the floor, legs crossed, control in hand before he answered.

"Shit, yes!" he said.

"No," I said, to nobody who was listening. "I don't have my memory back."

Dirk was focused on the game intensely. "What?" he asked after a few seconds.

"I was saying you look just like Zack," I said, "the eight-year-old from down the street who matches wits with Sam on the Xbox." Why had he bothered to come here? Sam giggled and Dirk took a second away from his frantic joystick maneuvering to smile at her. Great—those two were a match made in heaven they deserved each other.

# 13.
# thanksgiving drop-in

The next morning, I went downstairs and saw my mom, already in a tailspin, ordering poor Carmelita around.

"Can I help?" I asked.

"Don't I wish . . ." my mom replied.

"Well? You don't *have* to wish. I'm here to help. I *want* to help."

"I know you do, honey. But maybe if you just kept out of the way. Tell you what, go to the cellar and get me another bottle of wine just like *this* one," she said, as she handed me the bottle.

"Okay, but I'd love to help cook," I said.

"You don't cook, Jordan." That wasn't true. I could cook. I *did* cook. But our mother was such a control freak she wouldn't let me touch anything, God forbid I overmashed a yam.

I took the bottle down to the cellar and found a matching bottle. Having to match the label reminded me of some of the dumb mental games they had me play in the hospital, but this was clearly the maximum my mother would allow me to contribute to dinner.

Rather than adding to the aggravation upstairs, I walked outside through the basement door into the lovely autumn afternoon, crisp with the leafy, lawny smell. In the city, the stream of people becomes a form of scenery, and what you notice is the occasional tree. In the suburbs, it's reversed: on a day like this, the occasional human being stands out in bright relief to the landscape. Especially a stranger. I looked across the street and saw someone standing by a car. I recognized him immediately but couldn't place where I knew him from. Then it hit me—the angel. It was the same face I saw when I opened my eyes after flying heavenward, then hellward, off my bike.

"Hello?" I called out.

"Jordan Landau?" he said with his head cocked to one side.

"Yes . . . ?"

"Hi," he said, taking a few steps into the middle of the street. "Sorry . . . I'm Travis, Travis Andrews."

"Oh," I said. "The name on the cards."

"The cards . . ." he said.

I smiled at him. "The flowers. The chocolate . . ." It was no feat of memory to open my eyes and see all the ways he'd apologized and wished me well. So I felt completely comfortable for the first time since getting to Long Island. "Thank you. It's been really sweet, but you didn't have to do all that."

"I feel awful. I'm so sorry about what happened."

"I'd feel even worse about the size of my ass, " I said, and as I did, he looked around over his shoulder to take a peek at his ass. I felt horrible and rushed to explain, "No, not *your* ass, *mine*. The one that has grown exponentially since you've been supplying chocolate nonstop."

"Well, good thing that flowers aren't edible," he said. "And at the risk of sounding like I'm checking out your ass, which I'm not—I mean I *couldn't* because, well, it's behind you—it looks like it's a pretty good one."

My face felt hot. Even if I'd started it, this was beyond my comfort zone. "Can we not talk about my ass?"

"We can definitely not talk about your ass," he said with a laugh. "I'm sorry. How are you?"

"I'm okay . . . all things considered."

"Now *that's* a great thing to hear," he exclaimed. Nice guy. He felt so familiar to me. Not just because I'd seen him at the accident, but because I immediately felt like I knew him. Like I'd known him for a long time. But I was quite sure I hadn't. He'd have been hard to miss. He was tall with spiky black hair. Not moussed and jelled spiky, just out-of-control messy but perfectly messed. He had piercing blue eyes and a day's worth of stubble that showed up prominently against his fair skin. He looked like he'd be the lead singer of a band from the neck up, but the J. Crew sweater told me otherwise. It was the perfect blend, the amalgam most women will secretly admit they want most of all, like a guy's virgin whore fantasy: the rock star who's giving up touring to devote his life to you.

"Happy Thanksgiving," I said.

"Jesus, I'm sorry. Yeah, you too. Sorry . . . you're probably wondering what I'm doing out here. On Thanksgiving."

"Kind of," I said.

"I just wanted to make sure you were okay."

"I'm okay," I said, trying to reassure him. He seemed so lost.

"So I had time today, and I was going out east on the island. And you weren't in the hospital anymore. So your parents . . . I have this friend at the police department. Anyway, it's not malicious or anything like that. This is sounding really stalker, isn't it?"

I wondered if he had a family and thought about inviting him in for our dinner, but I knew my mom would have a fit.

"Okay," he said and then paused, as though that was all he'd come with. But more came. "Did you lose your memory?" he said abruptly.

"It's hard to say," I told him and looked away, feeling the creeping anxiety of my charade.

"You don't remember?" he said. It had been unintentional. Slow on the uptake, we both laughed. "I'm sorry. That's awful."

"I'm okay. Really." I couldn't figure out why I felt so guilty faking my amnesia to this guy. Probably because he was the one who'd caused it. Or *would* have been if I'd actually had amnesia. Anyway, I felt bad. He seemed so genuine.

And he'd said I had a nice ass.

"Do you have Thanksgiving plans?" I blurted out suddenly. I don't know why, and I knew he couldn't come in, so I regretted it as soon as I said it.

"No, not really. I was going farther out on the island. It's a funny story," he said. "Well, not really funny but . . . weird?"

"I like weird."

"My dad passed away a few years ago . . ."

"Sorry. Definitely not a *funny* story," I said.

"Yeah, that's not the funny part. A buddy of mine was trying to cheer me up and he bet me a hundred bucks that he could charm us into a stranger's Thanksgiving dinner. And he did. He has this magnetic personality, and he talked our way in with a bottle of wine."

"Wow."

"Yeah, so it became sort of a tradition. He'd really look forward to it—plan it for weeks. Always made it to dessert. I wonder if he still does it . . ." he said and trailed off in thought. "He was an amazing guy. Could sell you on anything."

He was staring. Not at me exactly but at my hand. I looked down and saw the object of his distraction. The bottle of wine.

Now, Jordan B.C. (before concussion) wouldn't have given all this a second thought. She'd have mumbled something terse or unintelligible at this point, turned in the wrong direction, taken a few steps, doubled back in embarrassment, and disappeared inside the garage. But she wasn't there. So Jordan A.D. (amnesia dabbler) spoke up.

"Where should we try first?" I asked.

Oh, the thought did strike me that if I disappeared into the neighborhood with my mom's wine she'd probably think the worst, call the cops, and never again let me out of her sight. And I was heart set on moving back to my apartment the next day. But he laughed the most darling laugh.

"Even if. *Even if.* It won't work. My friend isn't here anymore. He moved away."

"But *you* were there," I said, now stepping toward him with a look over my shoulder to make sure we couldn't be seen from my house. "How did it work?"

"It was really all him," Travis said. "He was an actor."

"Listen, I'm serious," I said after a pause. "If you don't do this with me, I'll sue you for everything you've got."

He scratched the side of his head slowly. "Well, I would hate to lose eighty-five dollars in loose change and free video-rental coupons." Then we looked at each other, our eyes wide with the rush of that manic moment. And I knew I had him.

"There are rules," he said with mock sternness and a sneaky smile as we got into his car and rounded the block, slowing down to scout our first foray. The car was nice but nothing out of the ordinary. He kept it well, but there was a stack of papers in the backseat under a small anchor. An anchor? Weird. But still, it was just quirky enough to be contemplated. I had no time to analyze it further. He had a healthy moderation in his sense of order, and I was buzzing with wonderment . . . at myself. A situation like the one I was in could be threatening or exhilarating, depending where you sat. I was in the front seat, passenger side.

"No threats. No crime. No sob story. Bring your A game." We screeched to a quick stop. "We are gentlemen and shall be received as such."

"Gentlemen?" I asked.

"Gentlemen," he said.

"So you never want to be taken for a burglar."

"Or a pervert, no, correct." He pointed at his pants. "So, slacks, wool or a wool blend." He kicked one foot up to show. "Shine on the shoes." He pulled open his coat for effect. "Belt matching the shoes, cotton button-down—no silk or exotics."

"Like what, mohair?"

He nodded. "It's family time. All cleaned up, face washed, hair combed. Smiling."

"I've got all that, and my Sunday best on to boot," I said, showing off my new pencil skirt, Ella Moss top, and Kors boots. "Well, Thursday best."

"You look great," he said. "And then the speech." He cleared his throat. "We are two gentlemen from the city. We'll change that bit. We were drawn here to this community in hopes of sharing the fellowship of the season with new friends. If you would permit us to join you, we would humbly thank you, not only with our gratitude but also with these spirits for your table."

I was silent for a moment. "You memorized that whole thing?"

"Yep."

"And they bought it?"

"Never had to knock on more than five or ten doors. In seven years."

"So this is how orphans get their jollies," I said.

He peered out and the car rolled forward again. "When do you have to be back?"

Back. As in, will I be on the news, a holiday-turned-tragic piece, by the time I get back? "I've probably got an hour and a half."

"Okay, it's about two, a little after, so we'll have to find someone who's sitting down early." We spotted a house with blue siding and white shutters, and a ragged turkey flag fluttering from a pole by the side door. A few more cars than seemed normal crowded around the place.

"First victim," he said.

He looked at me. "I'm Travis. You're Jordan."

"Are we related?"

"Jesus, you're worse off than I thought," he said.

"No, for the *story* here," I corrected.

"Ah. No—it's not a story. We are honest people with a simple, courteous proposition. So . . . We are two gentlemen—er, a lady and a gentleman—from the city. Remember?"

"We are . . . in your community," I began. Then I went quiet and pulled my lips in, and that made him nervous, I think.

"Just let me do the talking," he said.

We stepped up to the door, and a little round face wrapped in a drape saw us and disappeared. The doorbell rang inside. Then the door opened. A smile started on Travis's mouth, and he opened it to speak.

But I beat him to it.

"We are a gentleman and young lady from the city. We were drawn to this community in hopes of sharing the fellowship of the season with new . . . friends. If you would allow us to join you, we would thank you with both our gratitude and this bottle of . . . spirits for your table."

The man looked at me, then Travis.

"No," he said, and the door drifted shut.

I licked my lips and stared ahead.

"I think you ad-libbed some," he said. "But wait a minute—how did you . . . I mean, what about—" He spun his finger at his temple. I know he was asking about my amnesia, but he used the universal hand sign for crazy. I went with it.

"They tell me it's *retrograde* amnesia," I said. "People, things from before are foggy as hell. But I'm sharpy sharp on things *since* the crash."

We believe whatever we don't pay a lot of attention to, so he was on board—but he wanted to be clear: the next attempt was his. So we walked casually, confidently to the door of a split-level, totally out of place but homey anyway among the sprawling ranches with add-ons, mini-mansions, and doomed bungalows in the neighborhood. He took the bottle of wine. The door swung open and a very pleasant lady of about fifty with a headband on stood there.

"We are a gentleman and young lady from the city. We were drawn here to this community in hopes of sharing the fellowship of the season with new friends. If you would permit us to join you, we would humbly thank you, not only with our gratitude but also with these spirits for your table."

The lady stood frozen for a second; then her open mouth smiled and she looked back over her shoulder. "Well, all right. We don't eat till five, so you can watch football till then or play Nintendo with Lyle."

I was stunned. She was going for it?

"You're awfully kind," Travis said with a charmingly earnest grin. "But we're very hungry *now*, so . . . thank you anyway and happy Thanksgiving." And he turned and walked back to the car. I watched him for a moment before waving and smiling to her, wanting to retract my head between my shoulders into my chest, then ran after him down the sidewalk.

"Bye," she called out, as though it were a question.

"Oh my *God*!" I screamed when we'd slid back into the car and pulled away. "We were *in*."

"Told you," he said, doing a great job of hiding his own amazement at the early success, and—I thought—a little nervous that we might have just thrown away the prize. "But that dinnertime wouldn't do. This isn't a kidnapping." Something about the word seemed to stall him. He looked at me, and those eyes . . . I felt so strange. About *all* of it. Like I really *wasn't* Jordan anymore. At least not the Jordan I was before. Jordan B.C. "You have a schedule."

"You know, I'd invite you to *our* dinner, but my . . . " I trailed off. "I don't know that they'd get it."

"Please. Don't wreck the adventure with an easy out."

So we drove on, now about a mile from my house. Though it was still early, signs of gatherings were everywhere. We tried two more in close proximity. Both speedy rejections. The second one before the speech was fully out.

"You're gonna get that every so often," he confided as we stood on their sidewalk, looking back at them peering out at us.

"If you can't appreciate this art, I have nothing but pity for you," I said, shaking my fist at the house.

We got close at the next place, but the very old man visible down the front hallway looked terrified, so we didn't push the issue with the lady, sweet and apologetic as she was. After the next "no," I could tell Travis was slipping into defeatism or losing heart or maybe worried that I'd think he was obsessed and not wanting to push whatever luck this little adventure represented. So we talked a little more in the car. Then I saw it was nearing 3 P.M.

"One more shot," I said.

"You call it."

We went up and down two blocks. I told him to stop in front of a particularly unkempt place, a few extra cars in the drive, Indian corn on the door, plastic lawn chairs on their sides on the lawn. Fulfilling their destiny, I guess.

We stepped up and he cradled the wine in two hands. I assumed the silent-partner stance, slightly behind his right shoulder. *Ding-dong*. The front door opened, then the storm door, just a few inches. A man in a stretched sweater leaned out and looked at us, dead-eyed.

I seized the moment. "You're not gonna believe this," I said, throwing up my left arm to express my *own* disbelief. "It's really a total joke, but the joke's on us apparently. My brother here and I were going to *surprise* our grandmother, and just had our car break down on our way to Grammy's place in Philly, and now the truth is, we'll never get there in time for dinner at this point, so it's a total loss. Unless, that is, unless you could find it in your heart to let us eat with you guys, and we'd give you this wine we got for *her* . . . so there's that."

He didn't react at first, not at all. We half suspected, I think—*I* did—that we'd crossed some line and were now in for trouble. As though he was going to chase us out into the driveway with a rolling pin or something.

"Sure," the dead-eyed man said, now smiling, almost laughing. "We were just sittin' down. I was just gonna run out for wine, so you got good timing."

And for the next hour and ten minutes, we enjoyed an out-of-body experience in the company of Mitchell and Jeanine Verdanetti, little Mitch, Angie, Albert, Therese, someone else whose name I never got, and a pushy dachsund named JoJo. We listened much more than talked, so guilty did we both feel about my lie yet so amused by the whole affair. I complimented Jeanine on her cranberries and asked her for the recipe. Who knew candied pecans in cranberry sauce could be so good?

We ate fast, helped clear the table and load the dishwasher until Therese kicked us out of the kitchen, then we took our leave, thanking them so aggressively that I'm sure they thought nothing of our early exit—except as part of a great story for next year at the Verdanettis.

We drove back to my house in near-total silence. I thought he might be mad at me. It started to sour the experience almost, and I didn't know why, but I got choked up and thought I might cry, but then he looked at me and smiled and shook his head.

"I know you're currently lacking in the memories department. But I know *I* won't forget this, and I hope you won't either," he said.

"I'll try not to," I said.

He asked for my number, but I said I didn't *know* it, so he gave me his card and said to call him when I got settled back in my place. Then I found my business card and slipped it to him without another word.

"Lord, Jordan," my mother said when I'd come back up from the cellar and plunked down on a kitchen stool in her path. "I haven't seen you all afternoon. What happened to that bottle of wine I sent you for?" This was the reaction I'd hoped for, but still, I'd been gone for *two hours*. How could she not have wondered where her poor little amnesiac had been?

"We were all out," I said. "I just grabbed whatever cabernet was next to it."

She looked at the bottle. "That'll do. Now we're sitting down in a half hour—don't go far."

"I wouldn't dream of it," I said. And it was true.

I wish I could say my own Thanksgiving was as much fun, but it was mostly what you'd expect from any other dinner we'd shared for the past couple weeks—my mother loading up on the wine and pointing at people as she spoke to them, Walter cracking bad jokes, and Sam throwing curveballs at me left and right in failed attempts to trick me. Finally, she got so frustrated that she just lashed out at me.

"This is total *bull*," Sam said. "I may not be able to prove it yet, but she's faking it!"

"Samantha Danielle—stop it right now," said my mom finally, un-characteristically speaking up to defend me, in her full-on you're-in-trouble voice. "Your sister has had enough abuse for one night. She's not faking. It's clear that she doesn't have all of her faculties; this situation is very grave and very real and the power of attorney will allow us to pro-vide the proper care for her."

"Power of attorney?" Sam and I said at the same time.

"Yes," my mom said matter-of-factly.

"What exactly is that?" I asked, fully aware that I couldn't freak out on the outside like I was on the inside. I told myself not to panic.

"It's simple, dear," she went on. "The social workers and hospital staff agreed that we should set up a durable springtime power of attorney."

"I think you mean 'springing,'" said Walter.

"Walter!" she said crossly. That single word had more possible uses than any other in my mother's lexicon. Depending on the context, it could mean just about anything. In this particular case it meant, Shut the hell up, *I'm* the one explaining this.

"The social workers and friend of the court agreed it would be best if someone were looking out for you for a while. The springing means it springs into action if and when you become incapacitated."

"Oh, she's *sprung*," Sam interjected with a delicious smile.

Now the last thing I wanted was to turn over complete control to the Wizard of Odd. But my predicament was clear. Made even more so by my mom's next sentence.

"Now, Sam, do you honestly think Jordan would give up that level of control if she was *faking*? I've got the document right here," she said, and got up from the table to get the papers.

When she came back and put the document in front of me, I felt an ache in the pit of my stomach. I glanced at it, then at Sam and at Walter and back to my mom.

"It all just makes me afraid," I said. I ran through my entire repertoire in about twenty seconds flat: angst, befuddlement, confusion, denial. I wasn't even up to the letter E before Sam cleared her throat in my direction. I swallowed a few times and tried to speed-read the paper before actually signing it. "I just want to read a little bit of it so that I understand what it is—"

"Oh, go ahead and sign it, Jordan," Sam said. "You can't very well handle all of your affairs if you can't remember who you are."

Then I looked at my mother. "And you've been so wonderful," I said to her. "How could I *not* trust you?" How bad could it be? She was my *mother*. So she'd pay my bills for a while. Not such a bad deal after all. I was a little wary of her having me committed, but I figured that was a long shot. They'd greet us both at the door and probably take her instead of me.

I signed it.

# 14.
# looking up

The strange thing about attempting to get some R&R at your folks' place is that most people get infinitely more stressed out the minute they get around family. This certainly held true for me. Plus, every time I sat down at the computer to try to bone up on the subject of amnesia, someone would walk in and catch me. I could only say I was "trying to understand what was happening to me" so many times, especially with Sam breathing down my neck, trying to trick me into slipping up. But they were fruitless searches. I needed privacy, which was in short supply at Chez Landau. So I begged to return to my own home. I was sure they were as ready to be rid of me as I was them; and proving me right, they went for it.

My mom drove me back into the city. I kept up a visage of childlike wonder the whole way home and pretended not to know my apartment building when we got there. When we stepped out of the elevator on my floor, my mom all but plugged her nose as we walked toward my door. It was clear that she didn't like where I lived. But it was also clear that she wasn't there to help me move out.

I fumbled with my keys, pretending not to know which one opened the front door—then smiled sheepishly at my mom. Unfortunately I milked my uncertainty for a beat too long because Mr. Spandex-Dick-in-Your-Face came walking out of the elevator and approached us.

"Hey, neighbor!" he said. "Haven't seen you in a while."

I looked blankly at him and then at my mom, pretending that I didn't know who he was and hoping she'd ignore him and usher me into my apartment. But she noticed. *It*. The skyscraper in Lycra.

"Oh," she said, never content to leave well enough alone or opt for subtlety in moments like these. "My, my . . ." she said, eyes on the prize as I *willed* her to look away, LOOK AWAY! Finally she recovered. "Jordan had an accident. She has amnesia and can't remember anyone. Are you friends?" Damn her.

"Yes," he said. "I was teaching her self-defense." I couldn't believe what a gigantic fucking liar he was. Then again, who was I to talk? I just smiled and acted oblivious. But it was hard not to react to that. Believe me, it was hard.

"Good. Then you can watch over her."

"It would be my pleasure."

"Fab, because I'm double-parked," she said, already halfway back to the elevator. "You're okay?" she asked me, not bothering to wait for the answer. "Call if you need anything." And she blew me a kiss and disappeared into the elevator. Then I turned the *right* key into the lock and started on my way in.

"So, this week? A self-defense lesson?" he called out.

"Sure," I said, and shut the door behind me.

The apartment was a mess. Sneevil Knievel was the son of Satan. Or the pet that the Son of Satan had begged his father for that was now exacting on my universe his revenge for the little bastard's neglect. He'd not only thrown seeds all over my apartment, he'd taken to shredding the newspaper at the bottom of his cage. I get bummed out by the current state of affairs as much as the next person, but do I feel the need to shred the *New York Times* to bits? Okay, yes. But I rarely *act* on it.

"Hi, Sneevil," I said as I threw my bag of new clothes down. That was one small bonus. Sam was too small and selfish to share her clothes with me, so my mom had ducked out to Woodbury Common, an outlet mall for those unafraid of clawing their way for Chloé, and picked up some exceptionally wearable clothes. Certainly much nicer than my H&M wardrobe.

Sneevil immediately started to sing, and as mad as I was about him being in my apartment, making a mess and causing a problem with the neighbors, I felt bad for him. This was Sam's bird. I got that she wanted to trick me and thought that would be a good way to expose my fraud, but I hadn't taken the bait. Wasn't enough enough? Didn't she actually *love* the bird? Want her pet back? It bonded me to the little guy.

I hopped onto my computer, readying myself to Google *amnesia*, but was confronted with fifty-four e-mails in my in-box, nine of which were back and forth between my mom and Walter. Here was the cream of the crop:

From: wallygator317@hotmail.com

To: judypatootie521@hotmail.com

Subject: re: re: re: re: re: re: re: Chicken tonight . . . or fowl overload?

I've tried everything. Baking soda, Vaseline and rubber socks, sliding a hand cream–filled condom over it and leaving it overnight and still nothing. I showed it to a woman I work with and she said she'd seen the same thing on her husband. His doctor told him it was a toenail fungus. A little Lamisil should take care of it. I really need something. It looks like I've been soaking in an open sewer.

Eeeeeew. I decided, *again*, that the e-mail ccs were going to stop. The new Jordan could innocently suggest that they not copy her on every mundane, bizarre, or stomach-turning e-mail that passed between them.

The Internet didn't have much more to offer than the info Todd had already prepped me with. I felt like I had a good handle on it—all I had to do was act frustrated every now and then about having no memory and act guilty for not remembering the people, places, and things that I should.

I noticed a scent that seemed to be permeating my apartment. A scent that wasn't there when I'd left it. And it wasn't stale Sneevil, although that was no picnic either. This was nice. It smelled like . . . bread? The bread they served at . . . some restaurant. I couldn't place the restaurant, but they had delicious rosemary bread—that was it, the scent was rosemary!

And as soon as I took a minute to actually check out my surroundings, I noticed that there were little bundles of rosemary everywhere. And a note from Cat. She said she'd borrowed Todd's key to stop by and lace the entire apartment with rosemary because it was apparently a holistic wonder for the memory. There were also several bags of walnuts and a Post-it suggesting I eat some for snacks, every time I felt hungry.

Cat really was a true friend. I had been on the fence about whether or not to play amnesic with her along with the rest of my family. I wanted to tell her. I really did. The problem was, as loyal and self-sacrificing as Cat was, it really came down to the fact that she was too honest to be able to be a part of this kind of deception. Too open. Todd had just the right mix of loyalty and that almost criminal take-it-to-the-grave shadiness that one requires in a close confidant. I felt bad but decided it was really kinder not to drag her into my little deception. Besides, she was a doctor—it would probably violate some sort of Hippocratic (Hypocritic?) oath to play along with me.

I looked around—being back in my apartment felt very strange. It was my stuff, but I suddenly wanted to throw most of it away. And this wasn't the ordinary and omnipresent impulse to upgrade from my barely post-college appointments. It was more a feeling that the posters, tiny Simpsons erasers, dolphin magnet sculpture, bonnet-clad corn husk doll, and penis-shaped candle—well, they were all very nice and all, but they weren't *me*. While amnesia was pure affectation on my part, I'd begun to sense a difference in myself, slight but definitely there. Maybe like being in a bed with the covers tucked in too tight and then kicking them off and flopping around in freedom.

I suddenly wanted to get out of the apartment. The new me needed some "me" time—or maybe it was "her" time, because I wasn't exactly sure who we were dealing with yet. Some time not necessarily to spoil *myself* but to permit myself not to be focused on everyone else *but* me. And, yes, maybe a little spoiling was going to take place, but nothing extreme.

Just some garden-variety girl stuff. A manicure/pedicure. Maybe a haircut. A massage was on my wish list, but that felt a little too indulgent.

I definitely wanted to enjoy the city more. I'd lived in New York State my whole life and lived in New York City for years now, but I'd been cloistered in the same set of blocks, running between boundaries drawn by the same routines. Not to sound too much like a line in a personal ad, but I really never took the time to explore the city and I wanted to. (In formal attire or in jeans and a T-shirt—I didn't care.)

I took myself to the Central Park Zoo. For one reason and one reason only: the aviary. Not because I loved birds per se, and I was certainly getting my fill of bird with Sneevil around—but they had this little indoor tropical forest, and I was desperate to finally step inside it. My mom had taken us to the zoo several times growing up, but the birds were *always* off-limits. She complained about the humidity and her hair, and that was that—end of story. There would be no birds in our zoo experience. And even once I'd reached an age where I could take myself inside, I never gave myself permission to go in. The taboo of the humidity was engrained in my psyche. That was going to change. Pronto.

And it did. I went in . . . I saw the birds . . . I experienced.

*Christ*, was that place humid. I came out with a facial and a writhing-worm hairdo. But you know what? I didn't care. It was so freeing to just do what I wanted to do when I wanted to do it—frizz be damned. I could even frown right now if I wanted—my mother was nowhere in sight. Who was going to stop me? I did. I frowned. But then some maintenance man frowned back at me, so I snapped myself out of it.

I watched the trainers feed the sea lions and wondered if those animals were really *happy*. If the sea lions subscribed to Abraham Lincoln's theory of being as happy as we make our minds up to be, then damn straight they were happy. Of course they probably didn't know Abraham Lincoln from Abe the Madagascan Tomato Frog in the amphibian exhibit, and I'd always had mixed feelings on the whole animals-in-captivity thing, but they seemed to have a good life. From studying the expressions on their faces, I decided that they were indeed happy, or at least neutral. It was a mixed bag—the old safe-but-bored conundrum. Anyway, predators were nowhere to be seen. Except this one guy in a fleece coat that identified his team as Aéropostale. He was tracking me until I lost him by the lemurs.

I felt so good after my outing to the zoo that I vowed to spend the rest of my recovery time exploring the city like a tourist (sans fanny pack). I went to museums every day until I'd run out. MoMA was incredible and it was literally three blocks from the building I'd been working in every day for two years. I could get there faster than I could get to the deli where I got my sandwich for lunch every day. Why hadn't I taken advantage of this?

I went to the Empire State Building and took the trip to the observation deck. It was magnificent. A couple from Idaho asked me if I'd take their picture with the New York City backdrop, which I did, and then another couple asked for the same. Then a family. I became the observation deck photographer. But not because I was the *old* pushover that was Jordan B.C. I did it because it was fun. I was making a memory for myself: happily, finally getting to experience the view of New York's own precious eternity, and honored to help everyone else who was there document it for *their* own memories.

I went to Rockefeller Center and went ice-skating. It's overpriced, overcrowded, and overrated . . . but I'd never done it. And it was the season. The tree was there (again, I missed the actual lighting), and I wanted to experience the joy of waiting for about fourteen hours in the freezing cold so that I could rent uncomfortable skates upon which I could wobble around the rink a few times and perhaps fall on my ass as a bonus.

And I looked up. I'd never allowed myself to look up in *all* my years of living in New York. The ubiquitous "they" say you shouldn't look up, because it makes you look like a tourist. But what's so wrong with looking like a tourist? (Besides the fanny pack.) Tourists have the right idea. There I was, trying so hard *not* to look like a tourist, I was missing everything! All of the phenomenal architecture in the city—my God, some of the older buildings were just breathtaking. And I was ignorant of all of it—this incredible backdrop that wouldn't be available to me anywhere else, and I wasn't taking it all in every chance I got. Why?

In my time off I also did some reading—some for fun and some for inspiration. I picked up a couple of self-help books. It turned out I had been suffering all this time from low self-esteem. Who knew?

I read about Ted Turner and Bill Gates, whom one author mentioned in the same paragraph as Britney Spears, which seemed bizarre. It was talking about self-confidence and how these people focused on their goals and didn't let setbacks get them down. As it turns out, Britney Spears lost a talent contest when she was a little girl. She came in second, but she didn't focus on the failure. Something told her to forge ahead. She just continued to practice and build her confidence up. Of course, you can argue with that—and some messages from the cosmos are better left unheeded—but it came down to this: Without the oops, would she have ever done it again?

Seemed like my whole life until then had been a failed talent contest. But there I was, stepping up to the mic again, lip-synching my heart out. I knew I could have my Mouseketeers break and eventually my big hit. And I would always always wear my underwear.

Dirk finally stopped by again, and I was so over his feigning care that after five minutes of him trying to jog my memory, I pretended to fall asleep.

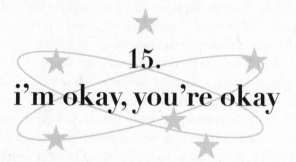

# 15.
# i'm okay, you're okay

You can do nothing for only so long without starting to feel like a waste of skin. So after two weeks of intense Jordan time, I decided I was ready to go back to work. I called Lydia at the number she'd given me and asked her for the address of our office. I even repeated it back to her incorrectly for effect.

I walked in feeling good. Confident. Their days of treating me like crap were over. Of course, there was the little matter of navigating their obvious doubts: How could I retain the skills of an ad agency staffer without a memory? And, this, overheard in the ladies' room a few hours in: "Seriously—she's, like, mentally incompetent, right?"

My stock answer (I should have had someone broadcast an e-mail): the damage was to subconscious memory, not so much to the hippocampal process memory that we call on to do our jobs. So I wouldn't remember all the faces and silly things we'd done together (a welcome relief from the endless retelling of those horrible Remember-how-drunk-she-got-that-time? anecdotes), but I still could outperform most of the dolts who padded payroll at this place.

As I passed through the halls, people were looking at me like I was Carrie soaked in pig's blood. But my bloodletting at the hands of Splash Direct was a thing of the past—they just didn't know it yet. Everyone I passed whispered to the person next to them and none too quietly either.

"I heard she tried to kill herself," whispered Charlotte, the uppity wench from payroll.

"Nope. You heard wrong," I said directly to her face, and then smiled like I'd said nothing at all.

"Oh," she said, totally flustered. "I wasn't talking about you."

"Okay, good. Then let's try to keep it that way, huh?"

She looked truly shocked. And why not? Normally, I wouldn't have said anything at all to her. They wanted to whisper about me, not my business. Well, now I was making it my business. And I'd be giving them plenty to whisper about—but I'd make sure they had their facts straight at least. I hightailed it to reception and pretended I didn't know where I was going.

"Hi, I'm Jordan. I'm not sure if you heard, but I had a bad accident and . . . well, I'm suffering from memory loss that leaves a few critical details out. You know me, right?"

"Yeah, Jordan Landau," the receptionist offered. "Traffic."

"Right," I said. "Traffic." It made me sick to think about what Lydia had done before I left, but if I was going to pull this off, I had to pretend nothing was wrong. "Can you let Lydia know that I'm here and ready for work?"

"Sure. No problem." She hit a couple of buttons and spoke into her headset. "Lydia? Jordan's here." She listened for a second, then disconnected. "She'll be right out. Need help finding your way?"

"No . . . funny thing," I said. "Certain things are perfectly clear. Like the layout. I could probably find coffee machine filters in the thirty-sixth-floor kitchen sooner than I'll remember . . . your name. *Sorry.*" Apologetic smile. Cue the awkward moment.

And as soon as I'd finished, there was Lydia, feigning a smile.

"Hi. I'm Lydia. I came to visit you in the hospital. Remember?"

"Yeah, I do. That was so nice."

"Let's go to your desk," she said carefully . . . slowly. It seemed she was back to the slow talking. And she led the way. As I followed, I looked back at the receptionist and smiled a thank-you.

"This is where you sit," Lydia said. "We call it the pit. And not because it's the 'pits.' " Great humor there, Lydia. "Your desk is that one—the one with the Hasselhoff poster. You're a huge *Baywatch* fan."

"I remember the desk. But, *Baywatch* . . . I am?"

"Sure," she said.

"Is that show even still on?"

"I don't know," she said.

"Is there any chance that I was poking *fun* at the whole thing?" I asked.

"I don't know," she said irritably. She was *done* talking about my love of a show that I'd actually never seen one episode of in my entire life. "My office is right in there. We're working on a campaign for VibraLens. The specs are on your desk so you can get acquainted with them."

"Great. I'll take a look at them," I said. And I looked around my desk. Nothing had changed really. I don't know if I expected it to, but everything was the same.

"Do that. We'll meet later this afternoon to talk about our big pitch Friday with the marketing VP of VibraLens."

"Okay," I said.

"Okay," she said.

"Okay," I said.

"Okay," she said again, her brow furrowing.

"Okay," I said again, noticing that she wanted to be the last one to say the last thing. I was finding it f'n hilarious not letting her do it.

"Okay!" she said, this time with a look on her face like a young child rejecting Brussels sprouts.

"Okay," I said again, trying my hardest not to grin the Cheshire cat grin that was welling up inside. Enjoying our last-word face-off much more than I should have been.

"Are you having an episode?" she said with venom. Now I *was* grinning. And this pissed her off even more. She turned and started to walk into her office.

"So I'll just look at those files then," I said. And she slammed the door behind her.

Todd saw me jump online and instant messaged me.

URAWANKER: Jordy!!

Jordalicious: Hey, babe! I'm at work. So far, so good . . .

URAWANKER: Somebody left bagels with TOFU cream cheese
in the conference room—disgusting. Way to ruin a perfectly good
bagel.

Jordalicious: Tell me about it. Sorry.

URAWANKER: It is what it is. *Nauseating*.

Jordalicious: Lydia just told me that I love *Baywatch*. Who knew?

URAWANKER: Irony isn't her strong suit, I take it?

Jordalicious: Backstabbing is. Gotta go.

URAWANKER: See you later?

Jordalicious: Yeah. Call me after work. xo

Just then Art, the mail guy, walked past me. He put up his hand to
high-five, and I almost did it, catching myself mid-arm-raise and running my fingers through my hair instead. Then I looked off distractedly.
I didn't know if he knew about the accident, and I felt bad. We didn't
have a verbal relationship, so he just walked away instead of explaining
our unspoken inside greeting.

Once again, Lydia's ideas for VibraLens were totally uninspired. I
started jotting my own ideas down, keeping the whole thing very secret
this time. I'd promised myself that I'd take better care of my property,
now that I'd forgotten how not to.

\* \* \* \* \*

I was this close to making it into my apartment when I heard the booming
voice of Tiger Schulmann's Manhood bellowing through the hallway.

"Jordan!" he exclaimed, startling me into dropping my keys onto my
teddy bear–themed welcome doormat. I reluctantly turned to face him.

"Oh, hi," I said, with as much enthusiasm as a girl greeting her most recent ex in a chance meeting on the street when she has no makeup on.

"Sorry about that. Didn't mean to startle you. But you *should* always be aware of your surroundings."

"True indeed," I said.

"Speaking of . . . how about that self-defense lesson?"

"Yeah . . . how about it?"

"How about now?" he said, not understanding that when I said How about it? I really meant, *Oh, you mean the lesson that I never said I'd take in the first place?*

"Now?" I hesitated.

"C'mon in," he said, and waved me over.

This was just the kind of bullshit that I'd expect from a creep like him. Taking advantage of some poor girl who's lost her memory. And he was going to pay for it.

"Great!" I said, and followed him into his apartment.

Even though he'd lived there as long as I had—longer even—there were boxes everywhere and it was sparsely decorated. He had a lot of karate paraphernalia and some kind of tarp covering most of one of his walls. There was a very small TV and a couch but no bed. I decided not to ponder where or if he slept.

"You can set your things down here," he said, and motioned to the top of a large Staples box as if it were a table. I put down my things and took off my jacket. "Now the first rule of self-defense is awareness. Always be aware of your surroundings and never allow yourself to be caught off guard. You want to always remove yourself from a dangerous situation if possible."

Like *now*? I thought, but what I said was, "Sounds reasonable."

"Now the only wrong move is no move at all," he said as he sidled up behind me and moved in close. Too close. "So if someone came at you from behind . . ."

He was coming at me from behind, all right, but not in a way I'd expect an attacker to touch me. He placed one hand on my right shoulder and the other gently on my stomach. I'd always wondered what that penis would feel like. And my knee was about to find out.

I turned around to face him and, in one swift motion, braced him at his shoulders and hurled my knee into his big fat crotch.

"Unghhhhhhh!" he roared as he doubled over.

"Oh, I'm sorry!" I exclaimed, like I had no idea what had just come over me. "Knee-jerk reaction, I guess." Hello, Jerk. Meet my *knee*. He opened his mouth to say something, but nothing came out. I grabbed my things and walked toward the door. "Oh, I should go. I'm so, so sorry about that!" I said almost merrily as I dashed out of his place and into my own.

Sneevil was singing some kind of aria, which I heard from at least three doors away before I got inside. I walked in and frowned at him.

"Sneevil, I hope you haven't been doing that all day," I gently admonished. He cocked his head to the side and continued to sing. I knew it was a problem—and not just because there was another note taped to my door.

"What's it going to take?" I asked him. "How 'bout I sing in *your* face for a few hours. See how that grabs you?"

And I did. I tried everything: talking to him, singing to him, playing loud music, covering his cage . . . nothing worked. Although when I started Kansas's "Carry On My Wayward Son" I could have *sworn* I saw him wince.

I was going to go from that to "Dust in the Wind," but my phone rang.

"Recognize my voice?" It was Dirk.

"No, I'm sorry. Should I?"

"It's Dirk. Your—"

"My boyfriend, right?" I said, finishing his sentence.

"Exactly," he said. "What are you doing?"

"I just came in from my first day back at work."

"How was it?"

"It was okay, I guess."

"You want to get together?" he asked tentatively. I *didn't* really, but I was so furious with him for cheating on me that I wanted to fuck with him.

"Sure," I said. "Why not?"

It would be my first "date" with Dirk since the accident. I pretended I was unsure of my surroundings so he'd be forced to pick me up instead of meeting me somewhere. I couldn't even remember the last time he'd come to pick me up before a date. Then again, I couldn't remember the last actual date we'd had.

True to form, Dirk picked me up and brought me straight back to his apartment. The place was all too familiar, but I was trying to look at it with fresh eyes. As far as he knew I was seeing it again for the first time, so I tried to actually do that—really look at my surroundings and all that was Dirk's place. He opened the door, ushered me in, and opened his arms gesturing to the "opulence" that was his apartment.

"This is the love palace."

"Wow," I said as I looked around at all the empty beer cans. This was not a love palace—it was a dorm room. I looked at the familiar Farrah Fawcett poster and, of course, as I had been trained to do, I noticed her nipple. I tried not to, but once you've had someone repeatedly point something out to you, it's where your eyes go by rote.

"You're lookin' at the nipple, aren't you?" he said, nodding proudly. What had I been thinking all that time? I was dating a simian. How did I let myself get away with it? He watched me, looking around, taking it all in. "Remembering anything?"

"No, can't say that I am."

"Remember this?" he said as he leaned in and started tonguing my ear. No warning. No warm-up. Not even a kiss or a touch. Just all of a sudden Dirk's tongue was thrashing around in my ear. It was revolting. I jerked away from him and his tongue, and looked around desperately for a Kleenex, which was obviously not going to materialize.

"What is that? What was *that*?" I practically shrieked.

"You loved it—used to at least. It was the patented Michael Dirkston Ear Extravaganza."

"You don't say."

"Nice, huh?" he said, nodding again. Pleased with himself. Someone had to do something. This man had to be stopped. All men had to be stopped. I was going to clear up this misconception right here, right now. I steeled myself.

"You know what? I know that guys probably do like that, the whole tongue-in-the-ear-thing, but I think I can speak for the entire female sex when I say that a tongue in the ear is not as erotic as you may think it is."

"You never said anything before. You liked it."

"I don't remember before, but I'll bet there's a good chance that I was just being polite." I was always polite before. But, dammit, enough was enough. Why should I tolerate beef tongue in my ear? I think I was actually nice about it, considering. I could have spoken volumes on the matter. I could have attacked his sexual prowess in general—which, I assure you, was lacking. Suffice it to say that Michael Dirkston thought that the clitoris was an ancient temple in Greece and mutual orgasm was a life insurance company.

Dirk was definitely thrown by the ear trick's not working. He looked down and twisted his mouth for a second, pulling at a loose thread from the rip in his jeans. I felt bad. I knew he meant well. No I didn't. I channeled the image of this "sweet boy" zeroing in on Hot Blonde at *our* restaurant, and I remembered Dirk was concerned with only one thing: Dirk.

As if reading my mind, he got up and walked over to the kitchen. Then he held up a box of De Cecco pasta.

"So should we make dinner?" he asked. "I have all the stuff to make that pasta primavera that you like."

"Okay," I said, knowing full well what the natural progression of this would be. I decided to head him off at the pass. "Go ahead."

"No," he said. "I meant you. You're the one who usually cooks."

"Really? I'm a good cook? Cool. But . . . ." And here's where I put on my own little-girl pout and looked up at him with apologetic eyes. "I don't remember *how* to cook anything. Sorry."

"Oh."

"Why don't we just order takeout?" I offered. "Or better yet, maybe you should take me somewhere fancy for dinner. You used to do that, *right?*" It was getting fun again. Dirk looked frustrated. He rolled his eyes. Right in front of me. I'm supposed to have amnesia. I'm not *blind*, moron.

"Yeah. Right," said a very annoyed Dirk. "I took you out all the time. *Really* nice places."

"Great. Then let's go to one tonight." I could tell he wasn't the least bit interested in wooing me again.

"I don't know. I'm kinda tired." Thought so.

"Well, maybe *you* want to make that pasta then?"

"Nah, never mind," he said. "I'm not that hungry."

"You were a second ago."

"Well, I'm not now."

"Well, I *am*. So maybe you can make some for *me*, then." He was getting totally annoyed.

"Forget the pasta. Let's just order in."

"Great," I cheerily said as he rolled his eyes again and pulled out a stack of menus.

# 16.

# reinvent your job

I woke up with one of those optimistic feelings that I guess normal people wake up with every day, but I just wasn't accustomed to it. It was so nice that I lay in bed for an extra ten minutes. Just because. And if I was ten minutes late for work? So be it.

When I got in, there were three yellow Post-its on my desk. All of them said, "Call me." All of them were from Lydia. This gave me pause. Three? I tried to re-create in my head what had gone on: She walks out of her office and down to the pit and sees that the person she wants to talk to—*me*—isn't at her desk. So she leaves me a note asking me to call her. What I can only imagine is two minutes later, she walks out again just to check if I am there yet. No, I'm not. But, what the hell, she's already standing, so why not leave another note saying the *exact same thing*. Then perhaps three more minutes pass—Christ, an egg could be cooked in that time. So up she goes to see if I have arrived yet. Again, I am still absent, so she decides that it would be an excellent idea to leave yet another note. Saying the very exact thing once again. Lydia gets paid a lot of money. This astounds me.

Then the phone intercom buzzed loudly.

"Are you in yet?" she hissed.

"Yes, I'm here." I looked at the clock. It was 9:07. I was only seven minutes late. All this dramatic note leaving took place within seven minutes. Lydia truly was a hideous beast.

"Why didn't you call me?"

"I just got here and I was reading all your notes," I said. "I didn't want to miss any. Were there more than three? I only saw three."

"No. That's all there were. Can you come in here, please?" All this was unnecessary by the way. One: Her office was two feet from my desk. Two: I could hear her equally well with or without the phone pressed to my ear. And three: She already had me on the phone, so why couldn't she just say what she wanted to say?

I got up and walked the two steps into her office. Her lips were pursed into such a tiny, wrinkled mold of bitter, I almost laughed at the sight of her.

"Hi. Good morning," I said.

She looked at her watch and then at me. "Gandhi said that lateness was an act of terrorism."

"Pardon?"

"You're late," she said. "It's terroristic." I wanted to burst out laughing but didn't. Again I was amazed, wondering how I managed not to react to that crap before.

"Are you sure that's what he said?" And are you sure that *terroristic* is a word? "I mean, I apologize for being late," I said, "but that's a little extreme, no?"

"Yes, I'm sure," she said as she googled Gandhi and then almost violently turned her computer screen to face me, reading aloud, "Punctuality is nonviolence. Tardiness is a theft of another's good time and therefore does violence.' "

I stood there and looked at her for a moment, not really sure how to respond to the sudden storm of fury. "Well, I'm very sorry. In the future I'll make it very clear when I'm *doing* violence."

"Fine," she said, brushing it off. "So I assume you went over everything?" Lydia raised her eyebrows. I raised mine back.

"Yup. Sure did."

"Good." She sighed. "I'm having a hell of a time with this one. The inspiration just isn't coming . . . " She looked up quickly with a pained smile. "Funny. You used to like knowing what was going on with the creative. Do you remember trying your hand at it?" she asked, almost admitting that I used to do her job for her but not actually saying it. What she was doing was trying to butter me up. A compliment before she asked me to do her job for her once again. "It's for VibraLens. I'm not sure about what I have, but maybe you can make them better."

"Sure," I said. "Lay 'em on me."

"Okay. What I have is 'VibraLens . . . The Eyes Have It.'" She looked at me to gauge my response.

"Very . . . clear," I said.

"Okay," she continued with mild annoyance, "and then I have 'Vibra-Lens. Eyes *Are* the Prize.' Which I don't know if that's the kind of thing you're having trouble remembering right now, but it's a take on 'Keep your eyes *on* the prize,' which is a pretty universally known phrase."

Yes. It was universally known. One of Martin Luther King's more famous phrases and totally inappropriate for a colored contact lens campaign. She sure was bringing the great spiritual leaders to the party today . . . Gandhi . . . MLK . . . I half suspected after lunch we'd be pitching birdseed with St. Francis of Assisi and a new brand of water skis with Jesus.

"Hmm," I said. And then there was a long pause. Normally, this is when I would have chimed in with all my ideas. Correcting hers but without seeming to. Making her shine. ("Ha," I'd laugh. "That's *so great!* It made me think of something else that I'm not sure if it's worth anything but I'll throw it out anyway . . ." I'd been the exact opposite of passive-aggressive. Was there a name for the act of manipulation in which you're trying to help someone but need to make yourself look like a bumbling idiot in the process so they don't feel guilty about taking advantage of you? I'd have to find the word so I could make a plaque declaring myself former world champion.) She was used to that kind of behavior from me. She was waiting for it. She leaned forward even. Cocked one eyebrow hopefully. Yeah, I had a couple of ideas. And if she thought I was handing them to her, then she was absolutely nuts. Those days were over, baby. But I waited an extra minute, just so it looked like I was percolating. And just when she was really chomping at the bit, I spoke up. "Those sound good to me! But I don't know what kind of a judge I am."

She was fuming. I could tell that she knew they weren't very good and she desperately needed my help. But what could she say? Nothing.

"I'll need them mocked up for the Tuesday meeting," she said disappointedly.

"Okay."

"And I'm going to let you sit in on the meeting."

"Neat," I said.

"And take notes."

"Okay."

"So you know where Caroline Keeps is, the art director, on the tenth floor?"

"I'm sure I can find her."

"Okay then," she said. "She needs this job bag back."

I wasn't sure if "Okay then" meant we were finished. That's not entirely true. I knew that we were finished. But I liked the awkward pauses. I liked watching Lydia get flustered. She had treated me like an idiot for so long, I liked watching her do it from this new perspective. So I stood there and looked at her.

"That's all. You can go now." That's what I was waiting for. I smiled, and my smile seemed to piss her off. Then again, everything I did that wasn't benefiting her somehow seemed to piss her off. She narrowed her eyes at me as I turned to leave.

\* \* \* \* \*

Todd met me at the concrete park across from my office for lunch. I shouldn't call it that. It was really a cute little park with a pretty garden. "Concrete parks" are what suburbanites call the city parks once they've moved out to the suburbs and turn up their noses at our little sanctuaries. They get spoiled with not having to actually work to get a little greenery. Even though it was December, it was one of those random warm days that you feel like you have to take advantage of. The bittersweet upshot of global warming.

It was hot dogs day. Todd and I usually had lunch together three times a week, and at least one of the three times we'd eat Sabrett's hot dogs. I know they're disgusting, but for me it was comfort food. When I was a little girl and my mom and Walter would take us into the city, I'd always get excited about getting a hot dog from a stand. I had no idea how many stands spanned the city and I actually thought we were getting hot dogs from the same guy every time.

So once a week I'd get a foot-long with the works—this time from the same guy. "The works," included a healthy topping of sauerkraut—which repulsed Todd no end. I don't know if I even loved sauerkraut all that much or if I just got pleasure from grossing Todd out, but either way it made for a tasty lunch. And every time, Todd had to make a stink about it.

Like clockwork, Todd watched me sink my teeth into my first bite and offered, "I don't know *how* you can eat sauerkraut. It's fucking disgusting. It's rotten cabbage!"

"It's not rotten," I said back, mouth full of food, as he shuddered. These were the little things that made me happy. Complaining about Lydia was always good times as well.

"Her ideas were completely pathetic. I mean—really bad."

"We have that at our agency too. People fail upward. It's part of life," he said.

"But her ideas can't have always been so insipid, so . . . silly and shameless," I said.

"Like for instance?"

"She's thinking of using Dr Martin Luther King to sell colored contacts."

He made a face. "Ouch. That ranks up there with the line she thought up for that new drug . . ."

" 'Kiss your genital herpes good-bye '?"

"Bingo."

"It's not fair." I sighed.

"What's fair, Jordan? Is there an overwhelming glut of fairness in the world? Most days suck. Most *people* suck. What are you gonna do?" he said, with a shrug of acceptance.

"I'll *tell* you what I'm gonna do," I answered. "Whatever the hell I *can*. Right now I have somewhat of a pass—carte blanche to do things I'd never have done before. And I can do it under the guise of not knowing it wasn't okay."

"Uh-oh . . . I smell a plan . . ."

"You always did have a keen sense of smell."

"Thanks. It's this new stuff I'm putting on after I shave," he joked.

"Which makes up for your dumb jokes."

"Anyway . . . what's the plan?"

"Well, after she not-so-politely excused me from her office, I got this idea. She keeps telling me how 'instrumental' I used to be and then gives me her lame copy to storyboard. She's also going to let me sit in on the meeting. Such *privilege*. Meanwhile, I'm getting zero credit for any of my previous ideas, which she blatantly stole."

"Corporate America."

"Yeah, well, the new Jordan doesn't just write it off as corporate America. The new Jordan doesn't get mad—she gets even."

"What evil have you planned?"

I smiled. He knew me so well. But this wasn't evil. This was me finally taking control of my life. By seeming just a bit *out* of control.

* * * * *

On my way back to work, I spotted Lydia and Kurt canoodling in an alcove between two buildings. I sped up my gait so they wouldn't see me, but it surprised me that they were being so careless—right near our office. I busied my mind by taking in the scenery. New York in December is something to behold, and I worked just blocks from Radio City Music Hall—home of the famous Christmas Spectacular, with the glittering nativity that suggests that since there was no room at the inn, the Holy Family just parked it for the night in a suite at the Four Seasons.

Back at the office Mr. Billingsly walked up to my desk and looked into Lydia's office, seeming distressed that she wasn't there.

"Where's Lydia?" he asked, as if I were her keeper. I felt this low-level panic in my stomach, but I didn't know why. I'd never actually confirmed that he and Lydia had a thing, but I was almost positive that at one time or another—if not still—they had. And what if one illicit lover should find her with the other? Call it confirmation that I'm basically a squeamish person that I wanted *no part* of it.

"She's at lunch."

"Well, can you make sure she knows that Tuesday's VibraLens meeting has been moved from two o'clock to one o'clock?"

"Sure thing," I said.

"That's an hour earlier," he added, in case I couldn't figure it out on my own.

"Yeah, I got that. Thanks."

"Getting back in the swing of things?" he asked. And then before I could open my mouth to answer, he shuffled away down the hallway.

I opened up my e-mail program and clicked *Compose*. At the very click of it I started beaming. You wouldn't think that writing an e-mail to your boss to let her know that a meeting had been changed from two o'clock to one o'clock would bring such joy, but it *did*. It did because Lydia never, never, never checked her e-mail. I was supposed to tell her everything verbally, and/or leave her a Post-it note, and/or send her brain waves to remind her in case actions one and two failed. But I didn't know that Lydia didn't check her e-mail. I had amnesia. So as far as I knew, I was being responsible and doing exactly as Mr. Billingsly said. It was perfect. I couldn't have orchestrated it better myself.

To: Lydia.Bedford@SplashDirect.com

Cc: Ted.Billingsly@SplashDirect.com

From: Jordan.Landau@SplashDirect.com

Subject: **Important** Tuesday Meeting—Time Change

The VibraLens pitch meeting has been moved up an hour. Instead of taking place at 2 p.m., the meeting will now take place at 1 p.m. Please note: This is an hour earlier.

J

Just typing the whole "hour-earlier clarification" that Mr. Billingsly had so kindly explained to *me* made me feel giddy. So giddy that I copied Billingsly on it as well.

*     *     *     *     *

Stu Elliot waltzed into the pit and sat on the edge of my desk.

"Hey, daredevil," he said. This was a reference to my riding without a helmet. "Didn't I tell you to wear protective gear?"

I wanted to say, "Yeah, Stu. You did. And if you wanna call me out on that, when I know for a *fact* that you took Lexi Kaye home from last year's Christmas party and spent the next afternoon in a pharmacy—we can talk about wearing protective gear. You sure you wanna have this conversation?" But I couldn't. Because I hadn't seen Stu since the accident and I wasn't supposed to recognize him.

"Did you?" I asked uncertainly.

"I'm sorry. I'm Stu," he said, and then put out his hand to shake. I took it and introduced myself back.

"I'm Jordan . . . but I guess you already know that."

"Yeah, we go way back." Stu cleared his throat and looked at my mock-ups, trying to move away from the awkwardness. "What are those?"

"They're for VibraLens. Colored contact lenses. I'm just playing," I said.

"They're good," he said as he looked through my ideas. They *were* good. I was looking at the colored contacts like my own fakery—and coming up with some slam-dunk ideas. He read a couple out loud " 'Change the way the world sees you.' 'A colorful new you' . . . they're *really* good, Jordan."

"Thanks."

"Colored contacts," he scoffed. "How about 'Pretend to be something you're *not*.' " Normally we would have shared a laugh over this. But I just stared at him, wide-eyed, for probably too long. I wondered if he was subtly trying to tell me something. That low-level panic I'd felt when I saw Lydia and Kurt came back tenfold. This time with good reason.

I froze. I guess Stu felt bad that I didn't seem to get the joke, so he tried to change the subject. "So we have our company Christmas party next week. You coming?"

Funny he should mention it. "I don't know," I said. "Should I?"

"It's a good ti-ime," he said in a singsongy cadence. "People get pretty trashed."

"Well, maybe . . ." I said, and we'd covered about all we could cover, so he got up and walked away.

The way Stu talked about the party made me think about the last good time I'd had. Thanksgiving. Not with my parents but with Travis. He'd given me his number and asked me to call him, but I didn't know if he'd meant it or was just being polite. And he hadn't yet called me, despite the business card I'd given him. I prayed it didn't have some impromptu shopping list scrawled on the back of it consisting of Dirk favorites. I don't care how down-to-earth you want to seem, it's *never* good for a girl to send the message that she's reminding herself to grab a six-pack of Pabst Blue Ribbon.

I pulled out his card and looked at it. He was an analyst in risk management at Goldman Sachs. I had no idea what that meant, but it sounded very corporate—not at all what I pictured him doing with his time. I wondered what risk management *was*. I knew that without risk there was supposedly little reward, but I also knew that I'd once risked everything to sneak out of my house junior year to go to Monique Anderson's party, and that hadn't provided any rewards at all. In fact, I'd gotten busted and lost driving privileges for three months. So which side of this thing was he on: Was it his job to create more risk and more reward or the opposite? And was that type of job rewarding? Since I was on the fence about whether to call or not, and the word *risk* was right there on his business card, staring me in the face, I decided that I shouldn't call. No matter what the potential reward. Another thing a girl should almost never do: appear interested.

"Hello?" said the voice I remembered from Thanksgiving when I called thirty seconds later.

"Hi . . . this is Jordan?" I said. Silence. "The girl from the accident?"

I added and then winced and held my breath until he spoke again. I was sounding like one of those people who raised her pitch at the end of every sentence like she's asking a question even when she wasn't.

"Jordan! I'm sorry, this speakerphone. I'm so glad you called."

"Good." Brilliant!

"Your business card turned out to be a frequent visitor card from a deli. Eight more punches and you've got yourself a free sandwich."

*Brilliant!*

"How are— Do you feel any better?" he asked.

"Oh, God, well, all the time, I mean my wound is improving," I managed to put together. "I'm still nervous about the memory thing."

"Absolutely, that would be— Yes, that's a difficult part."

"Of the accident. Yes."

With conversation this scintillating, we really should have just hung up immediately. But I was determined to right the ship, right then and there.

"What are you doing?" I asked.

"Just got out of a really tedious meeting. It's one thing to get tired after a marathon meeting about mitigation strategies and probabilistic risk models, but it's a whole new level of excitement when you actually start to fall asleep *during* the meeting."

"Yikes."

"In front of your managing director."

"Double yikes."

"And I thought sociology class was bad. That was like Vegas compared to the last three hours of my life—which I want back, by the way."

"So you *like* your job," I said.

"Actually it's not that bad, but it's certainly not the grand plan."

"I look forward to hearing what that is."

"And I look forward to telling you," he said. "What are you doing later? I know this great shabu-shabu place."

"Shabu-shabu?" I repeated, while I googled *shabu-shabu* to find out exactly what it was. I found that it's a fondue party of sorts . . . but there's no cheese involved—which didn't sound like a party to me at all—but before I could search the Internet further, he clarified.

"You cook the food yourself on a hot skillet in the middle of your table."

"Aha!" I exclaimed. "Sounds fun."

"You've never done shabu-shabu?" he asked, making me feel totally unhip.

"Oh, I've *done* shabu-shabu," I said cockily.

"Really?"

"No. At least I don't think so. It's hard to know for sure."

"Then we're on it. It's a plan, Stan," he said, and I used all of my will-power not to say "You don't need to be coy, Roy!" thinking it was too early to start being my usual goofy self. Plus, if he didn't recognize it as a "50 Ways" lyric, I'd have the awkward explanation to deal with and I didn't want to risk it. And was I supposed to remember lyrics? But there was that whole risk thing again, staring me in the face. And because I thought it, I felt like now I *had* to say it. Because the new Jordan took risks. And this entire thought process took only about four seconds.

"You don't need to be coy, Roy," I said.

"Just get yourself free," he answered, and the smile that spread across my face felt like sunshine warming me from the inside out.

\* \* \* \* \*

The restaurant was in the East Village, and when I got there Travis was standing outside, talking to another guy. We'd made plans to meet immediately following work, which was good because it didn't allow me any time to stress out over what I was going to wear, but it was bad for the same reason. The guy he was standing with was a couple inches shorter than Travis and was wearing a suit. He had tight curly hair and wore glasses. As I approached them, Travis stepped toward me and gave me a kiss on the cheek.

"Hi," he said. "Nice to see you again."

"You too," I said and looked at his friend.

"Sorry, this is Ben, a friend of mine," Travis said.

"Hi, Ben. Nice to meet you," I said.

"And you as well," Ben said. "Did you get any of your memory back yet?"

"Ah . . . you know the whole saga," I said, feeling guilty about the lie I was about to tell. "Little things, but so much is still not there. Some familiarity with the neighborhood, the coffeemaker, and the computer doesn't mystify nearly as much as it did—but people, things that happened . . ." I reached out tentatively, then smiled sadly. Guilt shmilt.

"I feel terrible!" Travis said, throwing his head back, looking up at the sky.

"Stop it—it's okay," I reassured.

"Did you forget everything or just a few things?" inquired Ben.

"It's sort of complicated," I said. "Some things are totally there—like song lyrics, and like how to brush my teeth, but names and faces . . ." I trailed off.

"Well, I'm sure you'll get your memory back real soon," Ben said.

"I'm sure I will too," I said to Ben. I felt like I was meeting the friends, so I needed to make a good impression. So it was a really good thing that I was *lying through my teeth*. Excellent first impression. I turned to Travis. "Please, don't feel bad about it. It's kind of weird, but kind of . . . incredible too. I get to start over." Ben looked at Travis like he was trying to tell him something.

"Are you joining us?" I asked Ben, hoping that he wasn't. I mean, it was supposed to be a date, I thought. I knew it felt like a date. What a cute meeting story we'd have. "How'd you two meet?" "Oh, he ran me over on my bike, which sent me to the hospital where he sent me flowers and candy while I faked a major head trauma and amnesia."

"Oh, that's nice of you," Ben said. "But I have dinner plans already. I just bumped into Travis here, and . . . I guess I'll let you two get to it. Nice meeting you."

"You too," I said, and Ben left us to shabu-shabu as a duet.

The restaurant was one of those places where they make you take off your shoes. I thanked God and everything that was holy that I was wearing cute socks (which *weren't* holey) when I stepped out of my boots.

Our communal table was recessed along with the plush cushion seats we sat on and our feet dangled below us. I was giddy with excitement—but I couldn't help noticing a smell permeating the restaurant. Hard to describe. I looked around and noticed the setup. There was a skillet built into each table, hot pots to cook some sort of stew . . . and it seemed that each table was given raw meat, vegetables, and some spices. I wondered if it was the raw meat that I was smelling, but it didn't smell like meat—it smelled like . . . feet.

I didn't know if I should say something to Travis because I didn't want to come off as a complainer, but it was pretty awful.

"Excited for your first—?" He stopped and sniffed. "Do you smell something?" he whispered.

"Thank God," I said. "Yes, I just wasn't sure if that was part of the shabu-shabu charm, so I didn't want to say anything."

We both looked around and under the table and in the same instant zeroed in on the culprit. Our tablemate. A man, late forties with his wife and twelve-year-old son. It *had* to be him. His socks looked filthy, and there was a hole in the left one with his big toe peeking out.

"Hole-in-one, twelve o'clock," Travis said, speaking in code.

"Roger that," I said. And try as I might have, I couldn't help but focus on that one renegade toe. "Kind of gross."

"I'll say. It's like he wore the same pair for a week just for the occasion."

"Well, let's just try not to focus on it," I said, trying to be upbeat and optimistic even though my eyes were practically watering.

"Sounds good," Travis said and snuck one last peek at the table. The son was flicking his retainer in and out of his mouth.

"So what's good here?" I asked.

"Not that," Travis said, with a glance at the kid. "On the menu? Meat. And meat."

"With a side of meat?"

"There's not a lot of variation on the menu—it's pretty much just how much of it you want to have."

"Gotcha," I said.

"This is too much effort," said Mrs. Stench. "If I'm going to a restaurant I want them to cook it for me." Travis and I shared a smile.

The waiter came over and took our order. The smell wasn't dissipating like we'd hoped. I took a sip of water and could swear it tasted like feet.

I didn't see it happen, but I definitely heard it—a plunk. And then a scream. The boy had flicked his retainer out of his mouth and into the hot pot in the center of our table. Then not thinking, he reached in to get it out and burned his hand. Then the mother started yelling at the kid for playing with his retainer, which she'd told him not to do "a *thousand* times," and the boy was crying, and the father was yelling that he just wanted to have "one nice God-damned family dinner once in my life."

The whole place was in an uproar. The stink, the retainer, and the mayhem were too much to bear. Travis grabbed my hand and helped me up. We put our shoes back on and ducked out of the restaurant.

"If you think I have good taste in *restaurants,*" he said, "wait till I pick our first movie."

It may have been the worst restaurant ever, but the promise of another date made it entirely worth it. "Our first movie." I liked the sound of that. We ended up on the corner of St. Marks and Avenue A, eating pizza and watching angsty, pseudo-punk rock kids beg for change and hiss at the people who didn't oblige.

"This is the real deal," I said as I took a dainty bite of my pizza.

"Who would have thought she'd prefer a meal totaling a whopping five dollars and twenty-three cents?" he asked and then stopped. "Don't look down," he said suddenly, staring at my chest.

Normally, any flattery implicit in a man's staring at a woman's chest is overridden by her anger at being reduced to a pair of boobs. But in this case, he was so obvious—and his gaze expressed so much alarm—it caught me off guard. Naturally, I looked down.

"Perfect," I said, now comprehending what he'd regarded with such dread. My "dainty" bite had resulted in a stripe of tomato sauce not much shorter than my forearm, in a neat diagonal across my shirt between my breasts.

"If anybody messes with us later, just tell him it's blood from the *last* guy who messed with us," Travis said.

I gritted my teeth and growled, but it couldn't completely disguise my smile.

*  *  *  *  *

When I walked into the boardroom at 12:59 P.M. the next day, every-body was already there. Everyone except Lydia. I'd timed it to reduce the odds that someone would send me hunting for her. The marketing vice president and president of VibraLens were seated next to Mr. Billingsly, who looked confused when I walked in alone.

"Where is Lydia?" he said quietly to me, with just a hint of concern.

"Not sure," I said, sharing the concern, putting my arm around it as if to say, I'm with you, brother—what the hell?

"I sent her an e-mail, notifying her of the time change," I whispered.

"Well, where's her material? Do we have that? Is Darryl around?" I smiled and pointed to the easel to reassure him, then shrugged about art director Darryl, knowing full well he hadn't been invited to the party. It didn't matter. Experience taught me Lydia rarely invited her art director on any given assignment to present, perhaps fearing to share credit even with the person who'd made her words come alive on the page or screen. We'd done boards and electronic mock-ups and I'd made sure everything was ready. *Everything*. Even if she wasn't.

Two other teams were on the pitch—a touch of creative excess Mr. B. always demanded from us for a new account and a strategy that some-times had the unfortunate side effect of overwhelming the clients and paralyzing their decision making. In this meeting, he was juggling the need to play host with the desperation about Lydia's absence, sending an assistant searching, to no avail.

Within forty minutes, both teams had pitched their ideas, none of which were blowing away the VibraLens suits. I had a little rule of thumb: If anyone's first words were "That's interesting," you were dead. And Splash had produced a load of "interesting" material. Mr. Billingsly looked in my direction.

"Okay then. Next, we have Lydia Bedford, who I know has come up with some great ideas. She's unfortunately been held up, so . . ." He looked at me, the idea not yet occurring to him—so I gave it a little shove into his line of sight.

"I can do the honors, Mr. Billingsly." I looked at him and smiled reassuringly. He announced me with a strained laugh, then muttered something under his breath which I wasn't positive I heard right. It sounded like, "Don't fuck it up," but I'm sure that was just my ears talking. I just smiled again at him and walked to the head of the room.

"Thank you, sir. I am Jordan Landau. Lydia was very excited about these mock-ups and I hope you will be too. The first concept plays to a demographic that came up earlier, a missed opportunity I think someone said—beyond the eighteen- to twenty-four-year-old vanity set. We're in a lawmaking chamber—maybe the floor of the Senate. Image is everything for these power brokers." I pulled up her first storyboard to show her lame-ass idea. It was a Senate hearing with one woman staring dead ahead with her impossibly bright blue eyes. "So, in this world, and in our target consumer's world, 'The Eyes Have It.'"

I looked around at the execs and saw that they probably thought what I'd thought. It was cute . . . but that was it. No reaction at all—they just seemed to be waiting for the next one. "Second, she evokes the powerful words of a great American leader but in a way that's not overly serious." I revealed the image—a table of dozens of multiethnic faces, eyes blazing with colored contacts that suggested a world in which every person had been forced to hand over his or her eyes, one person to the left. " 'Eyes *Are* the Prize.'" The room was deadly silent. But only for a moment.

"Interesting," the marketing VP finally said.

Mr. Billingsly shifted in his seat. The VibraLens camp looked neither happy nor unhappy, the worst-case reaction to a creative presentation. Indifferent. I wondered if they were aware of how awkward and inappropriate that idea was. I hoped so. And now was my chance. I steeled myself.

"If you'll bear with me, I'd like to continue with just a few very recent additions to our thinking on this . . . some things that were inspired by some experiences in my own life." I smiled to gauge the reaction, and Mr. Billingsly's eyes had widened to a point where I half expected them to fall out for lack of containment. Amazing how one eyelid extension could speak such volumes.

"First, the colored lens really holds a promise: that without much trouble, you present a new face to the world—and at last you're in control of that face. What did you say, Diane?" I pointed at the advertising manager. "That it makes your eyes a fashion accessory? That's at the heart of this concept." I revealed my first board. "VibraLens—Change how the world sees you."

Then I moved to the second. "A central part of your strategy is about breaking out of the commodity world of the contact and restoring the 'cool cachet' of the colored lens. So this concept builds not on how you look wearing VibraLens colored lenses but on how they change your outlook." I unveiled the second board, which Deb had done for me, thinking she was working on a crash concept for Lydia. It was a flowing image that changed from a blurry black-and-white photo to wildly colorful, crystal-clear Impressionist landscape. "See the world differently."

They seemed mildly interested. Then Lydia burst into the room.

"Hi!" she screeched. "The meeting was moved?"

Nine heads, four of them on the necks of clients, turned to see her. Billingsly tried to cover with a smile and an odd *khhghg* sound in his throat. Calmly, I replied, "I sent you an e-mail Monday about the change and then one again this morning."

She was wound tighter than a boa constrictor's grip on a rat. "But I never check my e-mail. You've known that for two years, Jordan." She was now screaming. Everyone in the room was getting uncomfortable. Except me. I was loving it.

"I'm so *sorry,*" I said, with a saccharine wide-eyed innocence. "I didn't remember. I assumed you'd read it. I'm *so* sorry." I was cool as a cucumber. Lydia looked like she was going to implode.

"Well, it's not a problem, we're just about through, so find a seat and we'll be back to it," Mr. Billingsly said, and then got in his characteristic late hit. "But I believe I saw the notice—so let's continue." Ha! Take that, snake woman! But then Mr. Billingsly said something that sounded like sweet, sweet music. "Jordan, please go on."

I shook off the Lydia intrusion and continued. "Right. Keeping with the same theme, I thought, we show a woman one way, possibly corporate, stuffy, buttoned up . . . and then we see the rock-star version of her. Not a total one-eighty and not ridiculous, but a definite change, highlighting her bright eyes. She walks in one way, dressed appropriately, and walks out completely different—and happier for it. 'VibraLens . . . Reinvent yourself!'"

Lydia looked like she was about to have a conniption.

"That's not my idea!" Lydia said loud enough for everyone to hear, straining mightily with a cracking smile to remain civil but utterly failing. She looked like she was in the early stage of a total breakdown. And as she melted, the VP of marketing for VibraLens clapped his hands together.

"Well, it should be," Mr. Billingsly said. "It's great!"

"Really?" I asked.

"I love it! Reinvent yourself!" chimed the VibraLens guy. "Jordan . . . "

"Yes."

"It's interesting. *No*, it's wonderful. It's just the kind of thing we need. Fun, hip. I even like the rock-star thing. Any others?" He smiled and leaned forward.

"Research told us that much of the resistance to your product among your target demographics is that colored lenses tend to be so noticeable. With ColorSense, you're toning them down, making them more like real eye colors, and avoiding the stigma of 'pretending.' Some places, they don't mind people pretending—people make a living at it. But we're casting our nets wider. For everyone who ever dreamed of altering eye color with contacts." I flipped to my last board. A woman looks seductively into the camera. "So subtle—no one else can see through them."

The room applauded. Mr. Billingsly smiled and acted as though he'd known it all along. The truth about Jordan . . .

"Jordan has always been our diamond in the rough. I think she's finally starting to sparkle." Was he serious? I went from "leave it in the gutter" to a diamond in the rough just like that.

Meanwhile, Lydia was mortified—which tickled me to no end. When everybody got up to leave, Mr. Billingsly put his arm around me with an off-balance hug (he had that post-positive-creative-meeting euphoria) and said, "How about this one, huh? Huh? Jordan, stop by my office this afternoon. I think it's time we start talking about your future here."

"Will do. Thank you!" I said, then mumbled but loudly: "Because I sure can't remember much of my past." And he actually laughed, long and hard, at my line. I was beginning to see and be seen differently.

# 17.
# curious jordan

Dirk had called again. After experiencing a heaping helping of the new, indifferent, and significantly less slavish Jordan, he'd called again with a swagger in his voice and I'm sure a glimmer in his eye. I couldn't be positive, though, since the initial contact had been a message on the phone (so delicious hearing him say, "Dirk? Remember? Dirk?"). He wanted to see me, and I believe that bears out the truest lesson about romance—at least when one of the parties is a brick head: Desire is directly proportional to disinterest. If you want him to come, tell him to go away.

But I had a mission, as I've earlier revealed. The secret part of my mission was that I was only wearing a mask of forgetfulness. The not-so-secret part of my mission was shoving aside anyone who had stood in my way before with an innocent shrug and forlorn smile. Fake ignorance was bliss.

So I agreed to get together for what I'm sure he imagined would become a torrid sexual get-reacquainted session. ("Unbelievable, dude!" he'd say. "It was like fucking Jordan and a total stranger all at once!") I had other plans. One last hurrah before I'd say good-bye for good. I'd agreed to meet him at Houston's, one of his firm's favorite restaurant bars. It wasn't high on ambience, but they had a great artichoke dip that I could always get into. I wasn't entirely sure what I was going to do to humiliate Dirk, but I figured he would give me plenty of opportunities to figure it out.

I got there about ten minutes late. Prior to that moment I was always on time or early for him. Punctuality was always a big factor in my life, and I'd spent the better part of my relationship with Dirk waiting for him to show up somewhere. Thinking about being late made me remember Lydia's inspired mangling of the Gandhi lateness-violence theory, and I laughed as I walked in. I'd incorrectly assumed he'd have a table for us, but he was seated at the bar, surrounded by people, his eyes glued to the television.

I called his name a couple times to no avail—then resorted to snapping my fingers in his face.

"Hey, *you*," he said, mouth full of some indeterminate snack food, fumbled, no doubt, through handfuls of fingers on the way into his trap.

"Hey, yourself," I said, smiling pleasantly to remind him I'd basically forgotten who he was. Dirk had already gone through one beer and ordered a second. His eyes were on me now, but the football game was a powerful temptress, and he succumbed over and over again to the urge to cast a look in her direction. He'd earnestly nod at me, say "yeah!" enthusiastically about nothing at all, stroke my forearm awkwardly—but you'd think the TV was about to attack him any moment, the way he kept eyeing it. Watching Dirk watch TV in a bar had definitely lost its appeal.

"Hi, there," I said again, more forcibly. He turned in his seat to face me.

"Remember anything yet?"

"Nope. Nothing," I said, but before I got through the "ing" in nothing, he'd already turned to watch the game again. "Although getting ignored in favor of a football game seems like something I'd remember. Or maybe I'm blocking it out on purpose."

"I was just watching that one play."

"So this isn't a usual thing with us?" I asked, counting up in my head the dozens of games I'd suffered through—not to mention how many times his team lost, which would result in an immediate depression and no victory sex. The converse being, his team would win and we'd have crazy energetic sex that made me wonder if he wasn't secretly picturing Derek Jeter or Tom Brady.

"Course not, baby," he said as he casually popped another nut in his mouth. Liar. "I actually wanted to talk to you about something."

"Really? What's that?"

"Well, it's something you and I had been talking about a lot before you caught amnesia."

Caught amnesia? Okay. You could call it that. I was pretty curious about what he was getting at. Considering we rarely talked about anything anymore, let alone talked a lot about something. "What is it?" I asked, all kinds of curious.

He leaned toward me, and it was all I could do to keep from recoiling. And then he looked side to side and got that mischievous half-mouth smile on his face. The one that had struck me as such an adorable, impish little grin before and that now only made me want to strike him.

"Women."

"Pardon?"

"Other women," he said. I was floored. Was he actually going to fess up to cheating on me? *That* I hadn't prepared myself for. It would be totally out of character—and why now, since he didn't think I had any recollection of catching him . . . Could he have developed a conscience? Was he sorry?

"What other women?" I asked.

"You were getting bi-curious," he answered.

Oh. No. He. Didn't.

"Pardon?" I coughed. "Did you just say 'bi-curious'?"

"Yeah. Believe me, I was as surprised as you are probably—but you were serious."

I nearly did a spit take. "You don't say."

"I do. Say. You had mentioned that things were great with us, but it was, like, the level of crazy that *we* were having was making you, like, hungry for even more. Like, you were thinking, whatever, like a three-way."

Like. "Wow. How adventurous of me!"

"Yeah." He took another swig of his beer. "So I was thinking that not tonight—tonight we'll just do normal crazy—but sometime soon, that . . . we could do that."

"Wow, soon?"

"Sure, why not?" he said. "You . . . me . . . and someone new . . ."

"Just us three?"

"Definitely," Dirk said, clearly getting excited just thinking about the possibilities. "Yeah, mix it up a little bit, you know? Throw a different ingredient, something else into the mix. But not"—and here, he sat up very straight and craned his neck way back, the picture of moral rectitude—"not trashy. Not anything to come between us."

"Huh," I said. Actually, I was sure he'd be flexible on the coming-between-us part if I agreed to go along with the plan.

"I mean, I was always happy with just you and me," he said, pouring it on even thicker. "At first I tried to talk you *out* of it because I didn't know if it would change things between us once it was all said and done, but . . . I just want you to be happy."

"Tell you what," I said, "make that third party a guy? And I'll think about it."

He made a face, trying to laugh but choked by instinctive fear of the subject. "Ho. Whoa. What am I? Some kind of fag?"

"I don't know. Are you?"

"Ha, no! God no. Fuck no! You *know* I'm not." If Dirk were a cartoon, steam would have been coming out of his ears. "Just forget I said anything."

"Are you sure?" I looked around, pointed at a good-looking guy in a flannel shirt. "What about *that* guy?"

"Right."

"I'm serious," I went on. "The two of you, going at me. It'll be different. It'll be *fun*. Someone else in the mix. I see what you mean . . ."

"Are you out of your *mind*? Did you lose some brain cells along with your memory?"

"I don't think so," I said. And then with my eyes locked on Dirk, and a new kind of smile dancing across my lips, I got up from my chair and walked over to the guy I'd pointed at.

"Hi," I said to the stranger in flannel. "I'm Jordan."

"Hello, Jordan. Mike," he said.

"Hey, Mike. This is going to sound weird but . . . would you let me kiss you? It's for a thing. Like a bet . . . kind of."

He looked, well . . . he looked like any man who'd just been asked for a kiss by a young and reasonably attractive woman in a bar. The preening was precious. "Who'd you bet?"

"Nobody. Actually, myself. I bet myself that I wouldn't go through with it."

"What do you get if you win the bet? And what happens if you lose?"

"If I win I get a kiss, some self-esteem back, and the pleasure of making someone pay for trying to take advantage of someone else's misfortune. And if I lose . . ."

He cut me off with a kiss. A good kiss too. Not like I saw fireworks, but it was pleasant *enough*, and it certainly caught Dirk's attention. He was halfway to where we were standing when I came out of it. I whispered to Mike to just play along.

"Hey, Dirk," I said. "This is Mike."

"Hey, Dirk," Mike said with a finger-trigger point.

"Mike's totally cool with everything . . ." I said to Dirk. "So how do you want to play it?"

"Jordan!" Dirk hissed. "Fuckin' forget about it, all right?"

"Fuckin' forgotten," I said as I held back a major laughing fit. "I guess, never mind, Mike," I said to my new friend. "But I'll let you know if anything changes."

That? Was awesome.

\* \* \* \* \*

After Dirk and I parted ways, I met Todd and Cat at the twenty-four-hour diner where we'd clocked so many hours together that they'd given us our own reserved table. Almost. Whenever we came, the owner or night manager would cast a weary glance at us and jerk his head toward our booth. If someone was there, the quandary set us back for minutes at a time. Once we stared a group of giggling teenaged girls right out of the place.

I was late—ditching Dirk had taken longer than expected. Still, to keep up the ruse, I called Todd on his cell phone and he pretended to give me directions so I'd know where I was going. I hadn't seen Cat in ages. I'd avoided her more than I'd have liked since my rebirth and I was feeling sixteen shades of guilty.

"Greetings," I said as Cat got up and hugged me tightly.

"I've missed you," she said. Make that seventeen shades of guilty. "I wonder—" Cat broke in, then stopped.

"Out with it," Todd said.

She arched her brows. "What it's like being in there. It's unbelievable that you can't . . . remember."

Unbelievable? Implausible, sure . . . but beyond belief? I hoped not.

"It's like . . . " I looked up for effect. "Like the first day of school, every day. I know I'll be okay. I know it's generally fine—I'm supposed to be there, I'll be able to handle the homework, do the math, fire up the Bunsen burner. But everyone is new. I don't know a soul. But"—I smiled hopefully—"I look forward to meeting everyone and making new friends."

"But what about when you got your arm stuck in that trellis in your backyard and Sam kept hitting you with her shoe? The baking cupboard surprise we used to make with the vinegar and mustard and cinnamon and chocolate morsels?" She scoured her own memory. "What, what, what about the bird . . . that flew into the car when you were driving? And you went up on the curb and took out the mailbox and blamed it on—" She caught herself. We'd blamed it on Todd and his minibike— and we hadn't yet found the perfect opportunity to tell him.

My body had a mind of its own, and it remembered every glorious moment with her, and it started to reach to slap her arm, and my eyes and mouth were about to go along with it in the hilarity of the moment, until Todd calmly interceded by horse-kicking me under the table.

"That's wild stuff, wild!" he said. "Hooo! Good times. And we can only hope that one day, God willing, she'll find her way back to us. For now, I think we have to tread lightly," and he used his fingers to tiptoe around the table.

So I swallowed hard and picked up again. "I've just been getting acclimated at work and trying to figure out who I was and who I'm going to be and how I used to live and if that's still gonna fly."

"And what about Dirk?" she asked. "Did you have a nice time with him tonight? You know, I hate to be the bearer of bad news—"

"You *live* to be the bearer of bad news," Todd interjected.

Ignoring him, she continued. "You weren't very happy with him before this happened to you."

"I know," I said.

"You remember what a dick he is?" Cat looked hopeful, as if I were having a breakthrough. I got nervous.

"I filled her in," said Todd. Always quick with the cover. God, I loved Todd.

"I'm surprised he didn't make you go home with him tonight," she said.

"Yeah, well . . . he did try to suggest we work some 'experimenting' into our sex life."

"Typical," Cat said. "Revolting."

"He's got some stuff to work out." I nodded.

"I'd think his idea of working something out would involve a couple thrusts, immediately followed by copious snoring," Cat added.

"Was that my idea of a good time?" I said. "I don't think that's going to get him anywhere these days."

"Good," she said. "Make him suffer. Make him beg! Conjure your inner diva."

I raised my glass. "To my newfound inner diva!"

"Hear, hear," Cat yelped. "I gotta pee so bad I think my bladder is going to explode all over this table."

"How 'bout you spare us the charming imagery and just go to the bathroom?" Todd said.

"Wow . . . hadn't thought of that." Cat got up and left, so Todd and I could have a mini powwow.

"You would not *believe* the shit Dirk was trying to pull."

"Oh, no," he said, "I would."

"Complete one-eighty from the other night with Travis."

"Who?"

"Travis."

"What's a Travis?" Todd asked, face contorted, shoulders inching toward his ears.

"The guy . . . whose car . . . you know . . ."

"Oh, the *florist*?" This was Todd's way of flexing his muscles. Any mention of any other men, and immediately his feathers started ruffling.

"Not exactly his occupation, but, yes, the guy who sent me all the flowers. Anyway, I've seen him a couple times and he's really sweet."

"Sweet, like how? Like a sweet old man? Sweet like a basket of puppies? A sweet three-year-old covering you with finger paint?"

"No, he's not a puppy. Or old. Or three. He's around our age, I guess. You know, I can't tell how old anyone is anymore." Cat came back in time to catch the last part of my sentence.

"I can't either," said Cat. "I swear everybody between the ages of nineteen and thirty-five looks the same to me." We all nodded in agreement. I wondered when that happened. I used to have a fairly good grasp of people's ages. I could tell more or less how old someone was by what they wore, the music they liked—that sort of thing. Now all the teenagers were dressing like twenty-somethings; and all the thirty-somethings were trying desperately to still look like twenty-somethings; and then the actual twenty-somethings, well, they looked their age, I guess. It made for some confusion though. "What did I miss when I peed?"

"Hopefully not the toilet," Todd said. "Jordan has a not-so-secret admirer."

"Really? Who?"

"The guy who ran her over," Todd answered.

"He didn't run me over," I clarified. "We *collided*. It was an accident. That's why they're called accidents and not *on purposes*."

"Porpoises?" Todd said. "I love porpoises! Is it porpoises? What's the plural of *porpoise*?"

"Could you *be* more annoying?" I asked.

"You know he *can*," said Cat. "Don't egg him on."

"Por-pie?" he murmured.

"Anyway, I wouldn't call him an admirer," I said, although I hoped it wasn't true. "He was just being nice. He felt bad about what happened."

"As well he should," said an indignant Todd. Then piling it on he added, "Causing our Jordan to concuss and lose all her precious memories."

"I probably won't even hear from him again," I said, but immediately said a little silent prayer, Please God, don't let that be true.

"I'm sure," Todd said with a knowing grimace.

"What about you, Cat? Tell us about you," I said.

"Is this where we start men bashing?" Todd asked sarcastically. "I love this part."

"No," Cat said. "Because I am a happily married woman with a baby on the way."

*  *  *  *  *

As I walked down my hallway—something was different. It didn't hit me until I turned the key in my front door. Silence. Total silence. Sneevil wasn't making a peep.

I quickly entered my apartment and ran to his cage—which was empty. I looked around, panicked, but didn't see him anywhere. My heart started racing, and then I heard a tap. I looked up toward the noise, and there at my window was Sneevil, nestled in a surrogate nest that he'd built on my windowsill. And on the other side of the window—a pigeon. Not just any pigeon—a pigeon who was looking longingly, desperately at Sneevil. And Sneevil was returning his gaze. Her gaze? Sneevil was so enamored with this pigeon that he'd moved house. And was that part of my new orange sweater amid the nest? Make yourself comfortable, Sneevil.

The pigeon tapped at the window again and Sneevil cooed and started singing. It was an avian Romeo and Juliet, but as I thought *avian*, immediately I got to thinking about the bird flu we've been hearing so much about and wondered, What if that pigeon was a flu-carrying carrier? I panicked and shooed him away. Or I tried to. He wasn't budging. He didn't even notice me. He only had eyes for Sneevil. And Sneevil returned his yearning gaze, inching forward, singing to it, leaning forward as far as he could—if it weren't for the glass partition they'd be out together dancing beak to beak.

I was pacing, trying to figure out what to do about the budding romance, listening to the messages on my answering machine. The first message was from Citibank. Shocker. They were relentless. You'd think they want you to pay them *every* month or something. They'd call at all hours, too. I'd received calls at 6 A.M. from the heathens.

My second message, though . . . that canceled out Citibank's annoyance.

"Hey, Jordan. Thought I'd put this number to use. Oh, it's Travis. The guy from the car. And Thanksgiving. And . . . shabu-shabu. Um . . . calling to see what your plans are for tomorrow night. Still feeling awful about the smell and the retainer and the late notice . . . This probably sounds like a really weird message. Anyway, I was hoping I could make it up to you. In a place where everybody has to keep their shoes on. Maybe you don't even remember the incident. I'm not sure which side of the amnesia that falls under. So if you don't remember, then great! If you do, then sorry . . . again. Give me a call. It's Travis. I said that already." *Beep.*

Could he have been more cute? He totally had that stammering-over-his-words Hugh Grant thing going on. But not annoying. Not that Hugh Grant is annoying, but we've seen him stammer through the awkward moment enough already. Travis, however . . . this was new territory. Move over, Hugh! This was the movie of my life and it had a new leading man. Cue the soundtrack.

Then my phone rang. And the only thing that could take me out of my blissful state of It's All About Travis more than Citibank would be my mother—which is who it was.

"Hello?"

"Hello, Jordan. It's your mother." This wasn't just her acknowledgment of the amnesia: She always identified herself to me like I wasn't going to recognize her voice after knowing her for my entire life.

"Hi, Mom. How are you?" Automatically I walked over to my freezer and took out a pint of ice cream. I didn't even realize I was doing it. I guess it was self-defense in the form of comfort food.

"I want you to set up some appointments for physical therapy," she said.

"Why?"

"It's going to be better for our case."

"What case?" I asked.

"Against the driver of that car, dear. He's going to pay big for what he did to you. And my attorney, and Dirk, said that the more bills we rack up, well, it makes the case stronger."

"No, Mom. I'm not going to physical therapy and I'm not suing him. I actually met him and he's really, really nice." And totally hot and going to have ten kids with me, so back the fuck up. And, P.S., why are you talking to Dirk?

"He can be nice while he runs half of New York over. It doesn't change what he did."

"Yes, it does. It was an accident!" Suddenly, I found myself saying the exact same thing to her that I'd told Todd just hours earlier. "That's why it's called an accident, not an on purpose."

"We'll talk about this later," she said and then paused. "Are you eating?" I *was*. I stopped. How did she hear that? It was fucking *ice cream*. That's probably why she called in the first place. Her radar went off. Somewhere in Manhattan, Jordan's about to stuff her face and it must stop. She'll get skinny like the rest of her family come hell or high water.

"I'm just having a snack."

"Ice cream?" she shot back.

Dammit. "No."

"Good. It's late to be eating anything at all, you know. You should try not to eat after seven."

"Okay, Mom, thanks."

"I'll set up an appointment for physical therapy tomorrow. Good night, Jordan," she said and then added, "Enjoy your Rocky Road or Chocolate Chunk. Which?"

I waited. "Chunk."

"Yes," she said. *Click.*

# 18.
# life is all pretty much improv anyway

I walked into the office and everyone was looking at me funny. It was reminiscent of the day when I'd been splashed on my way to work, but I was totally clean and they weren't looking like they felt sorry for me this time—they looked like they were in on a secret. That stupid look they'd get on somebody's birthday when they'd say, "Oh, Sally . . . they need you in the Bermuda conference room"—and Sally would show up to find a not-so-surprise cake and crowd waiting to celebrate her birthday.

Then when I got to my desk it was cleaned out—totally empty. Not a red Swingline stapler to be found, a conspicuous vacancy where the Hasselhoff poster had been. My heart started to pound and my stomach did the panic flip-flop that's usually reserved for when I get caught in a lie.

I looked around, but nobody would look me in the eye. Was I busted? Fired? Yeah, maybe I'd been a little deceitful, but I thought I'd kicked ass on the VibraLens pitch.

"Jordan?"

I turned and saw Lydia. "Hi, good morning," I said, but I nearly choked on my own saliva out of nervousness.

"What are you doing there?" she asked.

"Just . . . standing?"

"Wondering what happened to all your things?" Thump-thump, thump-thump. Can anyone else hear my heart pounding? I wondered.

"Kind of?" I said.

Then Laura J. Linvette, human resources manager and accounting manager (bad idea normally, but we were tiny by agency standards), appeared. "Congratulations, Jordan. This came quickly, so we didn't have time for a lot of planning, but I think you'll like what we've come up with."

"Really?" Now it *did* feel like amnesia. What the hell was going on? Then Billingsly turned the corner and smiled at me.

"Jordan! Here's my star," he said, stepping close. "VibraLens signed on to do print *and* broadcast with your 'Reinventing' campaign. They actually increased the buy after we laid out media strategy because they were so impressed by the creative potential here. And you, my dear, are officially in creative. You're on the Surf team. Starting today." At Splash, in addition to having conference rooms named after vacation islands, our teams were always named after water sports.

"Your new office is right next to Kurt's," Laura J. added. Someone else in her family was named Laura, so she'd come through life as Laura J. (Although I'd known a *few* HR managers who used middle initials. Maybe they fancied that the extra initial made them sound important?)

"Next to Kurt's?" Lydia piped up, and I could tell she wasn't entirely pleased about the whole turn of events. In fact quite the opposite.

I, however, was elated. "My own . . . office?"

"Right down the hall," Lydia muttered in her trademark annoyed fashion.

I walked down a few doors, reading the little signs with the names, and there he was. Not Kurt—David Hasselhoff. My poster, plastered on the front door of my new office. Kurt pushed off from his desk and spun around in his chair.

"Hey, neighbor."

"Hey," I said.

"Think we can *not* have that poster there so I don't have to look at it first thing every morning?"

"I think not," I said, confusing Kurt.

"You think we cannot have the poster in here . . . or we cannot *not* have it there?"

"He's been here longer than you have, Kurt."

"Okay, that's cool," he said. "Had to try. It kind of creeps me out."

"That's the point." I nodded.

I got settled at my new desk in my new office and the first thing I did was pick up the phone and call my machine at home to replay the cute message from Travis. Then I hung up and watched the clock while I calculated exactly when I would call him. Ten A.M. was way too early. Eleven? That was manageable. Not like I called the second I got up, but not like I was waiting all day to make him wonder. I decided to wait until eleven—11:30. . . 11:20. No, 11:30.

I picked up the phone at 10:47 and dialed.

"This is Travis," he said, when he picked up.

"This is Jordan," I replied.

"Jordan. Jordan—hey!"

"What are you doing?"

"Oh, you know. I'm just cookin' over here."

"I *love* a guy who can cook."

"That's me. Wearing an apron and a smile."

"That's quite a visual," I said, picturing it in my head.

"I'm actually fully clothed. Last time I showed up for work in an apron I got called in to human resources."

I laughed a little too hard at his joke. Then I rolled my own eyes at myself.

"When can I take you out?" he said.

Direct. I liked that. Then again I liked everything about him. What? You like to club baby seals? Me too! Let's book a charter flight.

"I'm pretty flexible." Shit. Play it cool.

"That's promising," he said. "We'll get to that later, though. Now, when can I take you out?"

"Aren't you clever . . ."

"How about tonight?" Hmmm, let me think about that. I was flexible but not totally available. In fact, I was practically unattainable. Not in his *dreams*! But tonight. Was there something I had to do tonight? Other than play hard to get?

"I'm yours." *Shit.*

\* \* \* \* \*

We decided that he'd pick me up straight after work. This could have taken on nightmare ramifications had I not anticipated the same-day date in my best-case scenario when I called him. I might not have shaved or I might have carelessly dressed, not worn a good bra and a top that would show off the effects of the good bra (thank you, Victoria, and all of your many wonderful secrets). But the new Jordan dressed on offense, not on defense—as though I were always anticipating that something good might happen, rather than something bad—and taking a little extra time every day to look nice. And I'd gotten up an hour earlier that particular morning to make an extra-special effort, just in case. So it was all working out according to plan. Nothing had ever worked according to plan for me before. I didn't even have a plan before. I was starting to love my life.

I darted out of Splash at 6:20 p.m., and as I started down the steps, I saw Travis sitting on my bench across the street. My stomach did an entire gymnastics routine and my knees felt wobbly. My heart pounded as I walked down the steps, and all I could think was, Please, God, don't let me trip and fall. And thank you, God, for introducing me to Travis. But next time, maybe we can skip the hospital part and maybe try a run-of-the-mill bump into in the grocery store vegetable section. He crossed the street to meet me.

"Hi," he said. "You look beautiful." And my face felt hot again.

"Hi, yourself," I said, and then we stood there awkwardly for about an hour (probably eight seconds in actual time). "So what's on the agenda?"

"Well, I was thinking that we could go to that new indoor games place and ride bumper cars . . . in honor of our meeting." I was smiling so big my face hurt. "And then, if it doesn't blow a diet of some sort, hand-mixed ice cream."

"Sounds like a blast."

"Until I ram you off the road," he ribbed.

"Wouldn't be the first time," I taunted back.

"Ouch!"

* * * * *

We had one of those near-perfect movie-montage first dates that you think doesn't exist in real life. We sped around in our bumper cars and yelled obscenities at each other.

"Payback's a bitch, baby!" I called out as I crashed into him.

"Women drivers!" he shouted.

"Oh, did I hear someone whining helplessly?"

We smashed each other up but good. And then when the novelty wore off we found ourselves with two impossibly large frozen ice cream drinks in front of us. I had a vanilla and he had chocolate.

"And what else?" Travis asked.

"That's it," I gurgled with a mouth full of ice cream.

"I want to know more about you. I want to know everything about you."

"Well, so do I! But I'm at a disadvantage since all I can tell you about me has happened since the day we met. Or should I say, first ran into each other."

"Rub it in, why don't ya?" he said with the cutest little pout, inspiring an incredible urge to lick the ice cream off his lips. I managed to resist.

"No, not at all. I was just saying . . . Tell me about *you*. Where's your family?"

"My mom lives upstate. My sister is married and lives out in Portland. And my dad died when we were in college."

"I'm sorry."

"Yeah, he was a terrific guy." He looked straight ahead, and it felt as though we'd stumbled onto something tender. "He was a lighthouse keeper."

"Really? That's not your average, everyday profession. Where?"

"Out on Long Island. But it doesn't work anymore. It's in desperate need of restoration."

"I've never even seen a lighthouse close up."

"They're . . . majestic. Wonderful, wondrous." Travis thought about this. For a second he was a million miles away. I guessed he was thinking about his dad, and I wanted to climb across the table and hug him or touch him or do . . . something. But he snapped out of it just as soon as he'd disappeared and changed the subject. "What else? Let's see. I don't believe in the colorization of old black-and-white films, I do believe in Santa Claus . . . "

"And you don't believe in artificial turf and the infield fly rule, I gotcha."

"Oh, *that* you remember," he said. Our eyes locked.

"Go on . . . tell me more," I said. The old Jordan would never have had the confidence to flirt this way, but it felt good to speak so freely.

"Okay," he went on. "I like André Three Thousand better than Big Boi, prefer running outside along the river over inside on a treadmill, phone calls instead of text messaging . . . and I can do wonders in the kitchen."

"Like levitate?"

"No, but I'll make the best damn whatever you like that you ever ate."

"Well, that shouldn't be hard since you'll be competing with memories of food that go back about two months," I said, giving him what's known in the airline business as the wave-in for approach. "And most of that was hospital food." He made a guilty face. He felt bad. Then I felt bad. "Seriously? You're a good cook?"

"That's something I *don't* joke about."

"Then I'm going to have to taste this cooking."

"How's Friday night?" he asked, as if on cue.

"I happen to be free," I said. For the rest of my life, my giddy mind shouted, in case you're not doing anything either.

# 19.
## slim-fast is a lot of things—"yummy" isn't one of them

Cat asked me to go to speed class with her before work. I feigned ignorance when she mentioned that we'd gone before and I'd loved it, and somehow locked myself into doing it again. Speed was a class kind of like spinning but you're on treadmills power-walking instead of on bikes. The only saving grace is that you're in a class full of other people doing it too, because—like black rubber bracelets, blue eyeliner, and crimped side ponytails—speed walking is one of those things that should have been confined to the eighties.

Cat wasn't spinning anymore because of the pregnancy, and better speed than spin, because the techno music that accompanied spinning made me want to kill someone.

"What does *cloud nine* mean?" I asked Cat as I increased the incline on my treadmill per the instructor's chirped order.

"It means you're happy as hell. You're in la-la land. You're a pig in shit. You're Dirk in a titty bar."

"I know what it means, silly. But where did the saying come from? Why cloud nine? Why not cloud eight or cloud seventy-two?"

"That I can't help you with."

"I could *really* like Travis."

"Sounds like you already *do.*"

"I know. He's not like anyone I've ever met. He seems really genuine, you know?"

"Genuine," she echoed. "That's important."

"Not like most of the losers I've dated. And, boy, I've dated my share of losers!"

Cat stepped up onto the sides of her treadmill and stopped walking, eyes wide. "Jordan! Who do you remember? Are you *remembering* stuff?"

"No! I mean . . . from what I can tell of Dirk . . . it doesn't lead me to believe I was very discriminating."

"Oh, yeah," she said, stepping back onto the still-moving rubber belt. "He's a total waste of skin. He's actually being more attentive to you since your accident. I mean, you wouldn't remember, but he was way worse."

"I didn't think that was *possible.*"

"Believe me. He treated you like crap. Frankly, I don't get the turn-around."

"Probably because I'm not letting him walk all over me. All of a sudden I must seem exciting or something."

"You see?" she said. "I've *always* said that. You're nice to them, and they shit on you. You act like a complete bitch, and they worship the ground you walk on."

"Now that's some messed-up logic. Anyway, he's making me dinner tonight."

"Dirk?"

"No! Travis."

"Well, look at you. Juggling men. I hate to say it, but I think that accident was the best thing that could have happened to you." I couldn't have agreed with her more.

"If you can carry on a conversation, you must not be working hard enough," scolded the instructor. "Don't make me separate you two ladies! Move your legs instead of your mouths!"

Being there was bad enough, but getting yelled at by the teacher made it worse. "I *liked* this last time?" I asked Cat.

"You loved it!"

"No, I think I'd remember if I loved it."

"You did," she said.

"Really? What did I say *exactly* that gave you the idea I loved it?"

"Ladies, perhaps you should take your conversation outside the classroom," said the instructor.

"Sorry," said Cat. "We were only talking about how much we loved—"

But before Cat could get out the rest of her sentence, I'd dismounted. Cat looked at me, perplexed.

"I love it so much," I said, "that I'm overwhelmed. I don't want to overindulge . . . seems almost selfish."

"O-kay," Cat said. I could tell she was annoyed that I wasn't sticking it out, but after the last class we took, I could barely walk for two days. Why did I have to do something I didn't enjoy?

"Meet you out front," I said, and hightailed it out of there.

Cat came out a few seconds later.

"I was too embarrassed to continue," she said, intimating that it was my fault.

"Sorry," I said not so apologetically as we headed outside into the freezing cold. "I need to go home before work. You?"

"No, I'm gonna shower downstairs. I brought clothes. I don't have a *date* tonight like you," Cat said with raised eyebrows.

I smiled at the thought of it. My date with Travis. He was cooking for me. Then I spotted a cab. But there was a woman standing in front of me—maybe ten or twenty feet—arm raised nearly out of its socket. I didn't see any other cabs up the avenue, and I really needed to get going. So I did something I'd only had *done to me* before. I stepped into the street, directly in front of her, and stole her cab.

\* \* \* \* \*

I was taking one of those amazing showers that you just don't want to get out of. I stood under my domestic waterfall, daydreaming about Travis, water beating down on me at the perfect temperature, and I swear I could have stayed in there forever—but through the pleasant, dreamlike gurgle began to intrude an angry buzzing. I had at times during my spell of amnesia—or what passed for it—started to sense that my little psychodrama was becoming psychosomatic, that my body had started to believe what my mind was shoveling. So I stuck my head out of the shower to be sure, and what a relief: It was the angry buzzing of someone downstairs, wanting to come up. So I stepped out, sopping wet—and good thing, because I was dangerously close to becoming beef jerky.

I got out, wrapped one towel around my head and another around my body. But before I could get to the intercom to ask who it was, I was startled by a knock at the door. A precise knock that could belong to only one person: my mother. Now, we had a fairly good understanding among the residents of my building about letting in nonresidents, stemming from one unfortunate incident with a lovelorn girlfriend who pushed her ex's flat-panel TV out his fourth-story window after being given access by his sympathetic neighbor. So it was a major accomplishment now to beat that system—but child's play for my smilingly insistent and cloyingly concerned mother. I clenched my teeth hopefully and peeked through the hole on the off chance that it was someone else arriving unexpected, uninvited, and unbuzzed in, with a big present.

But, no, it was my mother.

When I opened the door, she looked me up and down and her face twitched. Twitching is involuntary, right? Because, for some reason, that one tiny movement managed to exude pity, condescension, and disdain, and drum up about a thousand feelings in me—inadequacy at the top of the list.

"Mom. What a nice surprise."

"Hello, dear," she said and sniffed around almost like she was checking to see if I'd been smoking pot, but actually in an attempt to make me feel like my place wasn't clean enough. Or *anything* enough. Like me. "I was in the neighborhood and thought I'd stop by to see how you're doing." She did the two-second once-over of my apartment and I swear she twitched again. Was she developing a tick? Was she allergic to *me*? She looked at the pile of clothes on my floor. "What's the laundry plan?

Let the pile get so big you can't fit it through the door, then you do a bonfire and buy all new?"

"No, I'm *going* to do it. Although I *was* trying to go for a record."

"That's not funny, Jordan, it's just plain disgusting. How can you *live* like this?" In my defense, which is usually my place of choice when around my mother, the pile of clothes she was referring to was not all dirty clothes. Anyone knows a woman has to try on many, many outfits sometimes, just to find the one that works. This is on a regular day. Throw in PMS and you could go through ten outfits before you find the one that you are the least hideous in. This outfit is generally the first one you tried on, but that's another matter entirely. My point is that a lot of these clothes were clean. Just rejected. And because I'd spent so much time trying to pick an outfit I didn't have time to put them away. With someone else, I might have tried explaining all this. But none of it mattered to my mom, so I didn't bother explaining. I just nodded in agreement. How *could* I live like this?

"I don't *know* how I live like this," I said.

"I don't either."

"I know." I shook my head and shrugged, as if it wasn't me that we were talking about. And I was just as disgusted as she was.

"Well, at least it's more like the Jordan I know and love. Have you begun to remember anything yet?"

"No, not really." Yes, I remember the last time you stopped over uninvited and said the exact same thing. Why not just make a mental note that Jordan is a heathen and lives in squalor? Then you won't be so utterly shocked when you see it, and you won't have to bring it to my attention *every* time you invade my personal space.

"I brought you some goodies," she said, her tone now upbeat. I'd noticed the grocery bag in her hands, but I didn't want to ask. At least she came bearing gifts. Free food is always appreciated when one is living on the traffic salary and drowning in debt. My junior copywriter position came with a slight pay increase, but all it really did was allow me to eat albacore tuna fish sandwiches every day instead of the other kind. Still, like so many before me in a similar predicament, I hadn't gotten around to depriving myself of much yet. But the new Jordan looked around at her former life and knew somehow it was time. Stifle the occasional impulse purchase of the thing you didn't need and would certainly chuck in the garbage in six months. Have a bank balance climb into the triple and perhaps even quadruple digits. Have a plan.

She started pulling the groceries out of the bag. "I bought you some grapefruit, some prepackaged salad, and some of those yummy Slim-Fast shakes."

"Uh . . . 'yummy'?" I protested.

"You know," she said, trying to sound sympathetic and failing miserably, "it would be totally natural—not really your fault at all—if you put on a few pounds while you were lying around in that hospital bed."

"Oh . . . thanks."

"I also bought you some fat-free salad dressing and those mini-carrots, but don't eat too many of the mini-carrots."

"Why not?" I asked.

"Because they're not an *unlimited* vegetable. Stick to greens mostly and think of the carrots as a treat."

"Yeah, like chocolate truffles or Cheetos. Carrots are not exactly a treat, Mom."

"You're not exactly a *waif*, Jordan," she said. Thanks for pointing that out, Mommie Dearest.

"No, I'm not a waif," I said with a shrug. Ladies and gentlemen . . . my mother. Poster woman for subtlety. "But you know what? I'm okay with it. I'm comfortable with myself . . . weight included. And your obsession with *my* weight is just selfish and mean-spirited."

"I am your mother, and therefore your best friend. If I don't tell you these things, who *will*?" I loved it when she pulled that one. That was a familiar one in the repertoire. "You're frowning."

"Yes, perhaps I am. And perhaps I'll develop a wrinkle from it. I'm human. It's part of life. " She started looking between my eyes and then moved to the rest of my face. I started feeling flushed. Here she went. Inspecting me. As much as it felt good to stand up for myself, it was uncharted territory and it made me feel a little shaky. Maybe she wouldn't notice anything else wrong?

"Do you exfoliate, dear?" Maybe not.

"Exfoliate?"

"Yes," she said. "Do you?"

"Yes. All the time."

"What do you use?" Shit. She knew I was lying and I had no idea what to answer here.

"A scrub?" I said, more asking than telling.

"Yes, of course a scrub. Which one?"

"I don't know."

"Well, show me," she urged.

"I ran out," I bluffed.

"Right. Buy some exfoliating cream. Clarins makes a good one. I have to go. Sam is waiting in the car. There's a sale at Gucci."

"Samantha's here?" I asked. "Why didn't she come up?"

"This has been very hard on her, dear. You not having your memory and all that. She's been very upset."

"Oh, I'm sure she has been," I said. "You tell her I hope she feels better real soon."

"I will, dear. Kiss." And she air-kissed me, because physical contact is reserved for manicurists and masseurs.

After she left I looked out my window, which faced the street, and I saw my mom's car double-parked. Samantha was dancing to the car radio, leaning her head out the window, catching some sun. She did that twirly arm thing and sort of weaved her head. She was grooving, working through the pain she felt from worrying about me.

But I didn't care. Nothing could get me down. Because Travis was making me dinner. And if a piano had dropped on my head, I swear I'd have apologized sweetly to the movers for getting in their way.

*  *  *  *  *

When I arrived at Travis's apartment, I was greeted by the most vivid and beguiling aroma—garlic, sweet oils, herbs. Over his shoulder, the place looked amazing too. He'd set a beautiful table, with cut flowers in a cloudy-green glass vase as a centerpiece, and he was holding a tall candlestick when he opened the door.

"Is that a candlestick in your hand or are you just happy to see me?" I asked.

"It *is* a candlestick and I am *very* happy to see you." And I was a human candle, melting a little right then. He invited me to sit, but I wanted to watch, and it was a show of impressive synchronization, from cutting board to stove to sink. The man seriously knew his way around the kitchen. All six square feet of it.

We were midway through dinner and having an amazing time when he realized that the candle was still unlit.

"Dammit. I forgot to light the candle. "

Through my mind danced all the metaphors about lighting his fire, lighting his candle, shedding light. So I grabbed the matches on the table thinking, This'll be cute and lead to banter. And with such good intentions, naturally, I burned my finger and flung the burning match onto the rug, where he immediately stamped it out.

"Ouch!" I said and I shook my hand a little, to draw attention away from the rug (no harm done, it turned out). Without thinking, he took my hand and kissed my finger.

"All better," he said. Yeah, I thought. *All* better.

"This is delicious," I said, breaking a long yet strangely comfortable pause in the conversation. "You weren't kidding about your talents in the kitchen."

"It's—it's just something I've always been interested in."

"You're an incredible cook."

"Thank you," he said earnestly. "That's the kind of reaction I'm hoping I'll get."

"From?"

"From people who eat my food," he said quietly, not looking up.

"What people?" I asked. "Are you having a taste test?"

"Remember I told you about the lighthouse and my dad and all that? It's all part of my grand plan . . ."

"Do tell."

"Well, I want to open a restaurant. Right next to the lighthouse. A lighthouse-themed restaurant, you know, beachy, breezy, boat paraphernalia, stringed colored lights. Lots of fish on the menu. The whole nine—"

"And you'll be the chef?"

He nodded, smiling up at me shyly.

"Then with the money I'm making from the restaurant, I want to restore my dad's lighthouse, and who knows . . . maybe even turn it into an inn, like a bed-and-breakfast. Lighthouses are definitely an endangered species, but the stories behind them, the whole idea of searching and finding safe harbor, protection from the storm, a beacon in the midst . . . " He looked at me and winked. "People will just eat it up. And I'll be there with a cash register and a credit card machine."

"You joke, but what a great dream."

"Well, I'm going to make it real."

"I have no doubt," I said, the room growing warmer and warmer somehow. Watching him talk about the restaurant he hoped to open and restoring his dad's old lighthouse made him light up like the East River on the Fourth of July. But his face suddenly changed.

"God, I feel awful. Here I am talking about my dreams and you can't even remember yours. And it's because of me!"

Then, once again, I started to feel really uncomfortable. There he was, being the perfect guy, and there *I* was, totally falling for him and hoping that he was falling for me too . . . and it was all based on a lie. He felt guilty because of the accident, and I felt even more guilty about lying to him. It was great. Both of us completely riddled with guilt and nothing we could do about it. Or rather, something I could have done about it. I *could* have said, "Oh by the way, that whole amnesia thing, it was a *lie*. I'm fine." But I was waiting for the right moment. Perhaps in my will.

"Oh, stop," I said, trying to play it down. "I'm sure I'll get my memory back any day now. Really. Let's not talk about that. C'mon . . . how are you going to make this dream a reality? Tell me everything." He looked pained. I raised my eyebrows and gave an encouraging nod to say, I actually care! This is not bar or cocktail party talk. Lay it on me, every excruciating morsel!

"Well," he said, leaning closer to the table, "I've worked hard and been saving up for years, and I'm finally in a good place. I've got enough for a good chunk of the down payment, and with interest rates still reasonable right now, I can get a loan for the rest. I've got the plans for the restaurant ready to go. Blueprints, design, budget, menu, traffic studies for every season. I'm hoping to get started early next year."

"This could be huge. Cover story in *Food & Wine*. Lines stretching into the bay. People bitching about how they can never get a reservation. Huge!"

"I want to take you to the location," he said quickly.

"I'd love it."

So we just kept talking all night, and I swear there was not a single uncomfortable pause. Our words chased each other's in perpetual motion. We've all had those rare occasions in life of discovering another person we want to dive into and swim around in, and this was one of mine. And I realized that I was probably never once truly comfortable—not on any level approaching this—with Dirk. Maybe it was because Dirk wasn't comfortable with himself and Travis seemed to be the exact opposite. Maybe it was just because Dirk was wrong for me. Whatever it was, as we sat there, I felt so at ease, like I was following his light to my own home port.

The clock surprised us. It was extremely late, so late it was almost early, and I made my way to the door to say good night. I wanted a kiss so badly that I didn't know what to do with myself. I didn't know where to stand or how to act or what to do. I could tell that he wanted to kiss me too, but he didn't know how to broach the subject. He seemed nervous all of a sudden.

I put my coat on and he walked me to the elevator.

"I had a really nice time," I said as he followed me in. And now here came the pauses. Seven . . . six . . . five . . . "Your cooking is out of this world," I added. "Very impressive. You're gonna do it. And you should feel every bit as confident as I do."

"Wow," he said, seeming genuinely touched. "Thanks. And thanks for coming." Three . . . two . . . The elevator door opened and he walked me outside.

"It was my pleasure." Up went his arm and a taxi stopped for us.

"I'm glad," he said as he opened the door for me to get in.

"Okay then," I said, giving one last cue to kiss me. "I'll talk to you soon." Standing on one foot. Hand on the door, chin somehow still lingering.

"Yes, you will."

"Good night, then." *Kiss me!*

"Good night," he said. And I had no choice but to get in and close the door. No kiss. But I was still in a dreamy state of bliss. Probably better that he didn't kiss me. I'd be completely useless at that point. They'd have found me wandering the streets, marveling at window displays, fascinated to see vendors scraping overcooked marinated lamb across their griddles, waving gleefully to complete strangers. I'd fallen for Travis, for a second time. And this one was bound to mess me up even more than the first.

# 20.

## what if
### *when harry met sally*
## was right?
## or
## can men and women
## be just friends?

I jumped on my computer when I got home and started researching lighthouses. I was struck by how varied they were—fascinating, beguiling somehow, just like Travis had said. *Many* of them, at least. Others were quaint little cylinders of white, some charming with their conical hats, some like majestic castle towers, some bland and utilitarian . . . but I had a feeling the one his dad had tended would be pretty special. I stumbled onto a few very good lighthouse Web sites, dedicated to lighthouses all over—history, structure, keepers' odd lives and dirt pay (the traffic staffers of their day), the Sisyphean restoration efforts of the lighthouse faithful in little seaside communities, and how lighthouses were lit with wood and coal, then oil, then high-wattage bulbs, then extinguished altogether when modern navigation technology rendered nearly all of them wistful relics.

But actually, I'm not sure any of them ever *had* a practical purpose. I think they were all born metaphors. A beacon to bring the lost at sea home. Or guide them to safety around the rocky shoals in stormy seas. A light in the mist. A solitary sentinel. Designed not by architects but by poets. Shamelessly capitalizing on the ready-made romance was Henry Wadsworth Longfellow, in a poem called "The Lighthouse." It gave me an idea. I wanted to do something special for Travis, not because I was feeling incredibly guilty, which I *was.* I wanted to do it because suddenly, making Travis smile seemed like the most important thing in the world to me. I pictured his smile and it felt like a burnt orange sunset in my stomach. Then the phone rang.

"Hello?"

"Hi. Remember me?" asked a very annoyed-sounding Todd.

"No, I don't remember *anything,* remember?"

"Where have you *been*?" he snapped.

"Nowhere. Here. Why, what's wrong?"

"I've left you *three* messages."

Shit, I thought. I had become that girl who ignores her friends when she meets a guy. I hated that girl.

"I'm sorry, sweetie," I said. "I just got in now and jumped on the computer. I haven't even checked my messages yet. Everything okay?"

"Fine. *Now.* Let's go drink some caffeine."

"I would," I said, "but I'm so tired."

"That's what the coffee's for," he retorted.

I sat and thought about it. If I went, then he would feel better and I would feel better for finally paying some attention to him and everyone would feel better. I was just about to say I'd go when he asked, "Where were you, anyway?"

"I was at Travis's."

"Oh. Well. Say no more."

"What?"

"That *accident* sure has been convenient, huh? You get a promotion, a new boyfriend . . . Any day now Ed fucking McMahon will be pulling up at your front door."

"He's not my boyfriend," I began. "We haven't even kissed."

"I need to know this?" He was yelling now. "Please keep the details of your sex life to *yourself*!"

"What details? I just said *nothing happened*! What is your problem?!"

"No problem," he said. "I'm just not used to getting blown off for people who run you over. If I bounced a brick off your head, would I have gotten a call back?"

"Jesus, Todd. I'm *sorry*. You're obviously having a bad day, and I wasn't there for you, so let's talk about it. What's going on? "

"I'm going to get that cup of coffee now," he said.

"You might want to look into some decaf," I said back.

"Later."

"Todd, wait . . ." But he'd hung up on me. This more than sucked. I already felt guilty about lying to everybody. Todd was the only one who knew the truth, for fuck's sake. Now he was going to be mad at me too? Not that anybody else was mad at me per se . . . but they would be if they knew. Beyond mad. Soaring through life, buoyed by the freedom of not being me, I looked down for what seemed like the first time. And right then I felt like all my insides had fallen out. Everyone, everything would turn on me, I realized. Except Todd. And here he was, beating them all to the punch.

It was an unsettling shock, and just a little more drama than I was used to—especially coming from Todd. So I did the natural thing—indulged in some nervous escapism, refocusing on my lighthouse research and dreaming about Travis. And me. Me and Travis. Maybe I was dreaming so diligently because I was trying to forget everything I was pretending not to remember, but I was starting to feel as though I would never get tired of saying that. And if I did, then I could switch it around to Travis and me.

Then I got startled by a knock at my door. Not the aforementioned knock of my mother who was the only person who could con her way in without a downstairs key besides . . . Dirk? At first I thought if I ignored it, maybe he'd go away, but no such luck. The knocks kept coming.

"Jordan?" Dirk said, confirming my fear. I froze. Not that he could

see me, but any move I made, I thought, he'd hear, and I didn't want to
have to deal. "Jordan! I just heard you on the phone. I know you're in
there."

On the phone? Had the mighty man been anxiously pacing in front of
my door for the past ten minutes, deciding whether to take the plunge? I
got up and opened the door. Dirk walked past me and looked around.

"How *are* you?" I said earnestly, earnest having become my middle
name.

"Why haven't you called me?" he asked.

"I've been so *busy*."

"Busy?" he asked. "With *what*? You have no life."

"Are you fucking kidding me?" I snapped, and Dirk almost jumped.
He was definitely not used to the mouthy me. His eyes widened and his
arms started waving frantically, like he was trying to swat away what he'd
just said.

"That's not what I *meant*," he pleaded. "What I meant was, you can't
*remember* anything from before, so I just don't understand what you
could be so busy with."

"Oh, right." Dick. "Well, I've been promoted at work, so my workload has changed and I've been hanging out with my friends . . ." And
falling in love. "And just . . . you know. Trying to remember."

"You haven't called me," he said, as if he actually cared.

"You haven't called me *either*."

"But you used to be the one that called me."

"Really?" I said. "Well, as some wise man with a marginal voice sang
on the radio the other day, 'the times they are a-changin',' I guess." He
looked genuinely disturbed. I don't think it was because he missed *me*,
but I think he was confused as to why I wasn't being my usual doormat
self and begging him to spend time with me so he could treat me like
shit. Or maybe he just had a problem with radio stations that still played
Dylan. He looked down and around, and for a second he had that little-
boy look that was one of the things that originally endeared him to me.
I felt bad. He wasn't *pure* evil. He had a good heart under there. He
just needed a bypass to replace the punk artery that sometimes ruled
the roost.

"So I heard you're in a major lawsuit," he said. "You're probably going to get like seven figures."

"Where did you hear *that*?"

"La La Schneider told me."

"La La, my *sister's* friend?" I asked, not realizing I shouldn't have remembered that and quickly correcting it. "I think I met her when I was staying at the house." La La was the girl who'd had sex with Chris Tannenbaum in the seventh grade because they were "in love." They were *thirteen* years old. Meanwhile, I was sixteen at the time and I had never even French-kissed. Dirk and La La, huh? The way I saw it, it was a good news/bad news situation. Bad news: Dirk was now also cheating on me with my little sister's friends. Good news: I didn't give a rat's ass because I was crazy about Travis. Bad news: Dirk probably now had an STD because La La had contracted herpes at the ripe age of fifteen after sleeping with her seventeen-year-old camp counselor, her fifth sexual partner. Good news: I would not be touching Dirk again—ever. So as far as I was concerned, that thing could shrivel up and fall off.

"Yeah, I ran into La La at the roof deck at Bed."

He ran into her. Right. I'm sure he tripped and fell right *into* her. Meanwhile, I shouldn't have even remembered who the hell La La was, considering I had amnesia. This would have been a major slip if Dirk wasn't such a major dolt. But he was. Thank God.

"So you're gonna make us rich, huh?"

"Us?" I asked, cocking my head backward like I was dodging bad breath.

"You and me, baby. We're gonna be livin' *large*."

"Hate to break it to you, but I'm not suing anybody," I said, and thought out loud, "I thought I'd put the kibosh on that when my over-eager, money-hungry mother brought it up the first time."

"Actually, your mom confirmed it."

"Pardon?"

"Yeah," he said. "She did."

"Why are you talking to *my mom*?"

"I was checking on you. Just wanted to see how you were doing . . . and she knows I know how to lay down the law . . ."

"If you were checking on me, why didn't you just ask *me*?"

"Well, I ran into her."

"You 'ran into' my *mom* as well? You are doing a lot of running into people, Dirk."

"Sam had an after-party the night I ran into her and La La. At your mom's place." Images of Dirk, Samantha, and La La having a threesome were running rampant in my brain. It was making me feel ill.

"Well, I'm not suing anyone," I clarified.

"Jordan, you should. It's such an easy *win*. Trust me." Right. Trust *you*. Did he really think I was going to get rich off Travis? And that *he* was going to reap the benefits? He deserved every single herpe that was coming to him.

Dirk took a step closer to me. "Hey," he said, and then without any warm-up, he placed his hand on my right breast. Was that supposed to be foreplay? I started to crack up. "What's so funny?" he asked, and I just shook my head. I couldn't stop laughing. He reminded me of a monkey. I thought I was going to stop breathing, I was laughing so hard. Needless to say, Dirk wasn't at all amused by my hysterics. "You're whacked," he said, and with that he walked over to my door and let himself out. I actually laughed for a good five minutes after he left. I felt a teensy bit guilty about bruising his ego, but that was the most asinine attempt at seduction I'd ever seen. So perfectly conceived and executed, too—what with the "hey." Pathetic.

# 21.
# foghorns be damned

"Hello?" I said, half into the phone and half into my shoulder as I scrambled to choke off the electronic gurgle.

"I'd like to speak to Jordan, please."

The unmistakable tone and din of background voices, engaged in the same pursuit, told me it was my financial shadow, Cindy from Citibank. "I believe this is she."

"Yes, o-oh," the perky voice said, confused for a moment. "This is Cindy from Citibank."

"I didn't realize we were on a first-name basis, Cindy."

"Yes, Jordan, I'm calling again about your credit account, which is now nearly ninety days past due," she said, suddenly sounding a lot less perky. I knew there'd be a reckoning eventually. There was always a reckoning for me. But I just wasn't up to it. I wasn't dressed for it. I resented the calls, and I resented Cindy for being in the right. Besides, I still didn't have the money. So I decided to let my amnesia do the talking.

"Kimmy," I said. "I'm sure you know what you're doing, and you may even have good records to back it up. But the problem is, since the accident, I have no memory of you or your credit card or your company . . ."

"I'm calling from Citi—"

"Or any purchases I may have made on a credit card. I may *not* have, or if I did, I may not have been me exactly."

"When we talked before, you—"

"There you go again, Candy. I don't remember ever speaking to you. I have amnesia."

"Well, I . . . " She was flustered and took a moment to regroup. "That's not . . . Your account has been turned over to collection, i.e., me. And I've left several messages and we spoke months ago about this."

"I know you believe that, Carrie. And it may be true. But I can't remember, so I can't be of any help until I get my memory back." She was silent.

"Well, someone needs to be accountable for charges on your card," she chirped.

"I guess that's true. And come to think of it, it's *still* not me." Then I plunged boldly forward. "Maybe if you called my legal guardian. If you really need to get those bills paid, I suggest you take it up with her. Judith Landau. In Nassau. She's listed." It was a reprieve only, I knew, and not a noble impulse, but it beat a bankruptcy filing at that moment. "Oh, and . . . Cammy?" I added.

"Cindy."

"Lose my number."

I hung up and did a little victory dance. Yes, it was irresponsible, but getting rid of Cindy was so damned fun. Then the phone rang again. Maybe I'd danced too soon. I picked it up with major attitude.

"What part of *lose my number* didn't you get?"

"Is this a bad time?" It was Travis. Yummy, delicious Travis. And I'd just bitten his poor head off.

"Travis! I'm sorry—I thought you were someone else."

"That's okay," he said. "I thought I was someone else once too, but I worked it out in therapy."

"Funny."

"Bring a heavy jacket to work with you tomorrow. I'm picking you up when you get off and taking you somewhere."

"Where?"

"Good night," he said in an *I'm-not-telling* voice and hung up. I fell back into my bed and tossed for about a minute or an hour. I wondered where he was taking me.

* * * * *

I spent the next day at work watching the clock, nervously anticipating my date, waiting for the incredibly slow-moving day to end. And the hands weren't moving. Literally painted on, it seemed. When it finally hit five o'clock, I flew out the door, through the halls, into the elevator, and outside, where I saw Travis with a picnic basket in his hand and a smile on his face.

"I know *you*," I said as I walked over to him.

"Hi, gorgeous." I think I turned every shade of red. And he could tell too. He laughed at me blushing and put his arm around me and I kind of nudged him and burrowed into his side.

"Hi," I said.

"Let's go."

We walked over to the train station and took the subway to Penn Station. We watched the board for one of the trains of the Long Island Rail Road, and at that point I pretty much could guess where we were going, but I didn't give it away that I knew.

* * * * *

When we got to the lighthouse it was even more breathtaking than I'd imagined. A picturesque ocean-side view . . . sand dunes; a jetty; jagged gray and oatmeal-colored rocks. In fact, the dune atop the wall of rocks atop the water reminded me of a Napoleon dessert. A three-layer cake for the eyes. The lighthouse itself was magnificent—if a bit phallic—and certainly more awe-inspiring than I'd anticipated. It was like a tall, skinny castle, which reeked of girlish symbolism because Travis was, of course, fast on his way to becoming my prince. Anyway, the place was the height of cinematic romance.

"This is it," Travis said, arms outstretched.

"It's beautiful."

"*You're* beautiful," he said, and it made my insides feel like a gooey marshmallow. I loved the way he said it. He didn't say I was beautiful *to him*, or I looked beautiful *in this dress* or with my hair *that* way . . . He just said it simply, matter-of-factly. I was beautiful. And it was probably the first time I ever believed it to be true. "I just wanted to see you blush again."

"I don't *blush*," I said, suddenly feeling *less* beautiful and more like a turnip.

"How do *you* know? You don't remember anything about yourself," he teased.

"Well, I don't *think* I do."

"I'm sorry that you don't know for sure—and that it's my fault."

"It's such not a big deal," I said. "Really. Plus, not all memories are *good* ones. Maybe you did me a favor."

"I still feel bad."

"Can't you just forget about my amnesia?"

"Forget about it. Good one." He laughed.

We got quiet for a minute. "This place is incredible," I said at last.

"So what do you *think*? Good spot for a restaurant?"

"I think it's perfect. I mean, it's a *little* remote, but that's the point, right? What are you going to call it?"

"I think, The Beacon," he said. "I was thinking about Safe Harbor, but that sounds too much like a halfway house."

"Or a bad TV show."

"Or that." He smiled. "But I wanted it to be symbolic, so I think I'm going with The Beacon."

"I like it," I said. "It has a warmth. Ships lost at sea, looking for a safe dock . . . and here it is."

"That's right."

He moved in close to me, and there was some serious first-kiss tension in the air. I felt the usual kaleidoscope of excitement in my stomach, but he didn't lean in and go for it, so my nervousness forced me to just keep talking. My heart could take only so much.

"I think it works on so many levels," I said. "I mean it's perfect for your restaurant, but it's such a metaphor for the most basic human needs."

"Speaking of basic human needs . . . I've been wanting to do this for a while now . . ." He leaned in to kiss me, and I could tell it was going to be heaven . . . and *just* as our lips were about to touch, the most deafening foghorn on the eastern seaboard let one rip. I'm talking an ear-splitting, earthshaking *horn* blowing right that second. We both started to laugh. "Of course that wasn't exactly how I'd planned it," he said. I looked up at him and kind of bit down on my bottom lip, waiting for what would happen next. "I'm almost scared to try again."

"Don't be," I said, although it came out more like a whisper. And he leaned in and our lips touched, and the foghorn blasting my insides generously outdid the one we'd heard moments prior. In fact, all the foghorns in the entire world could have blown at that second and I don't think either of us would have noticed.

We came out of our kiss smiling.

"So, now comes the inevitable question," I said. "How come you don't have a girlfriend?" He looked thoughtful, then smiled before he answered.

"I think I *do*. I *hope* I do," he said with a shy smile. That? Was *so* the right answer. But not what I meant exactly. I was grinning nonetheless.

"You know what I *meant*."

"I could have asked you the same thing," he said.

"I beat you to it."

"I've had my share of relationships . . . but I haven't found someone that I really felt comfortable with. Or if I *thought* I did . . . it turned out . . . you know?" Oh, I knew. It was like he had read my mind. "And that's really important to me. I need to be able to just totally be myself and know that this person knows me inside and out, character defects and all, and loves me anyway."

"I'm sure that wouldn't be hard."

"You'd be surprised," he said with a hint of something creeping in. He'd been hurt. And that was the first glimmer of his past that I'd ever really seen.

I had no doubt that the more I got to know Travis, the more I'd fall for him. I was starting to have a needy moment. "So are you comfortable with *me*? I mean, I know we don't know each other that well yet, but . . ."

"Yes. I am. This is going to sound funny, but I was comfortable from the first time you opened your mouth. When you were lying on the street after the accident and you made that joke in the midst of everything . . . I swear I just felt something. Like I was meant to meet you."

"Well, you could have just introduced yourself," I teased.

"Where's the fun in *that*? I like to scrape my women off the sidewalk."

"Nice."

"You cracked me up that day," he said. "You always crack me up. Don't get me wrong, I think you're a knockout and attraction is important, but so is feeling like you can be buddies. And I feel that way with you." He got quiet for a minute. Then turned it back on me. "Why don't you have a boyfriend?" Hello, reality check. I *did* have a boyfriend. I told myself that Dirk was just a technicality at this point and that I'd take care of that soon.

"Well, I don't *remember* really. You know . . ." My convenient new fallback. "But I think it would be really important that someone get me."

"I think I get you," he said.

"Oh, you've *got* me all right," I said back. He smiled a mile wide and motioned to the picnic basket.

"Hungry?"

"Starving," I told him.

* * * * *

Travis got lucky. It was a case of perfect timing. I don't mean "got lucky" got lucky—although that did happen in due time (three weeks in, after date number five, with the window slightly cracked to let in cool air and the heater running on low speed in a probably futile attempt to cover the sound of our delirious joy and the bed frame knocking against the nightstand). I meant he'd got lucky by having the very good fortune to mow me down with his car at the precise moment when I'd hit bottom, when I'd lost all faith in love and its mirages. So even a so-so performance from

him might have earned my approval. But his was a tour de force of origi-
nality, cleverness, thoughtfulness, and happy coincidences.

You can say that I was the hungry diner to whom everything tasted
good—fine; then my advice is to go into every relationship hungry. Fed
up as I was with Dirk, Travis seemed like the antidote or rather . . . the
anti-Dirk. A good deal of it may have been ordinary early-courtship
glow, but you could pretty much slap any adjective beginning with *in-* or
*un-* on *Dirk*, then strip the prefix and you'd have Travis. *Uncaring, incon-
siderate, intolerable, unfeeling*—the list is endless.

We ate Moroccan food with our hands at a canopied private "kissing booth" table in a notoriously romantic restaurant—dark wood and
tapestry decor and belly dancers scattered about. There was the option
to close your canopy to the rest of the room, and from the sounds waft-
ing from our neighbors in the next booth over, we were pretty sure the
couple in question's main course was *inter*. Travis signed us up for a one-
night-only cooking class, so that I could embarrass myself attempting
to do something more than my famous pasta dish—a dish whose secret
ingredient started with *RA* and ended in *GU*.

This started our phase of what we called One Night Stands. Each of
us would choose something we'd never done or at least not with any reg-
ularity, alternating turns, and we'd make a night of it. His job was easier
than mine because all he had to suggest was *anything* and I'd pretend I
had no memory of ever having done it.

On my next turn I took us on the Staten Island Ferry at sunset. Travis
claimed to have been purposely trying to avoid Staten Island but agreed
to the round trip since technically, if we didn't deferry, he wouldn't have
been on the island. We held hands, took in the breathtaking view, and
watched a drunk guy puke over the railing. You sometimes forget to factor in the bonus joys of public transportation.

Inspired by the lush, I took us back to my apartment where I had a
bottle of wine, a foreign film—sans subtitles—and informed him that
the night's activity would be to make up the dialogue in English as we
watched. I somehow managed to turn the film into something Ed Wood
might be proud of. Travis insisted it was a *Western*.

Back and forth we'd take turns outdoing each other with *firsts*. We'd make plans for "sometime in the next few days" but end up together nearly every night. One bitter-cold evening in mid-December, he gave me his theory.

"Romo," he said.

"You have a dog?"

"Romantic momentum," he said. "Good things tend to get better. They pick up speed. Zing!" he said, shooting his hand directly past my right temple. "Things that are going nowhere get worse."

"Zing?"

"Don't fight physics, baby." He tilted his cup of hot chocolate toward me.

"Have you had this theory for long?" I asked him.

He sipped his drink. "Thought it up in the cab on the way over."

I didn't dwell too much on the theory, though it was typical, charming, offbeat stuff from him. And I kept secret my own theory: If you spend enough time with someone who treats you like a precious commodity—say, an open gas station when you're running on empty at 3 A.M.—and every time you see that person turn away, you want to tap him on the shoulder so you can see him again, there's a word for that too.

\* \* \* \* \*

It wasn't just my love life—work had been going great too. Lydia stayed out of my way, and I was getting credit for my own ideas, sort of. The truth was, as a junior copywriter (my title was "copywriter"), it was my job to make the senior copywriters look good, but at least I was working toward something and I was definitely on the right path. I was working on a new campaign for an Italian coffee press and I'd just come up with a brilliant campaign.

But before I could write it down, and just as I was thinking how nice it had been, not having to deal with Lydia, she walked into my office, smiling this tremendously awkward smile. I wasn't used to her smiling at me period, so it was totally creeping me out. She was looking around my office like she was all of a sudden interested in my life. She picked up a picture of Todd and me and looked at it. That picture had been on my desk in my cubicle outside her office for two years. She'd never paid it a moment's notice. I could tell she wanted to ask about it. She probably wondered if he was my boyfriend. I could have screwed with her and said he was my husband, which technically *was* true, but I didn't want her to even be in my office to begin with, so the idea of messing with her lost its appeal.

"Hi, Jordan. How are you?" she chirped.

"Fine." What the hell do you want? "And yourself?"

"Great. Did you have a nice weekend?"

"I did, actually. What can I do for you, Lydia?" I didn't know what she was playing at, but I wanted her to get right to it.

"Well, we used to work so well together, you know. And now, just because you're getting your own projects, I don't know why that has to stop. I mean, we're all one big team here at the agency."

"Rah-rah!" I said with as much sarcasm as I could muster. "Go team!" She looked at the picture of Todd and me again. Then she exhaled this big sigh.

"I have this pretzel campaign that's just killing me."

"Tying you up in knots?" I tossed out, mildly pleased with myself.

"Yes. I was wondering if maybe *you* had any ideas for it. Maybe you can think on it and we can get together later to brainstorm?"

"Let me look at my schedule. Lunch. Meeting from two to three." I paused for effect. "Nope, don't think I have time for that today . . . Sorry."

"Come on, Jordan," she came back testily, then composed herself. "I could really use your help."

"I'm quite sure that you could. But, frankly, Lydia, I think you've used me plenty *already*." Then with a quick change in tone in my best fake nice voice I asked, "Was there anything else?" She just walked out.

About an hour later, I looked at the picture of Todd and me for about the tenth time. Something was *definitely* up with him. He was acting all kinds of weird, and it was really bugging me. I called him and told him to meet me at Cozy's after work. They had the best pea soup in all Manhattan and I was long overdue for my fix. Plus, in the doe-eyed, Who-am-I? innocence of my fake amnesia, I was constantly having to pretend not to know the things I really liked and consequently having to dodge favorite items on menus and in stores when in the company of my concerned handlers. With Todd, I could slump back into the comfortable mode of me. And then there was the bonus that pea soup always grossed Todd out, and any chance I got to gross Todd out with my food consumption, I relished. Todd was playing hard to get. He said he was *busy* for the next two nights but would be available the next after that. We set a date for then, and hung up—certainly not a standard Todd-Jordan interaction. I looked forward to working out whatever was going on.

* * * * *

On my way to meet Todd at Cozy's I bumped into Lyric Lady. She raised one eyebrow when she saw me and sniffled. " 'If you see my reflection in the snow-covered hills . . .' "

I froze. She of all people would have no interest in me having or not having my memory—yet I didn't think it was a good idea to let on that I recognized the "Landslide" lyric or that I knew it was my turn to answer back. I felt guilty ignoring her because, really, what impact could she have on my life?—but still, I felt I had to protect my lack of identity. So, I brushed past her and kept walking.

"Humph," she muttered. I felt bad letting her down, but I choked back the answer, *The landslide will bring it down.* "I know . . ." she called out after me. At least I *thought* that was what she said, but I wasn't sure, and I didn't want to be sure because if I had heard her right, I didn't even want to begin to think about what that meant.

* * * * *

Todd had ordered the clam chowder. I was blissfully slurping down my pea soup, savoring the buttery sourdough croutons—pure heaven. He, however, was scowling at his bowl.

"This is the worst clam chowder I've *ever* had," he said. "The worst. What's in clam chowder? Clams and potatoes. I don't see a potato. Frankly I don't even see a *clam*. How are they even calling this a chowder?"

"You're in a mood," I said.

"I was fine before I was handed this consommé. I mean, what could be so wrong with throwin' in some potatoes and a clam or two. Just for shits and giggles?"

"You ever think about that phrase?" I asked. "Who came up with 'for shits and giggles'? What's it supposed to even mean? It's like someone just decided to make up a saying and put two words together that really have no business being together. Some anonymous moron who has no business making up sayings."

"You've put some serious thought into this," he said.

"No, it just hit me when you said it. That and I wanted to take your mind off your soup."

"Well, if the soup alone wasn't enough to ruin my appetite, dissecting 'shits and giggles' has done the trick. Too bad I wasn't eating chocolate pudding. Then I might even have cause to hurl."

"Sorry." He sat there looking disappointedly at his soup. And at me. And out the window. Something was up. And it had nothing to do with the lack of clams in his chowder. Although, I was about to find out that metaphorically, it kind of *did*. "Okay, so now you want to tell me what's really bothering you?"

"Ah . . . you've seen through my charade," he said.

"Which is?" I asked, still not knowing.

"You know. I mean, c'mon, Jordy," he said. "You must *know*."

"No, I *don't* know."

"This accident of yours. While it's been extremely convenient for your big master plan, I gotta tell ya, when I got that phone call . . . it scared the shit out of me. My entire life flashed before my eyes. Mind you, I wasn't even *in* the accident, but I realized . . . the best part about my life . . . was *you*."

I looked up, my spoon in my mouth.

"While you've been reveling in 'the new you,'" he continued. "I've still been madly and sadly in love with the old you. Pass me the crackers."

I was stunned. I really was. How do you come back from that? It was one of those big declarations that's supposed to make you realize that *this* is the person you are meant to be with. Or maybe you don't realize it until later, after you've gone through a bunch of stuff and made some more mistakes and then learned your lesson. Of course by then you'll be entangled with someone else or he'll standing at the altar and you have to make some grand gesture to win him back even though you had him all along. But this was veering toward the unrequited territory that would be heartbreaking for at least one party. Either way, this was some heavy shit. And of course my response was the height of lame.

"Todd. Todd, Todd, Todd! You're like my *brother*!"

"You couldn't come up with something better than that?" he snapped. "God, Jordan. That is so lame!"

"But it's true! I've known you since I was practically born."

"So, I'm losing this war based on familiarity? Shouldn't someone who knows you and loves you, the *real* you, be some kind of comfort?"

"It *is* a comfort," I said. "It's a huge comfort. And that's why I want you to always be there. If we were to ever get 'involved' and things didn't work out, as is inevitably the case . . ."

"Always the pessimist . . ."

"Seriously," I pleaded. "*Then* what? I lose my best friend."

"Who says it's *not* going to work out?" he asked. He had no idea how great things were with Travis. And even though I was about to try to prove my point that nothing ever worked out, I was hoping that in the case of Travis and me, things would be different.

"How many relationships have you had?" I asked. "Not counting the plethora of one-nighters."

"A few," he said. Defensively.

"And how many of them have worked out?"

"That's not fair!" he practically yelled. "They haven't worked out because I've been in love with you since we were in grade school!"

"Todd, don't do this. We know each other too well."

"Again I'm failing to see why this is a *bad* thing. Yes, we know each other very well. How is that bad?"

"Because I need you to be my *friend*. Can you please just be my friend?" What seemed like an eternity passed, but I'm sure it was only seconds. It sucked.

But Todd took it on the chin and responded in true Todd form. "Do I have a choice?" He smiled his trademark comforting smile, but I could see through it that he was crushed. I hated it.

I reached over the table and mussed his hair a little. It was beyond stupid. I may as well have said, "Way to go, champ" or something equally trite. "Thanks for being such a sport, buddy o' mine." I hated myself. But the last thing Todd wanted now was for me to feel sorry for him. So we struggled through our soups—or soup and consommé—said some hurried good-byes, and ran like hell in opposite directions, eager to put the horrendous evening behind us.

*  *  *  *  *

I needed to talk to Cat, whose apartment wasn't that far from Cozy's, but I couldn't bear to play up the amnesia charade just now. I tried to think of different ways I could call her and pretend to have no memory of our relationship or the fact that she was a shrink, yet use her for her shrink-ability. Just thinking it to myself sounded awful, but I needed to talk to someone with her perspective. Cat knew both Todd and me better than anyone in the world and I knew I could trust her. But how could I spill my guts to her about the shifting of my familiar and comfortable relationships while still pretending to be a detached amnesiac?

I called her on my cell—told her that I'd found her number programmed in my phone and I needed to talk to someone. She told me to come over and gave me directions, thankfully unaware of the fact that I was already halfway there.

When I got to Cat's office there was another emergency meeting taking place and it wasn't of the flustered-friend kind. The door burst open and I saw—and heard—a twelve-year-old girl there who was crying hysterically. Her hair was five different colors and looked like she'd cut it with a butter knife. Her nose was pierced, and she was wearing way-too-low-cut jeans. Her mother and father followed close behind and nobody looked pleased.

"Fuck you, I'll kill you in your sleep," the girl hissed.

"See? You see?" her dad said to Cat.

"Becky, that's a terrible thing to say," Cat calmly said. "I know you don't *really* want to kill your parents and so do you."

"You're right. I don't want to kill them. Because I don't want to go to jail. But I *do* want them dead. They should kill themselves! Make the world a better place!"

And my mom thought *I* was trouble. "Maybe I should come back another time," I said.

"Maybe you should go fuck a cow!" Becky suggested.

"Maybe I will," I calmly said back.

"You can't because cows are female, stupid *bitch*." This girl was twelve.

"Becky, that's enough," Becky's mom said. "I know our time is up. Thank you for all your help, Cat."

"Yeah, thanks for *nothing*," Becky said, and then turned to me. "Your turn, psycho. If I'm still seeing a shrink by the time I'm old like you, I hope somebody runs me over."

"Somebody did run me over, actually," I gleefully responded. And wanted to add, "but here's hoping that if it *does* happen to you and you get *real* amnesia, it will wipe out every memory of the wicked little person you are now."

Once they left, Cat gave me a big hug. "How's it going?" she asked, and then pulled back from her hug to look me in the eyes when I responded.

"It's going okay. Work is going good. Better than good, in fact."

"Great," she said. "But . . ."

"I know you mentioned before that you are a psychologist," I said hesitantly. "I didn't know what the protocol would be on needing a friend to talk to who could . . . help . . ."

"Please! Of course! Tell me what's going on . . ." she urged.

"It's about Todd. "

"What's up?"

"He told me he loves me. Over clam chowder."

"What?" she shouted at a decibel so high I was certain her little fetus heard it.

"I know! I mean . . . I think I do? I mean—that's new information right?"

"Brand-new," she said, mouth agape. "Shocking."

I wasn't sure how to play it, so I went with what I thought I'd do if I really did have no memory. "I didn't know what to do, but I had a feeling that he and I were just good friends . . . I mean . . . I don't know. You knew me before. Did I have feelings for Todd?"

"You loved him," she said, "like a *brother.*"

"That's what I said!" I exclaimed. "I felt awful."

"He's going to feel hurt and maybe angry. You need to prepare for that, but remember, you're not responsible for his feelings."

"But," I said, "I kind of *am.*"

"Really?" she asked. "You're that powerful?"

"Not powerful—I . . ."

"Don't put that on yourself. People may have feelings as a result of your actions, but you don't *make* them feel the way they feel—they just do. All you can do is be honest and treat people with the kindness they deserve. I'm sure you weren't mean to him."

"No, I wasn't."

"So maybe just give him some breathing room. Allow him to feel whatever he's going to feel, and let him make the next move and guide the two of you back into the friendship."

I looked at her stomach to see if she was showing yet, but she wasn't. Once we'd covered the Todd dilemma, it felt like there wasn't anything safe for me to bring up and she didn't know what to talk about either so we just got quiet.

"You want some tea?" she asked.

"No, I should let you go."

"You sure?"

"Yeah. I've had a long day and it's Christmas this weekend. I've yet to shop for anyone. Granted, I have no idea what people would like or *want*, but I have to get them *something*."

"It's the thought that counts," she said as I put my coat on, and when I was walking through the lobby of her building that's what kept ringing in my ears. "It's the thought that counts."

And feeling silly and brazen, I decided I was going to do all my Christmas shopping at Duane Reade. What did I know? I was just a memory-deprived daughter and sister, so for once my lapses in taste could be excused.

# 22.

## a partridge where a partridge shouldn't be

The lack of shame that came with supposedly not knowing any better brought a freedom that I'd never felt when shopping for gifts. I'd always been such a people pleaser and gotten so deeply panicked buying presents for my family in the past that my palms got sweaty at the thought of Christmas shopping. But wandering the aisles of New York's quintessential drugstore on Christmas Eve morning, I started to really get into it. If I didn't know these people and looked at them as the outsider that I was pretending to be, what would I see? What would I think they needed?

My dad was easy. In aisle two I spotted a rubber-clad waterproof flashlight and it seemed like a perfect "dad" gift. For my mom I went to the cosmetics section. A big bottle of Jean Naté, a cosmetics kit that was assembled in a stainless-steel box, and last, some face scrub, because I knew how important she thought a good scrub was.

Samantha was a little different. What do you give the girl who's got everything she ever asked for but nothing she truly needs? The girl who's made you feel *less than* for your entire life. The girl who's so busy blowing hot air, trying to trip you up, and make you fail that—and then it hit me . . . a blow-dryer. So she could blow her hot air all the livelong day. And not one of those expensive $200 T3 dryers that I'd heard Lydia touting even though her hair *still* looked like a mohair sweater and, if I wasn't mistaken, had started falling out since she got that fancy dryer. Sam was getting the Conair special: $15.99.

I took all my packages to the counter and threw in a roll of wrapping paper and a disposable camera so I could capture their expressions when they opened their gifts. I did a cursory wrapping job back at my place and then hopped on the train to join the fam for the festivities. I had my overnight bag packed for exactly one night. That was as long as I could stand.

My stepdad picked me up at the station. I looked out the window during the car ride home, taking in all the decorated houses, for a moment feeling jealous and wondering what it would be like to have been born into a different family. But as soon as I thought it, I came to a realization: Even though each of the houses we passed looked like a Norman Rockwell painting, I knew that behind most of the facades was probably just another dysfunctional family with its own set of problems. No matter how much greener the grass was or, in this case, how much more ostentatious their Nativity scene–decorated lawns and reindeer and Santa sleigh rooftops were, I didn't know what was *really* going on inside. And to that end, I thought, nothing is ever really as it seems, is it?

Which brought me to Travis. There was something a little too good to be true about him, and I hadn't let myself think about it, because I was too busy getting caught up in the cotton-candy dream haze that was the getting-to-know-you phase. But he couldn't have been that perfect. *Nobody* was. The only questions were, how deep the bad shit was going to go when it *did* finally surface, and would I be able to see past it? Embrace it? Or would my newfound, no-bullshit persona be less forgiving?

When we pulled up to our house, the familiar decorations brought back vivid memories, which I did my best to disguise with an expression of vague wonder. The lights outside, all white, because my mom thought colored lights were tacky; the wreath on the front door that, no doubt, was made by Mrs. Kornblut; and the jingle bells that hung over the fireplace screen, rung only once a year—a motion alarm to signal that Santa had come or gone.

"Hi, Carmelita," I said when I walked into the house and saw her looking frantic, little beads of sweat above her upper lip.

"Hello, Miss Jordan," she said.

"Need any help?" I asked, but before she could answer—as if tuned to her own jingle bell motion detector—my mom swooped in and ushered me out of the kitchen.

"Let Carmelita be," she said. "How was the train?"

"Lovely," I said. "Is there anything I can do before dinner?"

"Just stay out of the way, dear."

I did. I stayed out of the way for the next couple hours until the four of us sat down to dinner. I made a mental note that if I ever had hired help cooking a holiday meal in the kitchen, I would make sure there was a place at the table for that person to eat with us.

I also made a mental note of something else. Or rather, the lack of something else: the turkey. For my entire life we'd had pretty much the same Christmas dinner, which was, in essence, a rerun of Thanksgiving dinner—and it always involved a turkey. Green beans, mashed potatoes, roasted corn on the cob (cut off the cob for Princess Samantha), cranberries, stuffing, yams of some variety, and turkey. Instead, there were small individual birds on each of our plates. Birds that reminded me way too much of Sneevil.

"Lord, we thank you for this meal," Walter said. "We thank you for our health—"

"Most of our health, at least," interjected Sam.

"We thank you for blessing us with our *family*," he continued, "our friends, and we remember those who are less fortunate and spread the spirit of giving beyond our family." I looked once again at Carmelita, who was not at the moment on the receiving end of our spirit of giving, and thought about the hypocrisy of that last statement—again wishing she could eat with us. She was *more than* welcome to whatever this small bird on my plate was.

"Amen," said my mom and Sam.

"Amen," I said and then asked, "What are we having for dinner tonight?"

"It's quail," said my mom. "I thought we'd try something *different*."

"Ah, partridge on our plate, rather than in a pear tree," I said.

"It's not a partridge," Sam said. "It's *quail.*"

"Actually," Walter said, coming to my defense, "they are similar. The quail and partridge are interchangeable in most dishes."

It reminded me of a pigeon. I did not want to eat a pigeon. I also didn't want to complain. But here was one of those opportunities for me to be the person I *wanted* to be instead of the person I'd always been.

"I'm sorry . . . but is pigeon also in that interchangeable group?" I asked with no small amount of hesitation.

"Ew, Jordan. Duh, *no,*" said Samantha.

"I guess it is, yes, squab," Walter said, and smiled as he cut into his quail/squab/pigeon/partridge. I looked at Sam and made a face I'd only been on the receiving end of prior to that moment.

Sam pushed her plate away. "I'm *not* eating pigeon."

"Samantha," my mom said, "this is NOT pigeon. It's quail and it's a delicacy. You've had it before."

"I have?" she asked, needing reassurance.

"Of course," my mom said with a shake of her head.

I watched the interplay between Samantha and my mother. Sam may or may not have had quail before, and what was on the plate before her may or may not have been pigeon—but it didn't matter. Sam followed my mom's lead. If you'd seasoned and roasted a pinecone dipped in dog vomit and then called it a delicacy, you'd have won Sam's approval.

I, however, *didn't* follow. I couldn't. I never had and I probably never would. And even though Sneevil was *not* my bird, wreaked havoc on what was at one time (go with me) a borderline tidy apartment, and drove me crazy, he'd grown on me. And he was in love with a pigeon (whom I'd named Romeo) that had made my windowsill its permanent home, and for that among about a thousand other reasons, including the fact that the quail staring up at me might well be his—or her—relative, I was not going to be able to eat that bird.

The good part about being somewhat invisible to your family is that when situations such as having roasted quail on your plate arise, you can wriggle out of them with minimal distress. Everybody dug into the dinner, and I moved things around on my plate and ate *around* the bird, but managed to avoid having to cut into it. Then I somehow made telepathic eye contact with Carmelita, who in one deft move served me more yams, swiped Romeo 2 off my plate, and ducked into the kitchen—nobody the wiser.

\* \* \* \* \*

The next morning, I wiped the sleep from my eyes and trundled down the stairs. Sam, Walter, and my mom were already sitting under the tree, waiting for me.

"Merry Christmas!" I said.

"Merry Christmas," they all replied.

"We've been waiting for you," Samantha said as if I couldn't see the myriad gifts that had already been torn into.

"Looks that way," I said, and reached for one of the gifts I'd bought my mother. "Here, Mom. This one's for you."

"Well, you open yours first," she said, handing me a box that was obviously an article of clothing.

"Thanks," I said, as I opened it. For a split second I felt about twelve varieties of guilt—one for each day of Christmas—buying her present at Duane Reade topping the list of reasons. Then I opened *my* gift. It was a sweater that *I'd given her* the year before. I'd gotten it at Saks and it was her size and her favorite color: pink. I never wore pink, never liked pink, and haven't been her size since I was nine years old. Not only was she re-gifting, she was re-gifting my gift for her back to me . . . and doing it with a smile on her face because supposedly I had no recollection of giving it to her in the first place.

I put on my best poker face and smiled warmly. "I love it!"

"Is it your size?" Samantha said, trying to egg me on.

"Well, of course it's not my size," I said sweetly. "But that's not what matters. It's a lovely sweater from my mother. Something she picked out just for me. Thank you, Mom!"

"You're welcome, dear."

"Which one is mine?" asked Sam, and I pointed her to her box. "This one is yours from me," she said as she tore into her present and expected me to do the same.

I opened mine up to find a travel kit. But not just any travel kit. An American Airlines first class overnight kit. The kit they *give* you when you travel to Europe or somewhere far enough that you conceivably could sleep, if not crumpled into your seat like a used paper towel in a restaurant bathroom. "Thank you so much, Samantha. I'll have to take a vacation so I can use this!"

"You're welcome," she said, holding up her gift from me. "Uh, a blow-dryer?"

"Neat, huh?" I practically cheered.

"Yeah . . . neat," she said. "If the three that I already have give out, I'll go right to this one."

"Oh, you have one?" I said, slumping at the shoulders. "Sorry, I didn't know!" She looked at our mom, who shrugged and continued to open her presents from me, seeming nonplussed. Then we were all startled out of our wits when Walter yelled.

"Hot damn! This is *fantastic*," he said, and I looked to see him holding the flashlight up. "Jordan, I actually needed one of these. You *always* need a flashlight," he said, and he meant it, bless his amiable soul. "Thank you, sweetheart."

"You're welcome, Dad," I said as he touched my hair, tucking it just behind my ear, providing a feeling of safety and family (even if only momentary) that I never got to feel.

Memories are divine moments, painted over with emotions so they're hardly recognizable. No matter. I felt happy all of a sudden. And for that moment, and maybe no other, it was a Christmas I wouldn't ever pretend to forget.

\* \* \* \* \*

The Christmas gifts I *had* put a modicum of thought into were for Travis. We were still somewhat in the polite, getting-to-know-you stage, so I wanted to get him something thoughtful and sweet but not too much of a big deal because that might freak him out. It was a delicate balance: What if my present wasn't as nice as the one he got me? What if it was *too* nice? The good news was that it wasn't a birthday, so we were both in the same gift-giving boat—both equally at risk of scuttling the whole thing.

There's nothing worse than misinterpreting where you are in a relationship and being made painfully aware of it in the form of a gift exchange. Which actually happened with Dirk one Valentine's Day early on. I always did have seriously bad Valentine's Day karma.

I'd spent about an hour in the Hallmark store, trying to find the right card. Nothing that said I love you, nothing too mushy—just something cute and sweet. I bought him an oversize Hershey's kiss and a little red teddy bear. It was very mainstream, easily obtained, and not expensive, and it had no chance of suggesting I'd put too much thought into the decision, quite a feat after more than an hour of anguished hunting. It was just enough for where I thought we *were*.

Dirk called me about ten minutes before he was scheduled to pick me up and said he was running a few minutes late—never a good sign—which I didn't know would be status quo for the rest of our relationship. When I asked what we were doing, he said he didn't know. I didn't know if that meant that it was a surprise and he was being coy, or if he really hadn't put any thought into it, but I'd find out soon enough.

When Dirk finally showed up seventy-two minutes later, he had a casual air about him that immediately put me on the defensive. Or would have—had it not been Valentine's Day. But I figured that St. Valentine would be forgiving—how else does someone get to sainthood?—and so should I. I gave him a kiss hello and watched him as he took his tan leather coat off and walked over to my couch.

"So . . . what are we doing?" I asked.

"I'm kind of tired," he said. "Want to just order in?"

"Sure," I said, conjuring St. Valentine's magnanimous and nonviolent spirit once again.

We ordered Indian food and watched TV until it arrived. When the buzzer rang, I got up to get the door, pausing once to look back in his direction. A look that might have suggested, It *is* Valentine's Day, dear Dirk, so right about now you might think about getting your ass off the couch to come *pay* for this dinner.

Nothin'.

So I paid, thinking he must just be spacing out. He'll realize and jump up with his wallet at any time. Or the delivery guy will say, "Oh, one more thing . . ." and produce one more thing. *Some*thing.

I tucked the card, bear, and chocolate into the bag and then brought it over to the table. He unpacked it and smiled when he saw the gifts.

"Happy Valentine's Day," I said. He opened the card and smiled. I hadn't written anything too sentimental. I think I just went with the message on the card and signed my name.

"You too," he said, and leaned in to kiss me. I kissed him back half-heartedly as I wondered what was going through his head. If *any*thing.

And then he dug into the food. I sat there somewhat astonished and suddenly lacking appetite, but I choked the food down nonetheless. I mean, I'd *paid* for it.

After we ate, he attempted a bit of a make-out session, but I wasn't exactly into it, as I was still waiting for my teddy bear. Finally he gave up and said he was tired, put his leather coat back on, and left.

I always knew that having expectations was just a way to set myself up for disappointments, but still . . . it *was* Valentine's Day.

It wasn't that he'd completely overlooked the holiday after asking me to spend it with him, so much as it was the final blow—him leaving his card, candy, and teddy bear sitting on my table. You live and you learn. And you don't spend Valentine's Day with someone who says, "What's up?" *every single time* he calls you. You're calling *me*, Dirk—*you're* the one who's supposed to know what's up.

But what a difference a guy makes. This was Christmas and this was Travis. I had typed and printed the Longfellow poem. My big plan was twofold. I was going to have the poem copied on parchment paper and then burn the edges to make it look like some lost (then found) document. An artifact. Maybe even the original Longfellow manuscript. If they'd had computers back then (I didn't have much choice of fonts). I bought an antique wooden frame for it that I thought would go perfectly in Travis's restaurant and I was going to surprise him with it.

I was also having the prototype made for a T-shirt that was going to be part of a cute little marketing plan I'd thought of for the Beacon. I know it was a case of putting the cart way before the horse, but it would be something that would make Travis smile and maybe keep him going with his plans on a day when he was struggling.

Travis and I had agreed that we'd exchange gifts when I got back from my parents'. By then I'd have already been to Kinko's and made my little arts-and-crafts project and I hoped that the T-shirt would be ready. The place I'd hired to make it was used to doing big runs of thousands of T-shirts, and when I came in wanting just one, they weren't too thrilled with me. Then again, they charged me a bloody fortune, because apparently the setup fees to silk-screen one shirt were the same as if they were making a thousand. So they really could have used an attitude adjustment.

I stopped by Kinko's first.

"Hi," I said to the distracted guy behind the counter. "I was wondering . . ." He just kept looking down at the register, concentrating on it like he was trying to split the atom. "Hi. Hello?" Still nothing. "Brandon?" Then he looked up.

"How'd you know my name?!" Brother.

"Uh, your name tag," I said and motioned to the pin he was proudly wearing.

"Oh. Cool. Hey." And then he actually looked back down and started to mess with the register again.

"Um . . . excuse me? Do you have a minute?"

"Me? Sure." As in so many situations in life, it turned out be a matter of asking the right question.

"Yeah. I was wondering if you could copy this poem onto some parchment paper. Or parchment-looking paper. It needs to fit in this frame, but I'll do that part."

"We don't do framing," he said.

"Right. That's what I said. I'll take care of that part myself."

"Okay, cool." And he went back to the register, this time pulling the paper-receipt spool out and inspecting *that*. Every time I go to Kinko's and I'm met with this kind of stuff, I always think that I am being punk'd.

"Brandon?" I repeated.

"Hey!" he said, as if we were long-lost friends.

"I still need to make that copy."

"Oh, okay. What can I help you with?"

"Okay . . . I need this piece of paper copied onto parchment-colored paper."

"Sure. No problem. Would you like that on Sandstone or Desert Haze? Me? I prefer Sandstone."

"Well, if you prefer it," I said, thinking maybe if he was working with his preferred paper it would speed up the process. I picked up my cell phone and dialed Travis, who was now number three on my speed dial. I told him that I was running a little late but that I'd meet him downstairs at his place in twenty minutes.

Then I called the T-shirt printing place. I told them I'd be there in ten minutes. They informed me that the shirt wasn't ready. This wasn't good. I tried my best to stay sweet and asked how much longer they needed. A couple of hours, it turned out—which sucked. I figured that I'd just meet Travis and give him the framed poem at dinner and then we'd take a walk after dinner and I'd surprise him with the shirt.

Brandon came back with the poem. It looked great, but I still needed to burn the edges to give it that antiquated, distressed look. I took it outside and started to set it on fire. Brandon watched from inside and his eyes widened when he saw me take the lighter to it. He ran out.

"Miss! Miss!" I looked up. "I could have done it on Desert Haze! Sandstone was just *my* preference. If you didn't like it, you could have said something. I could have redone it on Desert Haze."

I marveled at his sudden conversion to a customer-service power-house and explained what I was doing. A relieved Brandon made his way back into Kinko's and I continued to set the edges on fire and then quickly blow them out. By the time I was done it looked perfect. Well, not perfect but that was the point. It looked haggard and ancient and pretty close to what I'd wanted. I'd actually burned into one of the sentences but the last letters were still legible and I thought it added to the charm. I put it in the frame and set off to meet Travis.

\* \* \* \* \*

When a man makes reservations for himself and his new girlfriend at One if by Land Two if by Sea, people familiar with this landmark New York restaurant are inspired to remarkable heights of inappropriate suspicion.

"What, are you getting engaged?" Todd asked me testily without an excited smile when I told him. I rolled my eyes.

"You keep leaping to such far-fetched conclusions, you're going to pull your groin," I told him.

"I may end up doing that anyway," he mumbled.

"What was that?" I said, though I'd heard.

I realized that I needed to temper what I shared with Todd—a realization that of course came too late and left my stomach feeling like I'd just tried to outrelish that little Asian guy who wins the hot dog–eating contest every year: bloated and nauseated with my own insensitivity and all the by-products that came with it. But I wasn't *used* to keeping things from Todd. And because he was the only one that knew the truth, this newfound *awkwardness* between us was that much harder.

At Christmastime, the ever-present threat of a marriage proposal is only part of the spectacle at One if by Land. And as I stepped out of the cab, I spotted another and felt a pleasant little chill—the twinkling lights on the Christmas tree through the beribboned window across the street. The restaurant looked to have been built into an old coach house, and the twisty street that it resided on—so unlike the broad, plain avenues we'd just left behind—made it that much more cozy. It was freezing outside, a few snowflakes were even making an appearance, but the restaurant had a fireplace going and a toasty holiday atmosphere that felt like home—the homes I've seen in magazines and woodcuts on the first pages of Dickens and Jane Austen novels, anyway. At my parents' house, the fireplace was bricked in, painted off-white, and then covered by a porcelain peacock. Not charming, but definitely low-maintenance.

I walked in and clumsily busied myself with taking off my coat and looking for the coat check so it didn't look like I was looking for Travis. It was silly and insecure, but it was one of those hold-over old-Jordan behaviors that I hadn't forgotten yet. I don't know why, but I'd always felt uncomfortable walking into a restaurant or walking off an airplane if somebody was there waiting for me. Having that *searching* look on my face—a look that would be totally normal and acceptable in those circumstances—made me feel nervous. Exposed. Maybe it came from a fear that nobody would show up and the hopeful, expectant look would turn to the shamed, disappointed look and strangers would watch me turn from awaited lass to stood-up loser. A little grandiose to think that complete strangers would be paying that much attention to me and my facial expressions, I admit. But I found the coat check, which was right behind the maître d's station and also where Travis happened to be standing.

As soon as we sat down and before Travis even had a chance to butter his bread, I put the wrapped frame in front of him.

"What's this?"

"It's not a really big deal," I said. "And it's twofold. And the second fold isn't here. It wasn't ready. But it should be by the time we get done with dinner."

"You didn't even have to get me *one* fold," he said. "But I'm happy that you did."

"The truth comes out."

He laughed and waved his hand in front of his face. "I meant, just because it shows me that you've been thinking about me. Whatever it is, I'll cherish it forever."

"It's last Wednesday's *New York Post* with a wad of used chewing to-bacco in the sports pages."

"Hmm," he said. "Did you include a gift receipt?"

"Stop it. I've been thinking about you, all right. In fact, some of that thinking has generated, *in my humble opinion*, some really fun marketing ideas for your restaurant . . . which will be opening next Christmas at a lighthouse near you!"

"I was hoping for a summer blockbuster," he said, smiling.

"Sleeper of the summer, it is! So . . . you're going to need to advertise. Which is where I come very much in handy."

"One of the many ways," he added. "Do go on . . . "

"Well, it doesn't matter how good the food is if nobody knows about it. So a new restaurant needs good buzz. We need to get attention . . . you know, like, like a foghorn blasting your eardrums out."

"Sounds inviting."

"An invitation! Exactly. To everyone who walks into any of the quaint little gourmet food shops and gift shops that every little hamlet in the Hamptons is lousy with," I said.

"People who overspend on food," he said. "Perfect."

"The gourmet foodies get a coupon good for twenty dollars at that market or that store. That'll get us in with the owners. We also give invitations to everyone who gets on the Hampton Jitney."

"The bus to the Hamptons," he said, growing intrigued by degrees.

"And everyone who comes to the restaurant gets their jitney ticket paid for."

"Okay, okay. But is that our clientele?"

"New Yorkers who like to go to the Hamptons will appreciate the twenty bucks and will come back talking about this great new restaurant? Yep. That's them."

"I like it . . ." he said, smiling.

"And for fun, the first five hundred or so leave with a T-shirt. The front says 'I know where you ate last summer.'" He laughed. "Or something silly like that."

"No, I like *that*."

"And then the back has the restaurant's name, The Beacon, in big letters."

"Huge letters!" he echoed.

"Lighthouse sized!" I replied. "*Totally* phallic. People wear them out—*free* advertising, and then more people will want them, of course, so you'll start *selling* them. All the profits, by the way, can go to the light-house-restoration fund."

Travis was shaking his head in disbelief. "I can't believe you thought of all this."

"Please." I shrugged. "I was bored at work."

"You're brilliant."

"But wait! There's more!"

"Call now and you'll throw in a *second* advertising campaign, absolutely free?"

"Yes! Actually, no. But . . . I was looking up lighthouses on the Internet and I came across this . . . " I pushed the wrapped, framed poem toward him. "It's really beautiful, and it needed to be yours." He unwrapped it and just stared at it for a minute. Then he started to read it aloud.

" 'The rocky ledge runs far into the sea, / and on its outer point, some miles away, / the lighthouse lifts its massive masonry . . . ' " Then he put the framed poem facedown and, staring over my shoulder dreamily, continued to recite it word for word. I was stunned.

"I guess you *know* it," I marveled.

" 'The Lighthouse,' by Longfellow," he said, still quiet, somewhere between melancholic and deeply touched—I couldn't tell which. "My dad used to recite this poem all the time. I'm not kidding. It was the first thing I ever memorized when I was a kid. That and 'The Star-Spangled Banner.' "

"Wow! Then I done good?" I said, sensing now which way the wind was blowing.

"You done better than good," he said, and I could swear he was almost hoarse. "This is really . . . special. I love it."

He leaned in to kiss me and stopped just short of my face to look at me. Then he kissed me with a force that I wasn't used to. It wasn't even as much a physical thing as it was emotional. I felt more connected to him at that moment than I ever had. I could feel how much it meant to him—how much *I* was starting to mean to him. It was one of those kisses that speak volumes, that say what can't be said in words. I was so happy that I got nervous. This was becoming a habit. Every time I thought about how incredible Travis was, and how happy I was, I remembered that I'd been lying to him all this time and I actually got chest pains. I had to tell him. But how? I was going to have to think of something. I hated having this big secret from him. He was rereading the poem, oblivious to my inner turmoil, thank God.

"I'm going to put this right up front in the entrance of the restaurant."

"Which will give the customers something to read while they're waiting for a table because it's always so damned crowded!"

He looked at me intently. "Have I told you how crazy I am about you?"

"No, but if you had, I don't think I'd get tired of hearing it."

"Good, because I think you'll be hearing it a lot."

We sat there, our faces inches away from each other, when suddenly he lurched backward.

"What's wrong with me?!" he screeched, and then pulled a little gift-wrapped box out and put it in front of me. "I was so caught up in my present I didn't give you yours."

"Don't worry, I'm glad," I said. "I'm thrilled that you like it."

"Here. It's just a little something. Open it," he instructed. And I did. I pulled out the most delicate gold locket I'd ever seen. With a J inscribed on the front.

"It's a locket," he said.

"I see that," I said back. "It's beautiful." I opened it to see if there was anything inside and there was. A tiny picture of a lighthouse.

"Oh, I *love* it!" I said.

"That's just temporary. You can put anything you like in there."

"I wouldn't change this picture for anything in the world," I said quietly, and I felt I didn't want to joke with him anymore.

"I was hoping you'd say that." He beamed.

After dinner Travis and I enjoyed a brisk walk toward the East Village. I was guiding us in the direction of the printing shop, because I wanted to pick up his T-shirt and give it to him and the guy told me he'd be open late. I'd pretty much ruined the surprise already by telling him about it, but I was awful with surprises and he didn't know I'd actually gone and had one *made*.

It was true, though, about me being bad with surprises. I could never buy anyone gifts ahead of time because I prided myself on giving good gifts, and whenever I *had* purchased something particularly groovy, I'd get so excited that I'd need to give it to that person right then. Even if it was a month before the event that I'd bought the gift for. Then—being a person easily and often riddled with guilt—I'd end up having to buy *another* present for when the actual day rolled around, because I wouldn't want to show up empty-handed or risk that person having forgotten that I'd already given them a gift. So the added bonus of being a bad surprise giver is that it also gets really expensive.

I actually put a self-imposed time limit on when I'm allowed to shop for people—usually falling between three and five days before the occasion. The downside to this restriction is that it guarantees I'm smack-dab in the middle of the frantic last-minute Christmas shoppers, getting pushed and shoved out of the way of the discounted cashmere sweater that I don't even want but end up buying anyway because I now have a bruise of honor and I don't want to end up with nothing to show for it. Pretty much a lose-lose situation.

Anyway, we were cutting through Union Square, where the booths in the Christmas bazaar had been, when I spotted Dirk and some bimbette. I took a moment to see what I was feeling. Was I hurt? Angry? Sad? I watched him from about fifty feet away, imagining him pulling his charming Dirk tricks, telling choice stories from his best-of arsenal—all of which I knew from experience were certainly enchanting hearing for the first time or two or six.

And I was elated to find that I didn't feel *anything* as I watched him. Of course it was jarring to see him with another girl—especially since we hadn't broken up officially, so he was blatantly cheating on me once again. But, thankfully, this time I didn't care.

That didn't mean I wasn't going to fuck with him, though. It was too good an opportunity. The funny thing was, what I noticed *first* was a man in an ugly black Patagonia jacket with purple and green trim—and

I wondered who was in charge of the color palate at Patagonia and why people allowed them to get away with it. It was only when I got a better look that I realized it was Dirk. In a new jacket.

"Could you excuse me for a second?" I said to Travis, and then walked over to Dirk and Bambi.

"Hi, Dirk!" I said as chipper as can be. Dirk looked up and turned white. He dropped the girl's hand and ran his own through his hair.

"Jordan, hi!" he said.

I turned to Bambi and put out my hand and smiled. She took it, we shook, and Dirk looked like he wanted the earth to open up and swallow him.

"Hi. I'm Jordan. Maybe Dirk's mentioned me to you. I'm supposedly Dirk's *girlfriend*, at least Dirk thinks that I think I'm his girlfriend, but I have amnesia. Apparently he does *too* because he's forgotten that he's supposed to be my boyfriend and, well . . . he's here with you."

"Jordan . . ." Dirk said, but I ignored him and kept talking to the girl.

"I'm sorry to say this, but you'll probably wish you had amnesia too after spending any length of time with him. He's good for some laughs, though. Good luck."

"I'll call you tomorrow," he said out of the side of his mouth in a lame attempt to disguise it from her.

"Really, don't. You see that guy over there?" I was pointing to Travis. "He's the best thing that's ever happened to me, so you just carry on. This all works out nicely. You with . . ." I looked to Bambi.

"Jessie," she said.

"Perfect. You with *Jessie* and me with that handsome gentleman you see over yonder and everybody's happy."

"But—wha—" Dirk, stammered. "Can you excuse me for a minute?" he said to Jessie and then motioned for the two of us to move to a more private location, approximately four feet to the left.

"What is it, Dirk?" I asked.

"I'm sorry," he said, and he looked like he meant it, but I didn't see the point. "I am. It's totally nothing."

It was interesting. I knew he felt bad and I appreciated what limited remorse he was seeming to muster, but I honestly didn't care. "It's okay, Dirk," I said. "Really. Go on and enjoy your night."

"Seriously?" he asked hesitantly.

"Seriously," I reassured with a chuckle.

"But what does that mean for *us*?" he asked, still not quite getting it.

"What do you think it means, Dirk? There is no more *us*."

"You're *dumping* me?" He recoiled in shock.

I couldn't help smiling at him ruefully. "Don't make it sound so completely unwarranted or unexpected, my big, dumb animal. I think we can both recognize the awkward circumstance we've happened upon this evening."

"That," he said, meaning *Jessie*, "doesn't mean *anything*."

"Well, I'm sorry for *her*, then. Because, as I said . . . *that*"—and I motioned over to Travis—"means *a lot*. And right now isn't the time to have this conversation anyway."

"Baby, this is all a misunderstanding. We've gotten way offtrack. I swear to God I was just telling Mike and Joe in the office that I was going to propose to you on Christmas." What?!?!

"What?" I said in disbelief. "Where is this coming from? We haven't even been *seeing* each other."

"You know it's what you *want*. And it looks good for me workwise if I'm settling down. I'm so close to making partner early and I know if we get hitched it will be just the push I need. Win-win," he said, and then held up his index finger to Jessie, indicating that he'd be just *one* more teeny minute. Because he's pseudo-proposing to his girlfriend. But he'll be back in a jiffy and they can continue their *date*.

"Do you not see the many, *many* levels of wrong here?" I asked calmly.

"Think about it. I'll call you tomorrow?" he asked.

"No, Dirk. Why don't we just let some time go by and then if—and that's a really big freakin' *if*—but *IF* there's anything we need to talk about, we can. Take care."

And I walked back over to Travis, took his hand, and led him away from my past. Dirk looked after me completely dumbfounded. Jessie didn't look any too pleased herself. But me? I felt happy. There are probably so few moments in life when people can truly say they're happy. And even fewer of them when that happiness is acknowledged. I wanted to savor it. Breathe it in. Really *feel* it, because it was the first time in a long time that everything felt right.

"What was that about?" Travis asked.

"Oh, just some unfinished business," I said. He looked at me inquisitively and I added, "It's finished now."

"Good."

And without looking back, we walked toward the T-shirt print shop and Travis's place. I told Travis to walk ahead and meet me in front of his place. I said that the rest of his surprise was coming.

"Another surprise? This is like Christmas and my birthday rolled into one!" He closed his eyes again and held out his hands and I pushed him in the direction of his apartment building.

"Shoo! Off with you! I'll meet you there in five minutes." And he walked off and I continued on my way to the print shop.

When I got there, the shirt was all ready and waiting for me. It was perfect. He was going to be so excited. I paid the guy and told him that we'd probably be needing a lot more of them down the line, so don't lose the design. (I didn't want *anyone* to have to pay that setup fee again.) The guy said that they keep records and templates for three years and that whenever we needed them, they'd have them.

"So this Beacon place . . . it any good?" he asked.

I smiled knowingly. "It's gonna be the best restaurant ever."

\* \* \* \* \*

When I got to Travis's place he wasn't out front, so I rang the intercom bell, then called his cell phone. No answer either time. I walked in front of his building, figuring that he'd just run off for a minute and he'd be back any second.

I thought I saw his friend Ben walk into the building, but then I thought it couldn't be him because he didn't even say hi to me. In fact it

almost looked like the person scowled at me. I continued to wait, calling
Travis every so often but still getting no answer.

After about fifteen minutes an elderly couple was coming home so I
followed them into the building.

When I got to Travis's apartment door I could hear voices from inside. He was home? What was the deal? I wondered. It was Ben that I
heard first.

"I told you not to get involved with her, but no . . . you had *everything
under control.*"

I knocked on the door. It swung open, and I took about two steps in.
But nobody looked happy to see me.

"Hi. What happened? I had a surprise for you . . ."

"I already got my surprise," growled Travis. "Thanks."

"Why are you acting like this? What's wrong?"

"Not much. Except that I'm being *sued*!"

"Oh my God!" I exclaimed. "By who?!" Travis looked at me like I was
insane.

"By *you*!" he shouted.

"What are you *talking* about?" He thrust the papers in front of me. I
took them and looked at them and saw the words right there before me,
but I couldn't believe my eyes.

It was all there. I was suing Travis. But I'd had *nothing* to do with it. I
was absolutely 100 percent as shocked to see those papers as he probably
was.

"This is bullshit! Travis, I promise, I had nothing to do with this. You
have to believe me," I pleaded.

"And it was just a coincidence that you told me to wait out there
when I was served papers?"

"Yes! It was," I said. "I swear."

"Not likely," Ben threw in.

"Dude, why don't you take off? I can handle things from here," Travis
said to Ben.

"As your lawyer, I would rather be present for any dealings with the
plaintiff." Plaintiff? He was referring to me as *the plaintiff*?

"Your lawyer!?"

"Ben, really. I'll handle this."

"Call my cell if you need me," Ben said and then left. He almost clipped me on my shoulder as he walked out.

I tried to reason with Travis. "Travis. Look at me," I pleaded. "It *is* a coincidence! I was getting your surprise." I waved the T-shirt in front of him, which he had no interest in whatsoever. "I had no idea about any of this!"

"Well, regardless of how I actually *got* the papers, it says here that you're suing me. Jordan, if you do this," he said, and then finished the rest without even looking at me, as though I were no longer there, "I can't open my restaurant. I don't have time or money to deal with all this. Plus, my already way-too-expensive car insurance will skyrocket. And I'm trying to save up."

"I'm not suing you! I promise! I would never!" I practically screamed. "God, this is so crazy. This is obviously my mother's doing. She's been trying to talk me into suing you since day one. She even asked me to start going to physical therapy so it would better the case—which I *didn't* do, by the way!"

He looked up. "And now, even to get a lawyer to defend against this—"

"And your lawyer? Ben? I heard you guys talking when I was at your door. What's his problem?"

"Same as mine now," he said, and then shifted his feet ever so slightly. "He never thought we should have gotten involved. He just wanted me to smooth things over originally. Just in case. He was looking out for my best interests."

Now *I* was pissed.

"Oh . . . I get it. It was just damage control all along? I had no intention of suing you, but *you,* on the other hand manipulated me into your little plan? 'Oh, you're so great, let's go to my romantic lighthouse, blah, blah, blah . . .' and I fell for it, hook, line, and sinker. Was this all just to make sure I didn't sue you?"

"Well, if it was, it sure didn't work—*did* it?"

"I can't believe you!"

"I can't believe *you*!" he said. I threw the shirt at him. He pulled it off his head and looked at it. He could see that it was the shirt I'd described at dinner, that I'd actually had it made. And there he was, standing there with the T-shirt in one hand and the subpoena in the other. But he said nothing. So I turned around and walked out.

\* \* \* \*

The minute my feet hit the pavement outside Travis's apartment I lost it. It was too much to even wrap my head around. I'd been worrying about how to tell him I'd never lost my memory—creating little scenarios in my head for coming clean about the whole thing and how he'd react and how I'd defend myself and how we'd ultimately work it out—but never in my little fantasies had a lawsuit filed by my mother entered the equation. I walked with two fingers in my mouth to keep from sobbing out loud and the other hand across my eyes to keep strangers from seeing them. From the side, I must have looked as though I was trying to twist my head off.

I *hated* my mother. *Hate* didn't even seem strong enough. *Loathed.* Was *loathe* worse than *hate*? *Despise? Detest? Deplore? Deplore* wasn't very strong. Generic hate would have to do. Leave it to her to take a perfectly good pretend case of scrambled consciousness and make it a *real* case of scrambled consciousness. Every chance she got.

I was walking down McDougal Street bawling my eyes out, literally wailing like a little baby, when something dawned on me (besides how stupid I looked and how badly I was embarrassing myself): It felt as though this was all happening *to* me. My modus operandi was to be the victim. Everything happened *to* me, people did things *to* me, I was suffering because he did that and she did this. But nothing was ever my fault. And that was all very convenient for the old Jordan because the old Jordan didn't take responsibility for anything.

Now that was forgotten. I had to figure out what *my* part was in it and what I could do to try to fix it. It was time to shed the victim status and stop subscribing to the belief that everything happened *to* me. Things just happened. And it was my job to turn things around—not sit back and take it as though I were a bystander in my own life.

I'd faked amnesia. Yes. Signed the paper giving my mother power of attorney? Check. But I *hadn't* granted her permission to bulldoze the beautiful, if slightly dishonest, relationship I was developing with Travis.

As I walked home, I thought about things my mom had done in the past, arguments we'd had, slammed doors and slammed phones . . . and I remembered a conversation I'd once had with Cat when she asked me why I had *anything to do* with my mother.

The answer was totally obvious to me: "Because she's my *mother*."

"What does that mean?" she said and added, "and don't give me biological statistics." Cat wasn't overly sentimental, and as far as she was concerned, just because someone shares the same blood as you doesn't give her the right to be an asshole. And her corollary to that rule was "Life's too short to deal with assholes that aren't paying you, and even *they* have limits."

"It means I love her, and she's the only mother I have," I said. And while it was still true at that second, I couldn't help feeling like I'd been somehow shortchanged in the mom department, and it certainly wasn't the first time I'd felt that way.

So that was the old me. Did the new me still feel that way? Did the new me subscribe to the belief that you don't have to have a relationship with someone who doesn't respect you—even if that person is your mother? I didn't know the answer, but I *did* know I was going to call the woman and demand some face-to-face time so I could figure it out. That and get her to cut out this lawsuit crap.

When I got back to my apartment I was emotionally spent. I fell onto my bed in a pathetic heap and heard a crinkle, rolling over only to find it was a printout of the lighthouse poem. Travis. That was the other variable. Besides being furious at my mother, there was the whole Ben-is-my-lawyer—you-are-guilty-until-proven-innocent—by-the-way-I'm-no-longer-that-perfect-guy-you've-been-falling-in-love-with-I'm-a-COMPLETE-ASSHOLE thing.

What was up with the Ben thing? Maybe Travis *wasn't* the guy I'd thought he was all along. Maybe he was just some jerk covering his ass so he didn't end up in a lawsuit. I didn't even remember going to sleep. I just cried and cried and when I opened my eyes it was the next morning. I called my mom and asked that she meet me for lunch. I forgot to be stern at first, given how angry I was at her—it was the old Jordan calling—but then she started to hesitate, and then I didn't ask anymore. I *told* her to be there. And after agreeing reluctantly, she was in the middle of upbraiding me when I hung up.

# 23.
# power(less) of attorney

When I got to the Blue Water Grill my mother was already seated and drinking. I imagined she was on her second "Whatever your best merlot is" with several more to come.

"Hi, Mom," I said with venom, and took the empty seat. The one facing the wall. I know you need to respect your elders and all that, but my mom *always* demanded she sit "facing out" so that she could have the nice view. I'm sure that's proper etiquette in dating—the man allows the woman to face out, but is there a rule that states your mother always faces out? I'm an adult female, which would mean that we're *both* women, no? So why did she always get the good seat? "Thanks for meeting me."

"It sounded urgent," she said as she sipped. "What*ever* could be so important?"

"You filed a lawsuit on my behalf against Travis."

"Travis?" she said, acting confused. Like she had to place the name. And there it was—right pinky to the bangs. A few pushes of the hair out of the eyes, and then the fingers would run in a line to the rear of her head, as though they were looking for an exit. The telltale part, I'd come to call it. The unmistakable sign that Mom was lying.

"Yes, Mom," I said in a tone she probably hadn't ever heard from me. "Travis. The guy you filed the lawsuit against. Unless there's more than one lawsuit you've filed on my behalf?"

"No, dear. Just the one. Sorry . . . I just didn't know his name off-hand." Bullshit.

"Well, you have to unfile it," I demanded.

"I'm sorry, Jordan," she said in an almost apologetic tone, "but we can't do that."

"I'm not suing him," I insisted. "Whatever you did. Undo it. Cancel it."

"No," she said.

It was a simple answer—one she'd told me all my life without any qualifications. It was never, "No, because of this . . ." or "No, and here is *why.*" It was always just plain "no." And I guess, as my mother, she had had the right to say no to many things throughout my life. Like when I asked to be an only child again at the age of eleven, five years after Samantha was born. ("No.") Or when I asked if I could have my own apartment at the age of fourteen, because she was constantly yelling at me for playing my music too loud and having my own pad would solve the problem. ("No.") Or at fifteen, when we'd gone to London for vacation, and I asked to have wine with dinner and argued (truthfully) that the United Kingdom stipulated that alcohol could be consumed (in the home) from age five with parental consent. ("You're working my last nerve, Jordan.")

And, fine—she had every right to nix those requests. But this was different. I was an adult. This was my life. And even though it had technically *been* my life since I'd turned eighteen, my life had really only become *my own* the day I got in that accident. And, as such, I needed more information before I could know how to respond.

" 'No,' what, Mother? 'No' . . . why? What's your reason?" I asked in as calm a tone as I could.

"We are suing him and that is the end of the story." She took a big gulp of her wine and motioned to the waiter that she'd be needing a refill by tapping her fingernail against the glass. "It's all filed. The ball is already in motion. There is a lawsuit taking place, and that is that."

"Okay." I said. "That much I understand. Yes, currently there is a lawsuit between him and me, but *I didn't file it* and I *don't want to sue him,* so I'm asking you to stop it. I'm fine."

"You are *not* fine, Jordan. You have amnesia!"

"Well, I *like* it, okay? So stop the lawsuit."

"No, I won't. I'm your mother and I care for you and this is best and you're not in any shape to make this decision." The waiter came over and refilled her glass.

"I'm not asking you to do this. I'm telling you to. I'm an adult. You can't file a lawsuit for me. I can stop it myself, but you did it with your lawyer, so just undo it."

"No. I won't. *We* are suing him. And while you may be an adult, you aren't 'all there' since the accident. Listen to yourself. You *like* having lost your memory? Do you even know what you're saying? I *doubt* you do. I am your legal guardian and as such have power of attorney, which now, in its most literal sense, gives me the power to hire an attorney."

She had a point. As far as she was concerned, I was gravely injured and grossly wronged, and she was trying to protect me and punish the person who'd inflicted this on me. But that didn't stop me from freaking out.

"You can't do this!"

"I've done it, dear. As I said, the ball's in motion."

"Well, stop the ball," I said, in a decidedly non*inside* voice. "Stop the fucking ball!"

"Jordan, watch your mouth!" A few people turned and looked in our direction. Tears welled up in my eyes, blurring my mom from my vision, which I was thankful for, because I couldn't stand to even look at her.

"Mom, *please!*" I urged. "You *have* to stop it. Please! I'm begging."

"Sorry, dear."

And I stared back at her, shooting paring knives since no daggers were at hand. "So, now I'm back in the cramped, hideous, Judith Landau dungeon that I suffered eighteen years to escape!" An amnesiac probably wouldn't have had that level of prepossession or pent-up anger, so I quickly added, "If *this* episode is any guide."

She slammed her napkin to the table. "That's a *terrible* thing to say."

"I'm sorry," I said. "I'm just—I just. You can't do this. Please listen to me. This is my life you're messing with. I'm not that hurt. Really and truly. I'm fine. And I'll find a way to undo this or die trying. He's important to me. And if you drag him to court, you'll spoil all his dreams."

"*His* dreams? What do I care about his dreams? I'm sorry, Jordan, but he's not my concern. You are."

"Then do this for *me*," I begged.

"I *am*, dear. You just don't have the clarity to see it right now." The waiter came over with menus. As he put them down, I got up.

"I'm not staying." My mom sipped her drink and shrugged at the waiter. "And I'll go see the lawyer myself."

* * * * *

I stormed out of the restaurant, picturing alternating images of my mom's and Travis's faces as I stomped on an imaginary game of hopscotch. I pulled out my cell and called Cat.

"I hate my mother," I said.

"Well, you weren't her biggest fan before either," Cat answered.

"She's killing me! She's suing Travis. How can she *do* this?"

"She thinks that she's doing the right thing, as twisted as that may sound."

"Don't take her side," I spouted.

"I'm not. I'm just saying—"

"She trapped me. I thought I could go and tell her to stop it, and she would and then everything would be okay. Now what do I tell him? I'm sorry but I'm suing you and there's nothing I can do about it?"

"It sucks, I know . . . but . . . yeah. That's the truth, right?" It was hard for me to even know *what* the truth was anymore. "You guys were really hitting it off, huh?"

"He's caring, considerate, interesting, ambitious, funny, smart—the anti-Dirk," I said. "Well, he *was*."

I gave her the quick and dirty rundown of the Ben situation.

"Isn't that a little sketchy?" she asked, almost reading my mind.

"I don't know. It looks bad. But if Ben is a lawyer, that's what he knows how to do."

"Make people hate each other?" she joked.

"No," I said. "We do that well enough on our own. Something tells me Travis was the real deal."

"Wow," Cat said. "That's quite an endorsement. We talking marriage material?"

"I don't know." I sighed. "He seemed to have all kinds of potential to be my awfully wedded husband someday . . . "

"Did you hear what you just said?" Cat asked excitedly.

Shit, I thought. I'd slipped again. I'd said *awfully wedded*. When we were kids we'd misunderstood wedding vows as *awfully* wedded instead of *lawfully* wedded. When Todd and I married, lo those many years ago, we'd even said it in the ceremony, thinking we were saying it correctly. I decided to just play dumb.

"What?" I asked, all wide-eyed and clueless.

"You said 'awfully wedded.' That's our inside joke! You remembered!"

"I did?"

"Yeah!" she said. "Oh my God, you're getting your memory back! Have you had anything else like this happen?"

"I . . . I don't know. Maybe it *is* coming back." Cat sounded so happy I didn't want to ruin it by pretending it was a fluke. I let her think it was coming back to me. Which was like choosing which lie fit the moment better. Or which dress to wear to your own funeral. Not fun.

But the more I thought about it, the better it sounded. If I got my memory back, then my mom wouldn't have guardianship over me and I could fix everything.

\* \* \* \* \*

I stopped by the office and was immediately struck by the lack of chaos. Granted, it was pretty much empty, save for the idiots like me who came in of their own free will over the holiday break, but I couldn't seem to shake that distinct calm-before-the-storm feeling. I didn't know if it was my own turmoil over my memory experiment starting to bubble over and burn me or if it was something else that lay in wait behind a midheight cubicle wall. I walked dead center down the hallways, looking side to side cagily.

The old Jordan wouldn't have been caught dead in the office over vacation, but after the Christmas break we'd be pitching the Rinaldi Coffee Company ideas for their new coffee press, and, although I had a good handle on my pitch, I wanted to make sure it was my best work yet. Just a few days before Christmas I'd come up with the tagline from heaven: "Get rich quick." There was no way Rinaldi wouldn't love it, I thought, and coming off my VibraLens heat this was just the thing to keep myself in the game as a major up-and-comer. All I had to do was work out a few different versions for my pitch.

But I couldn't focus. Not on anything other than Travis. The committed effort to blank my mental slate and get down to work kept devolving like this: I saw a rubber band on the floor and bent down to pick it up, which gave me a slight head rush, which made me touch my forehead, which made my shirtsleeve brush my locket, which made me think of Travis. So I tipped my mouse pad up on its edge to shake off the accumulated crumbs and shavings and who knows what else, and as they fell to the floor, some particles caught the light and sparkled a little, which reminded me of the snow falling through the nimbus of the streetlight in front of the restaurant where just two nights before we were . . . Shit.

Every time I tried to sketch out an idea, I'd unconsciously draw Travis and Jordan stick figures. Happy Travis and Jordan. Angry Travis. Jordan apologizing. Travis accepting. Travis not accepting. Jordan crying. Travis and Jordan flying a kite. Not sure why. I wound up with seven pages of strip-cartoon blocks playing out all the different scenarios of how we might resolve the mess, had we both been born stick figures.

When it was finally clear to me that I wasn't going to get anything done with work or anything else until I fixed things with Travis, I decided to pack it up and take the direct approach to fixing my life. And there was only one person who could help me now. I tucked my budding cartoon strip into my bag and took off.

* * * * *

I practically ran over to Todd's apartment. I knew that if anyone could help me find a way out of my mess, it was Todd. And even though his declaration of his feelings had knocked all the stuffing out of our codependent, mildly misguided friendship for a while, I knew we'd eventually get past it, and I needed him right then.

In the movie version of my life, I wouldn't have even made it all the way to Todd's before Travis tracked me down—totally out of breath—and declared his love for me.

In the *real* version of my life, I arrived at Todd's place, sans any grand gestures along the way, and was greeted by an unshowered Todd, who was not entirely happy to see me.

"Who comes to my lair uninvited?" he called out as he opened the door.

"It's me," I said sheepishly.

"Hi, me. To what do I owe this surprise?"

"I need your help," I said. "I know, I suck. I'm a selfish asshole and I should respect your feelings and leave you alone for now . . ."

"Agreed," he said and started to shut his door.

But I nudged my way past him. "However . . ." I said as he rolled his eyes, "this whole thing *was* your idea."

His mouth popped wide open.

"Well, what if it *had* been? You'd feel like hell right now, and you'd know how I feel." His mouth closed. "You're the only one who can help me. You're the only one who knows the truth. And the only one I trust."

He motioned for me to sit on his couch, and after I moved the two empty boxes of cereal and a leaning tower of *Adweek* magazines, I found a spot. About the fact that he was watching *Baywatch* in *Spanish*, I said nada.

"What's the crisis?" he asked.

I told him the whole long, sordid story about my swamp-beast mother and the lawsuit and the fight between Travis and me and my suspicion that maybe I was being had all along but I hoped in my heart that I hadn't been because I was feeling so happy with things, which taken together must have sounded like knitting needles to Todd's ears.

"Yeah," he said with an exhale so big I caught a whiff of his lunch. McDonald's, I thought. "You're in a pickle, all right."

"I have to fix it."

"So fix it," he said flatly. The lack of warmth was to be expected, I suppose, but it still stung.

"I *had* it all planned out. I thought I would just come clean . . ."

"Good. You *should* come clean. I hated this idea from the beginning."

"I know you did," I said. "I slipped up in front of Cat again—*another* person I'm betraying."

"Yeah, Jordan, the whole thing was . . . I don't even *know* what the word is. *Dishonest* comes to mind. Also *devious*." He thought for a moment. "And *shitty*. The fact that you pulled it off even for this length of time is the *only* impressive thing about it."

"Okay, I get it. You hate me. But can you table that for five minutes?"

"Tabled," he said.

"If I come clean that I never had amnesia, then there's no case and my puppeteer mother watches all the strings get cut out from under her. Plus, I can demonstrate I have all my faculties so she can't be my guardian anymore."

"Good. Do it. What do you need *me* for?"

"Todd, I *can't*! I'm supposed to just *tell* Travis that I didn't have amnesia and I've been faking this whole time? Lying to him? And all the guilt that he's felt . . . I mean, he's been feeling really bad about it . . . So I'm supposed to just come clean? And then he's miraculously going to say, 'Great! Let's put that silly amnesia stuff behind us and live happily ever after'? No! He's going to freak out. And be even more pissed that I lied to him. And probably think that I'm NUTS!"

"*Well*"—he threw his hands in the air—"you are."

"Thanks."

"Don't mention it," he said, and unmuted his television.

"I'm not nuts," I defended. He didn't even speak Spanish. He'd rather listen to a language he didn't understand than me—a girl he didn't understand. On second thought, maybe he knew exactly what he was doing.

"Right," he said, watching a surprise scene of someone frolicking a little *too* far from shore. "*Sane* people fake amnesia every day. Look, Jordy, you know I love you. And I don't mean that kind of love right now. I mean, you know I care about you . . . with all of your crazy little quirks and harebrained schemes. But this whole amnesia thing was a really crazy stunt."

"Well, I need your help."

"You keep saying that, but you haven't told me what it is that you want me to do."

"I need to find my memory," I said.

"Huh?"

"I lost it. Now I need to find it."

"Okay," he said and then waved his hands in front of my face. "Poof! You have your memory back. See how easy that was?"

"No, I need to regain it in front of Travis. I can't just say, 'Oh God! It was here all along' "—and I reached into my coat pocket and pulled out my glove—" 'right where I left it, see?' Plus, it'll be a chance to make him feel better about the whole thing. He was there the first time, he thinks it was his fault; he's been feeling guilty. This way, he'll be there when I get it back, so he's kind of like a witness again, almost a hero, and it's all come full circle. He won't feel bad anymore and everything will be better." Todd looked at me like he was waiting for the rest of the plan. "So I need to get hit in the head."

"Okay, I'm sold," he said and he looked around the room. "Do you want to put your head through a wall, or should I grab a vase or something?"

"*Pretend* hit in the head, like in wrestling on TV."

"That's actually quite real," he insisted. "But what are you brewing up here?"

"We need to stage some kind of fake accident. Like you can throw a flowerpot off a balcony."

Todd got up off the couch and started pacing manically. "Oh my God. Tell me you didn't just say that. A flowerpot? Seriously?"

"Well . . . yeah . . . ?"

"Okay, Wile E. Coyote, supergenius. Why not just make it an *anvil*?"

"Meep, meep?" I offered meekly.

"*Jesus!*" He exhaled.

"I'm serious. Hear me out. You throw the flowerpot. I'll fall down *next* to it, pretend it hit my head and black out for a second. And then when I get up, I'll remember everything. Nobody will ever know the difference."

"Then we break for a Cap'n Crunch commercial? You really *are* nuts. I mean it. Don't you think that's a little above and beyond? This huge elaborate ruse . . . for what?"

"For *me*?"

Todd looked at me and squinted a couple times. "No," he said. "I'm sorry, Jordy. You're on your own. I'm *out* of the fake-amnesia business."

"Okay," I said. "I understand. I do."

This moment was punctuated by David Hasselhoff saying, "Adiós, mujer," to Pamela Anderson in what appeared to be her last episode.

I was on my own. I'd instinctively reached out for the person who'd always been there for me, but I'd overreached with him too many times, and this was just too much of a stretch for him. It somehow never felt like lying—none of it, as bad as it got—if Todd knew. But suddenly I felt very sad and incredibly selfish. I shouldn't have asked, and Todd was right to reject me. No one was going to help me out of this; I was just going to have to brave it alone.

*   *   *   *   *

I mentally prepared myself for the deposition as best I could. Clearly, it would be a simple matter of declaring my self-sufficiency—and doing it in such a way that wouldn't suggest I was hysterical and crazy. The very phrase "I'm not incompetent" probably suggests just the opposite in certain contexts. Like this one. What's more, Travis would be waiting for me inside, and with my mom bound to spew her usual venom disguised by sickly sweet helplessness and wonderment at the legal machinery moving forward, there was a good chance that things weren't going to go as I'd have liked. Even knowing this, I was still completely undone

by the steely-eyed glare Travis focused on me as I walked into the law office conference room.

My mom was already there, hair teased up more than usual, seated
at one side of the table, next to a woman whom I recognized from the
early barrage of interrogations at the hospital and now assumed to be our
lawyer. Travis sat to the far left of her, along with Ben and some other
guy, a little older, paunchy, and red faced, with little strands of brown
hair sweeping upward to his bald spot, as if worshipping it. He was the
first to speak, and after some terse instructions were laid out, I was sworn
to the whole truth and nothing but (I set my hand on the Bible gingerly,
fearing a terrible shock or searing heat from the fire of eternal perdition),
and the thing began.

"I'm Adam Manning, and I represent the defendant," he said, and I
watched as the court reporter sat off to the side taking notes on her little
machine.

"Hi," I said. I looked at Travis, but he wouldn't look back at me.

"Please state your full name and spell it out for the record," Adam
Manning said.

"Jordan Landau. J-o-r-d-a-n L-a-n-d-a-u."

He asked me how old I was, where I lived, what I did for work. He
asked me a bunch of mundane questions and I answered, looking in
Travis's direction every so often, only to find him squeezing his fist open
and closed and staring into his lap.

"Please take me back to the date of the accident," he said. "What time
of day was it?"

"Afternoon." I knew from watching countless episodes of *Law and
Order* (truly the *Three's Company* of today for the sheer impossibility of
turning on your TV without landing on one of its reruns) that I was supposed to answer only what was asked.

"Where were you?"

"New York."

"Where in New York?"

I told him. We established, over the course of the next several minutes, that I'd been riding my bike in the rain.

"Was there traffic around you?" he asked.

"I guess. It *is* Manhattan."

"Do you use drugs?" he asked.

"No," I said, taken aback by the sudden turn in the questioning.

"Were you using drugs the day you drove into my client's car?"

"Objection," my lawyer said. "Draws a conclusion based on facts not in evidence here. She didn't drive into the car. He opened his car door into her."

"I'll rephrase. Were you—"

"No, I wasn't using any drugs," I said again.

"How much money do you make a year?" he asked me. I didn't know why it mattered and I was a little—okay, a *lot*—embarrassed about my salary.

"I make about thirty-five thousand a year. But I just got a promotion and my salary is increasing."

"Is it true that you're on the verge of bankruptcy?"

"Bankrup—" I looked at my mother's lawyer imploringly. But she blinked slowly, as if secretly signaling me to share it all.

Manning resumed, his head cocked far to one side. "Is it true that you have several collection agencies calling you regularly?"

"Yes."

"Would you say that you have a significant amount of debt?"

"I have *some* debt."

"Would you say that you need money?"

"Who *doesn't*?" I asked. Ben rolled his eyes and wrote something on a piece of paper and slid it over to Travis. I desperately wanted to know what it said, but I had to pay attention to the guy doing the questioning, whose head was now cocked so far to one side that I was starting to get sympathy pains in my neck. It didn't help that I found myself tilting my own head slightly just to maintain eye contact with him.

"Is it true that you don't even have an injury? That you're here today *not* because you're injured but because you need money?"

"No! Absolutely not. I don't even want to *be* here."

"Is it true that you're aware of Travis's finances and you're doing this for the money? That you didn't start this lawsuit until you knew what he had in his savings for his future business endeavor?"

"No," I said, on the verge of tears.

"Please tell me when you lost your memory."

"After the accident."

"But you remember the car door opening in front of you. You want us to believe that you lost all your memory for events that happened before the accident but you remember the *accident*?"

"I remember the accident," I replied, now so thoroughly confused that if my opportunity to establish my competency had landed in my lap, I wouldn't have noticed.

"Did you remember that you owed a lot of *money*?"

Had Travis put him up to this? Ben? I felt like I was going to throw up. "No," I said.

We took a short break so they could put in a new tape, and when we resumed it was *Travis* getting deposed.

"Please state your name and spell it for the record," our lawyer said. Then she started inching through his personal history, and I was bored by it but incensed enough not to be able to tear myself away.

"Have you ever been involved in a car accident before?" our lawyer asked.

"Object to the form," Manning said. "You may answer."

"Once, when I was seventeen," Travis said.

"Have you ever been sued before?"

"No," Travis said.

"Where do you live?"

"East Seventeenth Street."

"Do you live alone?"

"Yes," Travis answered.

"Are you married?" our lawyer asked.

"Objection," Ben spoke up, and Manning gave him a sidelong look. "Relevancy."

"I'm just establishing living situation," our lawyer responded. "It's a deposition, Ben. You can have it stricken if the objection is borne out, but this is just background stuff."

Ben looked at Travis.

"Are you married?" our lawyer repeated.

"Yes," Travis said.

# 24.
# the best laid plans
# and all that . . .

Take all of the hypothetical, overimaginative, nonsensical possible outcomes to the deposition, multiply them by sixteen, and then add in about five thousand other scenarios—nowhere in that vast panorama did I envision the prospect that the major finding would be a wife. For the defendant.

I was stunned, repulsed, saddened, infuriated. They say grief progresses through phases of shock, denial, anger, and acceptance. I'm not sure of the estimated arrival and departure times for each jaunt, but in this case, I tore through the entire itinerary, leaped clean over acceptance and made it back to shock before the court reporter's fluid fingers had hit the keys on yes. And that revelation was compounded by the fact that when Travis revealed the unthinkable, he looked at me and I'm pretty sure he smiled, a kind of flat smile, like he was introducing her to me. Some introduction.

I was upset before, understandably. He didn't seem to have enough faith in me to believe that I had nothing to do with filing the lawsuit. That was one thing. But I figured we'd work that out. That was a hiccup. A glitch. A silly misunderstanding.

This—this was another story. One that seemed to be jumping straight to "the end." Married? How in the world was that possible? What loving

God would allow that to be true? And in the tiny fissures opening between the shock and anger and denial, why hadn't I had even the slightest inkling that it was coming?

Then it hit me. Karma. I was being punished for my experiment. I'd taken to calling it an experiment because it seemed somehow less offensive. But not to whomever called the shots in the realm of Karmic Retribution, apparently. There, high on the mountain, it was known by a term as old as the human ability to give voice to thought. Lying. My pants off. Had I done this to myself? I wondered.

My mother took that shocking admission as her cue to push her chair back from the table at an angle and disengage from the deposition. Which was good, because this little movement distracted me from the certainty that I was about to pass out. If there were an audible sound that went along with a heart breaking it would have drowned out all the lawyer-speak that went on as we gathered our things and left the conference room. In one instant I saw my future with Travis disappear. In this model it was his fault, but in another it could have easily been mine. He could have found out I was faking and told me to make like my memory and get lost. But then I'd have had the opportunity to beg his forgiveness. To explain and grovel and . . . something. But this took it out of my hands completely. There was nothing I could say to explain his wife away. No amount of pleading or good deeds could reverse it.

*His wife.* I hated those words. Hated the pictures, too, that sprung into being—wedding, moving in together, laundry mingled in one hamper, groggy searches for toothbrushes on brittle mornings, warm embraces. The phone answering machine message:

SHE: Hi, this is Moojie Moo—

HE: And Travis . . .

SHE: We're not home right now . . .

HE: But leave a message . . .

SHE: And sure as the sunrise, we'll get back to you soon!

BOTH: Tee-hee!

ME: *Barf*.

How could he have forgotten to mention that one crucial detail? I couldn't help wondering what she was like. How'd they meet? Were they happy? They couldn't be. He had his own apartment. Or did he? Was he separated? Did they have kids? Was there life insurance with mutual beneficiary agreements involved? The questions raced through my mind at a dizzying pace. Just *how dumb* had I been?

*   *   *   *   *

Outside, I could barely breathe. Partially because it was so cold that the air stung with every inhalation but mostly because of the gut punch. My mom had offered to take me home, but I shooed her away, not wanting to be anywhere near her. It was one of those times that a girl really *wants* her mom too. I just didn't want the one I had.

Cold as it was, I was in no hurry to get home. I walked from the business district through various neighborhoods, finally winding up in the West Village watching some kids playing ball across the street, shouting, chasing, celebrating the mindless abandon of being kids. How lucky they were, to have no idea of the bullshit they had in front of them. Life was hard.

If I knew what being a grown-up was all about, I'd have milked every second of my youth. I'd have watched a little less TV, for one thing. And ignored more requests for help around the house. Not that chores are bad, but my sister had consumed the equivalent of both our childhoods in chore avoidance. Wistfully, with perfect hindsight, I thought in that moment that I'd have found this very playground and a game like this. One boy in particular looked back at me furtively, pretending not to notice me just a stone's throw away. He was red-faced in the cold, and his head seemed to be popping out of his coat from the immense pressure his collar exerted. When someone would charge at him, he would dodge and fall, then scramble up and quickly look back to see if I was still there.

And I was, stepping a little closer to the low fence without even thinking about it, dazed, sad, lost again, looking around me to see that this place wasn't home, not anymore, not hearing even the raucous rising tide of their voices when they shouted something I never heard. Until it was too late.

"Look out!"

There was only a wailing in the distance, like a siren, getting closer and closer and closer. Until I figured out it was my own voice.

# 25.
# who are you? take two

Eyebrows. Eyebrows were everywhere. Arched and in different variations of concern, above eyes I didn't recognize, set in faces I didn't know, peering at me through a funnel. The walls of the funnel were dimly white and soft blue, and pain was everywhere, throbbing in the faces that seemed more startled by me than I was by them.

"Honey, honey?" someone said, but it sounded more like "hoingy, hoingy." "Baingy, baingy," another voice said—"baby, baby" apparently—and "Norggin, norggin?" which I couldn't make out. Other variations on that pleading, nothing I could decipher. I reached up to poke the water out of my ear but couldn't move my right arm. Then I realized I couldn't *see* my right arm. Or feel it.

I looked around through hairline slits in my eyelids at the five people behind the faces, one in a white coat, and I had no idea what any of them were doing there—save for Whitecoat, who I assumed was the boss. The TV mounted in a corner and barely visible to me was playing a scene in a room with a bed and white and blue walls and people all around peering at the person in the bed, which made the situation all the more surreal. A hospital room in a hospital room. And a white coat that contained a doctor.

"Her CAT scan shows no internal bleeding," Whitecoat said quietly, probably so that I couldn't hear (but I did, the water seeming to clear out of my ears somewhat), to some of the other people as they looked at me with their arms tightly crossed and thumbs pressing up on their chins, "which is lucky since she was hit in the occipital region."

"Which is what?" a narrow woman said. "What does that mean?"

"That means it's not as protected by the skull," explained Whitecoat.

"But she's okay?" asked a skinny guy with a vein sticking out of his forehead and a T-shirt that read: WHO WOULD JESUS SUE?

"Well, that's relative," said Whitecoat. "She didn't suffer a hematoma, but what's happened is called a coup-contracoup injury. That happens when the brain is shaken from the back to the front and then back again."

"Jesus!" said Jesus Litigator aptly.

"But, as before, there's no discernible brain damage and I would deliver a very positive prognosis, except the—the lack of response, is . . . troubling . . ." Whitecoat trailed off.

Narrow Woman stood there, shaking her head.

"I just . . . It's remarkable," Whitecoat then said to no one. "The coincidence . . . and I've seen reinjuries before, but I've never seen one like this before."

"Meaning?" a little voice said.

"The course of the condition is always unpredictable, but this really amplifies the butterfly effect," he replied. "We'll monitor closely, but there's really no telling where this will go."

"Well, what does this mean?" asked Narrow Woman, a tiny thing in her early fifties who looked like she spent every waking hour with a personal trainer. Her hair was short and highlighted, and she was wearing what looked like a cashmere track suit.

There was Other Woman—just as tiny—who looked almost identical to the first woman, only this one was much younger, college age. It was frightening how much they looked alike. I figured they must be related. Then there was a man behind them, older, with thinning black hair that swept in every direction around his head. He hung back, but his eyebrows and eyes I remembered most, because they were squinting and he never seemed to look away. He was taller than them (which wasn't hard because they were extremely small people), and he was the only one who smiled at me when the three of them first walked into the room and joined Whitecoat.

"So wait—what happened?" asked Younger Clone.

"She's got amnesia," said Smiling Man.

"I *know*, Dad," the girl said as she rolled her eyes.

"No . . . *again*," the father clarified.

"So . . . then what did she forget exactly? The last month? Is it possible Jordan will forget that she's forgotten everything and just be normal?" That was the mini-me again.

Nobody had addressed me directly yet, so I tried to speak up. At first it was a terrific struggle to separate my tongue from the roof of my mouth, like separating a stack of magazines that have dried together after a spill. After clicking and murmuring for a while, which made them hush and lean closer, I managed a whispered word.

"H-ha-hi." They all looked at me. I looked at the tiny woman, who leaned closest. "Who are you?"

"Here we go again," said the young one.

"I'm your mother," said the narrow woman in cashmere. "This is your sister, Samantha, and this is your father." I scanned the three of them for something familiar, but I felt nothing. I had no idea who these people were. I wondered if I looked exactly like them too.

"Mirror?" I asked. Both my supposed mother and sister reached into their handbags, pulled out matching compacts, and thrust them toward me. I looked into the one closest, which was my mother's. I looked *nothing* like these people. I mean, not at all.

"You're my family?" I asked. I *was* lying in a hospital bed so I couldn't tell exactly how tall I was, but looking down at myself I guessed I was at least a little taller than these women, who were like five feet, five foot two *maybe*. And they looked like they never ate. There must have been some mistake.

Then another guy walked in who everybody seemed to recognize. Everybody but me, that is. He was good-looking in a studied, *Men's Fitness* sort of way, tall with a jutting chin and dark hair that was brushed up like surf. This guy was wearing a baseball hat, riding askew on that rising wave, and while I knew nothing about him, his look told me at the very least that he wasn't too much for individuality.

"What's *he* doing here?" asked Jesus T-shirt Guy.

"Well, I called him from the car," my mom said. "Hi, sweetie," she said to him and then turned to me. "Jordan, this is Dirk."

I said nothing but looked at his smiling face. Sorting out the roles was tough work, with my mind not locating names, not recognizing faces, not doing much of anything at a grade level above second or third. Someone was a love interest, though it was dislocating to know that I might be intimate with someone without any memory of it. Very strange sensation. Best I could figure out, the Jesus guy was maybe my boyfriend or husband or brother. I wasn't making any moves until I found out which.

"Hi, Buttercup," Dirk said.

Then *another* guy walked in.

"What are *you* doing here?" the mother person hissed at him.

"Todd called me," he said, looking at Jesus Shirt. I guessed that my brother's name was Todd. I looked in his direction.

"Todd?" I asked.

"Yeah, Jordy. I'm here," he said. He was shaking. He must have been a really good brother, I thought. He seemed to care more than the rest of my family.

"What did you do *this* time," said my sister to the new guy, "club her?"

"Sam, they *told* us—she got hit in the head by a baseball from some kids playing across the street from her," Todd said.

"You have no business here," the mother person said to the new guy. "Please leave." He looked really bummed out. He turned to my brother, Todd, and pulled him aside.

"Listen, it seems like she's in good hands, so I'm gonna take off," he said.

"All right, man," my brother said.

"I'll come back when it's a little less crowded." My brother nodded in understanding at the guy my mom hated, and he left. It was all very confusing.

"So she got amnesia . . . *again*?" asked Dirk.

"Yeah," said Todd.

"So she doesn't remember *anything* from before?"

"No, Dirk. *That's* what amnesia is."

"And since the last time, everything that happened since then?"

"She doesn't seem to remember much of *anything*," my father said.

* * * * *

After everyone had left it was just Todd and me. He kept looking at me with this really weird look the whole time everyone was there, like he was trying to ask me something or tell me something. But I had no idea what he was getting at. And frankly it was making me nervous. So nervous that I decided to close my eyes and go to sleep because I just couldn't deal.

When I was asleep I dreamed that I was at a dance club where everybody seemed to know me but I didn't know them. Everyone there was familiar with one another, and they were all dancing and trying to get me to join in. For whatever reason I was vehemently, almost violently opposed to the idea. I don't know if it was because I didn't know *how* to dance or if I was *against* dancing or maybe a combination of both—but I was being tugged and pulled in different directions and I was fighting it like crazy. I was yanking myself away from the octopus-like arms when I turned so quickly I woke myself up, with a plastic tube draped across my face.

Todd was still sitting there, watching me.

"Hey," he offered up.

"Hey," I said, a little embarrassed, wondering if I'd drooled. "I'm sure watching me sleep must have been thrilling."

"I'm just glad you're okay . . . sort of."

"You're *sort of* glad that I'm okay? Or you're glad that I'm okay, but I'm only sort of okay?"

"The second one," he said. And then he did that thing again. He kind of squinted and looked hard at me, like he was trying to decipher something.

"What?!" I finally asked. "Why do you keep looking at me like that?"

"Is this real?" he asked. "I mean, I *think* it is. I just need to make sure. It's just so weird! I mean, what are the odds?"

"What are you talking about?" I said.

"Is this for real?" he repeated.

"Is WHAT for real?" I said.

"Do you really not know?"

I didn't know what the hell he was getting at, so I just stared back at him. I figured that since he was the only one still there out of all of my family that I should probably appreciate his presence, but I still thought he was totally *weird*.

"Okay, this is going to sound really strange," he said.

"Okay . . . ?"

"Brace yourself," he said, and looked sideways and at the door to my room.

I crossed my arms over my chest and grabbed my shoulders. "Braced," I said.

He looked sideways one last time before he said in a hushed tone, "Up until a day or so ago, you had been *faking* amnesia."

This, of course, was the most ridiculous thing I'd heard so far—even *more* ridiculous than my being related to the two very small women. "What do you mean?" I asked.

"It's true. *I* was the only one who knew. It was a crazy plan you had, and I, being your best friend and all-around great guy—"

"My best friend? You're not my brother?" I asked, now even *more* confused.

"Your *brother*?" he said, cocking his head backward like it was a re-volting suggestion. "Who said I was your brother?"

I thought about it and realized that nobody had actually introduced him that way. "Nobody, I guess. I don't know . . . I just assumed."

"Seriously?" he asked, not waiting for a response. "That's *priceless*. Even your *subconscious* writes me off as a nonoption."

"Huh?"

"Nothing," he said. "I'm sorry. It's my own personal nightmare. But we were talking about *yours*."

"Oh. Yeah—I *really* didn't want to dance. Wait, had I told you that?"

"What?" he asked. "No. Dance?"

"Never mind," I said. "It was my dream. But I get it. You were talking about my real-life nightmare."

"Right," he went on. "Anyway, I was helping you."

"Helping me . . . ?"

"Fake the amnesia."

"I don't get it," I said. "Why would someone want to fake amnesia? I mean, this isn't a whole lot of fun. Does it look like I'm having a good time here?"

"No, it doesn't."

"So why would somebody want to do this on purpose? Or fake it even?"

"It was a do-over," he said, trying to rationalize his crazy story. "You wanted a do-over."

"That's very weird," I said. "I'm sorry, but I don't know if I believe that."

"Trust me. Yes, it was weird, but what goes on in that little head of yours, that's God's own private little mystery, and once you set your mind to something—*that's it*. I tried, *believe me*, but there was no talking you out of it."

"Why would I want or need to do that?"

He sighed and paused. "You didn't like the way your life was going."

"Was it that bad?" I asked. "I mean, what was I . . . some kind of *loser*?" I tried to wrap my head around the whole idea of someone wanting to fake amnesia and I couldn't. Any scenario I came up with was so bleak that it just didn't seem to make sense. Especially considering all the nice people that came to see me in the hospital. It seemed like I had a good enough life.

"No, you weren't a loser, but . . ."

"But?"

"You never stood up for yourself. You definitely didn't make the best choices in the *guys* you dated. You weren't crazy about your family. You were unhappy at work . . ."

The idea of it just seemed so completely strange to me. He could tell I found the suggestion completely freakish, so he brightened suddenly.

"Anyway, you *did* it! You turned everything around. And it was work-ing. Things were going really well for you."

I was sure that he was a nice guy, this *Todd*, but I just didn't want to hear this stuff right now. I didn't know him from Adam. I didn't know *me* from Adam. I certainly didn't know Adam. And what he was saying was making the whole thing even more confusing. I really just wanted to go to sleep and wake up and have my memory back and not have to deal with this crap.

"I'm a little tired now," I said. "Do you think we could talk some other time?" He looked crushed. I felt bad for him and sorry that his story wasn't resonating, but I just couldn't buy it. It was preposterous. And more than I could handle at that particular moment.

"Sure," he said. "You get some rest. But do me a favor . . ."

"What?"

"Don't say anything about what I told you," he suggested. "As weird as it sounds, you wouldn't want anyone else to know about it. Trust me on that one."

"Okay. Whatever you say. Bye."

"Bye, Jordy. Feel better." And he started off. But before he left, he looked at me like he was trying to *will* me to remember him or remem-ber anything. When I kind of raised my eyebrows at him, he stopped and left. I felt bad for him. He might have been a great guy—he *did* say he was my best friend—but best friends don't count for a lot when you have no idea who the hell they are. Plus, he'd just totally freaked me out.

\* \* \* \* \*

"Hi, beautiful," the good-looking one said as he leaned in and kissed me on my forehead. Dirk. My mother had called him Dirk the day before.

"Hi," I said back.

"It's Dirk, remember?"

"You were here yesterday. I remember seeing people here yesterday. That's unfortunately *all* I remember."

"I'm your boyfriend," he said as he took my hand in his. "Is this okay?" he asked, referring to holding my hand.

"Yes," I said. "It's nice." So that solved one mystery. The handsome one was my boyfriend.

"How are you feeling today?"

"Better, I think. I don't know how I felt *before*. I still have a headache . . ."

"That's to be expected." He had the sweetest expression on his face. I wanted to touch his cheek but didn't feel I knew him well enough.

"It's pretty universal to hate being in a hospital, right?"

"Definitely," he reassured.

I frowned. I wanted to say something about not liking the helplessness and the uncertainty and all the attention, but I honestly couldn't find the words. I wanted to point at myself and say, "See? This is how I feel," and hope people could fill in the blanks themselves.

"You'll get out soon. And I'll take you home. Don't worry about a thing. I'm gonna take care of you. Like always." Like always. That sounded nice. That was the first comforting thing I'd heard since I'd woken up in the hospital.

"I'm sorry, Dirk," I said. "I feel guilty not remembering you. You seem so wonderful. I'm sure you're a really great boyfriend."

"You never had any complaints."

"Then I must be really lucky." He smiled at me, and I could see why I would have fallen for him in the first place. He had a killer smile. It was confident and, yes, a little cocky, but he gave off the sense that he belonged to me so I had nothing to worry about. I couldn't fathom why Todd had told me I had bad taste in men. He was probably just jealous. Then a blond girl walked into my room.

"Hi!" she said to me. And then, noticing Dirk, she completely changed her tone. "Hello, Dirk." I wondered if there was something between them ever. Was she his ex? If she was, then why was she being nice to me? Was I friends with her? Was I friends with all his exes?

"So it's back to square one again?" she asked me, eyebrows raised.

I looked at her, not really comprehending but giving her—like everyone else who traipsed into the room—the benefit of the doubt. This must indeed be some kind of square one.

"Unreal," she said. "Seriously. I can't believe it! I'm surprised you're not a local news story. Hell, screw local—this is, like, *60 Minutes*."

"Much longer than that," I said. "They say this is *five days*, but I only remember today and some of yesterday." She smiled and then stopped suddenly. Then she picked up talking again.

"I'd go with the fifteen minutes of fame, personally. I'm *Cat*. We're best friends. Have been for, like, *ever*. We grew up living next door to each other." She pulled out a picture and held it before me. Two little girls wearing wigs. "This is us. You're the blonde. I'm the brunette. They're wigs. Not a very good look for eight-year-olds, but we thought we were pretty foxy." I looked at the picture of us and looked at her. Tried to see how her face had changed. I didn't know my own face well enough yet to make any kind of comparison. I'd seen myself for only that brief moment when I was trying to compare myself to my miniature mother and sister.

Then Cat flipped to another one of us when we were little girls. "And this is us—sans wigs—also a long time ago. As you can see, we are every bit as cute now as we were back then." She pulled out another picture. It was of Todd and her, making one of those chairs where you'd hold hands and cross your arms and a person would sit in it. I was sitting in the chair. "And here's a funny one." I looked at all the pictures and felt completely overwhelmed. I didn't recognize any of the people in them or remember any of the moments. I felt my nostrils flare and my chin quiver as I tried not to cry, but I lost control anyway and tears started streaming down my cheeks.

"I'm sorry," I said, wiping the tears away and sniffling back the drip in my nose—then regretting the disgusting sound it made. "I just . . . This is really strange." I didn't remember *any* of it—or them. It looked like I had all of these fun memories, but no matter how long I stared at the pictures or how hard I tried to concentrate, they meant *nothing* to me.

"It's okay," Cat said. "I know it's frightening not knowing anybody or remembering anything. But this will pass. You'll get better." Dirk looked a little uncomfortable. I guessed it was the crying.

"Sorry to get all *crybaby*," I said to him.

"Not at all, sweetie. This is very overwhelming. You'd have to be a robot not to feel scared and confused," Dirk said.

Cat jerked her head backward and smirked at Dirk. "*Speaking* of artificial humans, mind telling me what you've done with the real Dirk there, Rusty?"

Dirk ignored her.

"I'll let you two catch up. I have to go anyway," he said, looking at his watch. "I have a commitment."

"Ahh, my *apologies*," Cat said. "That's more like it—double booking a hospital visit and a date."

"Actually," Dirk told her, "it's a volunteer thing I'm doing. No big deal, but they do count on me being there."

"Really? That's *so* nice!" I said.

"It's about the only thing that could come between us now," he said and winked at me.

"Well, that . . . or any panty-clad ass on a barstool," Cat interjected.

"Cat, be happy Jordan here is still with us. Try not to be so bitter about two people who have found love," Dirk said with a sympathetic smile. "It's just uncharitable." Then he blew me a kiss. "I'll come see you later, baby."

"Ugh. *Gag* me!" said Cat after he'd gone.

"You don't like Dirk?" I asked.

"What's to *like*?" Something was definitely not right with this picture. She must have slept with him, I thought. Or *tried*. *That* was probably it. She must have tried to steal him away from me and he turned her down. What kind of friend *was* she? There was no way that my supernice, volunteering boyfriend could have done anything intentionally harmful to her. Of course I was clearheaded enough to recall that love and lust are capricious masters. My guess was that Cat had a bit of a bruised ego.

Then the guy they'd kicked out the day before came walking in with a gigantic stuffed bear with a goofy face and droopy eyes. All I saw at first was the stuffed animal, then I saw the guy hidden behind it, struggling to carry it in.

"This is Bartholomew, patron saint of amnesia victims," he said.

"He's come to look after you and help you get your memory back. And to remind you that there is somebody who is crazy about you waiting for you to hurry up and get better." How cute was *he*? "How you feeling, Curveball?"

"Okay," I said. Confused, I thought. Curveball? Was this some sort of password? Was I supposed to know the code word to say back to him?

"Hi, I'm Travis," he said to Cat, and put his hand out to shake. She took it and nodded her approval at me.

"Well," she said, as a smile spread across her face. "I've been waiting for this moment," she said to him. "I've heard *a lot* about you, Travis. It's very nice to meet you." Then she smiled at me and jerked her eyes at him a few times, as though she thought I couldn't see him and wanted to signal to me that he was there. "In fact . . . I think I'm going to go grab some coffee and leave you two. There's nothing better than some good old hospital cafeteria coffee. I'll be back." Cat left and then poked her head in the door and gave me a double thumbs-up when he wasn't looking.

"Sorry about the size of the bear," Travis said, looking disapprovingly at the mountain of fake fur. "They didn't have anything bigger. I figured I'd already gone the flowers and candy route last time . . . although, come to think of it, you probably don't even remember that, so I guess I could have done it again. Well, he seemed pretty cute anyway, so . . ."

"Thank you," I said. "He's great."

"And when I get you home, I've got an extra special welcome-home-get-better-soon dish that I want to make you."

"You cook?" I asked.

"You better believe it. I can clean too. If you're really nice, I might even do your taxes."

"Lucky *me*. Wait—do I have taxes?"

"You never were too good with your bills," Cat said with a smile, still hovering in the doorway. "Really leaving now. Be back soon."

"*Everyone* does," he said. "I'm actually pretty bad with numbers. But I would give it my very best and mess it up *real* good before you had to call in the pros."

"I appreciate it."

"I can't believe this happened to you." He brushed the hair out of my face, which made me a little anxious because of the unfamiliarity. But then he looked at me so sweetly. There was definitely something going on here. I had to ask.

"Were we . . . ?" I looked up at him, hoping he would catch my meaning.

"Were we what?" he asked, not seeming to know where I was headed.

"It seems like we, I mean from the way you're acting . . . Did we ever *see* each other?"

"God, I'm sorry. I thought you knew that. Yes," he said, and then smiled a shy sort of smile. "I'm crazy about you. I mean—there's some stuff—*a lot* of stuff that we need to talk about but . . . we'll work it out." I started getting cold and clammy again. I flashed back to when Dirk was in there earlier and how he told me that *he* was my boyfriend. I couldn't imagine what was going on. Was I some kind of two-timing tease? How many guys out there thought that they were my boyfriend? And which one did I really *like*?

"Wow."

"Wow . . . good? Wow *bad*?" he asked.

"I just . . . I'm sorry. I just don't remember."

"It's okay. Really. Don't stress about that. You can't remember *any-thing*. If you'd forgotten only *me*, then I might have cause for concern."

"This is all really strange," I said. "A lot to process."

"I know it is. I can't imagine what it's like for you. But we'll get all caught up. Don't worry. I'm not going anywhere."

"Good," I said, and tried to smile but I felt really nervous and guilty. He was so sweet. This amnesia business was not a good thing to have if you were indeed a man-eating two-timing slut.

Travis stayed with me until my visiting hour ended and then promised to come back. I drifted off with an image of him and Dirk standing side by side. Choking each other, then turning on the real source of their misery—me. Then I tried not to think anymore for a while.

\*   \*   \*   \*   \*

Later, a man in a blue cotton shirt and pants walked into my room and smiled at me.

"Hi, Jordan. How are you feeling?" he said as he checked whatever they had dripping into me intravenously.

"Don't tell me," I answered. "We're going out too?"

"No, but I'm game if you are." Everybody was a comedian. I, however, was confused and having a bit of a crisis. For all I knew I was cheating on everyone—with everyone else.

Then he took out a tongue depressor. "Say aah," he said. I surmised that he was another doctor. I opened my mouth, stuck out my tongue, and did as he'd requested. I wished I'd brushed my teeth in the last day and wondered what kind of dragon breath I was launching in his direction. He put the tongue depressor on my tongue and wrote something down on my chart. As he was doing this, he smiled.

"What?" I asked. At least I tried to ask, but it was hard to be understandable with a stick on my tongue. He took it out.

"Now *that* was impressive," he said.

"What? I have good tonsils?"

"No, your gag reflex. Most girls gag after five seconds."

"Oh," I said, not sure if this was even appropriate conversation. I mean, what was he trying to say?

"I did my residency in Los Angeles. West Coast girls have *great* gag control. Actresses. Go figure. But you're the best I've come across on the East Coast." My eyes widened. Were we really discussing my gag reflex? Had he really just said "come across"? And did I really have the talent of a porn star? I did apparently have two boyfriends, so the prizewinning gag reflex *would* be par for the course.

"Well," I said, "I'm not sure how I'm supposed to respond to that. Thank you for noticing?"

"How do you feel about dancing, Jordan?"

No *way*, I thought. Was he making a pass at me and my gag reflex?

"Um . . . I don't know," I said. "How do *you* feel about dancing?"

"I enjoy it."

"Fair enough," I said, not really sure where the conversation was going.

"I'm asking because I'm going to be sending you to Dr. Debra. She does something called dance therapy."

"Sounds like fun," I said. He shrugged and tucked his pen behind his ear.

\* \* \* \* \*

When I got to the dance therapy room, I hovered at the door, not feeling too keen on entering. But the teacher, Dr. Debra, knew me.

"Hi, Jordan," she sang as she ushered me farther into the room.

"Hi, Jordan," said some guy in his late forties. "Good to see you. Welcome back."

I felt this overwhelming rush of panic. Was I going crazy? Welcome back? The doctor had just sent me there for the first time.

"I'm sorry," I said. "Perhaps you have me confused with someone else."

"No, Jordan," the guy said. "We *know* you. You just may not remember us."

"But I don't remember ever being here," I said, looking around the room. "And I only got to the hospital a couple days ago."

"I know. We heard all about it. It's so terrible. I'm Paul," said the guy. "We—you and I—were partners in dance therapy before."

"Oh, we were?" I had forgotten that I'd supposedly been there before and that I'd already been suffering from amnesia. Or *had* I? If I bought Todd's story, then I'd been faking it. But why? Why would I want to hang around a hospital and dance with stroke victims? I had no idea what kind of person I was and/or how I got my kicks *before*, but I couldn't imagine that *that* was my idea of a party.

"It's good to see you again," he said. "You look well."

"You too, I guess."

Dr. Debra put on some New Agey music and asked us to start moving. And we did. I guess I was doing better than the last time because Dr. Debra said so.

"Excellent, Jordan. You're much *looser*. Good progress."

"Thanks?" I muttered. This was just beyond bizarre.

"Feel yourself. Feel yourself from the inside out. Move how you feel." Some woman started shaking like she was having an epileptic fit. I thought she was going to die right then and there—until I realized . . . *that* was how she felt. And as luck would have it, even if it *was* some kind of fit, she was in the right place. Someone would have just wheeled her to the right floor and taken care of it.

"Jordan, move your body!" Dr. Debra commanded. I'd been so busy staring at the shaker that I'd neglected to "dance how I felt." I didn't want to dance at first. I felt confused and scared and frustrated and annoyed . . . and then—for reasons known only to God and perhaps the inventor of Dance Dance Revolution—I *did* want to dance. There *weren't* any words that could express what I was feeling, and suddenly I felt a desperate need to express them. And I did. I danced. Crazily. Wildly. Totally uninhibitedly. I shook and swerved and twirled and shimmied to such an extent that sweat was forming in little beads all over my face, dampening my hair, and I didn't care. I didn't even notice that people had stopped their own movements to watch me, and when I finally started to lose steam and *did* make contact with the roomful of eyes, it didn't matter.

And even more surprising—everybody clapped for me.

"*Very* powerful, Jordan," said Dr. Debra. "This is the breakthrough we were hoping for last time. Congratulations on being *present*."

After dance therapy, I was sent back to my room. All the nurses knew me and said hi to me by name as I passed, but I didn't recognize any of them.

I sat in my room and tried as hard as I could to remember something. I pictured all the people that had come to visit me and concentrated on their faces, trying to bring back memories, something . . . anything. No such luck. All I got was a massive headache.

I started to wonder if I was crazy. I didn't *feel* crazy, but if I had done what Todd said I did—which I wasn't leaning toward believing—then there must have been something seriously wrong with me. What kind of person would fake amnesia?

* * * * *

I stayed in the hospital for weeks. The psychologist assigned to pull me back—that's literally what he called it, that or "pull me out" or "pull me up" or bring me back or up—anyway, I don't remember what he called it, but he held forth Monday to Saturday excluding Wednesdays in a sliver of an office on the seventh floor, beyond the locked corridors of the proper psych ward in what he called the outskirts. Or outlands or outlying areas. I wasn't much on details at this point. Anyway, something in his gentle enthusiasm always set me at ease, and on this particular day, I was in the mood for some easing.

My luck, he was out, but there was a general hubbub on the floor—it was the psych ward, and it was visiting hours. Some people didn't have anyone there to see them, and those were the saddest and the ones I focused on. I wondered how long they'd been there and why nobody was coming for them. I wondered about what landed them there and about being labeled "psychotic." What was the straw that broke that camel's back, the last alarming thing they'd done to get thrown into a mental hospital—or was it an accumulation along the way? And could it have been possible that one or more of these people's actions, while perhaps seeming irrational, was in fact a sane reaction to an insane situation? Just thinking about it terrified me. How could you tell the visitors from the patients, the civilians from the conscripts, without the ill-fitting blue gowns?

One woman caught my eye. She looked more bedraggled even than her ward mates, with worn skin and hair venturing off in every direction. She wore a dirty gray bandana tied around her right wrist. She was mumbling to herself. I could only make out every few words, but every time she finished a sentence, it was almost like she was waiting for a response from me.

"'Watch what you say . . . calling you a radical . . . liberal, fanatical . . .'" she said, and then cocked an eyebrow at me. Was she talking about politics? Someone called her those things? Had she been arrested at some kind of political protest and brought here? I couldn't help but think that, at least while she was staying in the hospital, she had a roof over her head.

I looked away, not wanting to stare, but that seemed to agitate her even more. She got up briskly from her chair, looked around, then took three long sidesteps toward me and sat directly across from me.

"'Won't you sign up your name,'" she continued insistently in my face.

"My name?" I asked. "They say, 'Jordan.' And I don't have a good argument against it."

She waved my answer away and went on, "'We'd like to feel you're acceptable . . . respectable . . . presentable, a vegetable!'"

"Well, a little memory loss, yes, but I wouldn't go *that* far," I said, backing up slowly.

"Hmm . . . ," she said. And then she walked away, whistling something to herself, leaving me as lost as ever.

* * * * *

When I got back to my room, my mother was there with my doctor.

"Before I send you home there's something I wanted to talk about," the doctor said to both of us.

"What is it?" my mother asked.

"As I said before, getting amnesia twice like this really is *unprecedented*. I'm wondering, just very curious, if this could be . . . a reaction. Something you might call psychological but really I just mean a response to something traumatic, rather than purely caused by the head injury, which it seems was not terribly severe in this case." So while I was visiting the psych ward, my mother and the good doctor were discussing *my* sanity.

"What do you mean?" I asked, fearing that I was headed for my own room on the seventh floor.

"Well, head injuries are notoriously unpredictable. The effects don't show up consistently based on the amount of observable damage. They're hard to pin down. So I've just been wanting to ask, were there any problems when you were growing up, Jordan? Did anything ever happen that you didn't tell anyone about?"

"I—I honestly have no idea," I said.

"What are you implying?" my mother asked in a not-so-friendly tone.

"I'm not implying anything. I'm suggesting that she could be trying to suppress something traumatic that may have happened to her at some point in her childhood."

"Like witnessing something terrible?" I asked.

"More likely, *experiencing* something terrible or shocking or frightening."

"I know what you're getting at and I can assure you that nothing ever happened to her," said my mother. "No uncles touching in the wrong place . . ."

The doctor looked directly at me. "I'm not implying something specific, some particular abuse, Mrs. Landau. Forgive me if it seems that way. This is a safe place, Jordan. You can tell us anything and nothing bad will happen."

"Thank you," I said, "but I still really don't have any memories of anything at all, so I have to go by whatever my mother says."

"I will say *this*," my mother added, "she *was* always a bit of the black sheep. You know, nothing like me. Or her sister, Samantha."

"I'm not saying she hasn't suffered some injuries here," the doctor said. "She has. But her brain's most immediate reaction seems to be to just shut down and *forget*. That type of response could correlate to a trauma—buried in Jordan's subconscious, perhaps. It's something to think about. I'm going to give you the number of a very good psychiatrist that you can call at your convenience."

"Thank you," we both said.

Then I saw Dirk in the hallway. He was talking to one of the nurses. She was writing something down for him—probably after-care instructions for me. He caught my eye and walked into the room.

"Your carriage has arrived," he said.

"And where is it taking me?" I asked.

"I'm going to take you home and get you situated. Make sure you're comfortable."

My mom smiled at Dirk and gave him a hug.

"You're such a good boy," she said. "Jordan is so lucky to have you."

As we were leaving I thought about Travis and the fact that he'd also said he was going to come and get me, but I didn't know yet how he fit into the picture. It could be that he was trying to make headway, and seeing my weakened state, he took it as an opening. Then again, Travis seemed so sweet and loving . . . it could have been the real deal with him. I just told myself that Dirk showed up first, and my mother seemed pleased, so that was who I was meant to leave with.

*   *   *   *   *

When we were getting into a cab I saw Travis walking into the hospital with what looked like a couple of tall coffees. He didn't see us and Dirk didn't notice him, but I watched him navigate the revolving door—a drink in each hand—and felt a lump in my throat. A lump of confusion, fear, uncertainty, and regret, put there by someone I couldn't remember any more than the cabdriver who indifferently whisked us away.

# 26.

# but then again . . . no

I don't know what I was expecting to happen when Dirk and I walked into my apartment, but nothing did. I guess I thought that being in my apartment might spark something. It didn't. We simply appeared there. In the apartment, I looked at pictures of Dirk and me, and Cat and me, and Todd and me, and my family. Framed memories that meant nothing, that might as well have been someone else's.

I'm not sure what I'd done to earn my release, considering I still wasn't back to myself—whoever that was—but my family had spoken to my doctor, and doctor to psychologist, and all of them in turns to social worker, and it was decided for me (my vote wouldn't have made any sense) that I should go home. Each time they'd asked, I'd correctly told them where I lived and where I bought groceries, where I took dry cleaning (although I didn't remember the lady's name or her daughter's, or that there was a lady or a daughter) and where the post office was. I knew the ATM I used but not my PIN; I knew the nail salon but not what colors looked good on me; I knew how to get to work but had to be reminded what I did. In my mental landscape were gaps and dark patches like a thumb had been on the lens when the pictures were taken. I can't express the strangeness of it all, but everyone has pictures like that—so maybe I don't have to.

"So, this is your place," Dirk instructed, just to fill up the quiet. "I cleaned it—well, I had it cleaned."

"You did?" I asked, suddenly ashamed, wondering what kind of state I'd left it in. "Was it messy? Am I messy?"

"No," he said, "just . . . you know. You hadn't been here and I wanted you to come home to a clean apartment."

"Thank you," I said as I looked around. The place *was* clean. Spotless, in fact. And small. Incredibly small. I knew it was mine, and I didn't recall thinking it was especially oppressive before. But through those clear, fresh, unschooled eyes . . . it was a damned cracker box. I looked at the bookshelf to see if anything I'd read would trigger a memory. It was then that I noticed there was a bird off in the corner.

"Hey!" I exclaimed. "Who is that?"

"That?" Dirk said, and I could almost have sworn it was the first time he noticed him too. "That's . . . your bird."

"I have a bird. Huh. What's his name?"

"His name is Tweet . . . Tweetie. Tweetie . . . Bird."

I walked to his cage. "Hi, Tweetie Bird," I said. "I'm sorry I don't remember you. I promise it's not a reflection on *you*." And in one of those instances that makes you wonder if animals really do understand more than they let on, right as I said that he pecked at his reflection in the little mirror in his cage. "Yes, *that* is a reflection of you."

Dirk came up from behind me and put his arms around my waist. I felt my face get hot and wondered if I was blushing. He guided me over to my refrigerator and opened it.

"Stocked it full of all our favorites," he said. Before I could open my mouth to thank him, he handed me a cell phone. "And . . . this is your new phone."

"New phone . . . ?"

"We couldn't find your cell phone anywhere on you after the accident, so I took the liberty of getting you a new one. It's your same cell phone number. I programmed my phone number in there already so whenever you need anything . . . just press number two. The manufacturers put voice mail on number one. So I'm number two on your phone, but number *one* in your heart."

"That is the sweetest thing . . ." I said.

And as if on cue, the new phone in my hand rang. I looked at Dirk, unsure of what was going on. Had he rigged it to ring at that second?

"I guess I should get that. I mean, it's my phone right?" I flipped it open. "Hello?"

"Hi!" said the voice on the other end. "Are you home? It's Travis. I thought I was going to come pick you up today. I guess they let you out a little early?"

"Yeah," I said, and I started feeling clammy.

"Who is it?" Dirk asked. I started feeling *very* clammy.

"It's Travis?" I said to Dirk as I covered the phone.

"That guy's a *dick*! Hang up."

"Um . . . can I call you back?" I said to Travis.

"Yeah, let me give you my work number."

"Okay, let me get a pen," I said, but then Dirk grabbed the phone out of my hand.

"She doesn't need your number, bro. Don't call here anymore." And he flipped the phone shut. I was completely shocked and felt really bad for Travis.

"That wasn't very nice, you know," I said to Dirk.

"Nice? Baby, don't you know who he *is*? That's the guy that hit you with his car, and then he tries to, to *bed* you so you don't go after him in court! We're gonna sue him for everything he's got. He's bad news."

Right then my mom knocked and then came in with a bag of groceries.

"Really? I had no *idea*," I told Dirk.

"You had no idea about what?" she asked.

"That Travis hit me with a car," I repeated.

"Oh, yes! Awful boy, that Travis!" she said. "We're suing him, you know. Stay away from him."

"Oh," I said. He seemed nice, Travis, unlike most reckless drivers you meet. Not that I'd met many, or maybe I had—there was no way of knowing. And he said that we were . . . at least he insinuated that we were dating. No, he definitely *said* we were dating. Was he lying? Was he that conniving?

"No matter," my mom went on, "I went grocery shopping! Dirk, honey, will you help me with these."

"Of course, Mrs. Landau," he said, "but I have to warn you, I had the same idea and the fridge is already pretty packed." He grabbed the bags from her and placed them on the counter. "You look very nice in that sweater, by the way." He seemed to know his way around my apartment and my family.

"Is he *best*?" my mom asked me. "You hold on to this one, dear. He's a keeper." She'd also said something along those lines when I was in the hospital and I wondered, What was with the Dirk agenda? "Don't mean to do a drive-by, but I have to run. I know you're in good hands," she said and then blew us a kiss as she walked out the door.

Dirk plopped himself down on my bed and patted the empty spot next to him for me to come sit. I did.

"How about a massage?" he asked.

"Oh, you don't have to do that," I said, feeling uncomfortable enough as it was *without* any touching.

"I meant *me*," he said, and then he pulled his sweatshirt over his head and lay facedown, shirtless on my bed.

"Oh!" I said, surprised, but then he rolled over and started laughing.

"I'm kidding! C'mon . . . lie back and let go. I'd tell you to forget all your cares, but you're way ahead of me."

Rather than argue, I just did as he said. I kept my shirt on, but I did lie facedown and let him rub my back. As nervous as I was, having this complete stranger/perfect boyfriend massage me, I somehow managed to let go and relax—and the next thing I knew my phone was ringing and Dirk was nowhere in sight.

"Hello?" I said.

"It's Cat. I'm downstairs . . . Can you buzz me up?"

"Is Dirk still here?" I asked, looking around my apartment. It was too small for him to hide, so I realized he must have gone.

"Huh? I don't know. Is he?" Cat said.

"No, sorry. I was just asleep . . . I got confused. I must have fallen asleep when he was giving me a massage. I hope I didn't snore. Do you know if I snore?"

"Um, Jordy? I'm *downstairs*. Can you buzz me up?"

"Sorry. I'm sorry. Yeah . . ." I said as I looked around for a buzzer. "Do you know how I do that?" I should have had a giant question mark tattooed on my forehead because that's how I felt most of the time.

"It's on the wall right outside your kitchen," she said. "You know, that little hallway with the stove in it."

When Cat walked in, she had that same look that *everybody* had since I woke up in the hospital. Like they were wearing five-pound earrings on only one side and they were weighing their heads down. They'd all say, "How *are* you?" with their tilted, feeling-sorry-for-me heads. I felt like a pity case.

"How *are* you?" she asked, as if on cue.

"I'm okay, I guess. I don't know. How am I? Do I seem okay?"

"You know . . . you seem *different* than you were the first time you had amnesia."

"Really?" I asked. "How so?"

"I don't know. I guess somehow the last time you were still like . . . *you*. Not that you're not you now, I mean, you're *you* of course. But you seem more . . . I don't know . . . lost this time. Do you *feel* more lost?"

"I don't remember last time, so I can't really answer that, but I certainly don't feel *found*."

"Your place is clean," she said, looking around. Then she noticed something. "Oh my God, you still have Sneevil? *Why?*"

"I don't know," I said, concerned, feeling like I'd kept a library book out too long or I was wearing something that was totally out of fashion now. "What's a Sneevil?"

"The bird. *Sam's* bird."

"Tweetie?" I asked.

"What-ie?" she said, scrunching up her entire forehead and cocking her head backward.

"Dirk said his name was Tweetie."

"Figures. Dirk doesn't know *anything*. That's Samantha's bird. Your sister?"

"Oh," I said, wondering who was telling the truth. Every time Cat was around and Dirk was around, I seemed to get a different story. I didn't know if I could trust her, and I still had a weird feeling about her and Dirk. She had such animosity toward him. It just didn't make sense.

"You wanna go for a jog?" she asked.

"Did I used to jog?"

"Yeah," she said. "With me."

"Did I like it?"

"Not really," she admitted.

"Well, that's something then," I said, relieved both that she wasn't a total liar and that I wouldn't have to jog. "Because going jogging right now sounds about as fun as a root canal. Maybe I remember that I hated jogging?"

"You did hate it," she said with a shrug, "but you did it anyway. I was hoping for more of a speed-walk anyway . . ." She shot me a hopeful look but I still wasn't interested in joining.

"No thanks," I said apologetically.

"What can I do, honey? I feel helpless," Cat said as she looked around for something to cheer me up.

"No, you're great—just for hanging out with me. I'm this blob with no recollection of anything. How *boring* is that? And here you are."

"You're not a blob, and you're not boring," she said.

"I am. I'm like a vegetable. No, worse—something even more vapid. What's lower than a vegetable? I'm *tofu*."

"You're not tofu. Stop it."

"I am pure soy protein, not fit for a bagel."

Cat got up and picked up a picture of her and Todd and me. "Listen, I was talking to Todd, who's been really worried about you, and he and I came up with a great idea. We told Travis too, and he's on board."

"Travis?" I asked, confused once again.

"I know—can you believe it? Todd and Travis banded together. They bumped into each other at the hospital after you left today."

"Okay, but Travis . . ."

"Listen—it's genius," she continued. "We want to have a party. For you. Like a *This Is Your Life* party. I think it's a great idea. We'll have everybody who was anybody to you there. Something is bound to trigger a memory."

"And what if it doesn't?" I asked.

"Then it's a good excuse to have a party!" she answered.

"And Travis, *he's* the guy who hit me with his car. Why is Todd talking to him? We're in a lawsuit with him. He probably shouldn't be— "

"Jordan," Cat interrupted. "I don't know *what* you're doing with Dirk again, but you really, *really* liked Travis."

"Dirk is my *boyfriend*," I said. "That's what I'm doing with him. I don't know what you have *against* him, and I don't mean to hurt your feelings, but I have to tell you this makes me a little uncomfortable."

"I'm sorry," Cat said, and chewed on her bottom lip. "It's just . . . ugh. He is such a scumbag!"

"Was there something going *on* between you and Dirk?" I blurted.

"Jordan—I'm pregnant!" Cat exclaimed. "Remember?" Was *that* it?

"Is it *Dirk's*?" I questioned. And judging from Cat's hysterical laughter, I could surmise the answer was a definite no.

"That . . . is a good one," she said, when she finally stopped laughing. "I promise you will meet Billy—my husband, who I love desperately—at your party. And then you will believe that I'm only looking out for my best friend. So, fine. I'll leave this alone for now. Even though I *know* that you'd want to know that you basically hated Dirk and were completely smitten with Travis."

I was starting to get a headache. "That's not what Dirk says. Or my mom."

"Okay. Fine. Well, can we do this party? I think it's a great idea."

"I —I don't know. Can I think about it?"

"I guess . . ."

"Thanks, Cat," I said, trying to swallow the exasperation so I didn't get it all over her. "I don't mean to seem ungrateful. This is just a lot to deal with and the idea of having a memory party is just a little . . . odd. But I know you're just trying to help me and I totally appreciate it. I'm sure you were probably an amazing friend."

"Well . . . naturally," she said. "And not *were* . . . *are*. I *am* an amazing friend. And so are you."

*  *  *  *  *

I was lying on my bed, frustrated that I had no tie to it. My bed in my apartment was supposed to be some sort of comfort, I thought, but it was just a piece of furniture in a room that was supposedly mine yet felt unfamiliar. No comfort. I felt like a visitor in my own apartment—in my own *life,* for that matter.

I wondered if there was any truth to what the doctor said—if maybe this *was* a result of some trauma, if I was suffering from post-traumatic stress disorder. And what if I didn't get my memory back? What was I supposed to do?

I didn't know what it meant to be Jordan Landau. Was it up to me to piece it all together from what everybody told me or was I supposed to follow my instincts and make new choices, become someone else? Wasn't that what Todd claimed I'd done? Faked it to reinvent myself?

I could understand the appeal of a clean slate and the freedom to do whatever I wanted with it to an extent, but completely losing my identity seemed like too harsh a punishment.

I was nobody. I didn't have memories of the house in which I grew up, my family, my friends, my job. No first day of school or favorite teachers or birthday parties or scraped knees. I could talk on the phone, cook a meal, work a key in a lock, and use my credit card—well, I knew to present it anyway, though in the account's current state, it didn't get much farther than the presentation phase and then Daddy Cash had to step in. "How" was more or less okay. "Who" and "what" were a washout.

The phone rang—startling me, thankfully taking me out of my head.

"Hello?" I said, hesitant—not knowing if I would recognize the voice on the other end.

"Hey, it's Travis."

Travis. Another question mark. I knew the name now, and from his visit to the hospital, I knew he was bound up in some inscrutable romantic triangle—maybe it was a square or pentagon—but it was the same as having a book on my shelf that I didn't remember reading or a piece of furniture that I didn't remember buying. Dirk had one version and Cat had another. He was obviously persistent and wasn't deterred by Dirk having hung up on him, so I figured I'd hear him out.

"Hi, Travis," I said.

"How *are* you?"

"Okay, I guess. Just trying to remember things. Like if I liked living in a cold-weather state and if so why?"

"Good question. Feeling the cold?"

"Hating it," I said.

"Yeah, it's brutal today. Are we *really* discussing weather?" he asked, but I thought I could hear a smile through the phone.

"Sorry," I said. "It's one of those immediate . . . relatable things. I don't know what else I'm *qualified* to talk about. They did some exercises at the hospital where they held up pictures and asked me about them. We could do that . . . but probably not on the phone."

"Yeah," he said, and laughed. "Probably not."

"Yeah . . ." I said back, and then there was a pause. He called me, so I guessed he had a reason.

"So . . . have you remembered things?" he asked hopefully. "People?"

"No," I answered. "I wish. People are a missing link."

"I'm sorry," he said. "I know it's hard. Can I say some things and see if they spark anything?"

"Sure," I said.

"The Beacon?"

"No."

"Longfellow?"

"Nope. Someone I know?"

"Not unless you're about a hundred and fifty years old," he said, "and I'm not sure that would be a turn-on. For me, at least. Let's try . . . Thanksgiving? Going with me to crash strangers' Thanksgivings?"

"No . . . did we *do* that?"

"Oh, yeah, we did," he said, and then laughed as he remembered. "You were *great*."

"This past Thanksgiving?"

"Yup."

"I wasn't with my family?" I asked.

"You were. You took a little break."

"Huh," I said, trying to keep up and failing. It got quiet again.

"Bumper cars?" he asked.

"Sorry," I said.

"It's okay. It's not your fault. But at least this time it's not *my* fault."

"Yeah," I said. "There seems to be some . . . stuff about that."

"Jordan, it's a mess. People are going to tell you all kinds of things . . . and we'd sort of had a fight. But—and I don't want to confuse you—we were really happy before the stupid fight."

"Okay," I said, because I didn't know how to respond to that.

"I know . . . it's a lot to process and you're probably getting different stories from everyone, but I care a lot about you. And there's an explanation for everything that went down between us—at least my part."

"You know," I said, "I don't remember what 'went down,' so I really don't even *know* what we're talking about."

"I know," he said. "I just had to say it. It had to be said."

"Okay," I said.

"I'll let you get back to whatever you were doing."

"Okay," I said again.

"And if you think you want to see me, or you start to remember anything, I just want you to know that *I'm* not mad and I can explain—" He stopped himself. Then started again, "Never mind . . . I already said it. Okay, Jordan. Good night."

"Good night, Travis."

\* \* \* \* \*

The next afternoon, Cat was back, and she was very pleased with herself because she had a plan. The plan? Try to get my memory back with negative association. Her reasoning was that during my *first* bout with amnesia—a phrase I don't imagine gets used very often—she tried to help me by making my favorite foods, taking me to my favorite places, showing me pictures of good times past . . . and none of it worked.

She decided that we'd do the opposite this time. First stop: Elton John. She popped in the *Greatest Hits* CD and cued up "Your Song."

"This is *pretty*," I said. "What's wrong with this song?"

"Wait for it . . ." was her response. We sat in silence, listening—and then at one point she stopped the CD. "*There* . . . did you hear it?"

"I don't know," I said. "What was I listening for?"

"That *line* he said—'If I were a sculptor . . . but then again . . . *no.*'"

"What about it?"

"It's ridiculous. What is *that*? It's always bugged us. You more than me, even. Did he change his mind mid-lyric? So why leave it in? It's like a P.S. in an e-mail. Just move the damn cursor up and put it in the message."

"I don't know," I said helplessly.

"Fine," she said, and took out that CD and put another one in. And then another. And another. Nothing seemed familiar, but I will say that—even hearing them for what seemed like the first time—"Macarena" and "We Built This City" are two songs I don't need to hear ever again.

When I finally got up the courage to ask that we stop the musical experiment, Cat willingly agreed and told me to grab my coat—we were leaving.

\* \* \* \* \*

Cat had this knowing smile on her face when we walked into a bar called The Lounge.

"This is going to do it," she said. "I can feel it."

"Did I dislike bars?" I asked.

"This is a *lounge*."

"Oh. Did I dislike lounges?"

"Not as a rule but sometimes. It's not the lounge per se . . ." she said and then edged her way up to the bar and ordered us a couple drinks.

I took in the people at the lounge and noticed one girl in particular. She was sipping her drink while dancing—eyes locked on various guys at the bar, one by one. She'd sip and shimmy. If she didn't get a smile or nod of encouragement, she'd move on to someone else. Her dancing had a clear message: If any of you gentlemen have an interest in taking me home tonight, I'm available and I'd love to show you my reverse cowgirl.

"Here," Cat said as she thrust a drink with a leaf in it at me.

"Thanks," I said, and took a sip.

Cat moved her face dangerously close to mine and cocked an eyebrow. If I didn't *think* I knew better, I'd have thought maybe she wanted a kiss—but she was waiting for my reaction to the drink.

"Well?"

"It's good. What is it?"

"It's a mint julep. You hate it."

"I do?" I asked, taking another sip, testing to see if maybe this sugary, minty confection wasn't as tasty on the *second* sip. It was just as good as I'd remembered it from thirty seconds earlier. "I like it," I said, feeling guilty.

"Well, so much for that," Cat said disappointedly.

A few hours and three mint juleps later (mine being the only ones with alcohol due to her present condition), we found ourselves wandering (more like staggering in my case) through the Meatpacking District trying to hail a cab—not having much success.

"There's one!" Cat shouted.

"That's not a cab," I corrected. "That's a PT Cruiser. And it's *purple*."

"So it is," Cat replied, squeezing my hand as we stumbled along.

Why did I know that a car wasn't a taxi, but I had no memory of this sweet but oddly persistent woman who, when you took the almost-attempted kiss and furtive hand-holding into account, seemed to be another in my growing string of suitors? Several occupied and off-duty cabs passed us, so we decided to walk to the next avenue. On our minitour of the Meatpacking District, we passed what may have been a transvestite—

what was definitely an impossibly tall woman with massive calves—two guys peeing—not on each other, thankfully, but still *we* didn't need to see it—and a side of beef, literally.

"Yuck," I said.

"That's *nasty*," Cat agreed, flipping her cell phone open. "Let's call Todd. This is fun. We need Todd."

"It's late," I said, too late.

"Todd, it's us! Me and Jordy. We're looking at a meat hook and thinking of yoooou!" Then she hung up. Machine, I guessed.

Finally, an empty cab was heading in our direction, but some girl in a parka was running for it.

"Hey!" Cat called out. " Hey! That's OUR cab! Get that cab—don't let her steal it!" she yelled at me. But the woman in the parka got it.

"I'm sorry," I said, "but she *was* closer."

"Great," Cat answered. "*Now*, you can't remember how to win a battle for a taxi."

\* \* \* \* \*

It had been a week since I was released from the hospital, and I didn't remember much more than I had in those first dim moments of consciousness. I was warned about an uncertain recovery path, but without the library of memories to keep me occupied, impatience seemed to be my main occupation. I wandered aimlessly around my apartment, talking to the bird on occasion.

"This is *my* apartment," I'd say, "but most of this doesn't ring a bell." And he'd look at me, then out the window, then across the room, just as clueless.

Another thing my feathered friend and I apparently did share was a landlord hostile to our presence there. The place wasn't totally alien to me, but I did have a jarring sense that this wasn't the kind of apartment I'd have chosen, had I been in my right mind. Apparently, I'd been a little short of punctual with the rent. Repeatedly. The credit card people could vouch for that. And there were other issues. In a series of error-ridden notes and letters, I was reminded that the bird was a "vialation," rent was "well due," "past overdue," then "aggrievusly due," then "payed in full—thank you Mrs. Landua." Don't be fooled: It turned out I wasn't legally married, just legally under the care of Mrs. Judith Landau. I could figure that out later, I figured. For now, I'd take the happy inding.

I started going through all my things, hoping something would spark a memory. But nothing was jumping out at me. I stared at pictures of me and my friends, trying to re-create where we were when the pictures were taken, but everyone looked like a stranger to me. Including *me*.

Todd had come over several times, and it was clear to me why we were as close as we supposedly were. He was a really good guy who always made me laugh. Cat had stopped by two more times to apply new tactics in trying to help me get my memory back, but all her tricks and schemes were amounting to nothing—unless making my head spin counted.

It had been explained to me that I wasn't terribly close to my family, so it surprised me when Samantha showed up at my apartment to see how I was feeling. She gave me a hug and really looked me in the eyes when she asked how I was doing. She *seemed* to care.

"I'm okay, I guess," I said. "Not really. I just don't know what to do with myself. I feel lost."

"I owe you an apology," she said.

"For what?"

"I was mean to you—before. When you had amnesia the first time. Do you remember anything from when you were staying with us at Mom's?"

"No," I said. And I wondered if I was trouble for them and why they didn't want me to stay there *this* time.

"I didn't believe you had amnesia. I thought you were faking it."

This was interesting, considering Todd said I *was* faking it. "Was there a reason you thought that?"

"No, not really," she said, picking things up and setting them down, "but I feel like I didn't support you then and now you're *worse*."

"Samantha, I'm sure that isn't the case."

"You can call me *Sam*. It's what you call me."

"Sam," I said, and smiled at her, trying to let her know that none of it was her fault. The bird started making noise, and Sam looked over at the cage. She looked guilty.

"Is that your bird?" I asked.

"Yeah, it is."

"What's his name?"

"Sneevil," she said, and half shrugged in embarrassment. "Sneevil Knievel."

"Huh," I said, and got lost in thought, wondering why Dirk had said his name was Tweetie.

"I'm sorry," she said.

"Oh, it's okay. I like him. He keeps me company."

"No, not about dumping the bird on you—which—I'm sorry for that too." She got up and looked out my window. Then she went on not looking at me. "I've always been jealous of you. You're smarter than me and you have a good job. And even though Mom and I have more in common, she respects you in a way that she doesn't me. Even my father, who you're not *related* to, likes you better."

"I am sure that's not true," I said, walking over to her. "It's not."

"I know," she said, as she cocked her head and sniffed back her humility. "But sometimes it *felt* that way." I felt like I'd just gotten a glimpse into the dynamic that was our sisterly relationship, and it wasn't pretty.

"Okay, then."

"Yeah," she said. "I guess I'll go."

"Okay," I said, and then looked at the cage. "Do you want your bird back?"

"Um . . ." she said and exhaled, blowing her bangs off her forehead. "No, you can hang on to him for a little while."

"Okay," I said. "That's fine." I looked at Sneevil and wondered if she'd ever cared about him and how she even came to have him.

"Do you own anything besides Pumas?" Samantha said, so I turned to see what she meant and saw Todd at my door.

"Every time I think I missed out not having a little sister I'm reminded how blessed I truly was not to have any sisters. God forbid I ever end up with a satanic sibling like yourself," he said to her.

"See ya, guys," Sam said and made her way past him.

"Hi," Todd said. "Is now an okay time?"

"Yeah, sure," I said. "For . . . ?"

"Oh . . ." he stammered.

"Don't tell me. I forgot something else . . . ? What now?"

"No, no," he said. "I'm stopping by unsolicited. No worries."

"Oh, phew," I said. "Then, it's as good a time as any."

I wouldn't recommend amnesia generally, but something about not remembering people made me see them with an intense clarity when they did poke their heads back into my life. Maybe it was because it felt like seeing them for the first time; maybe it was my mind playing catch-up in rebuilding impressions. Whatever the case, I drank in everything greedily—how they looked, spoke, and moved; what they did with their hands; how you could tell when they were listening and when they weren't. And after seeing him exactly twice since the accident, I had a feeling Todd was different somehow as he leaned against the doorjamb.

"You coming in?" I asked.

He dropped his arms and looked at his feet, and for a second, I thought he was going to turn around and leave.

"That was an invitation," I said. "Here, I'll make it official. Please, come in."

Still he stood, half smiling, awkwardly surveying the apartment's interior, which didn't take long. Sense of humor must be related to memory, because for the life of me, I couldn't summon a single funny thing to lighten the mood.

"Todd, come *in*!"

Here he looked directly at me as if awaking and at last stepped into the room.

"That's nice," I said. "Is it new?"

"What?" he said quickly.

"Then again," I mused, "I'll be saying the same about everything I see people wearing." And it occurred to me that amnesia *might* just have an advantage or two—for instance, a whole new wardrobe! (Or clarity with which to see the many blemishes in your current couture.)

But Todd regarded himself and his leather jacket, which was unscuffed and stiff and creaked a little as he walked.

"This? This I've had for . . . years. I don't know. I fished it out." He wandered around, looking at my candles and dried flower arrangements and plastic Buddhas, opening magazines and flipping through pages without reading anything. "You don't think this is unusual, do you?"

I tried to guess at the reference. "No. Actually, most people seem to come in here and do the same thing—look around at my stuff, like they expect the loss of memory to have produced a total apartment make-over." I picked up a John Deere keychain from a shelf. "Frankly, I'm not sure I'd have minded."

"No, I mean me coming over here unannounced. I *never* come unannounced. But you don't remember that."

"You're certainly welcome here. I'm not much company, not remembering anything about us, but they say that should get better over time."

He leaned against the small kitchen table. "If it's true that you don't remember—and I'm not doubting that it's true," he said, though it sounded very much like he doubted it was true, "then is it true you don't remember . . . you know . . ."

But I didn't, so I gave him a look to say I didn't.

"How it *was* between us?"

"Between you and me?" I asked.

"That would be *us*," he said, standing up again and starting over his circuit of the place. He pointed a Buddha at me, and the Buddha's up-raised hands pointed at me too. "You and I were kind of together. You were kinda into me and I had a huge crush on you too. We were just at the point of moving beyond our friendship to something more."

The crowd of suitors was getting thicker by the moment. It should have been a tremendous comfort, a jet-propelled ego boost, to have so many friendly, good-looking, put-together, and otherwise entirely suit-able men interested in me, but although it sounds ungrateful, I wanted to close my eyes and wipe my mind clear of the whole mess. Despite the fact that I'd only started to make fresh etchings on that mind. So I sat down on the couch.

We were quiet for a while. I looked at Todd, and I figured out what seemed different about him. He was half smiling all the time, half leaning, half standing, half looking at me and half not. Half and half. In between. In the hospital, he'd moved quickly, forcefully, almost crazily. He always seemed to be on the verge of stumbling, then he'd catch himself. Laughing too loudly, frowning, sticking his tongue out. Now he seemed like a kid who knows he's in trouble. I have to admit, though it was making me slightly uncomfortable, it was also somehow . . . cute. It was the type of thing that inspired adjectives like *boyish* and *endearing*. He sat down close to me and turned to face me.

"Jordan, if it's true" (there with the "true" again), "if it's true that you don't remember, I thought maybe I could do something that would remind you."

Without knowing exactly what this meant, I sensed something was up from the proximity. His knee was a thumb's width from mine. And the silence. The gaps between us speaking were relatively quiet, but who picks out the silence and listens to it? I did then. I heard it chewing up the time.

He moved so that our knees were touching, and then his hand reached out and closed over mine. It trembled and felt slightly moist. Maybe a lifetime of confronting situations such as this is supposed to give you the instincts to deal with it. But nothing came to me. I was terrified, yes, but captivated too. I simply didn't have any idea what to do in that slice of a second as he leaned slightly forward . . . inching his face closer to mine. Then he abruptly stopped himself.

"God," he said. "My God."

He bent forward, folding himself nearly in two and pulling me close, sweeping his arm around my shoulder and hugging me to him, his chin on my shoulder pressing down.

"What the fuck is *wrong* with me?" he said.

"I . . . don't know?" I offered meekly.

"Wow," he said, as he stood up and started to pace. "This will go down in history as the most loserish, creepy, scumbag thing I have *ever* done. You'll be allowed to get mad at me for this. But don't stay mad for *too* long."

I didn't know what he meant. "I'm sorry . . . What did you do?"

"Jesus," he said and hesitated for a moment. "I just totally lied. That was all a lie. We're not— We're friends. *Just* friends. I'm so sorry this happened to you," he said hoarsely. "I'm even more sorry that I tried to take advantage of the situation and I hope you forgive me. Oh my God, I hate myself."

I was so surprised by it all, so uncomprehending, that for a moment I just held my arms out. Then I hugged him back.

He pushed away to face me, and his eyes were wet and the half smile was full. *I* began to cry.

"Oh, stop. It's all right," he said, shaking his head. "What's between us will *always* be between us. You'll see. It'll come back. Or we'll make it again."

Todd. I wasn't exactly sure who he was, but I was sure I'd like him forever.

# 27.
# familiarity breeds contempt

"Happiness is nothing more than good health and a bad memory." Or so said Albert Schweitzer. According to a card Cat had given me on one of her visits. But I was in pretty good health—excepting the recent bump on my head—and had a *very* bad memory, and let me tell you . . . I was *not* happy.

People who looked *one* way, acted another way. There was no road map or Cliff's Notes for human decency. I guess that's true anyway, but when you have no memory about anyone's character, you tend to make bad choices, trust the wrong people. I wished that everyone wore signs like sandwich boards that would declare who or what they were. Character defects and assets. Just a one-word warning so I could get a heads-up and know who I was dealing with. This person is a: Liar. Cheater. Letch. Fraud. Manipulator. Backstabber. Felon. Narcissist. Scumbag. That person is: Dependable. Honest. Selfish. Conceited. Kind. Two-faced. Caring. Satan.

My door buzzer sounded off, nearly giving me a heart attack. When I pressed the Listen button, I was relieved to find it was only Dirk. He was at my door within seconds as if he'd heard my psychic stress signal, and he thrust a brown paper bag in my stomach.

I opened the bag. "What's this?"

"It was a late-night-ice-cream surprise," he said as he pulled out two pints of Ben & Jerry's ice cream—Peanut Butter Cup and Chocolate Chip Cookie Dough—"but now that I see how cute you look, it's maybe-we-should-step-things-up-and-move-past-second-base-since-we've-been-together-for-two-years-even-though-you-don't-remember ice cream."

"New flavor," I said. "They can fit all that on the carton?"

"Yes." He seemed amused.

"It's a very *sweet* surprise," I said as I shifted my feet and felt my jaw clenching. "And that sounds really . . . nice. But I just don't feel ready for that yet." I shrugged and winced a little. "I'm sorry."

"It's cool. I'll get spoons," Dirk said, handing me the Cookie Dough pint, then going into the kitchen to grab two spoons. I caught my reflection in the mirror—the light glistening off my necklace—and I moved a little closer to inspect it.

"Did you get me this?" I called out.

"What?" Dirk answered, handing me a spoon, flicking off his carton top.

"This pretty necklace?"

Dirk looked at it the same way he looked at Sneevil the first time he saw him, so I knew the answer was going to be no. As little as I knew him, I was able to recognize looks I'd already seen.

"No," he said.

"Hmm," I said, leaning into the mirror, opening the locket, and noticing the photograph in it for the first time.

"There's a lighthouse in here," I said.

"So there is," Dirk replied, and then raised his spoon for a toast. "To us and to new beginnings," he said.

We clinked spoons and dug in.

\* \* \* \* \*

Between my time in the hospital and my recovery time at home, it had been an extra four weeks since the break my job gave us between the holidays. I'd started a routine of twice-weekly physical and mental therapy sessions, so I felt somewhat occupied. But I was ready to restart my real life, whatever that was. So I wasn't too unhappy to receive a call one morning from Splash Media Human Resources, an extremely nice woman asking about when I might be able to return to work, and seeming a tad reluctant to point out—though she brought herself to do so—that I'd missed an awful lot of work in the past four months or so. I told her I was ready when they were. The next day, a follow-up call came from a woman named Lydia, who also seemed nice in the extreme and also seemed terribly interested in my plans for returning.

On the following Monday, feeling the love, I got dressed in gray wool slacks, a silk and rayon burgundy blouse, black loafers, and a black jacket—all very serious stuff—and set off to the office.

I walked into Splash Media and was immediately struck by the chaos. People were frantic and it was only 9 A.M. I passed a man who looked me up and down and laughed.

"Got an interview?" he said.

"I do?" I asked, not sure what he was saying.

"Oh, right," he said, wagging a finger at me. "Sorry, I forgot. I'm Kurt."

"Hi, Kurt?"

"The outfit," he said as he waved his arm up and down in front of me. "You don't usually dress like that. We always tease people who show up in suits. It's assumed that they have an interview at another company because we sure as hell don't dress up *here*."

"Oh," I said, feeling suddenly self-conscious and wishing I had a change of clothes with me.

"You look like you're gonna cry," he said. "Don't freak out. You look *nice*."

I wasn't going to *cry*. "Thank you," I said. "I'm okay. But some things are a little . . . less than clear. Like my office. Could you just get me going in the right direction, please?"

"Sure," he said. "You're just down the hall this way," he said, and I followed him through the halls until we reached my office.

I'd only been sitting at my desk for about three minutes when a woman stood in my doorway.

"Welcome back," she said. "I'm Lydia."

"Hi," I said as I thumbed through a pack of Post-its nervously.

"Look"—she sighed heavily—"I know that what went on may have given you a certain impression, and I want to correct that. Is that all right?"

"I'm sorry, but it's not working," I said, and she froze. I'd opened my mouth halfway, to say it was all right, then realized I had no idea what she was talking about. In the containers of my mind—some empty, some overflowing—the one labeled *Lydia* held very little. I knew her when I saw her, but whether she'd run the place or brought me coffee and Danish in the morning, I had no clue. I remembered that I wrote, and it seemed to me she'd worked with me in the writing—because her face was familiar—but it wasn't attached to a "Lydia" or any concrete experiences. Just etchings, like graffiti on subway windows, and I didn't know what they meant.

"I didn't mean to startle you," I continued. "I just, I don't have *any* impressions of you, one way or another. I'm so sorry. Right now, I can't remember anything we did together."

She brightened, and I mused happily that I'd touched something deep and tender inside her. "That's, well, *that's*— Anyway, are you settled? Ready to create some new magic together? *Partner?*"

"I just got here, but sure . . . what should I be doing? Or 'we'?"

"Well, your Get Rich Quick campaign took off, and while you were out it's really taken on a life of its own."

"Good," I said, not knowing what she was talking about but glad I'd done *something* right.

"So now you're free to work with me again."

"Sounds fun," I said. "What are we working on?"

"We're pitching a long shot but a dream—Harvest," she said, but the name didn't register. I guess my confusion showed because she then added, "It's insurance."

"Ah. Okay."

"They've had these campaigns with wheat fields everywhere that they're trying to get away from so, really, it can be anything. Just no wheat."

"Got it," I said.

"Perfect. I'll check back with you later and we can brainstorm," she said and then disappeared, only to reappear within four seconds. "Nice loafers, by the way," she said, and then took off again.

* * * * *

Todd called and asked me to meet him outside my office on my lunch break. When I got to the little park across the street I was greeted by Todd and Travis.

"Ambush," I said jokingly.

"Actually, it is," Todd said, and I was struck by how ragged he seemed. His eyes were sunken and ringed by dark circles, his hair was slick and bent in all directions, and he wore dark corduroys and an ill-fitting black shirt. He looked like a down-on-his-luck vampire.

"Yikes," I said. "What did I do?"

"That's what we're here to talk about," Todd said.

"Hi," I said to Travis, who hadn't said anything yet.

"I don't know," he said with a shrug. "Todd asked me to meet him here, so your guess is as good as mine."

"What's going on?" I asked Todd.

"Both of you need to keep an open mind," Todd said.

"Fine. What's up?" Travis said.

"Jordan, I'm doing this for your own good. It's about what we talked about—what I told you at the hospital," Todd said and then looked at Travis. "Travis, Jordan never had amnesia."

"What?" Travis said and scrunched up his face. "Of course she did."

"No, not when you hit her, not when you met her, not when you took her out. She was faking it."

"Why are you doing this, Todd?" I asked.

"Is it true?" Travis asked me.

I felt panicked and confused. I *wanted* to tell the truth, but I didn't know what the truth was. So I answered truthfully. "I don't *know*," I said.

"What do you mean you don't know?" Travis asked, slightly agitated.

"She *doesn't* know," Todd said, "because she really *has* amnesia now. I'm the only one who knows about before."

"Okay. A, why would Jordan do that and, B, why are you *telling* me this?"

"Because she *loves* you. And I love *her*. And Dirk is doing a number on her. And I just want to make things right."

Travis turned to me. "So you were *faking* the whole time? I don't believe it!"

"Well"—Todd jumped in—"let me just say that she felt horrible about you and having to keep pretending. Seriously. That's why she'd always downplay it. But when she got hit by that ball that was a freak coincidence, because she had actually just asked me to try to fake another, *different* accident so she could make it up to you."

"Right," Travis said with a bit of an edge. "Because otherwise I'd have thought you were both crazy."

"No chance of that now," I muttered.

"She wanted to plan this fake accident. To *supposedly* knock her memory back into place—"

"I think this is the stupidest thing I've ever heard—" Travis said.

"No, there's more," Todd continued, growing more excited.

"You're right. I should reserve my vote," Travis interjected.

"And she wanted *you* to be the hero. Like . . . to take the blame off you. You were there when she lost her memory, and now you'd be there when she got it back and she'd regain control of her custodianship—whatever it is that her mother got—and call off the lawsuit."

Travis now looked at Todd carefully. "She was doing that for me?"

"Well, she wasn't doing it for *me*," Todd said.

"Wow," Travis whispered.

"Yeah," Todd said, settling into a confident smile. "*Stupid*, but sweet."

The two of them seemed to have come to some kind of understanding, but I sure as hell didn't understand any of it. And they weren't really including me in the conversation, so I didn't get why they had asked me there except to humiliate me.

"Am I needed for anything here?" I asked. "Because I don't necessarily believe *any* of this and I really don't want to hear any more about it."

* * * * *

My stomach was grumbling because I'd skipped lunch after the ridiculous surprise attack, so I went back to my desk, unwrapped half a granola bar I found in the top drawer, and spent the next two hours or so reading the background deck and jotting ideas for the brainstorm with Lydia. I don't know if it was the shock of Todd's wildly imaginative confessions, the now-months-old granola bar, the clean slate of my wiped mind, the thrill of being back to near normalcy at my desk . . . Maybe it was the intoxicating inspiration of the insurance industry, but the ideas came remarkably easily. Exploded, really, like flashes from Cat's digital camera (she'd been on a mission to create new memories from the start, in case the old ones came back in bad shape). I knew from the woman in HR that I'd been doing well and my return had been eagerly anticipated in certain quarters, but I didn't expect to be able to pick where I'd left off with so little effort.

Late in the day, Lydia came into my office with a legal pad in her hand and sat on the edge of my desk.

"So . . . did you think of anything?"

I didn't want to seem overconfident, so I played coy. After all, brainstorming was spitballing ideas, to see what stuck. I could undersell the ideas and seem not only brilliant but unfazed by it all.

"Well," I said, "they've been on the consistency thing for a long time with the brand, but this marketing brief calls for a less conservative but still reassuring and embracing message to speak to the biggest consumers of insurance. Not Mapplethorpe but not Norman Rockwell. So here's what hit me."

I put my two hands together, side by side.

"Uh-huh," Lydia said and wrote something down.

"And then the tag: 'You're in good hands . . . with Harvest.'"

Lydia stopped writing. "So . . . like a send-up? Or a straight comparison? I don't know that they do comparison. But if there's humor, I suppose . . ."

"Well," I said, a little nonplussed that she hadn't thrown the pad into the air and embraced me, "it's not really a humorous approach. It's the two hands, together, carrying you, holding you up, like this—" and I formed a little cup with my two hands, as I'd seen so clearly in my mind's eye. "But, and this just occurs to me, it's also like 'We treat you right; you're in good hands with us.' Or 'the helping hands of Harvest.'"

She sucked on her pen tip. "Question," she said. "Does your next concept involve a wisecracking lizard?"

*SLAM!* I slapped my open palms on the desk. "That's *spooky*! Must be out there like . . . electrons in the air. This thing is going to write itself!"

The pad hung limp in her hand, and she regarded me, unsmiling. "I'm not sure it wrote itself, but it did get written," she said.

"You're not taking anything down? We don't want to *lose* this."

"Oh, it's not going anywhere," she replied.

I looked back to my pad, where I'd been jotting thoughts. "You're probably right. It would be hard to forget this stuff. It's just *flowing*."

"True that," she said, and she walked out, leaving me to wonder if I'd overwhelmed her.

\* \* \* \* \*

Because it disrupted any personal routines I might have had, amnesia left me in a perpetual waiting game. I waited for people to call, come over, make plans, break plans. I fed myself fine and did the laundry, but I didn't initiate. This left me vulnerable to all sorts of dubious outings—like tagging along on the shopping trip to Barneys with my mom and sister after work one day.

"Hi, Jordan," Samantha said. "Welcome to our world." When she said that, I stopped for a second—thinking that it sounded familiar to me.

"I *know* that . . ." I said. "What is that?"

"It's the song that played in FAO Schwarz," Sam said. Barneys seemed like the equivalent of an orgiastic romp through aisles of toys for grown-ups, tantalizingly out of reach, so it was fitting.

"Did we used to come here a lot together?" I asked. They looked at each other and laughed.

"No," Sam said. "You weren't much of a shopper."

"Well, what was I, then?"

"You were more of a . . ."

"An independent thinker," my mom finished.

"Was I a nerd?" I asked.

"You weren't a *nerd*, Jordan," my mom said. "No. Not a nerd."

"Yes, she *was*, Mom," Samantha interjected. "You weren't cool at all. That's why it was such a score when you started going out with Dirk."

"You guys really *do* like Dirk, huh?" I asked. It was weird. For every argument Todd and Cat had for Travis, my mom and Sam had one for Dirk.

My mom nodded. "He's a wonderful man, dear."

"And I was happy with him?"

"*Very.*"

"You spent a lot of time with us?" I asked.

"Well, no, but we knew you were happy."

"Look, Jordan," Sam said. "You're not going to do better than Dirk. Like . . . ever. So I wouldn't question it so much if I was you."

For the next hour, I watched my sister and my mother go after the same outfits, the same colors, and then argue over who saw them first, finally deciding that they would each get different colors and share. I watched my mom—my own dear bridge-and-tunnel bully—practically rip the last size twenty-four pair of Joe's Jeans out of some girl's hands (making them, not Joe's, not this poor girl's, but hers and hers alone) and not miss a beat.

I watched in awe as my mother and sister moved deftly through the aisles and targeted their must-have pieces. They could be at opposite ends of the store, but they'd somehow manage to pick extremely similar things. And then when they caught up with each other they'd say in tandem, "Where did you *get* that?"

I watched the salespeople recognize them both and call them by name and, even more scary, pull out a reserve selection that they had handpicked and kept on hold for them in anticipation of their next visit. Nobody at Barneys seemed to know who I was, though.

I looked at a sweater that was *sort of* interesting and checked the tag: $2,800. Was $2,800 not a lot of money for a *sweater*? Had I missed something when I hit my head? Did everyone go crazy and think it was okay to spend a vacation's worth of money on some knitwear?

When they were getting rung up at the register, the salesgirl gave them each a thong. Cosabella's new color. They were giving them to their best customers.

"They're complimentary," the salesgirl said as she tucked them into the bags and smiled. I picked up another pair and held them up in front of my face.

"You look fan*tas*tic," I said, in a funny voice as if the underwear were talking. "That's an excellent purchase you're making. The color really makes your eyes stand out." My mother took them out of my hand and put them back on the counter.

"What are you *doing*, Jordan?" she asked in a *most* disgusted tone.

"I was making a joke. She said they were 'complimentary.' Get it? They were *complimenting* you." They didn't laugh. The salesgirl took pity on me and, even though I wasn't buying anything, surrendered an extra one of the complimentary thongs.

\* \* \* \* \*

As if my day hadn't been long enough, when I got home, Todd was there, waiting for me.

"I'm sorry about the other day," he said.

"I'm really tired," I said.

"Please trust me. Everything I said was true."

I *did* feel like I could trust him, but I also felt so embarrassed. "Faking amnesia? That's a horrible thing to do to people! The people who care about me . . ."

"Hey . . . *your* idea," he said.

"I know . . . so you say . . . It's just so weird. Were things really *that* bad?"

"You were going through a rough patch."

"And what are the odds that it really happened to me!" I said. "Talk about karma! I'm a terrible person. I'm being punished. God is punishing me."

"God is not punishing you."

"God hates me."

"Stop." He laughed at me. "Jordy, you're the best person I know. We've just gotta get your memory back and help you see that." There was a warmth about Todd that made me feel safe.

"Let me show you something," I said, and I pulled out the thong that was still in my bag. Todd blushed a little.

"Okay, we weren't *that* kind of close before. I thought I cleared that up."

"No," I said, waving the thong around. "I have to get your opinion because I think you'll *get* it." I told him how they'd given out the complimentary thongs, which as I was retelling the story seemed even more strange to me. I mean, what kind of complimentary gift is that? What are you saying to your customer? Thanks for shopping here. Now, if you'd be so kind as to shove this up your ass . . .

The minute I said, "You look fan*tas*tic," Todd started cracking up.

"Complimentary underwear," Todd said. "Very cute. *That's* the nutty girl I know and tolerate." I felt so much better. Instantly. "You couldn't expect your pod-people family to get that though. They aren't the sharpest knives in the drawer. And when it comes to sense of humor, forget it."

"Then why do *I* have one?"

"Because you're awesome. Don't question why you are how you are and they're how they are. You'll only be forced to come to the conclusion that I came to a long time ago: You're adopted. But you have enough to deal with right now. We can revisit that later. Plus, you're not adopted. You're just amazing and unique and brilliant and funny and therefore anyone in your presence will appear to be a lesser form. Because they are."

"How did I get so lucky to have a friend like you?"

"Because I too am amazing and unique, brilliant and funny. People seek their own kind."

"I see." I nodded. Todd was a good guy, even without memories. "Thanks for . . . trying to help me."

"Least I can do. Just trust that I'm not the bad guy here?"

"I do," I said, but I wondered if that was supposed to mean *Dirk* was the bad guy. And why did there have to be *any* bad guys?

\* \* \* \* \*

Lydia's cryptic reaction to my "in good hands" idea made it all the more important that I wow her with some different ones. So the next day, when I walked into the office, I was armed and ready with two more equally good angles—one had just hit me the night before in the shower, and the other came to me when I was brushing my teeth that morning.

I was in the mini-kitchen on our floor, pouring stale coffee into a Styrofoam cup when Lydia snuck up on me.

"Creative juices flowing today?" she asked.

"Yeah," I said. "They are."

"Great," she said and followed me back to my office.

"Okay," I said. "We want to think about branding, right? What rings out more clearly in that background material than confidence and comfort?"

"Comfort?" she asked.

"Well, I, *for whatever reason*, really liked the ideas I shared already. Not because I came up with them—"

"Jordan, the joke has sort of been milked, and I *get* that you didn't come up with it . . ."

"Right," I said, not understanding but not wanting to lose momentum, "not because they're my ideas but because they work. When you think about your insurance, you want to know there are people behind the promises. So, to that end, I think we should do something bold for a brand that's always been about some vague notion of 'consistency,' and not known as dependable, personal, caring—you know?"

"Okay . . ." she said.

"So I had a couple thoughts," I went on. "One was like a neighborhood *watch*. But not like a volunteer security guard . . . more like a friendly watch. Your neighbor watching out for you . . . having your back."

"Uh-huh."

"So this came to me, 'Like a good neighbor . . . Harvest is there.' And there could be different variations of the whole good neighbor thing, like maybe—"

"Jordan," she interrupted, "can you hold that thought?"

"Sure," I said.

"I just want to get the boss man in on this," she said, and disappeared out of my office. It seemed that the old Jordan ideatronic may have started cranking out the hits once again.

A few moments later, Lydia returned with a man with white hair and the Kurt guy I'd met, who'd accused me of having a job interview.

"Hi, Jordan. Welcome back," the white-haired man said. "I'm Ted Billingsly."

"Hi," I said. "Nice to . . . see you."

"Jordan was just telling me some new and inspired ideas she has for Harvest, so I wanted you to hear them for yourself," Lydia said and smiled reassuringly at me. "Tell them."

I repeated my "good neighbor" thing, and Mr. Billingsly stood there looking blankly at me for a moment. Then he opened his mouth, but nothing came out. I looked from side to side and nervously just went on. Surmising this concept might have been too soft or subtle for present company, I decided to tell him my other idea—one I hadn't even sprung on Lydia.

"Then there's this other one I thought of. Kind of on the same line of thinking, you know, stability . . ." I rambled.

"Okay?" he said.

"Like a rock," I said, and then waited. But they said nothing. "Meaning," I went on, "that they are your rock. They're *there* for you." And I sang the words as I'd heard them in my head while brushing. "Li-ike a rock!"

Kurt *snorted* and then covered it up with a cough. I didn't know what was going on, but I had a sinking feeling and it was making my throat itch.

Mr. Billingsly smiled at me and then turned to Kurt and Lydia and said, "Could you give Jordan and me a few minutes alone?"

"*Told* you," I thought I heard Lydia say to Kurt.

"Do you know what State Farm is?" Mr. Billingsly asked gently.

"State Farm?" I asked.

"Insurance?" he said.

"I'm sorry, I don't. Did we do a campaign for them?"

"No," he said. "We didn't. But they have a campaign that's very similar to the one you just pitched."

"Have had for, what, thirty, forty years?" Kurt said obligingly, still standing there with Lydia.

"They do?" I asked, feeling the tickle in my throat again, more pronounced now. "I'm sorry. I wasn't trying to steal ideas. It just *came* to me."

"I understand," he said. "I think it's just your subconscious remembering existing campaigns."

"Campaigns?" I asked. "Plural?"

"Lydia told me you pitched her the Allstate campaign yesterday, and, well, the other *idea* you had today—the 'Like a rock' campaign—that belongs to Chevy. It's Bob Seger."

"Oh God," I said, my throat now closing. "I'm so embarrassed. I swear I didn't mean to . . ."

"It's all right," he said softly, and he motioned for Kurt and Lydia to leave. "We understand. We just want you to get *well*."

"Thank you," I said.

"But for now, Jordan, I don't think it's doing you any good to be here. So I think the best thing for everyone would be you taking a leave of absence."

I stood up immediately and started packing my backpack. I put the stapler in there without thinking—then quickly took it out and placed it back on my desk. "Yes. Absolutely," I said as I was shuffling papers on my desk and shaking. "I totally understand. How long?"

"We'll work through Human Resources and come up with a plan. I'm sorry, Jordan," he said and got up to go.

"Is this a *permanent* leave?" I asked, my voice quivering.

"Call us when you feel better," he answered—which wasn't actually an answer at all. Certainly not the one I was hoping for.

# 28.
# damnesia!

When 6 P.M. rolled around the next Friday night and Todd, Cat, and Travis showed up at my door, I was thrown for a loop—I'd seen the Todd and Cat combo and the Travis and Todd combo, but never had the three of them triangulated their way into my vicinity at once. Although I'd at some point agreed to my *This Is Your Life* party, I'd assumed that it wouldn't amount to much. Thankfully, they hadn't used me as a source.

"Get out," Todd said with a smile.

"You want *me* to leave?" I asked. "I thought I was the guest of honor."

"We want to set up some stuff," Cat said, "to surprise you."

"Surprise," Todd said, looking at his fingers and shaking them. "I think I've lost all circulation in my hands. Damn plastic bags. Damnesia!"

"Damnesia! I'll remember that," I said, peering into the bags and grabbing the first thing I could reach. "Sunny Delight . . . and nacho cheese Doritos?"

"Hands off," Cat said. "You're screwing up an experiment."

"In Proust," Todd explained, "the main character begins to experience vivid memories of his childhood when he has tea and madeleines. So we thought we'd prime the pump a little with the cuisine."

"Madeleines?"

"Shell cookies. But we grew up on SunnyD and Doritos."

"I didn't know you read Proust," Cat said.

"Don't," Todd replied. "There was an article about it in *The New Yorker*."

"I didn't know you read *The New Yorker*," Cat said.

"Don't. This girl at work was talking about it in a meeting."

"Impressive," she said, giving him a nod. Then she tore open the bag of Doritos with a loud pop and shoved a handful of chips into her mouth. "Pregnancy," she shrugged, mouth full. "I'm allowed."

Just then, I caught Travis staring at me, and there was something uncomfortable about it, so I picked up a magazine and pretended to be reading something. The more discomfort I felt, the more *familiar* it felt, like the memory of an emotion. Awkwardness, vanity, self-negation, shyness—I wasn't certain what to call it, but I'd been in that place before. It wasn't the first time since the accident that people had watched me, yet as I looked at his hands (he was flexing and unflexing his thumbs nervously), then at Travis, then at Cat (setting bags everywhere), then at Travis (pretending not to look but still glancing up), then at the floor (still under our feet, yep), then at Travis (eyes still finding me), I felt agitated. Strange. Something wasn't right with this man.

"You look very pretty, by the way," Travis said, and I dropped the magazine in my hands, then bent down to pick it up, lost my footing and bumped my head against a table edge.

"All right?" he asked.

"Of course, yes, fine," I said, laughing a laugh of pain.

"Then get out," Todd said, smiling again.

"Okay . . ." I said. "When should I come back?"

They told me to stay away for an hour at least but be back by eight because that was when the guests would be arriving. I wasn't sure what to do with myself for the hour, and it wasn't exactly warm out, so I wandered the streets for as long as I could stand (read: six minutes) and wound up in a drugstore, reading the greeting cards.

I picked up a birthday card with a freckled little boy in a baseball cap that said, "Happy 4th Birthday, Slugger." The kid on the card reminded me of Dirk. I wondered why *he* wasn't involved in the planning, but I just accepted that there were two different camps and not everyone liked everybody else. If my friends didn't like Dirk, well, it was unfortunate, but as long as I loved him, that was what mattered most. And I did. I thought. As far as I'd been told.

Taking my cue from the woman wearing the red scarf, blue rubber boots, and purple tights, who watched me with a curious scowl on her face, I decided I'd spent enough time in the card section. It wasn't *entirely* loitering—in fact I'd helped several people pick out just the right sentiment.

My front door was closed, but with the deadbolt extended, so people could enter without knocking. I could hear the sounds of a party—laughter, glasses, chatter, general party din—and, although it was my house and my party, I didn't feel right just barging in.

I knocked, softly at first, almost like I didn't want anyone to hear me so I wouldn't have to attend the thing. It was only when my knuckles hit the off-white painted door (which needed a cleaning) that I started to panic. What if this was it? What if this was my last hurrah? If this didn't work, would everyone give up on me? And who was everyone? What if it was revealed to me that I had no friends? And the only people who came were the people throwing it?

The door swung open, and Cat stood there with a goofy grin and a bottle of champagne in her hand. She ushered me inside, clearing her throat in the most obvious and obnoxious way possible, and everyone turned to look at me.

I scanned the faces, everyone smiling at me—eyebrows raised expectantly, looking for anyone who would remind me of something . . . anything. There were streamers everywhere and horrendous blown-up pictures of me at all different ages. I was shocked and appalled, but mostly embarrassed. There was a photo of me on some stage performing in a play, another of me and two boys—I can't be certain but it looked like we may have been break-dancing—and then there was one of me wearing a hideous red and blue uniform that had DOMINO'S PIZZA emblazoned across the chest.

"This is a little embarrassing," I said, trying not to seem ungrateful and covering up how mortified I was. "But *very* thoughtful. Just a little too much 'me,' you know? I mean . . . this is a whole lot of *me*."

"It's time you rediscovered 'me,'" Cat said. "You should do more for 'me.' This night is a 'me' fest, and on the menu, tonight's special entrée is 'me.'"

"We're talking about this *me,* right?" I asked, pointing to myself.

"Unless you turn out to be boring," she replied, kissing me on the cheek. "Then we'll transition it to *me* at about ten-thirty."

In no time, the entire place was filled with strangers, who were supposedly all very important to me at one point or another. I was surprised, and secretly pleased, by how many people came. My place was packed. Cat was pointing out the blown-up pictures to me, trying to jog my memory.

"Look at that one! Do you remember that? That was the summer of sixth grade. You were going away to summer abroad and you and your boyfriend at the time, Warren, slow danced to 'New York, New York' and you both cried! It was *so* sad!"

"Jeez," I said. "Sad, all right. Young love, huh? Dramatic."

"He's here!" She beamed.

"Who?" I asked.

Cat pointed to a guy and started waving him over. "Warren!" she said. The years had not been good to poor Warren. He was overweight, had a receding hairline, was pretty dorky, and had a mouth full of food when he spotted Cat waving. He waved back and started to make his way over.

"Please don't do this," I said. But there he was.

"Hi, Warren," Cat said.

"Hi," said a barely audible Warren with his mouth full of food still not swallowed and crumbs all over his face and collar. "Hi, Jordan. You look terrific."

"Thanks, so do you," I fibbed.

"Do you remember him?" Cat asked, eyebrows raised. Nothing like putting the pressure on, Cat. I strained. Looked at him, long and hard. Which wasn't easy because he was starting to drool. Thankfully his tongue darted out and he slurped it up. I shuddered.

"No. I don't . . . think so. I'm sorry. I wish I could say I did. I was only saying, you know, how *terrific* he looks, not compared to *before* but just, compared to—to . . . nothing."

"Actually," Cat said, in a voice low enough that only I could hear, "in a direct comparison, 'nothing' might just come out on top."

"That's okay," Warren said, and then leaned in and whispered loud enough so *everyone* could hear, "I *fingered* you the night before you went away."

"You don't say . . . ?" I managed to get out amid the shock and horror. He nodded a very self-satisfied nod, and I wanted a Jordan-sized section of my parquet wood floor to open up and swallow me.

"Good thing she ended up with amnesia, then," Cat said to him, smiling broadly.

Luckily, or unluckily, my sister walked over.

"Hey," Sam said. "These pictures are *classic. Love* the Domino's uniform."

"Yeah," I said, "but I don't look very happy somehow." My hat was down, nearly over my eyes, and my arms were folded tightly across my chest.

"Jordan worked there one summer," Sam said to Cat and anyone in listening range, "during the thirty-minutes-or-less campaign. I used to make crank calls from my friends' houses and give her the wrong address, then my friend would wave her over from the next house and we'd get free pizza and she'd get in trouble."

"How . . . *mean*," I said. I know she said she'd been jealous of me, but this girl was a nightmare!

"It was all in good fun," she said. "We were bulimic back then anyway, so there was no point in paying for food we were just going to throw up."

"That's horrible," I said.

"Jordan was bulimic too," Sam tossed out.

"I was?" I asked, surprised and saddened by the revelation.

"You *were*?" Cat said—tilting her head to the side, looking like she found that hard to believe, since she'd been around me practically since birth.

"Well, a *failed* bulimic," Sam said with a laugh. "She had the *eating* part down but forgot to exercise or throw up."

"I *knew* it wasn't true," Cat said. "You never change, Sam. Bless your little black heart."

"I gotta go . . . check something," I said. "Could you both excuse me, please?" And I made my way over to Todd in a hurry. He was standing next to an elderly woman and I couldn't imagine how she fit into this picture.

"Hey, Jordy. Good turnout," Todd said. "How are you doing?"

"Better *now*," I said. "My sister isn't the nicest person, is she?" I asked.

"She's wretched," he confirmed. Then we stood there, not saying anything for a little while.

"I met my sixth grade boyfriend," I said.

"Anything?" he asked.

"Uh, *plenty*! But, no, I don't remember him."

"Well, I was just getting caught up with Ms. Oakmin, our fourth grade teacher," he said. "Say hi."

I felt a little like a child, the way everyone was parading me in front of people and telling me to "say hi." I felt like any minute I was going to be asked to play "Heart and Soul" on the piano and then curtsy.

"You have grown so lively," Ms. Oakmin said in a thick German accent, "such nice breasts." This is the first thing she says to me after not seeing me since the fourth grade?

"I do?" I said, not knowing what the correct response to that would be. "I mean, okay. Thanks."

"You used to be flat like ironing board," she said.

"I was *nine years old*," I said, and found myself crossing my arms in front of my chest. As if it all wasn't humiliating enough without discussing my finally having grown some breasts with my fourth grade teacher?

"You were a very good writer. Do you write still? I hope you do."

"She does write," Todd said. "She's brilliant."

"Of course she is," Mrs. Oakmin said.

Among the fifteen or so people they'd heroically assembled (heroic considering that the phrase "three's a crowd" may have been coined in that very room) were other faces from the pictures. But I couldn't recall a name or a single moment with any of them—I was the literal embodiment of shallow. It was getting to me. So I pushed my way past all of the strangers/close friends. Everyone was tugging at me and trying to get me to talk to them and I just wanted to be alone. Then I spotted Travis. *God*, he was cute. I wondered what his deal really was. Was he the terrible person that Dirk and my family described or was he the great guy that Cat described? Or both? Was I really two-timing Dirk? Did Travis know? Did they both know? These were questions that I felt I couldn't ask anyone for fear of spilling the beans. Even though I didn't know if there really *were* any beans. I found myself gravitating toward him anyway, imagining that if I got close enough I might start to understand what we had between us by a kind of relationship osmosis.

Then Travis walked up to me. "How you holdin' up?"

"Do you think maybe you guys went a little overboard? I mean, sixth grade boyfriends? Fourth grade teachers? How far back are we going here?"

"You see that man over there?" Travis asked as he pointed to an older man in a tweed jacket and glasses.

"Yeah?"

"He delivered you." He paused for effect. "I'm kidding."

"None of these people are familiar to me," I said.

"I'm sorry. I'd hoped this would help." He looked around as if he was trying to think of something else that might trigger a memory. "Slide show?"

"Please, no!" We laughed. Now I felt more comfortable with him, more like he belonged among us.

Then Dirk walked over to us. I hadn't seen him at all and wondered if he'd just arrived.

"There's my beautiful girlfriend," he said as he picked me up and twirled me around.

"And there's my boyfriend," I answered back at last, and it was so exhilarating being spun—or perhaps my equilibrium just got fouled up—that I fell against him and laughed when he released me. Discombobulated as I was, with my past moving all around and so little of it familiar, I felt a little tingle of happiness, the first unadulterated glee I could remember in those weeks of recovery. I wanted to let them know. And so I did.

Todd's mouth fell open. Travis and Dirk looked at me too, and I thought I'd done something wrong. Then Dirk seemed to recover, but the other two didn't.

"Isn't she a sweet thing," he said, encircling my waist to pull me close again. Then he cocked his head and his eyes grew wide. "'*Why do birds suddenly appear, every*'—c'mon, you remember what I taught you—'*every time . . .*'"

I did remember. A few nights before, he'd said we used to lie around singing to each other. And he'd rehearsed one of our favorites with me, because he said those were his favorite times in his life, and he didn't care if I *ever* got my memory back—no, he almost hoped I *didn't*—because we had all the time in the world to create new memories.

"'*Every time, you are near,*'" I answered back in song, though I didn't know the melody. And we sang together, probably not getting any closer than a mile or two to the melody: "'*Just like me, they want to be, close to you.*'"

Travis's mouth had joined Todd's in the open position. I couldn't tell whether they were impressed or what.

"I'm going to be sick, right here on this floor," Todd said. (Or what, apparently.) He stuck his tongue far out and made a sour face. "I literally need a mint right now." He stepped around Travis, one step closer to Dirk. "First of all, it's 'they *long* to be.' If you're going to fabricate a precious moment, at least get the fucking *words* right."

Dirk also moved, squaring his shoulders to Todd. It was beginning to smell like trouble between them, and small as the space was, any odor quickly drew attention. A few heads turned over a few shoulders and drinks were suspended just short of lips.

"If you think I'm going to stand here while you try to brainwash Jordan into thinking you two were somehow close, that you're now somehow joined at the . . . unhip, you're an even bigger asshole than I gave you credit for."

Now, Dirk had about four inches, forty pounds, and half a foot of chest circumference on Todd. But maybe Todd had the edge in crazy, because surely as I thought Dirk would haul off and throttle him, he only smiled.

"I'm here about Jordan, as I think most people are tonight," Dirk said. "So I'm gonna let that slide. But don't make the mistake of thinking you know better than we do where this road is taking us, because we've never been down it before, and you wouldn't even know it if you had."

That stopped everyone for a moment, as we searched one another's faces for signs of comprehension. Todd was clearly overheated, but Travis said something to him I couldn't hear and they looked back at Cat.

"C'mere. I wanna talk to you about something," Dirk said close to my ear. He took my hand and dragged me away from Travis and Todd. I looked back at them, and I was struck not by Todd who had turned away, but by Travis, who now had the most heartbreaking look on his face. It was helpless and frustrated and just plain sad. Dirk saw me looking back and grabbed my chin. He planted a kiss on me and started to pull me into my bedroom, but then I felt another arm grabbing at me—more like a claw, attached to Cat.

"Jordy, I got it!" she said.

"What?" I asked.

"Your journal. You totally kept a journal."

"Okay . . ." I said. "Where is it?"

"I never saw a journal," Dirk said. "I cleaned the entire place—stem to stern."

"Well she kept one . . . and it probably told the truth about you about a thousand times," Cat hissed.

"Then I hope we find it," he said earnestly, actually looking left and right.

"*Cat*," I said, surprised by her freak-out. "Calm down, it's okay. If there's a journal, it'll turn up."

"I don't think there is one, sweetie," Dirk said.

"Yeah, because *he* probably burned it," Cat spouted.

"Can you excuse us," Dirk said, the picture of calm amid her accusations, and pulled me into the kitchen.

"Baby, I'm sorry about that," he said.

"I don't know why she hates you," I said.

"I *do*," he said. "Cat's interest in undermining our relationship is selfish and sad. I didn't want to tell you this because you've been friends for so long and I'd hate for you to lose a lifelong friend, but Cat . . . I've rejected her repeatedly."

"You *have*?"

"You and I have been together a long time, baby. And in that time, she's come on to me more times than I can even remember."

"Oh my God," I said. "That's really *surprising*. She's *married* . . . and *pregnant*!"

"She's hardly the first married woman who's tried, and I'm sure she won't be the last. It's not just sex she wants. She's claimed to be in love with me. That she'd be *better* for me. That she'd leave her husband for me. But don't *worry*. I could never love Cat. I love only *you*."

"Thanks," I said, feeling even more confused—if that was possible.

"But . . . speaking of loving *only* you, before we got interrupted, I was trying to steal you away to ask you something."

"Shit," I thought. He *knew*. He knew I'd been a cheating, lying, backstabbing girlfriend and he was going to ask me about Travis. I wasn't going to lie. I'd be honest. I'd tell him what I knew—that Cat told me I *was* seeing him but that I hadn't since the accident.

"Okay . . ." I steeled myself. "Shoot."

"I think we should get married," he said.

Not exactly what I was expecting.

I didn't know what to do. Was that a proposal, or was he throwing out a topic for discussion? "I don't have a ring yet, but I'll get one. And that's just a formality anyway. What matters is that we love each other and want to be together."

"Wow," I said, blown away. "Wow. Wow."

"I know," he said. "You're surprised. I am *too*. But it feels right."

"But I don't even have my memory back yet. I'm a wreck. I'd be a lousy bridge partner."

"I don't care. I know that I want you. I know you wanted me. We dated for two years and barely a day went by that you weren't *hinting* for a ring on your finger."

"Really?" I looked at my finger, trying hard to summon that feeling of naked-finger shame.

"Hell, yes! You were a one-woman Tiffany's campaign."

"At least I have good taste," I said.

"Well, you picked me, didn't you?" he said with a cocky smile. "Trust me. You were dying to get hitched."

"I was, huh?"

"Big-time. So, fine, I give in," he said, playfully twisting his arm behind his back. "*Uncle.* I wanna marry you too."

"Are you sure?" I said.

"Of course I'm sure." This was huge. I didn't know what to do. Here was this guy telling me I loved him and wanted to marry him, and my family I'm sure would corroborate it all, but I didn't even know who I was. I didn't know what to do. If I said yes, then I guessed eventually my memory would come back and I'd be overjoyed and we'd live happily ever after. If I said no, then what if my memory came back but he'd already abandoned the pursuit out of bitter disappointment and I'd lost my one chance at happiness? I wondered if I could ask him just to hold off until I got my memory back. But that would seem insulting. Like I didn't believe what he was telling me we had together. What if I said yes and my memory came back and I remembered that I really *did* like Travis? I couldn't do it. I couldn't just say I'd marry this man. I didn't know him. I didn't know me.

"Okay," I said. Getting ready to give him the spiel.

"Okay what?" he exclaimed. "You'll marry me?"

"Well, you didn't really *ask*, actually. You just said you thought we should."

And then he got down on one knee. "Jordan Landau . . . will you marry me?"

"Yes," I said.

I know. I said I wasn't going to, but he was down on his *knee*. And he *said* that I wanted to. In that condition, my system didn't recall how to generate an impulse like doubt.

"All right!" Dirk said and he put up a hand to high-five me. I obliged, and as his hand cracked into mine, I had the strangest sense—almost like vertigo—that I was watching him do this with someone else, not a solid object but a ghost or someone just out of frame in a photo, with Dirk dressed differently and seeming different, and the whole moment very unlike now.

Just then my mother walked over with a Hispanic man and woman. They were probably in their late forties, early fifties.

"Hi, Mrs. Landau," Dirk said. "Or should I call you *Mom*?" Travis and Todd were standing within earshot and turned at this. "Jordan and I just got engaged!"

"Oh my God!" my mom yelled. "I knew it would happen!"

"Oh . . . my . . . God," Travis and Todd said in unison.

"That's wonderful," my mom said and then hugged us both.

"Jordan," Travis said, "I think you should think about this before you give a final answer."

"Why are you even here, dude?" Dirk asked.

"Why *are* you here?" my mom added.

"Because I *love* her," Travis said.

My heart was pounding. Two men fighting over me. But it didn't seem like me at all, and I didn't remember either of them. It was confusing as hell.

"Not sure she's into bigamy," Dirk said to Travis.

"What?" I asked.

"Your loverboy here is *married*," Dirk said.

"He is?" I asked. "You are?" I said directly to him.

"Yes, Jordan," my mom said. "He is. We found that out at the deposition."

"The dude's a charleston," Dirk chimed in.

"Charlatan," Todd corrected with a derisive laugh. "Means 'fraud,' so I'm surprised you don't know it."

Dirk ignored Todd and went on. "He was only seeing you to get around paying a big settlement in the lawsuit."

"Jordan," Travis pleaded. "This is the thing I was talking about. It's not . . ."

"*Are* you married?" I asked.

His head dropped. "Technically, yes, but— "

"Why don't you take off, bro," Dirk said, and put his hand on Travis's shoulder menacingly.

"Don't do it," Travis said, looking back at me. My mom grabbed my arm and pulled me to the Hispanic couple.

"Jordan, honey, do you remember Esperanza?" People were gathered to see if I remembered Esperanza. And I all of a sudden started feeling dizzy. I'd just accepted a marriage proposal from someone I may or may not have wanted to marry.

"No," I said apologetically. "I don't think I remember you. I'm sorry."

"She was our housekeeper when you were a little girl," my mom said. "And this is her husband, Luis."

The woman spoke broken English and kept hugging me, nearly in tears, telling me she missed me, and she was sorry to hear I'd gotten "menesia" again. "Yordan!" she said. "You look so nice. So nice!"

"Oh, thank you," I said, "but I feel a little . . . like I need some air."

"Like a *lady*. I always remember when you are baby. Berry, berry messy."

"Oh!" her husband exclaimed. "She's the one used to throw her poop around?"

"*Ay, sí!*"

What? *What?* What were they saying in front of a room full of everybody that ever knew me? "Pardon?" I asked.

Sam took over. "Totally! Oh my God. She was so gross!"

"Was *you*? *Dios,* my *memory.* Anyway, we used to have to have a watch." Esperanza said, and suddenly I regretted even asking. "We take turns sometimes but mostly was me. I sit by your crib and I wait and I wait, and then Missis Landau call me for something and I get up for five minutes. But I come back and *Dios mío!* There's poop all over the place! Look like someone threw a chocolate cake at the wall!" Everybody was hysterically laughing. I was utterly horrified.

Cat, oblivious to what had just gone on, came walking up with a tray of chocolate cupcakes. Not exactly the visual I needed after that glorious tale of my smearing crap all over my bedroom walls.

"Cupcake?" she said as she offered them around. "Cupcake?" Nobody wanted one. Naturally. I looked at the cupcakes, my eyes wide in shock and horror, grabbed my coat, and just took off running.

# 29.
# awfully wedded wife?

I didn't know the depths of any previous humiliations prior to the Cupcake Incident, but I felt I'd be safe in saying that it was the most horrifying moment of my life up until that point. I heard someone call after me during my mad dash out of there, but I didn't stop because it didn't matter. Nothing anyone could say would make me feel better.

It wasn't *only* the whole Travis blowup that had pushed me over the edge—that was just the cherry on top of the shit sundae. It had all become too much. I'm sure people go through life and wonder about their limits. What's the mortification barometer? At what point do you cross over from throwing up a little in your mouth to wanting to move to a foreign country and assume a new identity?

A new identity. Interesting concept, I thought. Had I come full circle in the *Groundhog Day* version of my own life? Did I get to a point when enough was enough and decide to fake amnesia to reinvent myself? Over and over again? Was this where I was supposed to do it once more? And did I always end up getting legitimate amnesia at some point in the process?

Obviously not. The whole idea was ludicrous. But those are the things I thought as I ran down the stairs, out the door, and onto the street to breathe fresh air. I ran like someone was coming after me, even though I knew that the extent of the chase had ended with whoever had called my name when I darted out. I looked back once to see if Dirk was following, just to be sure, but he wasn't. I didn't allow myself to wonder why not.

I started getting winded about the same time I realized that my feet were killing me, so I slowed down to a walk and continued, having no destination and not wanting one.

I stayed out and wandered nearly all night. I know, it sounds dangerous and boring, too—it being New York and cold and all—but anyone who actually lives here knows that, as far as big cities or any cities go, New York is pretty damn safe. For one thing, there is *always* someone around, making it much safer than some desolate street in an indifferent suburb; most of it is well lit; and there are plenty of places open round-the-clock, where you can warm up when your feet get too tired or cold to carry you.

I smiled at passersby—people standing out in front of bars, smoking, couples on dates, the occasional homeless person—and it felt so good to be anonymous. To not know the people I passed and have them not know me either. It was exhausting having a bunch of people know me that I didn't know, and I was coming to really resent it. I wanted to blame someone and demand they fix me, but who? And how?

I walked through neighborhood after neighborhood, taking in the different flavors and scenery. Every fifteen blocks was an area with its own distinct feeling, and walking aimlessly through them in the dead of night gave me an appreciation for how truly remarkable New York City was.

At one point when I got sick of walking, I stopped into a dingy bar that didn't even have a sign out front. They had a jukebox with a lot of early country music mixed with hard rock albums and some punk. I stared at the titles and wondered why I could recognize almost every one of the songs but I couldn't remember my own mother.

The bar was pretty empty. There was one older guy wearing a trucker cap, unironically, and two girls who'd gotten all dolled up, perhaps thinking this was the night they'd meet the man of their dreams—or someone with enough money for a couple of apple martinis and a Caesar salad. I watched them look at the door every time someone new came in—which wasn't often. I saw the hopefulness turn to disappointment when it wasn't *him.*

I made myself at home on the last stool. The bartender, sEra, had her belly button pierced and a tattoo of a naked lady lying on a hamburger bun on her arm. She told me that she changed the spelling of her name from Sara to sEra when she was in high school, after she'd seen the movie *Leaving Las Vegas.* She thought it was cooler. Everybody wants to be unique—even if they're blatantly copying somebody else to do it.

By about 3 A.M. sEra and I were pretty tight. I told her that I'd gotten engaged that night and that I wasn't sure if I'd made the right decision. I told her about the amnesia—including the fraudulent case I'd forgotten—and that I still hadn't recovered my memory. I told her that there had been a party for me that night, which for all I knew was still going on, but that it was too overwhelming and I took off. I left out the part about Esperanza and the shit storm. And the cupcakes. No one needed to hear that. I wished *I* never had. sEra was a good listener. Then again, it *was* part of the job description, but it seemed like she was born for it—a bit of a sage. She had all kinds of advice for me and an interesting outlook on everything I threw at her.

On identity and my lack thereof, she said, "Nobody knows who they *really* are anyway. Most people are just trudging along—waiting for something to happen. True character doesn't even come out until people are tested—put in extreme situations . . . and most people spend their lives trying to *avoid* those kinds of situations."

"So I'm really no different from anyone else," I mused. "That makes it a little more palatable. Any thoughts on my engagement?"

"The fact that you have no idea who you are and what your behaviors were—rendering you essentially *not* the person your fiancé fell in love with—and he *still* asked you to marry him says a lot. He's willing to jump first and hope the net will appear. That's faith. And sounds like *love* to me."

"Wow," I said. I hadn't thought of it like that. Suddenly Dirk's proposal meant that much more to me. And even if I didn't know if I'd wanted to marry him in the past, I felt more certain that I'd made the right choice.

"Just my two cents," she said. "I think—once you find love, you should spare no expense . . . make *any* sacrifice." She was the embodiment of the wise barmaid. A cliché, no doubt, but clichés are usually born from some truth, and here was a perfect example.

"You have a beautiful outlook," I told her. "You must have a wonderful life."

"Don't believe everything I say," she said and smirked. "I'm pregnant with the bouncer's baby." She motioned to the door.

I looked to where she was directing my attention and saw a three-hundred-pound guy with no neck. She shrugged.

At 4 A.M., she kicked me out. Told me the bar was closing but said to come back anytime.

There are two kinds of people in this life. Morning people . . . and everyone else. I didn't know if I was or had been a morning person previously, but hanging out in a diner watching clubbers and night shifters wander in, then walking around until the sun came up, made me realize that by sleeping half the day away, you can miss out on a lot.

I sat on a bench and watched the early morning joggers, the construction crews building new skyscrapers, people setting off to work, bleary-eyed dog walkers. Everybody commencing a new day, rested and ready to conquer the world. I found myself wishing I remembered what it was like to have a day to start—what my rituals were, how I felt during each step, if there was anything I wanted to change or stop, if there was a favorite part of every day. What brought me joy? What bugged the hell out of me? When/if I did regain my memory, would I feel different from how I did right then?

By the time I got home, it was 7 A.M. and Todd was waiting there for me. He was half asleep, perched at my window. I could tell he'd been fighting sleep all night. Poor guy.

"Jordy! Thank God!" he said as he flew off the chair and ran over to hug me. He tripped on the carpet or his sneakers and stumbled on his way over. He was exhausted.

"You didn't have to wait up for me," I said.

"It's what I do best," he said, looking at me wearily.

"Seriously," I said, "go get some sleep. You wanna sleep here?"

"No. I wanna know where you *were* all night."

I told him about my night. About how much of the city I'd measured out by foot, about sEra at the bar, and about watching the sun come up and wondering as I'd done every day for over a month if *that* was going to be the day my memories came back. Todd wasn't pleased. Understandably. He had been worried.

"I'm sorry I made you worry," I said.

"You could have called."

"I wasn't thinking straight. I was embarrassed and I just wanted *out*. I didn't know you'd be here."

"Jordan, c'mon," he said.

"I didn't! I'm sorry. Will you forgive me?" I made puppy dog whimper noises and sniffled a few times.

"You know I always do."

"Actually, I don't. But I had a feeling. You want breakfast or do you wanna take a nap?"

"I think I need a nap," he said.

"I think I do too." And Todd and I both fell onto my bed without another word. I woke up first, at about 1 P.M. Todd was still sleeping and I watched him sleep. I'd just napped with this Todd person and it felt totally safe . . . comfortable. I trusted him. And I felt beyond lucky to have him in my life—really blessed to have a friend like Todd. He probably felt me staring at him because he woke up and frowned at me.

"What's that *look*?" he asked.

"I'm just happy that you're my friend."

"Well, you're not going to be happy when you hear what I have to say."

"Uh-oh . . ." I said.

"Yeah," he said and cocked an eyebrow. "Uh-oh." He steeled himself. "Jordan, you can't, can't, *cannot* marry Dirk."

"Ugh," I pleaded, flopping off the bed to brush my teeth, "Let's not get into this."

"We *have* to get into this. This is a huge deal. This is a cataclysmic nightmare."

"It's not *that* bad."

"You're right," he said. "It's *worse*."

"Todd, I know you think you know what's best for me —and I appreciate your concern—but I also understand that there are two different camps here. And I can't make *everybody* happy all the time."

"But you can make *yourself* happy. And I promise you that if you marry Dirk, you will not be happy." He seemed to be sure of this. But by deductive reasoning I thought there may have also been other factors at play.

"Okay, let me ask you something," I said.

"Anything."

"Did you have feelings for me before?"

"Yes," he said reluctantly. "But that has nothing to do with this. I swear. I'd much rather see you with Travis than with Dirk."

"Okay, then let me ask you *this:* When I was with Travis—like you people say I was—were you happy for Travis and me?" He got quiet. He pursed his lips and sort of flared his nostrils a bit. So obviously the answer was no. And I really couldn't trust Todd's opinion on this matter, no matter how good a friend he was or how much I felt I could trust him in every *other* matter.

Todd got up, grabbed his coat, and walked to the door. He stopped and looked back at me.

"No, I wasn't happy about you and Travis either, but—and this is a *huge* but—"

"Who's got a huge butt?" I tried to make a joke. It wasn't funny.

"I love you. As my friend and the girl I've cared about since I was seven freakin' years old. Yes, I had feelings for you and, yes, I acted like an immature asshole a lot of the time, because I'd always hoped that eventually you'd come around and see things my way and realize that we belonged together . . . but the bottom line is you mean everything to me. And so does your happiness. I wouldn't fuck with you right now. It's too important and you're too vulnerable. I'm not even putting myself into the equation here. The only thing I have to gain from telling you this is *your* happiness, which, as it turns out, is much more important than mine. But please hear me: You *don't* love Dirk. You love *Travis*. If you do one thing in this life, one thing, just trust me on this." And he walked out the door.

*   *   *   *   *

Cat showed up at about 3 P.M. and started opening drawers and searching cabinets. She was on a mission to find my journal, and no amount of my protesting would stop her.

Maybe ten minutes later, Dirk arrived, and Cat and he started going at it again.

"Look, Nancy Drew, there's no journal," he said. "Why don't you quit making up problems and just be excited for the happy couple?"

"That'll be a subzero day in hell," Cat said. "I don't know *what* this wedding stuff is all about. I mean—I get that he wanted what he couldn't have and that he's trying to make partner, etc. *That* I can grasp. But to actually push for marriage? When he'll be over you, once again, as soon as it sets in that he's *got* you . . . and the thrill of the chase is gone again? And it'll happen. I promise."

"Cat," I scolded in a tone I didn't recognize as my own, "I need you to be happy for us. Put whatever went down between you and Dirk behind you. If I'm willing to look past it, I think you can too."

Cat stood up and brushed off the lint that had collected on her pants from crouching and searching. She arched her back and stood with one hand on her belly in that way pregnant women do, looking out the window, then at Dirk, then at me, back out the window, at her feet, and back at me.

"Fine," she said. "Whatever. I'm here for you." Then she narrowed her eyes at Dirk, kissed me on the cheek, and left.

*   *   *   *   *

For whatever reason, Dirk wanted to have a very short engagement. He said that I would have wanted it that way, so our wedding date was set for three months from the night of my party.

For the next three months I was busy with a whirlwind of wedding stuff.

Even though I'd promised myself I'd never set foot in Barneys again after the Day of the Thong, we got my dress there. It was an incredible Christian Lacroix gown with the most romantic, whimsical, yet simple design—strapless silk tulle, embroidered ribbon lace, ruched bodice falling asymmetrically across the waistline . . . a dream manifested in a dress.

We had what seemed like fifteen fittings but was actually three. The girls who worked in the bridal salon at Barneys were remarkably interested and genuine even though they did this several times a day, every day, for different brides.

I had several hair appointments to do test dos and see what worked the best. We decided on an updo with some wisps in the front to frame my face. My mom seemed much warmer than she had before. She loved planning the wedding and threw herself into it completely. Walter told me it was nice to see us getting along so well, and I was glad *we* could share the excitement together because I certainly wasn't feeling much enthusiasm from Cat, Todd, and Travis.

My mom took mother-of-the-bride responsibilities very seriously, to the point of once explaining to a potential floral designer that she was the "Queen Bee, and must be served." I couldn't tell whether she was coming on to him or merely condescending, but in either case, it was inappropriate and unfortunately par for the course. Something about the prospect of riding shotgun rather than being in the driver's seat was drawing out her insecurities like pigeons on a loaf of discarded bread.

Cat finally shut up about Travis and me and agreed to be my maid of honor. She, my cousin Danielle—who I didn't remember, but who my mom insisted be in the party—my sister, and Mom were my bridal party. I wasn't about to argue since without cousin Danielle I'd have had just Cat, Sam, and Mom—and even though that made me related to three of the four people in my wedding party, it still seemed somehow less pathetic.

I never heard from Travis again, and Todd and I didn't see each other but a handful of times before the wedding. I tried to get together with him, but he just kept looking so disappointedly at me that it became too much to take. I felt the loss of Todd—deeply—but I didn't know why. Everything was happening at such a lightning-fast pace that I didn't have time to explore it.

It was go, go, go, from the wedding cake place (double-chocolate blackout cake with chocolate mousse filling and white buttercream frosting) to picking out the wedding band (and making the do-not-play list: no "Mony Mony," "Celebration," "Brick House," "YMCA," or "Hot Hot Hot") to color schemes, centerpieces, wedding favors, and reception plans (my mom and Walter's backyard decorated to the nines). I opted *out* of a bachelorette party because the lack of familiarity and wealth of relatives in my bridal party made it seem like it might be more uncomfortable than fun.

All the while, Walter looked concerned. I'd thought it was the certainty that his lawn would be wrecked just as it was getting its spring legs, but he was very accommodating to every request. It simply didn't seem to make him very happy—not any part of it. I assumed he was having trouble deciding what his role was supposed to be as stepfather, because he seemed always to be about to say something to me yet never did.

Before I knew it, April showers had given way to May flowers and it was the night before my wedding.

*   *   *   *   *

My mother was frantic. But to whatever extent I'd come to know her over the previous few months, it seemed like a good frantic. A thriving frantic. She was alive—more alive than I'd seen her in my short time since the accident—and even when little mishaps occurred along the way, things she'd deem a crisis, I'd always notice a hint of a smile when she dealt with them. And deal with them she would, making everything turn out the way she'd envisioned.

She'd really gone above and beyond. I actually wondered what she was going to do with herself once this day was *over*, because for the three months leading up to the wedding it was all she ate, breathed, and slept. And it showed. The church was breathtaking. She'd left no stained-glass windowpane unturned.

Cat, Danielle, and Samantha were visions in pewter. Their dresses were—dare I say—stunning. My mother had gone out of her way and had them custom-made, and they were decidedly more like couture, red-carpet fare than bridesmaid gowns. Cat had that pregnant celebrity look that had been all the rage during recent award seasons.

"You look so pretty," I said to them.

"We *do*," Cat agreed. "I never thought I'd see a non-hideous bridal party, let alone be a member of one. Someone should take a picture."

"Oh, I *am*," my mother said, camera blocking half her face and then blinding flash after flash.

"Oh, sweetheart," Cat said, choking back tears of wonder at the moment, "*you* look stunning."

"So . . ." Samantha said. "Is it time to *do* this?"

I raised my eyebrows wondering what *this* was, but when they all started reaching for wrapped boxes I realized it was the hoary yet indispensable tradition. Something old, something new, something borrowed, and something blue.

"Do mine first," Sam ordered.

I took the package from her and pulled at the ribbon, untying the bow. I peeked in the box and saw a hint of blue. I could tell what it was without even moving the tissue paper—a baby blue garter.

"From the bottom of my heart to the top of my thigh, thank you," I said, holding it up to show the girls. "Is this something new *and* something blue?"

"Just something blue," my mother said, tipping me off that the "something new" was coming from her. I pulled up my dress to slip on the garter and wondered if there was a *right* leg and a wrong one. But, already feeling self-conscious about the whole thing, I didn't bring it up.

"Wrong leg," Cat pointed out.

"I'm a lefty, and if anyone notices, we've got bigger problems than a little lapse of wedding tradition," I said.

"Open *this*," she said, clapping her hands gleefully.

I did as instructed and pulled out the most beautiful, delicate, pearl and diamond necklace I'd ever seen. Although . . . *had* I seen it? There was something familiar about it, like I was staring at a photograph—yet there it was in my hands. Cat helped me put it on and then pulled me to the mirror to look at myself.

I ran my fingertips over the stones and spheres. "It's so beautiful."

"It's something borrowed," Cat said. "*And* something old. It's my mom's."

"It looks good enough to eat," I said, and Cat took in a quick short breath.

"That's the exact same thing you said last time!" she exclaimed, as she pulled out a picture. "You actually put it in your mouth for a second, and if my mother had seen, I don't think we'd be here today." The photo showed me at age seven—marrying Todd in the backyard. I'd worn her mother's necklace that day too. I reached up to my neck to touch it. I knew she'd shown me the picture when I was in the hospital to jog my memory, so I couldn't be sure if I was remembering it from then or from when we were children. But I felt *something*. Like my brain was itching.

"My turn," my mom said. "Something *new*."

She handed me a small box, wrapped in silver paper. I carefully opened it, trying unsuccessfully not to tear the pretty wrapping, and pulled out a black velvet box. Inside were diamond stud earrings.

"Wow," I said. "They're *gorgeous*."

"I thought so. And every girl should have a pair," she said with an air of authority.

"Thank you," I said, although I'd started to feel almost like I was having an out-of-Jordan experience. Something strange was going on inside me, a mild combination of dizziness, nausea, headache, and anxiety. It came and went. I wanted to sit, then stand, then sit, then haul ass out of there and swing from a tree I saw that wasn't there. Wedding jitters, no doubt. I looked at the mirror and went to put the earrings on, but the little back slipped and fell out of my gloved hand. And as Sam grabbed it up and offered to help, I had a moment of intense fear that she was going to stick my lobe hard with the post.

"Jordan, hold still!" she scolded. "It's your day. I wouldn't hurt you if someone paid me—and I haven't had a decent offer yet. Besides," she said, cinching the molar-sized rock in place, "I'm *way* over that trick." That trick? I stared at her and stared, then rubbed my lobes a few times and turned my head to give her access.

My mother, Cat, and Danielle left the room to do last-minute checks, leaving Samantha and me alone in the room.

"So," Sam said, and kind of bobbed her head uncomfortably.

"So . . ." I said back.

"This is probably the part where I say some sisterly stuff and we get all weepy," she said.

"Okay . . ." I said and waited. There was an awkward pause as Sam kicked her left foot up and then swiped it back and forth a few more times.

Finally she spoke up. "Yeah, it's hard to know what to say, that isn't, you know, *insulting*." She pinched the top of her dress nervously.

Then a godsend—a knock at the door.

"Come in," we nearly shouted.

The door opened and there stood Dirk, looking very handsome in his tux, and . . . *looking*.

"Hey!" I said, suddenly aware of the implications. "You're not supposed to see me until I walk down the aisle! It's bad luck!"

"I'll leave you two," Sam said and slipped out of the room.

"Come here," Dirk said, and pulled me toward him. "*This* is for *good* luck." And he kissed me softly. Then his lips grazed my cheek, and my neck, finally settling on my ear. He started tonguing my ear like a starved dog lapping up the last of his dinner after not having eaten for a week. The soft kisses had given way to amateur hour at the ear canal. I didn't want to hurt his feelings, but it was *disgusting*.

And as I reflexively pushed against his arm and straightened slightly, I felt as though I'd been here before. The two of us in close quarters, my head turned sideways to him, eyes wide. I didn't know if it was déjà vu or if I was having an actual memory, but Dirk's tongue snaking around in my ear was an extremely unpleasant sensation that I was almost certain I'd experienced before. I pulled away and looked at him. I concentrated hard. Hard as I possibly could. Was I remembering something? Dirk winked as he said, "See you at the altar, baby." And then he was gone.

I stood in the same position in the middle of the room for what must have been a good ten minutes, trying to recall that moment, that *other* moment—something before the few handfuls of moments I was about to carry into that ceremony, down that aisle, into our life together. I had felt something just then. Something other than "now."

Walter opened the door and Cat leaned into the room, waving me forward with a trembling smile. I gathered my bouquet and stood amid the rustling of my bridal gown.

Then a phrase flashed in my mind, but it wasn't about Dirk. It was about ears. "Wise beyond your ears." As a child I'd misheard the phrase "wise beyond your *years*." I couldn't place the when or where, but it was a hazy memory that seemed to be floating in and out of my consciousness. I could hear my mother laughing and correcting me, but it still didn't make sense to me.

I didn't want to move. I got superstitious about standing in that very spot—since I thought the memories were finding me there—so I stayed for another few minutes, I don't even know how many, waiting for my memory, or even another word or a phrase or an image, to come back. Nothing came. Only the "Wedding March." I took it as a sign and readied myself for the biggest event of my life—and certainly of the life I remembered.

\* \* \* \* \*

Cat, Danielle, and Samantha scrambled to the entrance, to pair up with Dirk's groomsmen for the promenade down the aisle. My mom went next, and I laced my arm into the crook of Walter's, suddenly feeling all my muscles seize into knots—not knowing if I was going to scream bloody murder, faint, laugh, cry, or all of the above, though not necessarily in that order.

I had the distinct impression I was standing beside myself, a few feet away, wearing jeans and an old Dr Pepper T-shirt, watching a bride about to be given away, and I didn't know her, though she was me. Maybe at that colossal moment, with the vows lying in wait just a short walk away, every first-time bride and groom falls into a split second or two of shallow madness, shoved there by the stultifying awareness that life is about to change irreversibly. I'm not sure how many console themselves with the possible reversal that a divorce represents, but I certainly didn't. My mind drifted across a spotty landscape, partly barren, partly crowded with faces I'd known and places I'd been, abuzz with voices I couldn't understand and music that sounded as though it were being broadcast underwater. I felt half tempted to leave, but the bride stood still, next to a stepfather she barely knew, about to walk down the aisle and commit the rest of her life to a man that half her friends swore she hated.

We stood at the entrance, and Walter put something small into my right hand. A single orange jelly bean. "For luck," he said. I popped the bean in my mouth and chewed and swallowed. Then everybody rose in unison and turned to watch me leap.

"You ready, Jordy Belly?" he asked, and everything stopped. The voices, the thick chords of Mendelssohn careening off the high walls, the visual chatter of images riffling by like a crack-injected music video. The dreamlike haze I'd been drifting in for the previous half hour started to dissipate. All the near-miss memories connected, one after the next, the trickle becoming a tidal wave. All clear now. Blessing in disguise, with diamonds. Wise beyond her ears. Sam's adolescent assault on my freshly pierced lobes, improvising *new* piercings in a lifelong tradition of torment. Awfully wedded wife.

And Jordy Belly. I knew that. And I knew how I knew it. The tangerine jelly bean. I was born under the sign of Reagan, when Jelly Belly candies became all the rage, and in his love for the candies, the otherwise apolitical Walter had found something in common with the Great Communicator. From the supply he'd kept close by his desk in the home office, he'd always set aside the tangerines, for me, his Jordy Belly. I *remembered*.

Walter gave me a little tug and we started to walk down the aisle. I looked to both sides at the pews and recognized faces, not all but most. It was almost like a field with flowers popping up every other step—each flower the recognizable figure of someone in my life. Mrs. Winchell, the neighbor whom nobody liked but who always brought a fruitcake to our house every Christmas—which my mom would promptly re-gift to the Children's Hospital. Mrs. Redding, my piano teacher. I hadn't practiced in fifteen years, and there wasn't a shot in hell I'd remember how to play "Edelweiss" but I *did* remember *her*. Dirty Uncle Ritchie. He wasn't actually related to us, but he was Walter's best friend. He used to sneak me sips of beer, and when I came home from school one day and asked him what sixty-nine was—he told me but made me promise not to tell where I'd heard. And I'd wondered, how on earth could anyone hold a kiss for *sixty-nine seconds*?

And Dirk. There he was . . . looking as handsome as ever in his tux— the motherfucker.

Bad memories of our life together rained down—one sorry, sordid image after the next. I remembered the various girls he'd ogled, flirted with, cheated with. The forgotten birthday. Waking up in the hospital the first time—everybody dissecting me like a lab rat. And then waking up in the hospital for the *second* time. And Dirk pretending that we were still together even though I was completely, unequivocally, 200 percent over him. Memory after memory after memory . . . up until minutes before the wedding—Dirk sticking his disgusting cow tongue in my ear. The patented Michael Dirkston ear extravaganza. It all rushed back, borne on a raging river of saliva.

How did this happen? I thought. He caught my narrowed eyes and winked. I walked up the steps and found myself at the center of my wedding. It was totally surreal.

The priest nodded to us, to say It's time, and I took a deep breath. I didn't know when I was supposed to break the news that there would be no wedding. When would be the appropriate time to raise my hand?

"We are gathered here today to join Jordan Landau and Michael Dirkston in their blessed union," the priest said.

Right *then*, I decided. The second I heard the words "blessed union" in the same sentence as my and Dirk's names, the tragicomic farce had to be stopped.

"Father." I cleared my throat and raised my hand.

"Yes?" the priest said.

"I object," I said.

There was audible shifting in seats and a more than a few murmurs among the crowd. I turned to face them.

"Hi," I said to everyone. And I looked out into the church at everybody that was there for my wedding. *My* wedding. To *Dirk*. Repulsive.

"Hi?" a few confused guests answered back.

"It's me. Jordan. I mean—I know you know it's me, but I mean it's *me* me. I'm back. I got my memory back. Just now, and it's still coming back to me, but I *REMEMBER*!"

There were oohs and aahs and how wonderfuls abounding, smiles everywhere—except on Dirk's face. He looked eight shades of nervous.

"Dirk, I'm missing something. Where's my journal?"

"Your journal?" he said, in his best who-me? voice.

"My journal," I repeated. "It was under my bed. If you cleaned the place, you would have found it. And if you looked through it, you would have found *this:* You forgot my birthday last year. Or that time in July when you said I looked like the creature from the black lagoon when I was coming out of the water. Or when you cheated on me—the first time, and I cried so hard my tears soaked the page, and I circled the spot of dried wrinkled paper to note my tears."

Dirk looked out at our audience and smiled nervously. I looked out at the faces, recognizing so many of them.

"I remember you all!" I shouted. "Hi, Mrs. Dunlap," I called out to the woman wearing a straw bonnet with a big satin ribbon in the third row. "I remember you used to make us broccoli casserole. It was *awful*, but I didn't say anything. Nice to see you."

I felt manic. I'd gone from white-hot anger to soaring happiness. "I remember! I remember everything!" I started pointing at people. "I remember you, and I remember you and you—" And then I spotted Todd, who looked like he was holding his breath. I walked down the steps, back up the aisle toward where he sat. "And I most certainly remember *you.*"

"You do?" he said.

"How could I forget my first husband?" He smiled and looked like he was about to cry. The priest, however, wasn't too pleased to hear of my previous nuptials. "We were seven years old," I said to the priest, who just sort of frowned.

"Hussy!" said some old woman in the front row that I didn't even recognize. I looked back at Todd.

"How could you let me almost marry this creep?" I asked.

"I *already* objected," he said. "But you weren't buying, so I was just sitting here, holding my peace, praying you'd wake up."

"I'm sorry for what I put you through—and not believing you," I said and then looked at Cat, who was looking back at me expectantly, waiting for me to say something to her.

"And of course I remember my best girl!" Cat ran up and hugged me.

"You're back," she said. "I tried to stop you . . ."

"I know," I said.

A sudden movement distracted me. It was Lydia standing up and looking like she'd like to be anywhere but there. What the hell was she doing trying to sneak out of the fifth row?

"Lydia?" I said in a high-pitched squeal. "You stole the ideas for KidCo from me. And you're sleeping with someone fifteen years younger than you."

"Ouch," someone said. I looked out to see who it was and realized it was a room full of nobody I cared about. And, more important, nobody who cared about *me*.

Then I spotted Esperanza, who had accused me of throwing poop! I knew I wasn't one to talk about rewriting history, but that *wasn't* me. "And, Esperanza," I said as I wagged my finger at her, "it was Sam who threw her poop, not me! *Sam.*"

Samantha rolled her eyes as if she didn't know what anyone was talking about, but that one I wasn't going to let go.

"Oh . . ." Esperanza slowly nodded. "Jes, I think you're right."

Ya think? "I know I'm right. Because I *remember*," I said victoriously. "I don't know why most of you are even here. I'm looking at all of you and having trouble finding more than a handful of people who have ever even been *nice* to me."

I looked at my mom. "*You've* treated me like an unwanted stepchild for nearly my entire life. Yes, you've thrown me a lovely wedding. Thank you for that. But how could you sell me out like this? You *knew* I loved Travis!"

My mother stepped toward me and in a hushed tone said, "This is not the time or the place, Jordan."

"The time or place?" I asked incredulously. "But it *is* the time and place for me to marry someone that you knew damned well I'd broken up with before I lost my memory?"

"I was only looking out for your best interests," she said.

"*My* best interests? That's priceless."

Then I noticed Samantha, who seemed to be eating this up. "Sam, why so smug? You've taken advantage of me since you learned how to walk." I paused for effect and then added, "No *wonder* your father likes me better."

I turned to Walter. "You at least always *meant* well," I said, and then turned out to everyone in the church. "But most of you people treated me like shit for my entire life! And by the way? I faked my amnesia the first time because I needed a do-over. I wanted to forget about all of this, all of you! Because I'd let practically everyone in this church walk all over me so much that it seemed like the *only* way out was to start fresh." I raised my arms to the heavens. "So forgive me, Father, for I have sinned. I lied! But not anymore."

"That's enough," my mother said.

"You're right. It's more than even *I* can stomach. So while you're looking out for my best interests, you can go ahead and apologize to these poor people for wasting their time today by inviting them to this sham of a wedding. And it would be in your best interest to forget about suing my *real* boyfriend if you want to continue to have anything to do with your daughter. I've got my faculties back and there will be no power of attorney and no lawsuit. Travis isn't even at fault for anything. He did nothing. Except *love* me."

And as soon as I said that, I thought about Travis. I had to get out of there and find him as fast as I could.

"I guess the wedding's off?" Dirk said nervously. This was the idiot I was supposed to be marrying? *Awfully wed* took on new meaning.

"Yes, Dirk," I said. "The wedding is off." And then I turned to everyone else, "You hear that? No wedding today. Nothing to see here, people. Now, if you'll excuse me, I have to go find the guy I'm actually in love with."

# 30.
# to the lighthouse

On any given day, you can see pretty much anything on the streets of New York City, so my running out of the church, up Broadway a few blocks until I hit Union Square, and finally finding a cab to Travis's apartment, while still wearing my wedding dress, didn't create much of a stir. Sure, I got a few points and stares, but it didn't matter. I was on a mission. I'd dialed Travis's number the minute I got outside and got a disconnected recording, which made me even more frantic.

There was a guy walking into Travis's building as soon as I got there, so rather than wait and call up, I conspicuously followed him inside, smiling (for future reference, a wedding dress might be a perfect cover for a major burglary), and took the elevator up to Travis's floor. I ran to his door and started ringing his doorbell and pounding like a crazy person.

The door opened and there stood . . . *Ben*. Not who I was expecting. Nor was he expecting me. He looked me up and down in my wedding gown and guffawed.

"What, did you fall off your *cake*?" he said.

"Where's Travis?" I gasped, totally out of breath.

"He's not here," he said. "He doesn't live here anymore. I took over his lease."

"Where is he?" I asked.

"Who wants to know?"

"Who do you *think*?"

"Why don't you leave him alone, Jordan?" he said. "How about you just *forget* about him. You're *good* at that."

I didn't have time for this. The last thing I needed was Ben and his attitude. "Ben, *where* is he? Tell me," I urged. "I need to find him. Where does he live now?"

"I don't remember," he said smugly. "I must have forgotten. *You* know how that is."

"Hilarious," I mocked.

"Yeah, I thought so too. Thanks for stopping by," Ben said, and then started to close the door. I squeezed myself in between the door and the jamb and stopped him.

"Please, Ben," I begged. "Please just tell me where he is. I need to talk to him. And I think he'd want to talk to me too."

He sighed. Some combination of my newfound lucidity and apparent lunacy must have overwhelmed his resistance. "He moved onto his dad's old boat. He wanted to preserve his savings to fix the lighthouse and open the restaurant, in case he's got anything left after the lawsuit gets resolved."

"Oh, it's resolved!" I said grimly. "Do you know his phone number?"

"He doesn't have a phone."

"How is that possible? Just give it to me—please!"

"He *doesn't* have a phone," he said again.

"Well, do you know where the boat is?" I asked.

"They're generally found on the water," he said.

Tears began to form in my eyes. "Ben, please."

"It's in a marina somewhere, I don't know. *Really*, I don't know," he said and I could tell that he really *didn't*, so I thanked him and left.

I'd find him somehow, if I had to scour every marina from Maine to Miami.

\* \* \* \* \*

I took a taxi to Penn Station, a train out to Long Beach, and then another taxi to the marina. I was banking on the fact that there probably wouldn't be too many people living in the boats. I'd imagined they'd be lined up like ducks in a row and that I could walk up and down and peer in until I saw Travis.

Of course, I was *stupid*. For starters—all the boats were out in the water, moored in star shapes in the harbor, and there was no way I could get to them. Add to that the fact that they were spread out over about a two-mile area, and there you have it. Me standing on the dock in my wedding gown. Ridiculous.

Frustrated and overwhelmed by the day's events, I wasn't in a hurry to take two taxis and another train, so I took off my shoes and walked along the pier. I'd been so focused on getting to Travis, making up with Travis—Travis, Travis, Travis—I hadn't even *thought* about what would be next for Jordan.

The euphoria of coming clean and casting aside Dirk had worn off. I found a quiet spot, slumped down on a bench, and stared at the sailboats' bobbing masts, marveling at the train wreck I'd wrought.

\* \* \* \* \*

I got off the train at Astor Place and saw Lyric Lady, lighting a match. As soon as it sparked, she blew it out. Then she lit another and did the same thing. I didn't know if I should be happy for her getting out of the psych ward or not. I just wanted her to be safe. I cleared my throat as I neared her to make my presence known, and she looked up at me and frowned.

I walked exceptionally slowly as I passed her, giving her the maximum amount of time to toss a lyric at me. But . . . nothing. I don't know why this mattered so much to me, but it did. I felt this oddly poignant sense of loss. Probably how she felt when I stopped playing along—first selfishly, to cover my tracks and then because I didn't know better.

Then as I was just about to turn left on Broadway she cleared *her* throat. I stopped and turned.

She stuck her chin out defiantly. " 'I got . . . nine lives . . . cat's eyes . . .' " she said.

"'Usin' every one of them and runnin' wild,'" I answered. And I was *back*. "Back in Black." She raised her kerchiefed fist in the air, and on an impulse I ran back and hugged her.

Then she looked me over again and nodded. "'Nice day for a white wedding.'"

I nodded back and confided, "'It's a nice day to—'"

But she beat me to the finish, tossing her head back and bending her whole body forty-five degrees. "'Start agaaaain!'" she sang out. It was good to be home.

I got to the apartment at around midnight and Sneevil cocked his little head at me and let out a tiny chirp.

"Sneevil," I said aloud, "remember me?"

I walked straight over to his cage, and for the first time, I raised the gate and reached in—and though canaries don't like to be handled, he cautiously let me pet his tiny feathered head. He even leaned into my hand and nudged me.

"I'm sorry I didn't remember you, little guy," I said to him. "But I'm back. And you're *mine* now."

The red light on my answering machine was blinking and I didn't want to know what kind of vitriol it had in store for me, so I opted to ignore it. Not just ignore it but delete it—unheard. That was the past. Cliché as it sounded, my new life started when I stood at the altar and came clean. Although it may have been selfish and disruptive, I needed to do it so I could start over . . . again. This time not *faking*, not *lost*, but assembling all the information I'd gathered under both circumstances and coming up with a responsible plan for my future.

I picked up the phone and called Todd. I wanted to hear what had happened after I left my wedding. Turned out that my mom hyperventilated and nearly passed out from all the excitement, Samantha insisted that they go on with the reception since it was already paid for, and Todd and Cat went to the closest bar, where she matched him shot for shot (even if hers were ginger ale).

"Well," I had to ask, "was my mom okay? After she hyperventilated?"

"She's fine," he said. "Nothing five glasses of merlot won't fix."

"Okay . . ." I said, waiting for more info, but none was forthcoming. "So you don't even have any gossip for me? You just *left*?"

"*You're* the gossip, nimrod! Did you think something *more* exciting was going to happen after you left mid-wedding?"

"Guess not," I admitted.

"So?" Todd said. "Are you going to tell *me* what happened after you left? I'm judging that everything didn't go perfectly as planned or you wouldn't be calling me right now. What's up with Travis?"

"He moved," I said, "onto a boat. In a marina. *Somewhere*. But I don't know where."

Man overboard. Relationship over.

*　*　*　*　*

Obviously, the first official sit-down of the Three Musketeers was going to be awkward, but I needed to apologize to Cat in person and wanted to say some things to Todd as well.

We met at Cozy's, and although I'd prepared a bit of a speech, it all went out the window when I saw their faces. Cat was trying not to be angry, but I could see the hurt seeping through the warm smile she met me with.

"Cat," I started. "I'm so sorry. I know deep down that I could have trusted you. But I knew that you'd be horrified and I'd never be able to keep it up. You'd be the voice of reason. The one who put her foot down. I know it sounds dumb, but I respected your sense of right and wrong too much to bring you into it. And I wasn't willing to deal with what would have been your totally appropriate disapproval."

I started playing with the napkin dispenser because tears started blurring my vision and I needed to distract myself. I pretended to be wiping a finger smudge off the aluminum, but I was only making it worse.

"Hey," Cat said, and reached out to touch my hand. "It's okay. I mean, yeah, I was pissed at first . . . but Todd and I threw a few back at

Chumley's in lieu of your reception . . . and as much as I hate to admit it—I probably *would* have ruined your scam."

"You're just saying that," I said.

"No," Todd chimed in. "She *would* have. She really sucks at stuff like that." Cat play socked him in the arm and we were silent for a minute. "You're just too solid, Cat. We all bow down to you, pathetic bumblers in the presence of true goodness."

"The actual amnesia was never part of the plan," I said. "Thanks for trying to talk me out of the Dirk thing. Sorry I didn't listen."

"How weird was that, though?" Cat asked. "Not the actual getting of the amnesia—which *was* superweird yet obviously *karma*—but the Dirk thing. Talk about a clinical approach to life."

"By any means necessary, no less. *So* uncool," I agreed. "When my memory came back and I realized I was walking down the aisle to marry *Dirk* . . . ?" I did an exaggerated shudder at the thought.

"He had you, he blew it," Todd said. "Then he lost you, and he wanted you back. Now that you've woken up from the nightmare—"

"Damnesia!" I inserted.

"Right!" Todd smiled back. "And now that he's lost you for good, I wonder what his next move is."

"I don't," Cat said. "I saw him hitting on your cousin before they shuttled off to the reception."

"The reception?" I repeated. "My God—what a total mess I made. I didn't even think of all those things—the cake and the booze and the band and the tent rental. And return policies on gifts have gotten *awful*!"

"Coulda been worse," Todd said, winking, and I couldn't help laughing, and Cat couldn't either.

We sat there, me slurping pea soup—which I have to say tasted even *better* than I remembered—and all of us apologizing to one another for various missteps over the previous months, and when all was said and done, we were back to normal. Todd was even seeing someone who'd lasted *past* a week's time. All was right. Except for things with Travis.

That was wrong. Very wrong. But I wasn't giving up on us, and Todd and Cat agreed to help me.

* * * * *

My first stop: the DMV. Probably the last place you ever want to go, but Todd suggested that instead of wandering aimlessly on the docks in a wedding gown, I should look up Travis's registration. I didn't know if they'd actually give me any information, but it was worth a shot. Here's what I found out:

1. The DMV really is as stereotypically awful as it's made out to be.

2. If you operate a boat in New York State, you must register it with the DMV.

3. However, the DMV will not give you information about anything that isn't yours (okay, reasonable).

4. They won't even be nice about it.

5. Desperation isn't always a ticket to sympathy.

I was complaining to Cat about the dead end I'd hit, and how I was *never* going to find his boat, when she just started tossing out ideas at random.

"Stand on the dock with a megaphone?" she suggested.

"I don't think so," I said.

"Message in a bottle?" she said.

"Not so much," I replied.

"Smoke signals?" she said, again jokingly, but that was *it*. Not smoke signals but the beacon. The lighthouse. If I couldn't go to him, I'd make him come to me.

* * * * *

Rather than continue to spin my wheels, I decided to do some Internet research. I sat at my desk at home (I missed you, desk, I thought), logged onto my computer (missed you too, computer!), ready to choose a search engine, and came face to computer screen with an e-mail in-box filled with 168 unopened e-mails.

I warily clicked the little mailbox icon to take a cursory glace and make sure I wasn't missing anything important, and, lo and behold, there were a zillion messages from my mother and Walter to and from each other—none, gathering from the subject lines, having anything to do with me (*I did not miss this*).

I decided to open and respond to *one* of them and delete the rest. The one I opened went as follows:

From: judypatootie521@hotmail.com

To: wallygator317@hotmail.com

Subject: I forgot!

I remembered that I wanted to tell you something but couldn't remember what it was. Maybe I'll remember later. If not, it probably wasn't important.

Yet, it *was* important enough to share in an e-mail about *nothing* and blind copy me on it. It wasn't a huge deal, but it *was* taking up the majority of my in-box. And the more I thought about it, the more I realized that all I had to do was ask them to stop. Simple. Yet, like so many other not-yet-dealt-with issues, I'd feared the confrontation and not taken any action. I hit *Reply All*.

From: JordanLandau@yahoo.com

To: wallygator317@hotmail.com, judypatootie521@hotmail.com

Subject: re: I forgot!

Dear Parents,
Please do not cc me on your e-mail exchanges. I appreciate your wanting to include me in your correspondence. However, if it does

not pertain to me or if it is not "to" me, I would rather not receive
them. I realize that there is a lot we will have to discuss, but I've
been meaning to ask you to stop ccing me for a long time, so I
wanted to do that while it was fresh on my mind. Thank you very
much.

*Send.*

\* \* \* \* \*

I was browsing the New-York Historical Society, the conservation society, and the municipal authority, trying to figure out who could best
help me get the lighthouse up and running—if it was even a possibility.
I'd only been searching for about seven minutes when I heard a ding in
my in-box.

From: wallygator317@hotmail.com

To: Jordan.Landau@yahoo.com

Subject: re: re: I forgot!

Dear Jordan,
I understand completely and will stop ccing you unless it is rel-
evant to *you*. Glad to have you back and look forward to the next
phase of this family.

Love,
Wally (Dad)

*Seriously?* I thought. That was all it took? I was dumbfounded. A simple, calm, concise communication. Problem solved. No assumed identi-
ties. No abandoned memory. Huh.

After a series of dead ends and "you don't need *us*, the people you
want to contact are . . ." I finally garnered some useful information after
being on hold for about seventeen hours. A woman named Brenda at the

Long Island Power Authority caught me singing along to the hold music in a state of utter delirium, and she took a liking to me instantly.

"Sounds like you were pretty into that song. I can put you back on hold," she offered, but I declined. She giggled and admitted to doing the same thing when she was on hold.

She told me that the Redding Harbor Lighthouse's power had been shut off in 1988 and it hadn't operated since.

"Wait," I said. "So the power could be restored?"

"Yeah," she answered. "If somebody approved turning it on again."

I *did* have a rich history of trying to negotiate with the utilities company. But, really, who among us has been successful in *that* endeavor? Certainly not I. With my credit history, my power had been shut off so often, at times the view from across the street would resemble that of a strobe light—off and on, off and on, with blinding repetition.

But Brenda and I had a connection. We'd bonded over my rendition of "Because the Night (Belongs to Us)," so surely she'd help out a fellow on-hold crooner. I just wasn't sure what the best way to go about asking was.

"That is *very* interesting," I said.

"I guess," she said in a singsong, and exhaled—waiting to see if I was going to say anything else. There was a lull in the conversation, and while I can appreciate those quiet unspoken moments as much as the next person, Brenda may *not* have.

"Very, *very* interesting," I repeated, trying to fill up the emptiness.

"So, um . . ."

"Jordan," I said, finishing her sentence and trying to make things more personal.

"Yes, okay, *Jordan*, is there anything *else* I can help you with?"

"As a matter of fact there *is*," I said, finally mustering up the confidence to ask.

*     *     *     *     *

If you didn't factor in that I'd be out at the edge of the earth as I knew it, alone at a deserted lighthouse in an area with no cell service, and the very distinct possibility that Travis wouldn't even come, there was nothing wrong with the idea.

Of course, Cat and Todd disagreed.

"I don't like the idea of you all alone out there," Todd said warily.

"Alone isn't the worst thing I could be," I said.

"It's really romantic and all, but don't you think it's kind of extreme?" Cat asked gently.

"It *is* extreme. Yes," I said.

"So we all agree on that," Todd chimed in.

"He needs to meet me," I said.

"He can't meet you if he doesn't know when and where he's supposed to be," Cat said.

They weren't getting it. "Not that kind of *meet*," I explained. "Meet *me*. Meet this version of me. He's known me when I was faking who I was, which is closer to who I am—but too contrarian and too caffeinated—and he's known me when I didn't know who I was, which is mildly embarrassing, but he hasn't ever met the real me."

"Have any of us?" Todd said. "How many versions of you are there, by the way? Is *this* your final answer or is there going to be a new version in the coming weeks?"

"Maybe," I said. Todd threw his hands up in the air and Cat sighed dramatically. "But nothing *crazy*," I reassured. "I just mean that I'll be the best version of me I can be. I *may* change . . . but hopefully only for the better."

"Like a go-go dancer you?" Todd asked hopefully.

"I'll let that go," I said. "I didn't even really know who I was until now. And, *yeah*, I made mistakes, and it was pretty awful at times . . . but they say the most painful times bring on the most personal growth."

"My older brother used to beat the hell out of me all the time," Todd said, "and I must admit, it did grow . . . tiresome."

"Point is," I said, ignoring Todd, "I want the chance to show Travis who I am. To see if we have a *chance*. Without any lies or lawsuits or hospitals. And we may *not*. But the old Jordan wouldn't have *ever* done something like this. She'd have accepted that she made too many mistakes and she deserved to suffer for it. I'm not her anymore. Can you guys back me up on this?"

"Of course," Cat said. "Go get him."

Todd was silent. He took a long deep breath and exhaled. Then he finally spoke. "Fine. Go for it. Of *course*, I just want you to be happy. But remember *one* thing. You sang 'Close to You' with Dirk in public and without any irony . . . and I will *never* let you live that down."

∗   ∗   ∗   ∗   ∗

The train ride out to Redding Harbor isn't exactly short. It's at pretty much the outermost tip of the island—as far as you can go, and that kind of alone time lets you run through only so many songs on your iPod before you have to confront what's going on a little farther between the ears.

There was a little boy sitting next to his mother—sneakers untied, scrawny legs dangling—his hands covering his eyes. They were playing peekaboo. He'd cover his eyes and say, "Where's Mommy?" and then re-move his hands and giggle at the excitement of finding her again.

I hated peekaboo when I was little. The only game I hated more was hide-and-seek—probably based on the same reasons. In peekaboo, there's an element of momentary fear. Where *is* your mother? And then relief. *Ah . . . there she is.* I never felt comfortable, because I never had the faith that she'd definitely, for sure, without a doubt, be there when I opened my eyes. So I cheated. When I played peekaboo, I always peeked through the cracks in my fingers to make sure nobody pulled a fast one and ditched me. Technically it *was* called *peek*aboo, so my logical defense would be that I thought *peek* meant "peek."

Hide-and-seek was another matter entirely. I hated it because I never felt worthy of being found. And I was always scared that if I picked too tough a hiding spot, they'd just give up and go about the rest of their day—leaving me tucked away in some dark place, wondering if the game was still going on. So I always picked an easy spot. I picked such lame hiding spots that I may as well have just stood there out in plain view wearing a sandwich board. I didn't know why I did what I did at the time, but suddenly I understood it better—I understood myself better.

And in essence, there was a certain element of hide-and-seek to my having faked amnesia and even getting it for real. The first time, I was hiding who I was. Hiding the person I'd grown ashamed of from everyone, and also from myself. I didn't like who I'd become and I didn't necessarily want anyone to find the *old* Jordan, but I did want them to find the new-and-improved one in her place. Consciously, the first time, and unconsciously the second. Both times—not feeling proud of what I'd done and who I was.

But this time I wasn't hiding—in fact I was doing the exact opposite. I was trying with all my might to be found. I was about to try shining the brightest, most intense, dazzling, blazing light in an effort to signal my not-so-hiding spot.

I was doing what sEra the bartender had described to me—jumping without a net and having faith that the net would appear. The net being Travis. And there certainly were unanswered questions—his being married being the *biggest* question—but in my amnesiac state he'd promised that there were explanations, and I trusted that there were. I just had to get him to trust me enough to explain. More important, I needed him to just *show up*.

\* \* \* \* \*

The lighthouse was dark when I rolled up in the rental car I'd appropriated for the second part of the trip (no small feat when you have no credit card) on the chosen Saturday afternoon. As I approached it, I saw for the first time how rundown and forlorn the place looked. If part of the lighthouse cliché is desolation, then Travis's beacon fit the bill.

Because he'd been there to guide me the first time I'd come, and I was so focused on *him*, I hadn't seen the crumbling foundation, peeling paint, shattered windows, and the twisted mass of thistle, sickly juniper, and exhausted vines creeping around the place. It looked beaten. And as I pushed hard against the door and practically fell into the cold and stony emptiness of the ground-level vestibule, I felt a chill of doubt and defeat too.

I don't know why I expected it to be lit when I got there, but my breath grew short and my heart sped up as I climbed the stairs. In my turbulent emotional state, it didn't occur to me that, in addition to neglecting every friendship, working relationship, financial relationship. and basic code of decent human behavior during my bouts of amnesia, I'd also neglected to hit the gym. I was terribly out of shape and now losing faith in the project, which began to take on the proportions of a harebrained scheme in my now-memory-besotted brain. I told myself that it would of course be dark until someone physically turned it on—but I still had a lingering fear that maybe my impassioned plea for a one-week electricity window had been finally met with a yes only to get the crazy girl off the phone. And not because I'd told her she could indeed save my life with the flip of a switch.

It turned out not to be as simple as that, of course, but not as convoluted as you might imagine. The service restoration took a week, and beyond that, I was on my own. After a few calls I'd learned the location and operation of the main circuit breaker and lantern room switches. As these things go, the lamp was of a fairly recent vintage, and after a few trips up and down the stairs, peering into the box, poking around the controls, following directions in the manual I'd pieced together, everything seemed to be in order.

Sure enough, when I got to the lantern room and prepared to be dazzled, the lamp wouldn't turn on. *Perfect,* I thought. More punishment. I messed with it for a few minutes, trying to get it to illuminate, and I began to realize at last that I was no longer the Jordan who'd faked amnesia, and certainly not the one who'd *had* amnesia. I wasn't feeling sorry for myself. I was okay with whatever the outcome would be. I could recognize my part in all the mess I'd created and I was actually proud of myself for simply taking the action. I had no control over the result. I had no control over *anything*.

And I believe it was as soon as I really accepted that in my heart— well, maybe not *as soon* as that, more like a good while later actually, because I struggled with the giant lightbulb for a long time, but it's a lovely metaphor—that the light sprang to life. It glowed low and timidly for a moment, then despite the accretion of dust and grime on the outer surface of the lens, it became a blazing brightness so intense that I half thought it would wash me over the railing and out to sea.

Now, I'm not saying it turned on by *itself*—I gave it one last shove, but it *worked*. And I laughed a laugh of idiot joy and held my open palms up to the blaring beacon. Acceptance? Was that what I'd been lacking all along? So if I accepted that I'd never lose those last ten pounds, would they suddenly come off too? Maybe? Maybe not (but it was worth a shot).

Reading material is crucial in times of waiting, e.g., doctors' offices, airports, train stations, any situation where you're in an extreme rush or anxious for something to happen. And this qualified as one of those instances where I wished time would compress, as in the nature shows where a germinating seed becomes a blooming flower in five or six seconds. But I was destined to watch for Travis at the pace of grass growing. In my mad dash to get out to the lighthouse, I'd neglected to bring anything with me. (And, yes, I *accepted* that I had no reading material, and, *no*, a book did not magically appear.)

So after my first several minutes of joy and wonder turned to simple pondering and then to borderline despair, I paced. I paced and I thought. And I sang. And I sat on the floor. And I tidied up the place a bit. I did jumping jacks. And then marked off the tower one foot at a time, counting how many steps it took to get all the way around. And I did one handstand. And I paced some more. I was bored. But I wasn't giving up.

It started to rain. I wondered what it was like to be on a boat in the rain. I pictured Travis on one of the many boats out in the distant harbor—reading or doing whatever he did . . . and then looking out the window and spotting the lighthouse. Lit. I pictured it about a thousand different times and a thousand different ways before I realized how late it really was and that maybe he wasn't even on the boat. Or maybe his boat wasn't in that harbor anymore. And maybe this was a really, *really* bad idea.

I stepped tentatively onto the deck, which was worn and warped with age and slippery from the rain, and found a new area to pace. I didn't mind getting rained on. It felt good—cleansing—until it started to really pour. Then it was just miserable. Thick gray fog had settled all around, so I could see less and less. It felt like I was crying, but maybe it was just misery, hopelessness, and night closing in.

And then I heard a car. In the mist, I saw uncertain headlight beams and what appeared to be a beat-up pickup truck rounding the curve on the little jutting promontory that held the lighthouse. It stopped a distance away. Then someone opened the door. And my heart, wanting to see, made its best effort to leap out of my chest by way of my throat.

I couldn't make out if it was him or not but it was *someone,* in a desolate area with not a whole lot to do, and the chances of that someone being Travis were pretty excellent. I got so excited, I ran to the railing to get a better look. And I *slipped.*

It happened so fast that I couldn't stop myself. I felt my legs shoot forward and then the rotted outer edge of the platform gave way beneath my feet, and a pain soared through my thigh muscle as it stretched beyond my only semi-athletic reach. I slid down and banged my two elbows on the battered rail, then the adrenaline tensed my arms and curled my hands into claws, and the next thing I knew I was dangling from the lower ring of railing. I felt intense pain in my legs and arms and the unmistakable chill of blood flowing somewhere, but something else bothered me more. What if it wasn't even Travis down there but some local stranger instead, oblivious to me hanging up here, just out for a stroll or curious about why the lighthouse had sprung to life?

This is some high irony, I thought. The girl who'd tried to escape herself was about to vanish permanently. I'm going to fall and die on these rocks and nobody will know. Maybe it's a fitting end. Maybe I deserve it.

"Jesus!" I heard someone scream. And I couldn't help wondering if that was it. If I'd missed the dying part and gone straight to the afterlife. After all, apparently Jesus was already there.

I certainly couldn't look down to confirm. I was bruised, bleeding, *terrified,* hanging on to a rain-slicked, rust-encrusted metal railing that seemed poised to give way with just a little encouragement from me. The platform was at the back of my head, and my legs dangled free. When I tentatively pulled on the rail to hoist myself, it creaked and sagged. So I closed my eyes and felt the pain leaving my arms, taking my grip with it. Then my savior screamed again, but the voice was close enough to touch me. "Jordan!"

And his hands *did* touch me—or grabbed me by the arms, and I looked up, and it was Travis.

His fingers vise-gripped me below the elbows, and as the grip pinched I yelped loudly, but he pressed forward, or more precisely fell *backward* as he too slipped, and we tumbled onto the deck.

"Hi," I said.

"What's a nice girl like you doing hanging around a place like this?" he asked.

"I thought I saw you . . . I saw *someone*. I got excited. I was just trying to get a better look."

"Next time don't be so excited to see me," he said, standing up but not letting go of me.

I chewed on my bottom lip while I tried to find the right words to say.

"Is it *you*?" he asked. "I mean, the you I knew before the amnesia?" Then he cleared his throat. "The real thing?"

"I got my memory back, yes," I said, feeling ashamed but relieved that at least he was smiling.

"You're all *wet*," he said.

"It's not so bad," I said, barely audible through my chattering teeth. He took his jacket off and put it around my shoulders.

"I guess pneumonia beats falling to your death." He looked into the lantern room at the light. "*You* did this?"

"It's what it's for, right? For people lost at sea to find their way home?"

"Or to keep them from getting too close to trouble," he said, staring at me. "But it didn't work. I followed it right *to* you."

"I was hoping you'd see the—" I said, but I realized what I was about to say.

"The light?" he inserted. We nodded together, and he smiled a mocking smile. "But it's a remarkable feat. Unbelievable almost."

Travis glanced around as though a stranger to the place. "Honestly, I don't think I'd ever have come back if I hadn't heard someone say the old lighthouse was signaling again."

I turned to him. "But I thought bringing it back to life was your dream."

He smiled and sighed. "I woke up. Like you did. The memories here . . . they're vivid and important to me, but this wasn't a happy place. My father . . . he lived under the spell of the isolation, like a prisoner of his own past here. He pretty much ignored my mother for years and withdrew into himself. And he died alone. In a way, I was trying to fix that somehow, return it to its glory for him."

"It was a nice dream," I said quietly.

"The way I honor him is by breaking with this sad, beautiful thing," he said, running his hand along the low masonry wall encircling the lantern room. "Maybe it's a project for someone else. I'll bring the memories along. To the East Village. Maybe the Lower East Side."

"You're moving?"

"Opening a restaurant," he said, and now his smile was lighter. "When I look back on my past, I want to see more than this place."

He took a step closer to me and I thought for a split second he was about to kiss me, but he stopped himself. "How was the wedding?"

I held up my left hand to show that there was no ring. "Didn't happen," I said. "Although I came uncomfortably close. I guess I should ask you the same question?"

"Right," he said, and didn't look down or away or anywhere but in my eyes. "My marriage."

"Yeah," I said, eyebrows raised.

"Jamie Reingold," he said. "My friend from college and a few years later my girlfriend and then, well. She and I went to Vegas with five other friends, got a little drunk, and thought, what the hell, let's get married.

I'd never even *talked* about it with the girl, but after a few Jäger shots, it sounded like an excellent idea. So we found the closest chapel and had a guy in a polyester shirt with a Miller High Life logo on the back marry us. We were young and restless and stupid—"

"And in Vegas," I said.

"And in Vegas . . . not really thinking too far ahead, but, anyway, we did it. And we were okay for about two years." He seemed to count in his head. "Maybe a year and a half. I don't know. When we realized one day that it was *marriage*, and if you met someone that was more of a match for your maturing self, you couldn't pursue that person, which we both started to want as we grew apart, then we started to resent each other. Ridiculous, but we didn't want to be married to each other."

He looked out across the bay. "We were almost surprised by the need for a divorce, because we hadn't been entirely serious when we'd said 'I do.' We should have asked for clarification of the question. In this case, what happened in Vegas *didn't* stay in Vegas. It went wherever we did. We'd figured we could just get it annulled, but that didn't work, so we thought, okay—divorce. Turned out New York law doesn't take marriage as lightly as we did and getting divorced was a freakin' nightmare."

"I *see*," I said.

"One year separation, court filings. It's happening, though," he reassured. "We did the paperwork. We're legally separated. Haven't kissed her in years, by the way."

"Haven't kissed me *either*," I said.

"Not in *way* too long," he said, and he smiled, and he leaned in and grazed my mouth with his lips, while looking right into my eyes—his eyes crinkling at their outermost edges as he smiled. And then again he kissed me, this time relaxing into it and closing his eyes. Then we kissed again. And again—ignoring the easing rain, embracing the future. And for this soaked, bloody pulp of a girl, whose memory of her love for this man grew clearer as a moonlit night asserted itself through the fog, all was right with the world.

\* \* \* \* \*

I'd like to say that after the whole ordeal, my family underwent a total metamorphosis: My mom became a nurturing übermother, my sister and I turned into best friends, and my dear dad grew more of a backbone. But that didn't happen. Something better happened instead: I changed. You know that person about whom you say, "When I grow up, I want to be like her"? Well, I did. And now I am.

I learned to accept my family for who they were and understand that, though they might be limited in certain areas, they all had good qualities that I could appreciate. Hating them for not being who *I* wanted them to be was only hurting me. Holding on to resentments, a wise person once said, is like taking poison and hoping the other person dies. Plus, if that happens—and I'm not sure he thought of this part—then that person's not around later to give you the satisfaction of watching him fall on his ass.

I reimbursed my mother for the rent she'd covered, got whole with the landlord (and kept the bird), and also cut a chunk off my credit card debt (you should have heard the shock in Citibank Cindy's voice when *I* called *her*), using part of a loan from Cat. Yes, I know about the hazards of lending and borrowing with friends, but it'll be paid back in six months with interest—first two payments have already been made. Cat's got more money than Bill Gates, it turns out, so she offered, and knowing that I, Jordan Landau, was now good for it, I accepted.

The next time I saw my neighbor in his Tiger Schulmann finery, I was carrying my recyclables to the trash room. He lit up the moment he saw me, not knowing which "me" he was going to get but certain that—memory or no—there would be an angle to play with pliant Jordan Landau of apartment 5E.

"Hey, Jordan!" he said with a toothy grin. "Remember me?"

"Yeah," I said, looking down at his spandexed package and then back at his face. "Put some *pants* on, for Christ's sake."

I tossed my garbage into the receptacle and walked back to my apartment—not bothering to gauge his reaction.

\*   \*   \*   \*   \*

At work, things got back to abnormal quickly enough. With the lid blown off her affair, Lydia broke up with Kurt, the secrecy of the thing apparently having been its primary attraction for her. He got a production job at another agency. And, not long after, she was jettisoned for having taken creative license—or let's just call it taking creativity—in a few situations having nothing to do with me. Just as well. It allowed me to slip back into the stream as a senior writer within a few months, not exactly wiped clean of my sins but seen as more of a daring forger than a dim-witted fake. Even Art—of high-five fame—welcomed me back with a hand-stinging slap, perhaps my combination punishment and re-initiation into the land of the living.

He forgave. They all did. So I did, too. I learned to stop blaming the passengers for where the S.S. *Jordan* was headed and just take the wheel and navigate for myself. That's the surest way to get to the best version of me—Jordan Version 3. I finally understood that you can't run from who you are, but you certainly can *change* who you are. Every *day* you get the chance to decide who you want to be. And that's as far as it goes.

Your family may seem to consist entirely of people you couldn't stand to have around for ten minutes if they didn't have all sorts of damning details to use against you. Then again, they may occasionally feel the same way about you. And since it's the only family you get, somehow, in an imperfect permanent way, you fit together. And find a way to love each other.

And fortunately, we get to *choose* our friends.

\* \* \* \* \*

I was riding my bike in the city a little while later on a gorgeous morning in early June and I passed the wall right near where Travis and I had our first accident. I remembered it—the one with the message scrawled in spray paint. It still said:

GOD IS DEAD.
—Nietzsche, 1883

But I hadn't noticed what it said right underneath:

NIETZSCHE IS DEAD.
—God, 1900

I could tell that it was going to be a good day.

# about the author

What can I say in this bio that you didn't read in my last one? Wait—you *did* read *Stupid and Contagious*, right? Well, not too much has changed since that came out. Writing has a way of consuming every second of your life, partly with the actual writing and the rest with worrying that you're not writing enough. Oh, I quit coffee for a while, which is *big* news. But then I replaced it with about twenty-seven cups of green tea per day. (Probably making the whole quitting-coffee thing moot.) People say writing is 10 percent inspiration and 90 percent perspiration. This is nonsense—it's pretty much 100 percent caffeine. At least in my case. So while I may have switched seats on the *Titanic*, I'm still drowning (although vivacious and alert) in a sea of stimulant. But here's a new book to show for it!

I still have the same parents: My amazing mother, Tina Louise, my number one champion and the bright spot on the dreariest of days. My brilliant father, Les Crane, perhaps the only person with a darker sense of humor than mine. I still have two dogs: Chelsea and Max. Chelsea turns sixteen this year. Which means she can finally drive. Legally.

My years spent writing for MTV didn't do a whole lot for the intellect, but did nurture my profound love of music. *And* I got to meet Beavis.

Then it was time to pursue a few dreams—founding a record label, creating a line of jewelry, and finally moving full-time into writing creatively. Or at least fictionally.

And that's pretty much it. Nothin' to see here, people. I'm still just writing away: Screenplays . . . stories . . . letters to the editor . . . cookbooks . . . computer programs . . . term papers for undergraduates . . . prenuptial agreements . . . and the very book you're holding.

I hope you enjoyed it.

Keep in touch at: www.capricecrane.com.

# top ⭐ things

## i wish i hadn't forgotten

**5** The minibar is not complimentary.

**4** That call was on speakerphone.

**3** Vegetarians don't like being served foie gras. Even as a joke.

**2** Nobody actually wants to hear objections during the wedding ceremony.

**1** Dance like nobody's watching—but not at funerals.